THE
DEAD
SUMMER

HELEN MOORHOUSE

POOLBEG

rted.

1

A catalogue record for this book is available from the British Library.

ISBN 978-1-84223-470-9

Typeset by Patricia Hope in Sabon 11 / 15

Printed by CPI Mackays, Chatham ME5 8TD

www.poolbeg.com

About the author

Helen Moorhouse, originally from Co Laois, lives in Drumcondra, Dublin, with her husband and two young children. She has worked behind the scenes, and occasionally on air, in radio, for the past thirteen years.

Helen's interests include a TV obsession, cinema and reading when she gets time. She is fascinated by the idea of ghosts while simultaneously being terrified in case she ever meets one. *The Dead Summer* is her first novel.

Acknowledgements

Firstly, I'd like to thank Paula, Sarah and the team at Poolbeg for liking this book enough to publish it and then making such a lovely fuss over me while doing so (although I'm still bewildered!). I am also so grateful for your friendship and support during all that has happened – it has meant the world to have you on my side and to know that you have stuck with me throughout.

Enormous gratitude is also due to Gaye Shortland, my editor, for whipping *The Dead Summer* into shape and at such short notice too, and for dealing with my total technical ineptitude and making sense out of what's perfectly clear in my head (which is probably somewhere no one else really wants to go) but is complete nonsense on paper.

To my mother, Claire, for the bedtime stories and also ensuring that my library card was never out of date. Sleep tight and God bless.

To my father, Seán, for his unswerving belief in me and his enormous devotion and pride throughout my life.

To the Laidlaws, the Wexford Keenans, the Sligo Keenans, the Comerfords and O'Neills for your belief and love, in particular my siblings, Margaret, John, Tony, Rose and Angela, for teaching me that toys come alive at night, that spiders come down the chimney to get you, that the noises in the dark probably *are* something to worry about and for placing writers like Stephen King and all the others into my hands.

To the Heads for your critical eye, and especially, to Petrina, for your constant friendship and support over the past twenty-one years. For taking me all the best places and introducing me to the best people. PS, it's still not a comedy novel . . .

Special thanks also to my wonderful in-laws, Avril, Alan and all the Moorhouses, for your continued support and love through thick and thin.

To all of my friends – you know who you are – for troubles shared and glasses raised over the years. You all knew I could do it, even though I didn't.

To my colleagues and friends at UTV Radio Solutions and Cork's 96FM and C103, Beat 102-103, Dublin's Q102, FM104, Galway Bay FM, Limerick's Live 95FM and LMFM for your encouragement.

A special thanks must go to the doctors, nurses and staff at the Children's University Hospital, Temple Street, because without you all this book wouldn't have happened – especially Darach Crimmins and the dedicated, hardworking, committed and amazing nurses and staff of St Gabriel's Ward – I can never thank you enough for taking me out of the darkest place that I have ever been. For the 4 a.m. coffee, the constant hugs, the encouragement, the reassurance and for the incomparable medical care that you gave and still give to my darling daughter – there simply aren't enough words to thank you.

To Florence, the Sequel – thank you for the smiles and the sleeping and the unbelievable joy. Lots of love from the lady who peers at you over the laptop.

To my incredible husband, Daryl, for thirteen years of tolerance while I floundered around and procrastinated, trying to find my voice; for your unwavering belief in me, your constant practical and emotional support, your love and for taking care of me just as you promised from day one. I can't begin to thank you enough.

And for Daisy, the inspiration, my hero. You made me want to be a better person for you and triggered the switch that made it all click into place, and changed my life incomparably in the process.

For Daisy – my inspiration and my muse

1

May 28th

It was a balmy evening in Martha Armstrong's garden in London and she and five friends were drinking champagne.

"To Martha!" said Polly Humble and lifted her glass, insisting then in clinking it in turn against each of the five other glasses. It meant that she had to stand up out of her seat and lean over awkwardly to reach some of the others, but to Polly it had to be done this way or the toast hadn't been done correctly at all.

"To Martha!" chorused the other five.

"On her great country adventure!" added Polly, who thought the whole thing a great lark indeed.

All six took sips of champagne. Polly pretended to shudder with delight and rolled her eyes to the sky. Fiona smacked her lips loudly and Sarah said "Mmmm . . ." in an exaggerated fashion.

Standing behind Fiona, Sue Brice made a face at Martha and stuck out her tongue at each of the people at the table. Martha looked downwards, trying to suppress a giggle but also feeling sad at the sham of it all.

It took Claire Smith, one of Martha's ex-colleagues, to finally say what the others were thinking: "So, Martha, what does Dan think about all this?"

Sue opened her eyes wide at the question and cast a worried glance at Martha, who never flinched.

"Oh, I think he's actually quite pleased, to be honest," Martha said casually. "Me moving to the country gets the fly out of his ointment, the elephant out of his room so to speak."

There was silence for a moment.

"And is Ruby all excited about packing her case and moving away with Mummy?" chirped Polly in an exaggeratedly high-pitched voice, as if she were talking to a child or an idiot.

Sue rolled her eyes, unseen by the group.

Martha fixed Polly with a stare. "She's six months old," she replied drily. "She can't really tell the difference between moving to the country and next Tuesday fortnight."

Polly looked sideways under her lashes at Fiona and Sarah. Martha observed the glance, thinking that they couldn't wish to be gone any more than she wanted them to be.

"Are you sure that this is what you want to do?" asked Sue later when the others had gone and it was just the two of them left. She stood by the back door, smoking a cigarette out into the garden, while Martha shuffled about the kitchen making coffee for them both.

Martha stopped pouring milk into the two cups, picked up an envelope which had been tucked in beside the microwave and held it out to her friend.

"What's this?" said Sue, opening the envelope and drawing out a document. "Oh."

"Yup," said Martha. "Decree Absolute. Arrived this morning." She looked around her at the bare kitchen, all of the furniture sold or gone to Dan's new home, save the white goods which were remaining for the new owners. She sighed and handed Sue her coffee. "Oh, Sue, you know as well as I do that there's nothing left for me in the city."

"Your friends –" offered Sue.

"Who?" Martha cut in. "Polly Humble? Fiona Oldham? Sarah James? They're all wives and girlfriends of *Dan's* friends, not mine. They only turned up tonight to tick the box, as it were. I know for a fact that Sarah had Dan and Paula to dinner when I was five months pregnant!"

Sue blew out a cloud of smoke. "Oh yeah, forgot about that, sorry," she said apologetically.

"As for Claire . . ." continued Martha, sipping her own coffee and wandering over to join Sue in the doorway. "Well, she's been a good old sort but I know tomorrow she's just going to go into the office and get into a huddle with Liz and tell her that I'm storming off to the country and giving up my job because I'm all bitter and twisted about Dan. She'll make it sound all juicy and then by next week I'll be 'Remember Martha?' and pretty soon Claire will have moved on as well."

Sue dropped the cigarette butt and ground it with her foot. "And you're not at all bitter and twisted of course!" She picked up the butt between her forefinger and thumb. "What do you want me to do with this?"

"Oh, plant it somewhere and see if a ciggie-tree grows! I don't actually care any more – it's not my house, right?"

Sue smiled and flicked the butt out into the garden.

"Oh, sod this!" said Martha and turned back into the kitchen. She poured her coffee into the sink and opened the fridge. "This was for the new owners but, screw it, let's have a proper drink."

She took another chilled bottle of champagne out of the fridge and handed it to Sue who promptly ditched her own coffee and made her way back out into the dusky garden. Sue popped the cork and watched it bounce off the trellised wall and disappear into a flower-bed. She poured it into the two glasses Martha had set on the table.

"Of course I'm bitter and twisted!" said Martha. "I was with the same bloke for ten years for heaven's sake – had it all, I thought – the wedding in the country manor, the big house in the suburbs, baby coming along two years later, like I'd planned it. Shame it wasn't what Dan had planned in the slightest. His plans only extended to when he could next do the dirty with Paula Bloody Gooding!"

"Here," said Sue, familiar with the routine of letting Martha rant since she had discovered her husband's second relationship eight months previously. She topped up Martha's glass and lit herself another cigarette. "To keep the midges away, of course," she said, grinning at Martha.

Martha sipped her drink and inhaled Sue's second-hand smoke deeply, wishing at that moment she had never given up. "You know what bugs me the most, Sue? It's that he carried on with everything that we had planned and he'd have carried on forever if I hadn't found out. If Tom Oakes hadn't commiserated with me when he saw them at the Ad Awards, then I'd probably still be blissfully unaware my husband had a long-term girlfriend. It was only when he got caught that Dan actually grew the balls to admit that none of this was 'his bag'." She glanced back at the four-bedroomed terraced house that she had spent five years lovingly turning into a home for her family, then pointed at the window over the kitchen. "The only good thing that came out of that marriage is asleep in that room and her father doesn't even want to know her. And I think that he loves Paula Gooding more than he ever loved me, and more than he'll ever love Ruby, and that absolutely *kills* me. So yes – in answer to your question I think I am absolutely doing the right thing in selling up and getting out of Dodge. At least for six months or so to get my head straight, instead of just moping around here trying to . . . to catch a whiff of the nasty, leftover stink of my marriage." There were tears in Martha's eyes which she was trying her hardest to fight back. "You know what else kills me? That my little girl will never have a brother or sister who calls the same man 'Daddy', that she'll always feel left out at nursery or at school when kids talk about their dads – and what does she do if, say, they're making cards for Father's Day?"

"Relax," said Sue. "I don't think they do that any more – there are plenty of kids like Ruby with no dad, or kids with two dads, or twenty 'uncles' or two mummies."

"That's true," said Martha, comforted by this thought.

"Of course you're doing the right thing," said Sue reassuringly. "I'll just miss you both so much. We've never lived more than ten miles apart since we were at university." She rubbed Martha's hand lightly with her own.

Martha drained her glass. "That's another thing, Sue. I've got to do this writing thing as well, and everything in London is so tied up with the divorce that I can't get down to it with a clear head. I mean, I've left my job to finally write the book I've been promising myself I'd write since I was a kid. I've got to give it a proper go, now that I can finance it with this . . ." she indicated the house which she would leave forever the following morning, "and with the maintenance, provided Mr Lover can remember to pay it. I've brought Ruby into a broken home – I have to be able to offer her the best, be a mum who is trying her hardest to fulfil her own potential if I'm to be any example to her. I can't be someone who's face down in a bottle of wine every night because I'm trying to blot out the thought of going to work in the morning. You know I hate advertising with a passion and this is my chance to get away, start afresh. My life's just a great big bloody – *toilet* here in London."

Sue smirked, recognising that a combination of champagne and tiredness was beginning to speak instead of Martha. "Albeit a very nice toilet with a new Audi and lovely clothes and tons of handbags and shoes!"

Martha grinned, glad that her friend was there to bring her back down to earth. "Okay, so it's a gold-plated toilet with a thing that whirrs around to clean the seat for me!" she laughed. "But a toilet nonetheless, good madam! Seriously though, I've got to give this the best shot I can and if that means moving away then that's what I've got to do."

Sue nodded. "Pity Party over?"

Martha nodded. "Yes. Pity Party over. And please don't use that phrase around me again. It's going on the banned list along with 'twenty-four seven' and 'do the math'. Oh, and another one – 'so over it'!" She grinned. "I'm like totally so over that one!" she said, and the two laughed.

"To Martha and Ruby!" said Sue, raising her glass.

Martha followed suit.

"May your stint in the countryside be as fulfilling as you dream it can be," continued Sue, addressing the trees and shrubs in the darkening garden. "And may you bloody well cheer up soon!"

2

Eyrie Farm,
Shipton Abbey,
Norfolk,
England

February 1st, 1953

Dear Caroline,

*Happy St Brigid's Day to you and Happy 17th Birthday to me!
Who would have thought when we spent my last birthday
together that this year would see us so far apart – and not just by
miles? We never thought we would ever be separated, did we?
We were always so close since we were infants as we lived so near
to each other, what a tragedy for me when you were four and I
was three and you disappeared off to big school! But look at us
now! We arrived here at Shipton Abbey in Norfolk about a week
ago. You'll be surprised, I'm sure, by the address at the top of this
letter, but it's true, this is where I will be living for the foreseeable
future, until Daddy decides it's time to go home, when the
trouble has blown over.*

Worry not, Caroline, it's not me who's in trouble, but the trouble is certainly the worst kind. I pray that you can keep this a secret, and that the secret is not a burden to you as it is to me, but it is Marion who is in trouble. As she will undoubtedly begin to show very soon, Daddy has sent us here to Norfolk, to the care of an old friend, until her time has come and we see what's to be done. I am here as her companion – you know what she's like unfortunately. There's no keeping her out of harm's way but as the time draws near she'll be less and less able for her old antics, we hope. And when the baby arrives, so too will sense and we may eventually be able to come home to Dublin, please God.

I hope, my darling friend, you won't be too shocked or disgusted by what I have revealed to you here. On the one hand I know that you are now Sr Agnes, a novice in the Brigidine Order, and as such you are more blessed than those of us who haven't had the fortune to be called by Our Lord into his service. On the other hand, however, I know that a part of you must still be Caroline, my friend since childhood, from whom I have never kept a secret and from whom I could no more keep this secret than cut out my own tongue. What I am trying to beg of you is not to condemn us, please – I feel that I am implicated in my sister's guilt by being here with her and have to keep reminding myself that I have not sinned! Can you forgive us, do you think? I beg you, please!

Do you mind me unburdening myself upon you, Caroline? I had no one else to turn to while there were troubled waters at home in Clontarf, and I have had to beg God's forgiveness for asking Him in a weak moment to send you home from the convent to me so that I could see a kindly face.

It all started a month ago when Marion began to be ill all the time. I thought she would die she was so unwell, her face paler than milk, and I confess that I took to listening at doorways to hear what Mother and Father were saying when they talked about her. I know it was dishonest and sneaky but I feared I would lose my sister and, no matter how bad she can be, she is my only one and I should die myself to lose her.

7

Daddy was in a terrible mood all the time as you can imagine. He was slamming doors and coming in at all hours and going out again early in the morning. I found out then that he was making arrangements for Marion to go to a convent in Kerry of all places, a place where girls who have got themselves into trouble go until their babies are born and then the babies are taken from them and they can go home. Mammy, in turn, was upset as well – she didn't want Marion going to the nuns – the nuns in Killarney, Caroline, I mean – if your good sisters took in girls in trouble then she could have rested easy, knowing that Marion was as good as in the hands of Our Lady and St Brigid themselves.

Then the fortunes took a turn on us and Daddy received a letter from an old friend of his, a man called Charles Mountford, who was in the army with him during the war. After the war ended, thank God, Daddy and this man worked together on the building sites where they learned their trade until Daddy had enough money to come home to Ireland and start up the building company. As it happens, this man Charles Mountford did the same and started to build houses and factories and all sorts around here in Norfolk. He is very rich now, it seems. So he and Daddy had many hushed conversations on the telephone.

In the heel of the hunt, I was told two weeks ago to pack my bags, that Marion was with child, Lord save us, and that Mr Charles Mountford of Shipton Abbey was very kindly allowing us to live for a time in his cottage there. I was to travel with her and take care of anything that she needed because she was in a very delicate condition.

And so we are here, Caroline, without a farewell to a soul. Marion has been very unhappy – she is very ill and when she is not being ill in a pan by her bed she sits by the fire in the kitchen which I must keep lit for her at all times. Sometimes she goes into rages and I might make her a cup of tea to make her feel better and she'd smash the cup on the ground and make me clean it up. Or she might miss the pan sometimes and I have to clean that up as well. I am probably wrong to tell you these things. I'm sure they're just a sign of her condition. Mammy said that her humours might be funny sometimes but that everything will be all right when the baby arrives.

Daddy sends us some money to live on – the first of it has arrived today and I am to leave now to go to the village and do our shopping for the week. It is too cold for Marion to go outside, even if she were well enough. And, besides, Daddy says that she is not to be seen by anyone other than myself or Mr Mountford until the baby arrives and then he will decide what we should do. God willing, the baby will come near the end of the summer and then maybe I can return home and see you. I must go now and do my messages. Marion will need her lunch at one and I have nothing for her.

I pray for you every night, Caroline, that your life as a Bride of Christ is making you happy, although I know that our happiness is secondary to serving the Lord. Mammy says that by taking care of Marion I am serving the Lord and if it is His will then I will be able to come home soon to finish my Leaving Cert and go to secretarial college. You are so lucky that you have the Leaving Cert over you!

Write soon and tell me your news!

May God be with you,

Lily

3

May 30th

With the sun streaming in the tiny leaded windowpane, Martha smoothed down the duvet on the guest bed again and took a final glance around the little room at Hawthorn Cottage. This would be Ruby's room but, for the moment, her cot was set up in Martha's room.

It was only a matter of an hour or so before Sue arrived with Ruby. It was the first time that Martha had been away from her little girl for even a single night but they had agreed it was best that she travel alone to Norfolk first to sort out the cottage and that Sue and Ruby would follow the next day. It always made Martha smile that Sue, of all people, should be Ruby's most eager baby-sitter when needed. To the casual observer, Sue Brice was adamantly footloose and fancy-free, but Martha knew that she would always be there for Ruby, as she had proven throughout the messy period of the divorce.

Martha had stumbled across Hawthorn Cottage by accident on the internet, while idly skimming through rental websites at work one day. In the seven months since the divorce proceedings had started and the six since Ruby was born she had toyed with the idea of finally doing it – making a break, getting as far away from Dan and Paula as she possibly could – but she hadn't

10

thought about it seriously until she found the picture of her new home. It was a picture-postcard whitewashed cottage near the Norfolk Coast. She was mesmerised by the pictures of the tiny rooms upstairs, the large kitchen and dining area and the view of the garden with its lavender bushes and mature trees around. A phone call to the owner later and she began to formulate a plan. Martha couldn't help but feel a slight sense of pride as she looked out the window over the driveway now. She had done it, actually done it. Her new life was beginning.

"Everything okay for you then?"

Martha jumped. She had forgotten that the owner of the house was still here, doing some last-minute jobs to complete the recent renovation.

She turned and smiled at the stocky man who filled the doorframe of the little room. "Oh, hi, Rob – yes, everything looks great now, thank you very much." She could never get over how tall and broad the man was, with his sandy hair and permanent stubble.

"I've been having a problem with this, though," said Rob Mountford, striding across the little room in two long steps.

Martha cringed as she spotted the dusty prints his boots made.

Rob rubbed his huge dirty hand along the chimney-breast. "The fireplace was bricked up years ago," he said. "Don't know why. Ugly old thing, and a terrible job, so I just put plasterboard up over the whole thing. The plaster's caused me nothing but problems though – just won't stay put. Hopefully what I've done'll stick this time." He gazed at the wall and then turned to smile at Martha.

She noticed he had to stoop slightly in the room because of his height against the beamed ceiling, one side of which slanted. The sunshine continued to flood in the window which was set into the slanted roof, adding to the quaint beauty of the house.

"I'm sure it will, Rob – thanks very much for everything," said Martha. "You'll send on the bill?" she added, eager for him to leave so that she could finish the preparations for the arrival of her friend and daughter.

"Well, it's all taken care of by your landlord!" replied Rob, pointing to himself as he did so, grinning at his little joke.

"Oh, of course it is!" Martha found it difficult to remember that she wasn't an owner any more and not responsible for repairs and building work. For a split second she felt very sad.

Thankfully, Rob actually was finished and Martha walked him down the stairs, assuring him along the way that, yes, she would contact him for anything at all. She sighed with relief when she heard the crunch of the Land Rover's wheels on the gravel of the driveway. Her first task was to run back up the stairs with a cloth, wiping away the dusty footprints as she went. Everything had to be perfect when Ruby arrived at her new home.

Martha was in her room rearranging Ruby's changing gear on the unit when she heard the crunch of the gravel again and groaned. What did Rob Mountford want now? She stood and peered out the window and her heart leaped at the sight of Sue's green Citroën pulling up outside, her blonde head peering out the open window.

Martha paused only long enough to check her appearance. At thirty-five, she looked younger, her five-foot three-inch height and slim frame certainly adding to the illusion that she was in her late twenties. Her dark hair was cut short in a pixie crop and her fringe was tucked into a decorative clip over her left ear. She smoothed down the patterned tea dress that she wore and then ran down the stairs as quickly as she could in her green ballet pumps, tearing out through the front door to greet the new arrivals.

Martha swept her daughter out of the car seat and into her arms before Sue could straighten her legs after the three-hour drive from London.

"Hello, pigeon!" shrieked Martha, covering Ruby's tiny blonde head with kisses, and holding her out in front of her face so that the baby could see who she was. When the little girl registered that it was her mother who was there, her mouth spread open in a wide beam and she jigged up and down with excitement. Martha pulled her towards her for another embrace, but it was a hug too far for Ruby who gave a grunt and tried to struggle free, looking over her shoulder at Sue who was extending her arm to hug Martha.

"Don't know how you tolerate her, Ruby!" said Sue. "All that hugging and kissing – *bleucccchhh*!" The face and noise made Ruby giggle.

"Has she been good?" asked Martha, snuggling her face into Ruby's soft neck.

"You know yourself," replied Sue, opening the boot to begin disgorging the buggy, steriliser and other Ruby-related items. "Makes a great cup of tea but then leaves the bag in the sink – *and* I caught her smoking twice. My fags too!"

"Oh Ruby!" said Martha in mock horror. "I thought you'd quit!"

Ruby looked at her mother, beamed, and batted at her nose with a chubby little hand.

Sue straightened, having placed the buggy on the driveway. "What a cracking spot," she observed, nodding at the cottage.

Martha turned to look also. "It's lovely, isn't it? Told you!"

The cottage was, indeed, idyllic. Set back three or four hundred yards from the main road along a gravel driveway, it looked even more inviting in the sunshine than it had in the pictures the friends had seen on the internet. Intended as a holiday cottage for rental, Rob Mountford had renovated and modernised it over the past couple of years and was delighted to have a continuous tenant for six months for the first letting.

Martha thought the cottage looked as though a child had painted it in a picture. The outer walls were whitewashed and the woodwork painted an inviting shade of teal green. The front door was in the exact centre and inside it lay a hallway with a wooden floor, the stairs slightly to the left inside the door. Off the hallway were a number of doors – on the right a cosy living room, further on Martha's study. To the left, under the stairs, a small door led into the dining area and beyond it was a door to the kitchen. At the very end of the hallway, to the rear of the house, another door led into a utility room where the washing machine and dryer lived, and the walls were lined with shelves for household bits and bobs. The dining room and kitchen were separated by a folding partition which Martha chose to keep open, spreading daylight throughout the long room from the bay window to the front of the house and the small conservatory attached to the kitchen at the side. The living room also had a bay window and Martha had already envisioned staying until after Christmas, and maybe having her dad and stepmum along with Sue to stay, with a huge real tree glimmering in the window, like a picture on a Christmas card.

At the top of the old wooden stairs was a landing area, with what looked like the original floor varnished a dark colour, the doors to the rooms the same. The ceilings throughout the upstairs were beamed. There was no window at the end of the landing which was a pity, as that meant it had little natural light when the doors leading off it were closed. But, inside the two little bedrooms, two front windows jutted out from the slanted roof, leaded like the bay windows downstairs.

Martha was to sleep in the room to the right of the stairs, Ruby to the left, directly across from her. Beyond Ruby's room, over the kitchen, was a small unused room that Martha had used to store all of the empty boxes from her move. Beyond Martha's, the bathroom with its old-fashioned suite and claw-footed bath. The house brimmed with character. Martha's room, the living room and dining area all had original fireplaces which worked. The doors upstairs were original, the walls throughout the older part of the house bumpy with age but freshly painted.

Outside, the back garden was huge, leading around the side of the house to the small conservatory whose door was the sole exit to the rear of the house. Although Martha knew she would enjoy the conservatory, it was the one thing she felt was incongruous, the bright modern white frame out of character with the original cottage. Through it, however, she had a delightful view of the garden, all freshly landscaped and planted with mature shrubs and flowerbeds, and separated from the fields beyond by its surrounding lavender bushes and the mature trees which stretched high into the sky.

On this last day of May the sunshine beamed down and Martha felt it was all a dream come true, and with her daughter back in her arms she felt in one piece again.

"Pretty isolated though," observed Sue.

Martha turned back to her – she had almost forgotten that her friend was there. "It's not too bad," she replied. "There's a farm out the back, about half a mile across the fields, and the village is the same distance away to the right when you come out the drive. And, before you say it, I know I'm a city girl at heart but –"

"You always said you'd never live *anywhere* where there wasn't a Tesco within walking distance!" exclaimed Sue, closing the boot of her car.

"I know, I know! But look at this place – it's absolutely perfect! You never know – I might turn into a total Wurzel and move here forever!"

Sue gazed at the house. "And Ruby might recite Shakespeare over dinner," she said sarcastically and trudged toward the front door, cases in hand.

Martha laughed and followed her.

Martha plonked a third bottle of Pinot Grigio on the glass-topped table in the conservatory and moved the empties down beside the wicker couch where Sue lay barefoot.

"If I can't see them, then we haven't drunk them and I won't have a hangover when Ruby wakes at five in the morning!" she explained, plonking herself into the wicker chair opposite Sue, slurring her words slightly and giggling.

"At least you won't have far to go if she does wake," observed Sue, equally glassy-eyed. "I'm sorry to be ousting her from her room. You sure it's okay?"

"Oh, for sure," said Martha, spilling wine on the table-top as she filled up their glasses. "I'd have kept her in my room with me to settle her anyway. 'Sides, I've really missed her and I'll probably lug her into my bed when I go up anyway."

"That'll be pleasant for her with the amount you've put away tonight!" giggled Sue.

"Not to mention my garlic breath!" added Martha.

The two laughed and Sue struggled to her feet and padded over to the open door of the conservatory for a cigarette. The evening was still balmy though it was nearly ten thirty. "God but it's quiet," she remarked, gazing at the silhouettes of the trees surrounding the house and listening to cattle lowing gently in the distance.

Even though the cottage wasn't far from the main road, only the occasional sound of traffic reached them. All around, the fields lay dark and silent. Inside the house too, it was dark and silent. Apart from the glow of lamplight in the conservatory and a dim nightlight upstairs for Ruby, the house lay in total darkness, the occasional creak coming from the settling floorboards.

"So who lived here before you?" asked Sue, looking back in at her friend while trying to blow smoke outside and failing.

"Not a soul," replied Martha. "The place was derelict apparently until the local builder bought it three years ago and did it up bit by bit to rent out. Some of it apparently dates back centuries but, in saying that, which bits do and which bits don't," she smiled and indicated the modern conservatory, "are anyone's guess. There are walls knocked through, bits added on."

"What was it originally then?"

"Farmer's cottage, I think."

"So, nothing special then?" Sue sounded disappointed. She loved a good story.

"Nope, nothing at all," replied Martha. "Just an ordinary old cottage in the countryside."

Sue flicked her cigarette butt out the door and stepped after it to grind it out with her foot. She bent to pick it up but, as she did so, heard something that made her turn sharply and look back into the conservatory in disbelief.

Both women turned to stare at Ruby's baby monitor as the lights indicating a live link to the unit in her cot danced all the way up to red, indicating maximum volume, and what sounded like a long, rasping sigh was transmitted into the room. Martha felt the hairs on her arms stand up as the sound continued, filling with voice as it did so and ending loudly. If she hadn't known better, she would have called it a growl.

Martha and Sue stared in stunned silence at the monitor as the sound died away and silence once again filled the room. They were transfixed for a moment or two, both of them trying frantically to process what they had just heard.

Then Martha was out of conservatory, racing through the kitchen, along the hallway and up the stairs. Heart hammering, she threw open her bedroom door.

All was still. Ruby's little nightlight cast stars and moons around the walls, rotating slowly and silently. And Ruby lay peacefully in her cot, soother in mouth, one hand thrown above her head clutching the stubby tail of her teddy bear, Hugo.

Back downstairs, Sue was standing in the kitchen, waiting nervously.

"She's fine," said Martha shakily, her heart still pounding with the fright. "But I wish I could say the same for me."

"Jesus H, Martha," said Sue, "but your kid sure makes some funny noises in her sleep!" She gave a half-hearted laugh as she spoke, stepping back into the conservatory.

Martha was grateful for a rational explanation, and began to laugh herself. Yes, that was it. Just Ruby making one of her sleep noises. After all, when she was newborn, she used to emit bloodcurdling squeals and Martha would fly to her side but all would be fine, the tiny girl sound asleep. Just like now. That's what it had been for sure. Just Ruby making a noise combined with the unfamiliar acoustics of a new house.

Sue sat back down on the couch, pretending that her knees wouldn't support her and fanning herself. "Phew! That frightened the *wits* out of me! At this rate my nerves will be shattered from my 'peaceful' weekend in the country."

She laughed again and Martha joined her, laughing a little too loudly but the sound making her feel better.

"Speaking of nerves . . ." Sue went on, and launched into a rant about country drivers in a transparent bid to change the mood.

Nevertheless, both women jumped when there was a grizzling cry from the monitor some time later.

"I'll just go take another peek, shall I?" offered Sue. "Just to make sure she hasn't turned into a werewolf or anything since you came back down?"

"Okay," said Martha hesitantly. "Thanks, Sue."

Sue stood and left the room, crossing the kitchen in darkness and going out into the hallway.

Martha heard the wooden boards of the stairs creak and the floorboards yield underfoot across the house. She looked again at the monitor, crackling now as it picked up Sue's footsteps. She was glad her friend had offered to go and check this time because she had started to tremble again and wasn't actually sure if her legs would have carried her up the stairs. She felt sober and cold. She stood and pulled the door of the conservatory shut, bringing her own reflection round to face her, and that of the open doorway to the kitchen behind her. She instantly regretted doing it, suddenly filled with an irrational fear that she would see someone, or something, behind her when the door closed. The door clicked into place, the reflection remaining thankfully empty but for her own image. Martha turned the key in the lock and then, for security's sake, went and hung the key on its designated hook inside the kitchen door.

Martha heard Sue flush the toilet upstairs and took a deep breath. She went back into the conservatory and sat back down. She smoothed her skirt and took a mouthful of wine to calm her nerves. That strange noise . . .

It was just Ruby, she thought. She does make funny noises in her sleep sometimes. It's the only possible explanation. You're going to do this. Six months, show everyone you can manage, make a new start.

Her pep talk made her feel slightly better, as did the return of Sue who was smiling.

"All shipshape upstairs," said Sue breezily. "The Mistress of the Night has her soother in her gob and that teddy bear over her eyes and we're a werewolf-free zone."

Martha smiled, now reassured, and drew her feet up underneath her as Sue plonked herself back down on the couch and began a rant about the misuse of roundabouts.

Martha glanced at the monitor and back at her reflection in the conservatory glass. All fine, she thought, pushing aside the tiny voice raised by her fright which asked her over and over what the hell she was doing here.

4

May 31st

The next day dawned sunny and warm again. A trip to the village of Shipton Abbey for an excellent lunch at the Abbot's Rest and a stroll around the historic ruined abbey before returning home did much to dispel both Martha and Sue's hangovers along with the memory of their fright from the night before. The more Martha thought about the noise from the monitor, the more she reasoned that of course it had just been Ruby – but the amount that she and Sue had to drink had made it seem infinitely worse than it was, and what had scared her was, in fact, alcohol-induced.

In the light of day, it made her feel ashamed that they had drunk so much wine with her baby in the house and she made a mental note to cut down. After Sue had gone home, of course, she thought, as the two enjoyed a local cider in the garden of Hawthorn Cottage later that afternoon while Ruby tried her best to sit up on her playmat in the shade. Martha leaned back in her chair and let the sun warm her face. She could already feel the glow of a mild sunburn on her arms for staying out too long but she didn't care. This, she thought, was bliss.

They retired early that night, exhausted by fresh air and scrumpy. Sue knew she had to get a good night's sleep in order to drive home safely the following day, and Martha knew that she couldn't face another late night and early morning with Ruby who had woken at six with the sunshine streaming into Martha's room through the light curtains. The sooner Ruby could go into her own room with the blackout blinds the better.

Sue didn't really like how dark the blackout blinds made Ruby's room. She had stubbed her toe rather badly getting out of bed to go to the loo the previous night and she disliked the way that when she turned the light out the darkness actually seemed thick over her face, like you could touch it. She had lived in the city for all of her adult life and was used to the orange glow of street-lights at night-time.

The noises of the countryside were something she couldn't get a handle on either. "I thought it was supposed to be deafeningly quiet," she had complained to Martha earlier. "It's just bloody deafening and I can't tell what any of the noises actually are! It's all crunching and crackling and rustling and squeaking! And then last night there was a noise like a baby screaming!"

Martha laughed but had to suppress a shiver at the words. "It was a fox," she said, trying to sound reassuring.

Sue gave her a sideways glance. "Whatever it was, it was blue, bloody murder! And then that dawn chorus! People get mugged by gangs on my street and it's still quieter! And what's with it happening at four in the morning?"

Sue knew that she would find it hard to get off to sleep with the blackout blinds down, but it was preferable to a four o'clock start with the birds and the first approach of light. She switched off the main light in the room and felt her way back to the bed in the thick darkness, feeling almost stifled by the blackness that surrounded her. When she lay down and looked upward it was so black that she began to wonder if her eyes were actually open or closed.

A moth suddenly began to beat its wings against the window where it had become trapped by the blind. Sue sighed, but tried to ignore it and turned over onto her stomach to sleep. She finally managed to block out the moth but that noise was almost immediately replaced by another.

Sue lifted her head to listen. At first she couldn't place where the noise was coming from, being completely disoriented by the darkness. Straining her ears, however, she reckoned that the source of the sound was the blocked-up fireplace in the wall along her left-hand side. It was a scratching noise, starting slowly but becoming faster from time to time. She listened as it changed in frequency from a gentle scrape to a frantic scrabble. Bloody rats, she thought, and turned over in bed. She had stayed in the country with relatives when she was a child and remembered that during her stay a rat had become trapped in the walls of the old house. For days they had all listened to it run through the old walls from room to room, scrabbling to find a way out. It had eventually fallen silent and the sound was replaced a few days later by an unpleasant smell coming from the wall outside the parents' bedroom. She couldn't remember it being removed – the novelty of the rat in the wall had worn off when things fell silent – but she recalled the freshly plastered patch of wall on the landing.

The scrabbling continued, growing more and more frantic but not moving from the patch of wall where the chimney-breast was. Sue made a mental note to remind Martha to get her landlord back, with a rat-catcher, as soon as possible. Still the scratching continued. Sue lay there in the darkness, becoming increasingly restless. She rolled onto her side, pressed one ear into the pillow and jammed a hand over the other. Eventually she rolled onto her back. The moth had again begun to beat its tattoo on the window and the scratching from the fireplace had reached fever pitch.

Sue sat up in bed, bright red with heat and frustration. "Shut *up*!" she whispered as loudly as she could, not wanting to wake Martha and Ruby across the landing. She clapped her hands sharply together as if trying to scare a bird away. It worked – on the scratching at least. The scrabbling stopped immediately, even though the moth continued its incessant flapping.

Sue listened for a while. When the scratching noise didn't start again, she lowered herself back down on the bed. "One out of two ain't bad," she whispered to herself. She could sleep through the moth with a fist in her ear.

When she woke again, the room was bright but Sue knew that

there was something wrong – that the brightness couldn't be daylight as the blackout blind was firmly drawn. The memory of the moth from earlier in the night crossed her mind and she realised that it was silent, finally. In fact the whole place was silent. Sue wondered if this was what had woken her.

She came to fully, noticing that what was illuminating the room was in fact the overhead light that she was sure she had switched off before getting into bed. She remembered back to earlier in the night, feeling stifled by the darkness. She remembered clapping her hands at the noise in the wall in complete darkness and drifting off to sleep.

She rolled onto her back, registering the bulb lit up above her head. Had Martha turned her light on and looked in on her? And then forgotten to turn it off again? That didn't make sense.

Then Sue realised something else. When she breathed, for some reason she could see her breath in puffs coming out of her nostrils.

She blew air out through her nose again, another puff of steam. She opened her mouth and exhaled deeply. A cloud of vapour formed and then dissipated in the same way as it would on a February morning when the ground was thick with frost.

Sue realised that the entire room was freezing and that, not the silence, was what had woken her.

She pulled the duvet up toward her chin and turned on her side, drawing her legs up into a foetal position. A thought struck her and she craned her head around to see the small thermometer that Martha kept on the bedside table to ensure Ruby didn't overheat. She blinked, couldn't believe what she saw. Minus 2° Celsius. As cold as a January night, but it was almost June. During a heat wave that had lasted almost two weeks. London had hit 30° that day, for heaven's sake. And the temperature at 5 p.m. on the sign outside the village pharmacy had read 26°.

Sue sat upright. The cold enveloped her immediately, sliding around her back which was exposed in her sleeveless pyjamas. More clouds of vapour came from her as her breathing grew faster and shallower and she looked around the room in the glare of the overhead light. She could see that she was alone but for some reason it didn't feel that way. Her gaze was drawn again and again to the doorway but the old-fashioned wooden door with the latch remained firmly shut. No one was there. No one was anywhere in the room. But Sue was sure of two things. She didn't feel alone. And it was minus 2° Celsius.

Sue didn't scare easily. She had worked as a journalist since leaving university and it had made her hard and logical when she needed to be. There had to be a reason for this feeling she had, but she couldn't think of one. Usually unflappable and imperturbable, she realised now she was scared.

She scanned the room again. "This cannot be fucking happening," she said and half-pushed herself from the bed to get up and get out of the room.

All of a sudden she began to feel heat flooding the room – no, that wasn't right. It wasn't heat coming into the room, it was the coldness *leaving* the room, and leaving through the door where her attention had been drawn. She swivelled her head back around to the thermometer as the goose-bumps began to die down on her back and arms. For the second time that night she couldn't believe what she saw. The thermometer showed the temperature changing, rising up and up at speed – 6 degrees, 7 degrees, 8 – the numbers were changing almost too quickly for the device and they would stall from time to time and then jump up the 3 or 4 degrees it had missed while stopped. It eventually settled on 19° Celsius – about right for the extremely warm night and the time of year.

Sue sat stock still on the bed, trying to figure out what had just happened to her, and what to do next. She didn't want to stay in the room – her arms and legs were trembling with shock and fright. What scared her more than staying, however, was the thought of heading toward that doorway. The doorway through which the cold *had been sucked out*.

She felt weak in the aftermath of the experience. She sank back onto the bed, numb, and there she remained, staring at the still-lit ceiling, trying to figure out what to do until she fell into a fitful sleep.

5

June 1st

It was nearly ten when Sue eventually appeared in Martha's kitchen. She had slept through after the strange experience in her room, but still she felt exhausted and couldn't banish the thought of what had happened from her mind. Her concern now was how to tell Martha when she couldn't explain it herself.

Martha was sitting in the conservatory – gazing into space, a cup of coffee clasped in her hand – while Ruby was napping upstairs in her bed.

"Morning," said Sue, almost sheepishly, realising as she saw the tiny frame of her friend that in her terror the night before she hadn't even thought to check if Martha was alright, or worse still to check on tiny Ruby. She eased herself down on the wicker armchair, her body feeling all over as if she were getting flu. "Sleep alright?"

Martha looked up in surprise, only registering Sue's arrival in the room at that moment. "Oh, hi," she said, giving a half-hearted smile.

Sue felt sure that her friend was exhausted and distant because she had experienced the same strange occurrence as she had.

"Like a log, actually," Martha went on, "but you look like shit!"

Sue looked closely at Martha. She didn't want to bring up what had happened bluntly if Martha hadn't had the same experience and, looking at her now, she realised her eyes were red-rimmed from crying, not necessarily from lack of sleep. She decided to bide her time in mentioning it. There was plenty of time left in the day to get a case packed and get Martha back to London. Sue was sure of one thing, and that was that she was uncomfortable with her being alone in this house with Ruby.

"Think I'm coming down with something," said Sue. "But what's up with you? You don't exactly look full of the joys of spring?"

Martha lowered her eyes and when she raised them again Sue saw that they were filled with tears. "Oh just ignore me, Sue," she said, rolling her eyes upward as if trying to reabsorb the tears that welled in their corners. "I'm just feeling a bit, well, sad, I suppose."

Sue leaned over and grasped Martha's hand. "Why are you sad?" she asked gently, knowing that Martha would need prompting to talk, partially hoping that she would announce how stupid it had been to move to this place.

Martha sniffed. "I'm sad that you're going home today. I'm sad – really sad, that Ruby's got to start crèche tomorrow – I mean, someone else is going to get to see all the things that she does and they're not going to appreciate it one per cent as much as I do. I'm sad I'm not married any more. I'm sad that I'm here instead of cooking a fry-up in my kitchen at home – I'm sad those daisies over there need watering – like I said, just ignore me. I've got the collywobbles, that's all."

Sue saw an opening and took it. "Then come back to London with me," she said, squeezing Martha's hand.

Martha looked completely taken aback. "What?" she asked incredulously.

"You can stay with me," continued Sue. "Till you sort something out for you and Ruby. Something new and modern – with no dead daisies and dodgy plastering. We can see each other all the time, like before – what do you say? Just pack a case for you and Rubes and we can come get the rest of the stuff next weekend."

Martha looked stunned. "But you were all for this yesterday! All full of how great this place was and how you were so proud of me for taking things in hand and putting Dan behind me – why the hell are you trying to get me to back out now, Sue?"

Sue thought carefully. She thought about saying 'because your spare room has something weird in it and I don't want to leave you alone' but then thought better of scaring Martha, just in case her plan didn't work. She'd save that until everything else failed. "Because . . . I don't think . . . this place is right for you . . ."

Martha gave her a long look, then released her hand and walked into the kitchen.

Sue heard the kettle go on and the sounds of Martha spooning coffee into mugs and then adding the milk and stirring before pouring in the hot water. There was silence for a while and then Martha carried the two mugs back to the conservatory and placed one in front of Sue before sitting down with her own in her hands.

She spoke eventually. "Sue, there is absolutely nothing I would like more than to come back to London with you," she said, slow and measured.

Sue's heart leaped but then fell again as Martha added her 'but'.

"But I am absolutely one million per cent determined to do this and to make it work for six months minimum. I want to be able to look at Ruby when she's older and tell her that I took her to live in the country by ourselves when she was six months old and that while we were there I wrote my children's novel. This story – it's been buzzing round my head since I was a kid – the characters are there, the story is mostly there – it's time for me to finally get it out of there and onto paper. More than that, I need to do this for me – I mean, look at you, you've always wanted to be a journalist and now you're not only that but you're one of the most sought-after freelance feature writers in the country. You dance to your own tune – do exactly what you want to do

27

and you're the happiest person I know in their job. I've *never* had that, working in that damned agency. I've spent my life licking so much of other people's bums that I couldn't get the taste out of my mouth till I'd been on maternity leave for three months!"

Sue forced a grin. "You can write in London," she tried.

"I know I could. I could write on the moon but being here at Hawthorn Cottage is a whole package. I've never lived on my own before – I'm finally being independent, taking control of things. And this place is *beautiful*." She gazed outside, taking in the view of the garden, a lazy butterfly hovering around the flowerbeds.

Martha had a look of longing in her eyes like she was pleading with Sue not to take her away and it made Sue's heart melt. She had never seen Martha this passionate about anything other than Ruby, not even about Dan back in the early days. She knew that Martha was a talented writer – she'd known since university – but then Martha had gone into advertising and spent her time trying to keep everyone else happy at her own expense. Sue couldn't count the number of times she had seen her friend angry and stressed, the number of consolation bottles of wine they had shared over the years as Martha ranted on about her job. Sue couldn't imagine not loving what she did. It made her angry to see Martha so unhappy, and also that she had put writing on the back burner for so long. Queen of Procrastination, she called her. Over the years Martha had always promised to write – once her wedding was over, once things had calmed down at work, once she was on maternity leave . . . Here in the countryside it was finally going to happen for her because Martha had made it that way. Sue finally understood what it meant to Martha to be here and it was then that she knew no amount of pleading could get her away from this place. She almost felt jealous of the passion that Martha was showing in her eyes and she suddenly grabbed her in a bear hug.

"Alright, alright – enough of this!" she said, forcing a smile. "Stay here in the bloody godforsaken middle of nowhere then, if you bloody must!" She released Martha from the hug and saw that she was smiling bravely through her moist eyes. "But if anything at all happens – *anything,*" she warned, "you are to ring me, day or night and this time I'll come get you."

Martha grinned. "I will, I promise," she said. "Oh, someone's awake." She stood to go get Ruby who they could hear stirring on the monitor.

The rest of the morning was subdued, Martha making preparations for the week ahead and Sue packing to return to London. Sue said nothing about the night before, the warmth of yet another glorious day making the memory fade and making her wonder if it wasn't some odd local weather anomaly. She knew that the sea was nearby, and that there were marshes and flatlands and she wondered if the hot weather somehow had created some sort of weird fog or temperature drop that had made her experience what she had felt. It didn't however explain the light being switched on. She had asked Martha if she had come in for some reason and turned it on, but she had shook her head and thrown her a bemused look. Sue wondered if she had maybe done it herself, or if the wiring was faulty or if it was on some sort of timer that Martha was unaware of.

Many times throughout the day she thought about telling Martha but, knowing how fervently her friend didn't want to leave, she felt it would be unfair to tell her anything that would make her nervous. When the time came to leave that afternoon, Sue decided to stay silent and pray that nothing like that would happen once she had gone.

Going down the gravel drive, Sue kept a wistful eye on Martha and Ruby in her rearview mirror. Martha was making Ruby wave by manipulating her hand up and down, while Ruby stared intently in the opposite direction. Twice, Sue nearly slammed on her brakes and went back for them but she fought against the urge, remembering the look in Martha's eyes as she described her intentions. They went out of sight, hidden by an overhanging bush, as Sue reached the end of the driveway and she turned left for the motorway, feeling sure that she had just done the wrong thing.

6

Eyrie Farm,
Shipton Abbey,
Norfolk,
England

March 12th, 1953

Dear Caroline,

*I must start by apologising for taking so long to write to you
again. I knew I wouldn't have a reply from you soon because
your time is taken up with Jesus and your duties as a sister, but
that's no reason for not writing to you myself to tell you our
news here in Norfolk.*

*How has the weather been in Dublin? Are you allowed out
sometimes? I wish I knew what your life was like, so I could
picture you as you go about your business. Maybe if I describe
what it is like here, then you could do the same for me? It would
give me comfort to think you were thinking of me because it is
very lonely here, despite having Marion for company all day.*

The weather here has been bitterly cold. Myself and Marion are frozen to the bone and as it is very important for the baby that Marion stays warm she spends much of her day in bed. I have given her my covers, other than a single blanket for myself, and suggested that we share her bed at night-time, like when we were small and Mammy told us that to huddle together would keep us warm. Marion says that she doesn't want my cold feet near her in the night, though, so I stay in my own bed in my little room upstairs.

There are a lot of good things about being here in Shipton Abbey. Our little house is lovely, if draughty! And it's very good of Mr Mountford to let us stay here – he is a very good friend to Daddy. The cottage used to be a farmhouse – it's not any more you'll be glad to know! I'm not spending my days milking cows and shearing sheep as well as looking after Marion! It's still called Eyrie Farm, though, as there are lots of rooks' nests in the trees around. Thank God for the big trees as they shelter us a little bit from the winds coming in from the estuary. Did I tell you we were near the seaside? It's not the sort of seaside you'd go paddling in, mind, like Dollymount at home! I've been to the village shopping every week but I haven't seen the sea yet. From what I hear it's very muddy and people come there to watch all sorts of birds.

Our cottage is small, just two rooms downstairs and two upstairs and an outhouse at the back. Downstairs we have a little parlour and then our kitchen which is where we spend our days – except when Marion keeps to her bed. We each have a bedroom upstairs and there is even a very small spare room at the back, behind my own room. The rooms are set into the roof so the ceilings in them are the inside of it and we have to stoop right down if we want to go into any of the corners! Both of the bedrooms have little fireplaces, which is a good thing because once I can keep the one in Marion's room going then she and the baby are warm at least.

I hope you don't mind that I talk about the baby, Caroline. I know that Marion has committed a deadly sin and that she will have much penance to do. But, in my own selfish way, I feel that the better things are for Marion and the baby, then the easier life is all round.

Her humour is no better than before, worse if anything with the terrible weather and her being cooped up inside all the time. You know yourself that Marion has always preferred to be out and about than at home, and I think it troubles her greatly that she is here with only myself for company each day, especially when she still feels so ill. She can barely eat and even the smell of me cooking the dinner can send her into a rage. The sooner the baby gets here the better, I think. Then maybe we can go home and Marion will calm down and not be so vexed all the time.

Mr Mountford came to see us on Tuesday. It was a huge honour to finally meet him and guess what, Caroline? He brought us a bicycle! Our very own bike with a basket on the front so I can carry the shopping home from the village without having to walk half a mile carrying the bags. He said it used to belong to his daughter Iris (isn't that a beautiful name, Caroline? I wonder, if the baby is a girl, would Marion call her Iris maybe?) but that she has her own motor car now and doesn't need it any more. They must be very rich indeed if Iris has her own motor car, come to think of it. Anyway, Mr Mountford may as well have given me my own motor car I am so delighted. And the best thing about it (God forgive me for being selfish!) is that with her condition Marion couldn't cycle it, so I have the bike all to myself and sure isn't it a great way to keep warm, pedalling all over! It'll be no time at all before I go to see the estuary proper and explore the big old ruined monastery that's in the village. I'll tell you all about that when I go there.

Mr Mountford is a lovely man, really, and I was at pains to tell him how grateful we are for his help. Marion said she just didn't want to see anyone and stayed upstairs. She got cross with me when I told her we had to let her fire go out for a while to light the one in the parlour for his visit (he had sent word in a note that he was coming). I had to put my foot down though – we're not made of firewood and I couldn't let the man into the house without taking him to the best room.

Mammy has said she'll box up some ornaments that she doesn't need, and a picture of the Sacred Heart so we can make the place more of a home for ourselves. Mr Mountford seemed happy enough though with the fire lit and a cup of tea in the parlour. He had one of my scones as well with some creamy butter – he brought it with him, would you believe, from his own rations, and gave it to us as a gift and it went very well with the gooseberry jam that Mammy gave me to bring with us. That was the last of it, of course, and Marion went mad when she found out for she says it's the only thing that she likes to eat. But I have written to Mammy to see if she can send us another jar in her next parcel. She is sending some old clothes of Granny Flynn's to see if I can make anything of them for Marion as she will soon outgrow her own clothes and were I to go into the draper's in Shipton Abbey then our secret would be out.

Marion is very low, I am afraid. God forgive her but she told me last week that she wasn't a bit sorry for doing what she did to get herself into trouble and that she'd do it again in a heartbeat. I tried to reason with her and tell her that it was wrong when she wasn't married and then she gave me the biggest shock. She told me that the baby's father was a black sailor that she met at the docks. I couldn't stop crying at her, Caroline. Imagine if the baby is black? But, before, she told Mammy and Daddy that it was a married man who Daddy knew. She has no shame now, I'm afraid, but I feel she'll come round when she realises what she has done. Hurry up, baby, so my sister will get some sense into her head and Daddy will tell us what to do next. I pray for the spring, Caroline, so that the summer won't be far behind and the autumn after that and this will all be over.

With lots of love,
May God be with you,

Lily x

PS I don't know if this will reach you in time but Happy St Patrick's Day! Do write and tell me all about the parade if you see it!

7

June 5th

The next few days passed in a whirlwind for Martha. By Wednesday, she wasn't crying any more when leaving Ruby with Mary Stockwell at the small local crèche and nursery she ran called Lullabies.

Ruby seemed to be settling in well from what Martha could tell and even though she was still a little jealous of the time that Mary had with her baby, she realised that the time had come for Ruby to leave their little bubble and give her the chance to experience life away from her mother.

At nine each morning Martha was sitting at her desk in the small study across from the kitchen, ready to begin doing what she had dreamed of since she was a child. The outline of the story had lived in her head for years – a unicorn, the last of his type, living a lonely existence in a forest in an imaginary land. She had mapped out in her head the solitary adventures of this Lonely Pony, as he thought he was, having only ever seen from a distance the king's horses and thinking himself the same. But somewhere along the line she would create an event which would lead to his becoming aware that he was in fact the most magical creature of all. Martha had adored stories like this when she was a child. The urge to write had simmered inside her for years. Now that all the other factors were in place she felt compelled to finally begin the children's tale – and if it were never published, then if nothing else she had the story for Ruby alone.

She found writing difficult at first – on Monday morning, fully alone in the house for the first time, the black screen of the laptop had proved too daunting and she had slunk from her study, intimidated, and found herself wandering from room to room, noticing little features in the house that she hadn't taken in before. A solid oak beam set into the wall in the living room that served as a mantelpiece, picture-rails along the study walls, and the little bedroom windows upstairs. She shifted the bed where Sue had slept into a recess alongside the chimneybreast and rearranged the furniture to accommodate the cot but decided to keep her baby in with her for a while longer. Outwardly, Martha reasoned that it was until Ruby got used to her new surroundings but in her heart she knew it was because she wasn't yet ready to let her free from under her wing.

It was eleven when Martha realised the time. She chastised herself and returned to the study where she eventually pushed aside her laptop and took up a pen and paper. Soon, a little inspiration began to flow and Martha finally began her story about the lost unicorn with a scene where the unicorn stared at his reflection in a lake and thought how lonely he was.

At one she set off to collect Ruby from crèche, stopping at the end of the drive to check if there was any post for her.

It had bothered her to learn that the postman left her letters in a hollow in an oak near the road – he had dropped in a note informing her of the fact after she first arrived. She had assumed at first it was because to come up to the cottage would add more distance to his route. But Hawthorn Cottage was a bit of a delivery black-spot in general, she had discovered – the butcher also refused to deliver, citing the distance of the cottage from the village as the reason. Yet she was sure that she had seen his delivery van in Bickford once, over five miles away. It was puzzling. She had begun to wonder if some of the locals had issues of some sort with Rob Mountford.

Evenings were her busiest times. With Ruby bathed and bedded in her mum's room by eight, and then housework to be done, she found herself exhausted but satisfied by bedtime. Fresh laundry on the line overnight, fresh purées in ice-cube trays for Ruby's meals in the freezer, bottles ready for the following day, floors mopped – Martha knew it was probably just a house-proud phase and before long she'd be catching up on herself at weekends, but for now she was nesting and loving every minute of it.

She didn't feel lonely in the first few days at all, despite thinking that she'd miss London terribly. In the evenings, out at the washing line down the end of the garden, she'd take a moment to breathe in the air, its smells of grass and distant salt from the sea. Evening, she noted, had a different smell from morning and afternoon and it was her favourite. Despite the isolation, Martha felt finally some semblance of peace for the first time in months. And of pride as each day passed and she grew stronger in her new life.

Ruby was settling beautifully. Each morning she greeted Mary with a smile and beamed with excitement when she came to pick her up. She was eating well, unphased by the new surroundings and was particularly impressed with lying on her playmat under the pear tree in the garden and picking at clumps of grass which Martha had to intercept on their way to her gummy mouth. She was sleeping well in Martha's room, but was now taking her afternoon naps in the room that would be her own, in a nest on the bed made of pillows and Hugo, her teddy bear.

By Wednesday, Martha decided that it was time she bit the bullet and moved Ruby to her own room to sleep. "Or else you'll still be sharing with Mum when you're twenty-five and no boy will want to marry you!" Martha explained while tickling her nose with a daisy in the garden.

Martha mentioned the move to Mary Stockwell when she went to pick Ruby up on Thursday.

"Just take the bull by the horns and do it," said Mary. "Isn't that right, little precious?"

In the buggy, Ruby beamed and kicked her chubby legs and then reverted to trying to take her sunhat off.

"I know you're absolutely right," said Martha with a sigh. "I suppose I just needed to hear someone else say it."

The two women sat on the low wall running between the crèche playground and the attached community-centre car park.

"You know you've got her in your room as company for you and not the other way round," chided Mary playfully.

"It's worse than that," confessed Martha. "She generally ends up in my bed with me, and not because she's the one who needs a cuddle!"

Mary feigned outrage. "Oh my goodness!" she said to Ruby, making her giggle. "Your mummy is going to *ruin* you!"

Mary Stockwell was in her forties and had run the crèche in Shipton Abbey for five years but had taken care of children, including her own four, on and off for most of her life.

"Can't say I blame you," she said to Martha. "You're a brave girl living up there on Eyrie Farm all by yourself."

"What did you call it?" asked Martha in surprise.

"Oh dear, I didn't mean to call it that. It's the proper name for the cottage," explained Mary. "I know Rob Mountford calls it Hawthorn Cottage – it's a prettier name for a holiday let than Eyrie Farm. It's called after the nests though, in the tall trees at the back – you know, meaning the nest of a bird of prey – e-y-r-i-e, not the other one."

"God, it's still not a very nice name when you say it out loud. Think we'll stick to the prettier one."

"You're dead right. Well, I'm glad you're coping up there by yourself . . . only . . ."

"Only what?" said Martha. "We're doing great, aren't we, Ruby-Doo? The weather's been amazing, Ruby loves it and everything's gone really well for us so far."

"That's good. It's just . . . well . . . a wee thing like you up there on your own with a little baby . . ."

Martha saw that her face was worried, and her words sounded as if she were trying to say something other than what she meant.

"If you need any help at all," continued Mary, "then just let me know."

"Thanks, Mary," replied Martha, touched by the sincerity of her offer, if a little puzzled by what she couldn't read in her face. "Why don't you call up sometime if you're passing? We could do with a bit of company, couldn't we, Rubes? And to be honest, I'd like to show the place off a bit!"

Mary's face grew very animated at the invitation. "Oh, could I? I'd love to see it – I mean, it's always been a bit of a ruin and no one would really go near it before . . . well, it was most likely dangerous, wasn't it? I'll definitely take you up on that sometime soon."

"Done. Now, I'd better let you get back to work and get this madam home for her lunch and hopefully a nice long snooze so I can do some writing out in the garden – I feel I absolutely must make the most of this weather."

"You're right – forecast says it's to break at the weekend. Then it'll be back in your wellies up at Eyrie Farm – sorry! – Hawthorn Cottage," laughed Mary.

Martha pushed the buggy down the slope toward the road with a wave. "See you tomorrow, Mary!"

Fortified by a perfect afternoon – a long session with her unicorn story in the shade while Ruby snoozed, followed by a simple salad for dinner with a chilled glass of locally made lemonade – Martha decided that it was time to take Mary's advice and move Ruby to her own room.

The little girl kicked her legs in the air and watched from the safety of her mother's bed, as Martha dragged the cot gently across the landing and stood it in the centre of the opposite room. Ruby's changing unit was pulled under the window and the small bedside table that was the home of the thermometer was placed at the head of the cot, near the chimney-breast.

Martha had decorated the walls with framed photographs that she had taken herself – some bright green acorns, pink and purple gerbera daisies in an earthenware pot, Ruby herself, close up and grinning at four months. On the chimney-breast itself she hung a huge black-and-white picture that Sue had taken –

Martha holding Ruby above her head as the baby beamed at the camera. Sue had it framed as a moving gift and Martha loved how it was the centre of the room.

The little bedroom was inviting by the time Martha had arranged everything and popped Hugo in at the head of the cot to wait for Ruby. By eight, the little girl had joined him and was sound asleep, her soother discarded by her face as was her habit. Martha felt reassured as she saw how peaceful she was. The room was dark with the blackout blind pulled and Ruby's little nightlight cast rotating stars and moons around the walls.

Martha was grateful for the peace and quiet. She hadn't before spent time at the dining table so she took that day's newspaper, closed over the folding partition between the dining room and the kitchen and sat down at the huge antique table that filled the small space. She realised that she hadn't read a newspaper since the previous week and soon lost herself in a feature article about stressed working mums juggling the nine to five along with their children, and she allowed herself to feel very smug.

She was disturbed by a sound from above her, from Ruby's room. She was used to the house settling at night-time, old houses did – even new houses did it – but this sound was for all the world like a footstep just inside the door of Ruby's room. It was loud enough to unsettle her and she glanced up at the ceiling uneasily before returning to her newspaper.

There it was again, another creak that sounded like a footstep. Martha sat back in her seat and listened, rationalising what she was hearing. She had never sat in this room in the evening time before, of course, and that was when the old house made its loudest creaks – she'd just never heard them from this angle. She listened again. Of course, she'd been dragging the furniture around as well so there was bound to be some adjustment in these wooden floors. Her shoulders relaxed and she returned to the paper. They tensed up again as quickly, however, when what sounded like another footstep creaked over her head. She shuddered. She knew it was only old floorboards creaking but it *really* did sound like there was someone creeping into the room, pausing between steps so as not to wake the sleeping baby. "Bloody hell," she whispered and looked once again at her paper. Another step. She couldn't concentrate and stood to go upstairs and check on Ruby.

"This is bloody ridiculous," she said aloud and headed out through the small doorway under the stairs. She paused as she heard another step. She couldn't help it – she was starting to feel really scared.

She looked upwards toward the landing. She could see nothing, but the last creak had convinced her that there was definitely someone upstairs. She must have left the conservatory door open and someone had got in through the kitchen and down the corridor without her noticing. The front door was definitely locked so the conservatory was the only means of entry. Martha suddenly began to burn with anger instead of fear. Who the *hell* was in her house?

She looked around frantically for something with which to arm herself. The closest thing to her was the fire extinguisher from beside the front door so she picked it up and, with another glance upwards, started up the stairs.

Her chest grew tight with tension and she held her breath as she silently negotiated the steps on tiptoe. She had no idea what she would do when she confronted whoever had got in. All she knew was that she had to get to Ruby and if whoever was upstairs was intent on harming her baby she felt full sure that if she had to she'd kill them with her bare hands.

Silently, she reached the top step and gingerly paused outside the bedroom door which was ajar. She could see the moons and stars rotating gently around the walls. Raising the fire extinguisher to the level of her face, Martha took a deep breath and pushed the door open as hard as she could.

For a split second everything went blank as a massive surge of adrenalin coursed through her body. Then, nothing. Literally. When she finally registered the room as a whole, Martha saw that there was no one there apart from Ruby who was so soundly asleep that she hadn't even flinched at the door being pushed open. Martha stood there, stock still, the moons and stars still rotating silently, the only sound her breathing as she panted in the doorway.

Martha swung around. Logically, the intruder now had to be behind her. She charged across the landing – the bathroom – empty – as was her own bedroom. The small box-room was also empty, even the linen cupboard.

She returned to Ruby's room, unnerved, and checked the room again before pulling the door closed behind her and walking down the stairs. Her legs trembled as she replaced the fire extinguisher and checked over her shoulder again. Still nothing. She made her way back through the kitchen, and out to the conservatory door which she found definitely locked. It gave her some relief to know that the sounds from above had been just creaks after all, but they had sounded so like footsteps.

Martha shivered as she boiled the kettle and made herself a cup of tea which she took upstairs and drank sitting up in bed, under the covers but fully clothed, before she tentatively climbed out and undressed. It took all of her willpower to force herself out onto the landing and into the bathroom to clean her teeth, all the while listening for any more sounds from Ruby's bedroom, or anywhere in the house There was nothing to hear.

She returned for a last look into Ruby's room and gazed at the sleeping baby, longing to scoop her up in her arms and bring her into her own bed where she could lock them away. With a deep breath, Martha steeled herself. There is no one in the house, she reasoned. We are perfectly safe and you're imagining things that aren't there. She crept from Ruby's room and across the landing, feeling suddenly exhausted from her fright. She climbed into her own bed and turned to sleep, leaving her bedside light on.

8

Eyrie Farm,
Shipton Abbey,
Norfolk,
England

April 15th, 1953

Dear Sr Agnes,

*I start my letter again with an apology. I have been addressing
your letters to Caroline Devlin but of course your name is Sr
Agnes now. I am truly sorry. I only realised when my letters
arrived back here at Eyrie Farm. It means you won't have read
any of my news so far so I have enclosed the letters with this one
– read them in date order and you'll know what is happening. I
promise I'll address you correctly from now on. I asked Mammy
in my last letter what was the best way to address the envelope
so that's why it's addressed to Sr M Agnes Devlin but please
correct me if I'm wrong. I don't want any more of my letters to
go astray. To tell you the truth, I am surprised – and Mammy is
too – that they wouldn't know your lay name at the convent. At*

42

least the Reverend Mother would, surely? Mammy thinks that maybe your Reverend Mother doesn't want you to correspond with me because of my situation here with Marion. She could have opened my letters – Mammy says Reverend Mothers do that sometimes, or the Novice Mistresses do – and of course you are still a novice and they will be guarding you from outside influences.

I start this letter in very bad form, Sr Agnes. Marion is trying my patience and indeed she'd try the patience of a saint, although I think she's probably tried the patience of your patron saint already with her complete lack of chastity. I should try to be forgiving, like Jesus tells us, but I think that's very hard at the moment and hopefully writing this letter will calm me down.

In my last letter I told you that Mammy was sending over clothes that belonged to Granny Flynn for me to alter for Marion when she gets bigger. I did my best, Sr Agnes, I truly did, but you know that seamstressing was never my skill. To tell the truth, the clothes were a little old and they were all in black which was all that Granny Flynn wore after Granda Flynn died. Marion didn't like any of them. I told her that she didn't need to like them, that no one would be seeing her until after the baby was born and then she could burn the clothes if she wanted as she wouldn't have to hide herself any more.

What she did then was nearly a mortal sin. She leaped up from the chair by the fire and wouldn't calm herself down. She picked up the scissors that I'd been using to sew and didn't she start to cut up the clothes I was making for her! I was trying to pull them away and she was holding them out of my reach and waving the scissors around. I thought she'd stab me stone dead, so I did, with the way she was holding the sharp scissors. But worse than that! She ripped one dress clean through the middle and then took the scissors and held it over her belly and, God forgive her, threatened to stab herself! "I'll rip my belly open," she said, "and cut this babby out and burn it on the fire!" I started to cry – I'll tell you that I didn't know what to do!

When she's been like this before at home I've always called Daddy or Mammy and they've taken care of it, but here I was,

alone with her, begging her not to hurt the baby or herself. I
know that to kill herself would be a mortal sin, but what kind of
sin would it be to kill the baby when it's still in her before it's
baptised and freed from sin?

I told her to calm down and pray to the Baby Jesus not to be
so angry, and that her penance would be over soon. Oh, Sr
Agnes, that made her even more cross and didn't she go flying
out of the house without a coat on her and hopped onto the bike
– my bike I've come to think of it, even though Mr Mountford
said it was for both of us to share. I ran down the lane after her
but she wouldn't stop when I called her and she went out onto
the road. To make matters worse, what was she wearing only her
nightdress still! I was so worried about her, thinking she'd be
frozen to the bone, and what if the baby was harmed, or if she
fell off the bike or a motor car came along and she was killed
stone dead.

I ran out to the road after her but she was gone – I didn't
know which way she had turned and couldn't see a thing except
the barley fields around us. I ran a little of the way in one
direction and a little in another but she was nowhere to be seen.
I cried, Caroline, thinking that was the end of her. I started to run
to the neighbour's farm, then changed my mind and turned back
and headed toward the village. But then I thought she might be
hiding somewhere nearby – that surely she was and her in her
nightdress! – and if I caused a great hue and cry I would bring
even more shame on us needlessly. In the end I could think of
nothing better to do but go back into the cottage and sit by the
fire and pray she came back. Daddy would kill me if anything
happened to Marion – she's his pet, his oldest girl, despite all that
she's done.

I sat there for two hours, watching the clock as if that would
bring her back. Thank God, I thought, the evenings are a bit
longer now. Maybe that'll save her. I was out of my mind with
worry and had my coat on to go and search for her again when
I heard, of all things, a motor car pull up outside. Oh dear
God, it's the police, I thought, but it wasn't. Who was it only Mr

Mountford in a big shiny black motor car and Marion sitting in the back of it, with his overcoat on her shoulders, like she was the Queen of England! I nearly died of shame, Caroline, sorry, Sr Agnes.

She sat in the back seat and waited to be helped out of the car, like a lady. If I could have got near to her I'd have dragged her out, baby or not. There were two young lads in the car with her, Mr Mountford's sons. Robert, who is the same age as me, and Charles Junior who is about fifteen or sixteen. I was mortified and didn't know where to look. Mr Mountford held the door open for her and she had the nerve to hold her hand out to be helped down from the car. That did it for me! I grabbed her and told her to go in and upstairs as quickly as possible and she did. Just flounced into the house like Lady Muck.

Thank God Mr Mountford said nothing. He just told me to watch her more carefully, got back in his motor car and drove away down the road again, but the two young lads were staring at me out through the back window. I thought I'd pass out with the shame.

And do you think Marion was sorry? Not a bit of it, she went to her bed and barked orders at me to bring her bread and jam, that she was starving and no dinner ready for her. And she the one who hasn't eaten a dinner in weeks!

It gave me a terrible fright, the whole thing, and though she's been as good as Marion can be since, it makes me nervous to think what she might do or say. Sometimes I feel like I am the older one – she doesn't act a bit like she's nineteen years old, nearly twenty!

Please pray for me that she behaves herself between now and when the baby is born.

With lots of love,
May God be with you,

Lily x

9

June 19th

It was the first of many sleepless nights for Martha. Ruby began teething in earnest, waking during the night or early in the morning, crying for her soother, and then losing it five minutes later when she fell back to sleep and it dropped from her mouth, often falling through the bars of the cot. Frequently in the night, Martha would have to find a fresh one for her as her previous one would go missing as she tossed and turned. She had taken to placing a bank of five pacifiers on Ruby's bedside table at night-time so that they were convenient for her in the dark. Then as Ruby lost them through the night, she'd have a fresh one to hand. Martha also began to empathise with Sue's hatred for the dawn chorus as morning after morning it kept her awake between trips to Ruby's room.

The heat, too, was making it difficult to sleep. There had been no let-up in the heat wave and what had been so enjoyable at first was now oppressive and stifling. To top things off, some nights a bizarre and irritating scratching noise had started to come from the direction of the fireplace in Ruby's room – mice or rats most likely, who went on the move at night-time when the house was quiet. She was relieved to see that there were no signs of mouse-holes or droppings, so obviously the pests weren't emerging into

Ruby's room. However, Martha couldn't sleep through the persistent scrabbling when it started, hearing it through the baby monitor.

Finally she decided it was time to call Rob Mountford.

He arrived mid-afternoon on a sticky Thursday. Martha was puréeing food for Ruby in the kitchen, oblivious to the fact that he had come in through the open conservatory door. The hand-blender whizzed noisily, blocking out any sound so she didn't hear his footsteps behind her. She tutted as she splattered some puréed carrot out onto her arm and, as she turned to reach for a cloth, she saw Rob out of the corner of her eye. She screamed with fright, and dropped the blender, knocking puréed food all over the counter top and onto her clothes. Ruby let out a long wail of fright.

"Jesus!" Martha said and then, spotting that it was her landlord, her hand shot to her mouth. "I'm so sorry," she said loudly. "My *God* but you gave me a terrible fright. Oh, I'm sorry, Ruby." She bent to pick up the little girl whose eyes were fixed on the huge shape of the stranger inside the doorway.

Rob Mountford looked mortified. "I'm sorry," he said. "I knocked but you didn't hear me."

As well as being startled, Martha was slightly annoyed by his assumption that he could just walk in, but she didn't say anything. This was the country. Not London where you had to book a visit weeks in advance and then almost ring from outside the front door to say you were there. Ruby calmed slightly in her arms, although she still regarded the man with trepidation.

"It's fine," laughed Martha. "You just startled us. Would you like a cup of tea?"

Rob Mountford smiled, showing huge teeth. He was at least six feet four, reckoned Martha as she looked up at him.

"Yes, please, that'd be just the thing," he said.

Martha noticed that his cheeks were a little pink and wasn't sure if it was from the sun or if he was blushing. "No problem," she smiled, settling Ruby back on her playmat in the middle of the floor and turning to the kettle.

"I'll just nip up and take a look at the wall," said Rob and took a step toward the doorway. His eyes were fixed on Martha and he narrowly avoided stepping on Ruby's arm as he turned to leave, but didn't seem to notice, and Martha heard him stomp up the stairs in his dusty boots.

She plugged the kettle in and popped two teabags into a pot before going to the fridge for milk. She set down the carton on the worktop and then picked Ruby up, popping her into her high chair. "Best to be out of harm's way," she whispered to the little girl who giggled and reached out to tug her mother's hair. When Rob eventually returned, Martha was glad she had made the wise move to lift her daughter to safety as he stomped back into the kitchen and stood on Ruby's playmat, his steel toe-capped boots coming to a halt exactly where her head had been. Martha handed him a cup of tea. It looked like one from a doll's tea-set in his giant hand.

"It's all quiet up there at the moment," he said, refusing a chocolate biscuit.

"Yes," confirmed Martha. "It only starts at night, presumably when the house goes quiet. I hear it through Ruby's monitor."

"Annoying," said Rob and slurped his tea noisily.

Martha imagined that he could probably inhale the drink in one go and then crunch the cup between his teeth.

"Have you seen any droppings?" he asked.

"Thankfully, no," said Martha and shuddered. "I've actually got nothing against mice except the incontinence. We used to get them in London and I'd just spend all my time bleaching everything – *eurgh!*"

Rob seemed not to hear her. "Right then, no droppings. Sounds like it's confined inside then. It's these old houses – vermin find all sorts of nooks and crannies, bloody buggers pardon-my-language."

Martha tried not to grin. The 'pardon-my-language' was simply an extension of the word 'buggers', tacked on out of habit to negate the swear word. The man looked like he could kill you with a single swing of his fist and yet he apologised by rote for swearing.

"There's a bit of a crack in the breast as well," continued Rob.

"Pardon?" said Martha, unsure if she had heard him correctly.

"The breast. The chimney-breast. There's a crack in it." He looked at her as though she had asked him to explain what his shoes were. "Bang anything off it?"

Martha turned around to the sink so that he couldn't see her grin. "No," she said, barely able to prevent herself from giggling.

Rob seemed not to notice. "Right then. I'm going to have to take down the whole thing and start from scratch."

That was sufficient to wipe the smile from Martha's face. "How long will that take?" she asked, dismayed at the thought of the intrusion.

"I should get to you in about three weeks. Got a lot on with a new development."

"But when you actually start, how long will it take?"

"Can't really say," replied Rob. "We'll have to try to flush out whatever's nesting in there first and then close up all the places that it can get to and then we'll have to . . ."

Martha wasn't listening. "Oh look, it's fine. Once you promise to get in and out as fast as you can when you start. I work from here as well as live here and I can't really afford too much intrusion."

Rob shrugged. "We'll do our best. Can't do no more'n that."

"I suppose not," replied Martha resignedly.

There was a moment of silence, broken by Rob handing her back the cup that looked so tiny in his hands. "Thanks for the tea. I'd best be off."

Martha took the cup from him. "Well, thanks for coming to check it out."

Rob turned to go, then hesitated in the doorway of the conservatory. "I don't suppose you'd like to come for a drink in the Abbot's on Saturday night?" he asked, timidly.

It was the last thing that Martha had expected him to say.

"Oh," she said in surprise, her cheeks turning pink. "Wow. Um, well . . . yeah, sure. Why not?" She instantly regretted accepting but it was too late, the words were out. She hadn't been out with anyone since Dan, and sure as hell didn't want a relationship on the agenda along with everything else. A part of her felt that it might be a good idea to accept, however, if she wanted the rodents out of the walls sooner rather than later.

"Oh!" said Rob, clearly taken aback. He had obviously been expecting rejection. "That's great. I'll pick you up here round eight then?"

Martha was about to nod when a light went on in her head. "Oh hang on," she said. "I can't. I've no baby-sitter!" She was so thrown by the unexpected invitation that she had momentarily forgotten Ruby.

Rob's face was crestfallen. "I could see if Alison Stockwell is available," he suggested. "Mary's daughter. She's about fifteen, baby-sits for my sister occasionally."

Martha's smile slipped a little. "Perfect! See you at eight then!"

Rob's smile returned. "Brilliant," he beamed. "If there's a problem I'll let you know – what I'll do is bring Alison with me to mind your little boy when I come."

With that he turned on his heel and left before Martha had time to correct him. She looked at her daughter who was engaged in rattling a small toy as hard as she could.

"Oh dear, Ruby-Doo," said Martha as she put the teacups in the sink. "It looks like Mummy's got a date."

10

June 21st

With no call from Rob Mountford by five on Saturday, Martha assumed that Alison Stockwell's services had been secured. She hadn't mentioned the date to Mary the previous day at crèche in order to keep it as low profile as possible. Hopefully, something would go wrong.

Sue hadn't been at all sympathetic.

"But I don't *want* to go!" wailed Martha down the phone eventually, having patiently listened to a long lecture from her friend about 'getting back out there' and being 'back in the saddle' and other clichés.

"Nonsense," said Sue. "Of course you want to go!"

Martha heard her exhale a long puff of smoke. "Aren't you in a hotel room?" she asked with a shocked tone in her voice.

"It's got an open window. Anyway, stop trying to change the subject. Even if it's not the romance of the century, at the very least it'll get you out of the house and meeting a few people."

Martha sighed as she stood in the shower while Ruby napped. She didn't object in the slightest to meeting a few people – it was having drinks with her landlord that made her wary. Apart from the fact that he was at least three times her size, she was nervous that he wanted more than she was prepared to give, and that if it went wrong she might never get the rats out of her 'breast', as Rob might put it.

The lights flickered as she stepped from the shower. She wondered had the break forecast in the weather finally come, and padded back into her bedroom, wrapped in a towel, to look out the window. The sky in the direction of the motorway was slate grey although it was still sunny in her garden. There was a storm on the way, most likely.

It took almost an hour to get Ruby to bed. She knew something was up, having seen her mum blow-dry her hair and apply make-up. She knew that her mum didn't smell right either and Martha kicked herself for spritzing on perfume before the baby was asleep.

Eventually she settled, her moons and stars circling the walls, and Hugo in his habitual position by her head. Martha stood in the kitchen wearing jeans and a floaty chiffon top and poured herself a large glass of wine. As she did so, a bright flash of lightning illuminated the darkening garden and she jumped, feeling the static in the air. She was wondering if she should go and cover up mirrors, when the doorbell rang. Five to eight, she noted on the clock. Someone's eager. She turned to go and answer the door.

"On second thoughts . . ." she said aloud and turned back to the countertop, picked up the glass of wine and knocked it back in one. Then she opened the door to Rob and the baby-sitter.

Alison Stockwell was a chubby teenager, dressed in skinny jeans, a long T-shirt and cardigan, a scarf, and scuffed ballet pumps over which her feet spilled slightly. She had a friendly smile underneath her bed-head hair and patiently took in Martha's long-winded explanation about what to do should Ruby wake, stir, or even breathe loudly. Alison recognised a new mum, not used to baby-sitters, but Rob was showing signs of impatience.

By the time Rob and Martha were leaving, thick raindrops were beginning to plop down onto the windscreen of Rob's Land Rover and he was muttering about being late. Martha wondered how on earth they could be late for a simple drink but the rain began to bucket down suddenly and she stayed silent while Rob tried to negotiate down the lane through sheets of rain that the wipers couldn't keep pace with.

Martha usually loved the route into Shipton Abbey – a short half mile but beautiful. The country lane off which Hawthorn Cottage was situated ran parallel to the shoreline four or five miles away across green fields filled with ripening corn and barley, the sight of which Martha adored. Tonight, though, she was glad to finally make out the Shipton Abbey sign and begin the descent down the hill to the little village, dominated by the ruined abbey overlooking the estuary which brought the sea curling round the land and almost right up to its walls.

At the bottom of the hill, Rob turned the Land Rover into the sheltered car park of the Abbot's Rest. A sheet of lightning lit up the car as the storm grew closer overhead. Martha looked at Rob and made out a look of grim annoyance on his face – presumably at having to drive in difficult weather conditions. He pulled up as close to the front door of the fourteenth-century building as he could and dashed out to open Martha's door for her. He seemed disappointed when she determinedly pushed it open herself and ran for the door of the pub, taking shelter in the outer porch while he lumbered through the rain, locking the Land Rover with his key fob.

The pub was relatively deserted when they stepped down onto the flagstoned floor.

"Oh my goodness, that rain is something else!" said Martha breathlessly, going through the rituals of stepping out of the rain like shaking her hands and smoothing down her damp hair.

Rob ignored her completely and instead peered worriedly down the bar, looking for someone. Martha was taken aback by this rudeness and wondered if his annoyance had in fact been at her and not at the difficult driving conditions.

"Sorry we're late," said Rob suddenly to a man who appeared behind the bar.

"No problem at all," said the man and smiled at Martha. "John Farnley. Landlord and proprietor of this establishment." He looked back to Rob. "We're very quiet tonight with that weather so there's no pressure. Come through."

Martha glanced at Rob and for the first time took in what he was wearing – charcoal-grey slacks, a white shirt and a black cashmere V-neck sweater with shiny black loafers – very smart compared to her jeans and top, and she wondered what the hell was going on.

Martha followed Rob through the pub, giving the other customers a cursory glance as she did so. One old man at the bar, an old lady on her own staring at them as they went by, a biker couple with pints of cider. Martha thought it all looked decidedly grim.

John Farnley had stepped out from behind the bar and was holding open a small wooden door at the back of the pub with a sign saying 'The Refectory' on it. "Here you go, folks," he said.

At first all Martha saw was candlelight in the dim room but as Rob walked her through the doorway she made out that she was in a small dining room, each table lit with tea-lights. The ceiling was low and beamed, like her cottage, the windowsills deep and the walls whitewashed. To her right was a huge open fireplace freshly stocked with logs, with a mantelpiece lit by more tea-lights. There were no more than eleven or twelve tables, some with benches for seats, others with ancient-looking chairs, all with gleaming white linen tablecloths and shiny cutlery. John Farnley indicated that Martha should follow him to a secluded booth created by two high-backed church pews.

The table sat beside one of the small, leaded windows, lashed by the thundery rain and lit up occasionally by flashes of sheet lightning. So this is what they were late for. It was all very cosy and romantic, indeed. Oh shit, thought Martha as she scooched in toward the wall and Rob squeezed into the pew to sit directly opposite her. As he did so, he shifted the table with his knees so that it tilted precariously and Martha grabbed her drinking glasses to prevent them falling into her lap.

"Do you like it?" asked Rob grumpily when he was finally seated and nothing was broken.

"This is lovely, Rob," she said. "I never knew it was here actually. You shouldn't have gone to all this trouble – a drink

would have suited me fine. I'm sorry for making us late though
– I thought a drink was all we were coming for."

Rob's huge face softened a little at the apology and she found
herself faced with the same man who had asked her out in the
kitchen.

"I thought you might like a meal to say welcome to Shipton
Abbey," he mumbled.

Martha realised that she was, in fact, very hungry and it
would be lovely not to have to cook for herself. "That's really
thoughtful – thanks, Rob," she smiled.

The Refectory was an absolute treat. While not Michelin-
starred, it was Michelin-recommended and Martha was very
impressed indeed. There were only three or four other diners,
creating a gentle hum of conversation which added to the
atmosphere. Martha ordered a goat's cheese and beetroot salad
to start and scallops with asparagus risotto for her main course.
It was a little difficult to enjoy, however, as she found herself
having to do most of the talking.

Rob seemed to be working from a list of questions that he had
memorised: "So, how do you like it at Hawthorn Cottage?", "Is
your baby boy settling in?", "Oh, you're divorced, that's a shame –
how long?" and so on, with Martha giving answers that seemed to
get longer and longer as Rob stared blankly at her, never taking
the cue that Martha had finished speaking. She found herself
continuing to speak to avoid the long silences.

In turn, Rob wasn't very forthcoming with answers to any of
the questions that Martha managed to sneak in. "How is
business doing?" – "Fine"; "Have you always lived in Shipton
Abbey?" – "Yes"; "Is there a Mrs Mountford?" (Stupid question,
she thought. If there was, it was unlikely that she'd be sitting here
with the Man Mountain.)

She got a break when Rob went to the toilet after the main
course. It afforded her the chance to pick up her knife and fork
again and demolish the rest of her scallops. They were slightly
cold by this time, but still delicious.

This place really was perfect, she thought, looking around her.

If you were on a date with someone you actually wanted to be there with, of course. It wasn't that Rob was bad – scrubbed up, he was actually very handsome with his tanned face against the crisp collar of his shirt. His eyes were a charcoal grey, similar to his expensive trousers, she'd noted. There was just no chemistry between them – partly because she wasn't looking for a relationship, partly because they had nothing in common in the slightest. And, despite the amount she talked, she got the feeling that none of it was going in. She sighed. What a waste of a perfectly romantic situation.

There were things about Rob that rankled with Martha also – like the way he constantly referred to Ruby as a boy and had already called her both Rudy and Reuben during the meal – when he bothered at all. It was clear that he wasn't remotely interested in the little girl and totally unaware that this was a problem for Martha.

Another fly in the ointment was the way he spoke to the waiting staff. They were flawless by Martha's standards and in her ten years in advertising she had dined at some of the finest restaurants in London. Rob, however, spoke down to the staff as if he had been taught that this was the correct thing to do by someone from a different era.

Martha was mortified when he returned from the bathroom and spotted the main-course dishes still on the table.

"They haven't cleared away yet?" he bellowed, clearly outraged by the sight. He was still standing up when he bawled toward the kitchen doors. "Can we get a little *service* in here!"

"No, Rob, sshhh! It's my fault," said Martha, glancing around to see if the other diners were staring at them. They were. "I had some more of my scallops when you went to the loo and the staff didn't clear up because I was still eating!"

Rob didn't listen and looked agitatedly around him until the friendly waitress appeared. He instantly ordered her loudly to "Clean this away and bring us the sweet trolley."

Martha cringed, and smiled apologetically at the girl who said, "Of course, sir" to the rude request.

Rob sat down again, looking pleased with himself and his control of the situation. Thankfully he didn't object when the 'sweet trolley' turned out to be a menu of delicious-sounding desserts and ordered himself a chocolate brownie. Martha couldn't resist the Sicilian lemon tart and savoured every mouthful.

Rob was silent after the meal, to Martha's relief. Despite her protestations of tiredness, however, he insisted on having another drink at the bar before they left. John Farnley's house white was excellent by pub standards but Martha felt brought down to earth, having enjoyed the wines in the restaurant which were chosen to complement each course.

They sat in silence for a while at the bar, Rob sinking a pint of ale. Martha presumed that he would order them a taxi to get home. She then decided it was her turn to try again to make conversation.

"So, Rob, who was it lived in the cottage before it was left derelict?" she asked.

"Not sure," came the reply.

She was sure that she detected something more behind the response. There was something in the way his eyes shifted to the right as he answered. She decided to probe more. "Mary tells me it was called Eyrie Farm before," she said. "That could be taken as quite a spooky name, couldn't it?"

Rob's eyes shifted again to his right. Martha followed them and saw them directed toward the old lady who had stared at them when they arrived. She was staring at them again and as Martha's eyes met hers she stood up, resting a crooked, wizened hand on the table to balance herself. She started to move unsteadily toward the bar, shuffling round the table where she had been sitting alone, negotiating her way around the bar stools.

"Right," said Rob. "Time to go."

Martha looked back at him as he got off his bar stool and saw that he was deliberately pretending not to see the old lady approaching. She saw, too, that he had taken his keys from his pocket. "You're going to drive?" she said in disbelief, her attention drawn from the old woman.

"Of course," he said distractedly and, turning, walked away.

Martha slid off her bar stool. "But you've . . ." she started.

She was interrupted by a crackly voice in her ear. "There's a boy up there," it said.

Martha turned to see the old lady behind her. She was tiny, even smaller than Martha, her face lined with a thousand creases, her watery eyes sad and blue. She slurred her words when she spoke but Martha could detect a hint of an Irish accent.

"At Eyrie Farm," she continued.

Martha stared at her, mesmerised by a strange fear, trying to take in every aspect of the ancient face. "What boy?" she asked.

"A little boy," the old woman said, gesturing as if Martha should know what she was talking about. Her eyes were glazed.

Martha was about to ask her what she meant when she was startled by a bellow from the doorway.

"Come *on*!" shouted Rob gruffly.

Momentarily stunned by the tone of his voice, Martha scurried after him and, like a scolded child, stepped quickly through the door he held open for her.

In the Land Rover she kicked herself – firstly for allowing herself to even step into a vehicle with someone who was clearly over the limit, secondly for allowing herself to be spoken to like that. She sat in silence, staring out the window, knowing that to ask who the old lady was and what the hell she meant would either get no answer at all or at best an unintelligible grunt. This made her even angrier and she seethed silently while Rob leaned over the wheel, deep in concentration. It was getting harder to see again – the storm had abated while they were in the restaurant but now seemed to be returning and gathering strength as it came.

The short trip back to Hawthorn Cottage was quiet and tense and seemed to take forever. An anxious Martha was relieved to make out the gap in the hedge that was the start of her driveway and relaxed a little as Rob negotiated the turn carefully. She could hear a low rumble of thunder overhead as the cottage came into view. There's something wrong, thought Martha. Why is it completely dark? A sudden flash of lightning illuminated the scene before her and she shrieked in fright to see a dark figure standing at the bay window of her living room.

"*What?*" shouted Rob gruffly as he himself jumped and pushed down on the brake suddenly, twisting the wheel sharply to avoid Martha's own car parked in the drive.

He had barely come to a halt when Martha flung herself out of the door and pelted across the gravel to her front door, fumbling in her bag for the keys as she ran. She had just reached towards the lock when the door swung open and she was greeted by a clearly terrified Alison Stockwell, Ruby crying in her arms.

"Thank God you're home, Mrs Armstrong!" said Alison.

Martha fumbled to take the crying Ruby from her. "What happened?" she asked, breathlessly. "Is Ruby okay?"

"She's fine, Mrs Armstrong, but –"

"Why is it dark?" demanded Rob, appearing behind Martha, clearly annoyed and reaching over Martha's head to flick the hall light-switch on and off.

"I don't know," said Alison, her voice trembling. "It went all dark about an hour ago and Ruby was crying and then there was this huge crash from her room – I didn't know what to do!"

Martha felt herself grow annoyed as Rob charged past her and up the stairs. "Why didn't you ring me?" she demanded of the teenager.

Alison started to cry fresh tears. "My battery went dead – I don't know why, it was full when I got here. I couldn't use the landline with the power gone – I've just been trying to keep Ruby calm but I think she's scared of the dark or something."

Martha jumped as the lights suddenly came on around her. She could now fully see Alison's terrified, tear-stained face, white with fear and worry, and instantly felt sorry for her. "You poor thing," she said. "I'm sorry for shouting." She put an arm around the teenager's shoulders. "You must have had an awful fright. Come in and tell me exactly what happened."

She guided the frightened girl back into the living room where the TV had flickered back into life and the lamplight was warm. Alison shakily sat down on the armchair beside the fireplace and

Martha sat on the couch, gently lying Ruby down beside her. Ruby was instantly calmed by the brightness and her mother's presence and started to play with her feet. She stared across at her baby-sitter.

"Look – she's calm as anything now so don't worry about her," said Martha. "What time did she wake?"

"You see, that's the thing," replied Alison, her eyes red-rimmed and wide. "She's been awake all evening – or at least that's what it sounded like. I could hear this awful crying coming from her room – terrible sobbing and gasping like she was trying to catch her breath, so I'd run upstairs to get her but when I'd get into her room she'd be sound asleep."

Martha nodded. "She's teething. She gets really upset sometimes if her soother falls out but she can sometimes get it back in herself before you get there."

Alison looked at her in disbelief. "This wasn't teething pains – I've worked with my mum in the crèche and I know what teething pains sound like. This was more like someone was trying to hurt her – it was a screaming and gasping for air sort of crying."

Martha nodded again. Alison might be used to babies but she was clearly embellishing the story. "So when did she wake up properly then?" she asked patiently. She could hear rumbling and scraping upstairs as Rob did whatever he was doing and she wished he'd stop.

"When the lights went out. She started to cry properly then so I went up to get her. I picked her up to try to comfort her but – well, her room felt funny so I brought her downstairs."

"What do you mean the room *felt* funny?" asked Martha, rubbing Ruby's tummy.

Alison hesitated. "This sounds stupid but like there was someone else in there."

Martha dismissed the thought. "That was probably static electricity from the storm. It can make you feel all tingly sometimes. Besides, it can be very disconcerting with the blackout blind in that room."

Alison looked at Martha with a dismissive look of her own. "It was freezing cold up there as well. Much colder than down here. I brought Ruby down to keep her warm as much as anything. Then there was that massive crash from her room – I was too scared to go up to see and my phone wouldn't work so I just stood at the window and waited . . . it was so dark . . ."

Martha put her hand out to touch the girl's knee. "I don't blame you for being scared, you poor thing. Thanks so much for looking after Ruby – you did all the right things."

Alison gave a weak smile and looked up as Rob stamped into the room.

"Bloody bugger plaster's off the wall," he growled. This time there was no apology for the swear word. "Brought this down with it." He thrust out his hand which held the smashed frame of the photo of Ruby and Martha that she had hung on the chimney-breast.

Martha took it from him and looked at it in disappointment.

"That was the bang you heard, I reckon, Alison," he continued. "Power's fine though – the trip-switch had been flipped. Lightning must have caused a power surge or something. Plaster's gone where you've been hearing that scratching. Whatever's doing it must be dislodging it or something, I dunno."

Martha shuddered as if someone had walked over her grave.

"I'll try to get it sorted for you as soon as I can," said Rob. "But I'm very busy at the moment. You right there, Alison?"

Martha noticed that he hadn't once looked her in the eye as he spoke. Alison stood up meekly and followed Rob out into the hall.

"Wait," said Martha, remembering that Rob was over the limit. "You can't –"

But he was gone. Alison looked back almost apologetically at Martha and followed him. Still on the sofa with Ruby, Martha heard the door click closed and, as the outside sensor light came on, through the window saw Alison step into the passenger side of the Land Rover and watched as Rob executed a clumsy three-point turn and drove away.

11

June 22nd

The sun was beating down again the following afternoon, as if the storm had never happened. A fresher breeze blew through the open door of the conservatory, however, which was a huge relief to Martha whose head was thumping as she lay on the wicker sofa while Ruby thankfully had a long sleep upstairs.

Martha wasn't hungover from the fine wines at the restaurant but from the half-bottle she had drunk by herself at home after Rob and Alison had left. Ruby had settled to sleep happily in Martha's bed and then Martha had gone into the other bedroom to survey the damage. It was messy – a pile of rubble lay at the base of the wall where the hearth was encased and some red bricks were exposed. Rob, of course, had made the mess worse by tramping through the rubble, pressing it into the cracks between the beams of the beautiful wooden floor and kicking it far and wide under the cot and over to the changing unit. The unmistakable trail of his dusty footprints was everywhere. Martha scanned the scene and swore under her breath. She'd clean it up tomorrow. She went back downstairs and almost absent-mindedly poured herself a glass from the open wine in the fridge. She was seething still – at the fact Rob must have done a shoddy job in the first place for this damage to happen and at the fact that he had created even more mess for her to clean up. Her thoughts turned to the disastrous date – the way he had spoken to her, to the waitress and the drive home. The deceit in asking her for a drink and then actually taking her for a candlelit meal – the damned *presumption* of it all. She was annoyed too with Alison and her tales of gasping and screaming. What was she trying to do – frighten the wits out of her?

Martha realised she was dwelling on her anger because if she was angry then she couldn't give in to what was actually bothering her. The simple fact was, she was scared. All these creaky floorboards, scratching noises, thunder and lightning, Alison's stories about the room feeling like there was someone else in it. It was ridiculous but it was starting to unnerve her. She poured herself a second glass of wine and looked around the walls of her living room. She wasn't easily scared but she was finding more and more that Hawthorn Cottage – Eyrie Farm – was putting her on edge.

But as she lay now, her head splitting, in the conservatory, she was more concerned with how awful she felt than with how the house made her feel. She reached her hand out to the pint glass of water on the table beside her and grimaced as she took a mouthful and realised it was warm. With a sigh, she pushed herself off the couch and was about to go into the kitchen when out of the conservatory window she saw the familiar shape of Mary Stockwell heading for the front door.

Martha groaned. She really didn't want company, especially that of a woman who was undoubtedly going to berate her for leaving her daughter alone with a crotchety baby in a storm and then not paying her. Martha picked up the envelope with Alison's baby-sitting wages in it, which she'd forgotten to give her the night before, and shuffled toward the front door.

Mary's face was surprisingly friendly as Martha opened the door.

"Mary, how nice to see you," said Martha. "Before you say anything, I am so sorry about last night – poor Alison –"

Mary cut her short. "'Poor Alison' is fine," she said quickly.

"It was nothing that a four-hour conversation with one of her school pals didn't sort out."

Martha noticed she was peering eagerly down the hallway behind her.

"I didn't come about Alison," Mary went on. "I came to see how you and Ruby were doing after it all – are you okay?"

Martha looked puzzled as she stood by for Mary to come through. "Us?" she said. "We're fine – apart from the mess in Ruby's room and my thumping headache!"

Mary looked relieved as she stepped in. "Oh good," she said, glancing up the stairs behind Martha's head. "Whatever happened? All I got from Alison was a rather jumbled tale of gasping babies and collapsing chimneys!"

Martha smiled. "Come and see," she said and led Mary up the stairs to Ruby's room, signalling for her to shush so as not to wake the sleeping baby.

Martha opened the door wide and pointed silently at the wall. Only the barest glimpse of exposed red brick was visible. She had tidied up that morning and stood a large picture up against the wall to hide the damage. "I cleaned up what I could," she whispered. "And that hideous thing was the best I could find to hide the bricks. Neither Dan nor I wanted it from our house but I lost the toss unfortunately – typical where it concerns my marriage, it seems!" Martha grinned, realising she was sounding bitter. "Sorry for griping. But seriously – a giant picture of a hare in a massive white frame!"

Mary laughed softly and crept further into the room, to Martha's surprise. She silently crossed to the damaged wall and peered behind the picture, then leant it back against the wall and crossed again to the doorway.

"Of course Rob Mountford made a right old mess tramping around in the debris," continued Martha.

"That'd be Rob alright! I remember him when he was young playing with my neighbours' kids next door. He was always walking allsorts into the carpet there too – mainly dog or cat allsorts!"

Mary grimaced and Martha wrinkled her nose and laughed.

"I can't help but be mad at him, though," she said then. "If he'd just done the wall right in the first place before painting it then none of this would have happened."

Mary looked puzzled. "That's what I can't figure out," she said. "Big Rob Mountford may be many things but a shoddy workman isn't one of them. He's very thorough, and excellent at what he does. His reputation round these parts is second to none. And he put so much into this place – spent a couple of years getting it right so I just can't see him doing a rubbish plastering job. Anyway – you promised I could have a snoop round – can I take you up on that?"

Martha smiled. "Absolutely," she said and stretched out her arm. "This way for the guided tour, madam!"

When they had finished viewing the house, Martha made tea and they sat in the conservatory to drink it.

"Robbie's certainly done a super job on this place," said Mary admiringly, then added with a smirk, "Speaking of Robbie, how did your romantic meal go?"

"How did you know it was a meal?" asked Martha, aghast. "It was only meant to be a drink and when I got there it was all candlelight and wine! But 'romantic' it wasn't! It was impossible to even talk to him – he had a list of questions he seemed to have learned by rote, and other than that he was monosyllabic!"

"Oh dear, my fault, I think," said Mary, sipping her tea. "When he called to ask Alison to baby-sit he sort of cornered me and asked me for advice. He was insistent on the surprise table in The Refectory – I couldn't get him to stick to just the drink. I *did*, however, advise him to take an interest in what you had to say – ask a few questions and that. Rob was always what you might call literal about things."

Martha nodded, finally understanding some of the previous night's events. "Now it's a bit clearer alright," she smiled. "He's not going to get all *serious*, is he? I'm just out of a really horrible divorce and I can't even think of a relationship at the moment, no matter how much of a cliché that sounds."

"I understand completely. Hopefully Rob will too. He can be a nice guy, you know."

"I know you've known him a lot longer than me but I've found him a little, well, rude sometimes."

"You mean arrogant?" smiled Mary.

"That too!" Martha fired back, her face spreading into a grin.

"Oh dear," sighed Mary. "That'll be his dad, and his grandad, I suppose. Rob was always told to just go out there and take what he wanted and his forefathers led by example. They were self-made millionaires and I think Robbie was brought up thinking greed was good and all that 80's stuff. He was a late baby as well which didn't help."

"That's exactly what I thought had happened."

"It's not Rob's fault he's the way he is," said Mary. "It was just him and his sister and his dad growing up – his mum died when they were small and she was much younger than his dad. There they were, growing up in that massive house over the far side of town – have you seen it yet?"

Martha shook her head.

"Take a look at it – it'll explain even more." Mary rolled her eyes. "Rob had hard work beaten into him from a very young age but he was also told that if he worked hard he could have pretty much anything he wanted. Charlie – his dad – made him go to work for Mountford Construction the minute he left school. He let him take over six years ago and then gave him this place as a gift when he made his first million by all accounts."

"So he didn't just pick it up as a derelict site, then?" asked Martha, startled, thinking back to what she had originally been told.

"Oh no – it was run down and unoccupied but not derelict. And it's belonged to the Mountfords for years as far as I know. It was really Rob's baby over the past while though – first thing he ever did as a hobby actually. Got him out of old Charlie's hair for a while. Poor Rob still lives at home and I think he's under pressure to find a Mrs Mountford. I think Charlie's pushing for little Mountford heirs and heiresses as well!"

"Oh dear heavens," laughed Martha. "I guess I was lucky he didn't produce a ring and a vicar then!"

"Too right!" laughed Mary. "Bless him, he'll get the message eventually. Just don't go sending him any mixed ones."

Martha sat upright. "He won't get *any* mixed messages from me, trust me!"

"Keep it that way!"

"I will."

"Oh, Mary, I forgot this." She pulled the envelope with Alison's baby-sitting money in it out of her pocket. "Alison was ushered into his Land Rover before I got a chance to give it to her."

Mary waved the envelope away. "No need to worry about it," she said. "Mr M took care of the baby-sitting bill."

Martha groaned. "Dammit! I'll have to pay him back now. Letting him pay for Reuben's baby-sitter would never do!"

Laughing at Mary's puzzled expression, she explained Rob's difficulty with both the name and gender of her daughter.

"Speaking of little boys actually," she said then, as she walked Mary around the side of the cottage to leave, "maybe you can fill me in on something."

"What's that now?"

"Well, there was an old lady in the pub last night . . ." Martha thought that she saw Mary stiffen slightly. "She made a point of coming up to me to tell me there was a little boy in the house – what was all that about?"

Mary sighed. "That'll be poor old Lil Flynn. Tends to be a bit fond of the sauce, poor old thing. Used to be a seamstress, lives out on the marshes. I wouldn't pay her any attention."

"But what did she mean? She singled me out to tell me that?" Martha had a feeling that Mary knew exactly what Lil Flynn meant.

"Nothing to worry about," said Mary. "Oh listen – there's Ruby awake!"

Martha thought that Mary looked somewhat relieved by the interruption.

"I'd better head off then," said Mary. "You're sure you're both alright?"

"We're both fine," said Martha reassuringly.

"Right then. I'll see you both in the morning!"

With a wave, Mary turned and walked down the driveway, leaving Martha watching her, and feeling that she was missing something.

12

Eyrie Farm,
Shipton Abbey,
Norfolk,
England

May 25th, 1953

Dear Caroline,

Many thanks for your kind letter of May 1st last. I understand that you do not wish to receive any more letters from me because of our particular family situation and appreciate that you are praying for my immortal soul and that of Marion. Thank you for returning my previous letters to me, so now I have a complete record of everything that has happened to us here in Norfolk.

I understand, Caroline, that it's not you saying that you don't want to hear from me, that it's Reverend Mother who as we know from our schooldays is a right old battleaxe, as they say here in Shipton. I can say that to you now because I won't post any more of my letters to you, not even this one, but I will keep them in case some day you will be able to read them without fear

69

of harming your own immortal soul by association. I can also mention another thing now, which I didn't before because I was ashamed to, but indeed you must have put two and two together yourself and realised that I haven't been to Mass since we came here. I know that normally that's a mortal sin but Mammy says it's all right as I am caring for a sick person. I hope she is right. I should have asked you before as you could have asked the nuns about it.

Well, to turn to everyday matters, things have been quiet here since last I wrote. Marion never again referred to that day she ran away and neither did Mr Mountford, although as he hasn't called again I fear that we have made a show of ourselves and he is sure to turf us out on our ears before long. I don't know what we would do in that case. Would we go home and then Marion would have to go to the nuns, or would we stay here in England and try to find somewhere to live?

Now that the weather is better, I have dug myself a little piece of ground at the back of the house and planted some onions and some other seeds that I got in the village. I'm not sure why, as we will be home by the time they are ready to be harvested, but it was lovely to be outside here with the smell of the sea in the air and the lovely warm summer beginning. The digging and hoeing made me see that time is passing and soon the baby will be here.

I wonder what Daddy will tell us to do afterwards? Has he arranged maybe to have the baby adopted in England or will we bring it back to Ireland to have it adopted there and then myself and Marion can go home, say that we've been staying with an aunt or something like that? I am full of questions these days. Thinking about them keeps my mind from what I should be doing, which is studying for my Leaving Certificate.

Marion has decided that she wants to keep the baby and return home. She tells me now that the father is an actor in the Gaiety Theatre and she wants to live in sin with him and cause a great scandal. I am blue in the face telling her that the baby will have to go to live with a deserving family, a couple who can't have babies maybe, and who will love it. It makes me sad to think of that. I am so tired of telling Marion these things that I have stopped and just stay quiet when she tells one of her tales. I have learned that she might not be telling the truth. Next week the father might be a circus acrobat.

She is a dab hand with the scissors these days. Thank God she hasn't threatened to harm the baby again but we needed to have haircuts in these past weeks and I cut hers short, like the new fashion. It was her turn to cut mine and I asked her just to trim the ends but what did she do? She didn't even cut the whole thing short, she just cut one side to my ear and left the other to my shoulder! She laughed herself sick, and danced around holding the scissors out of my reach before she put it somewhere I couldn't find it. I looked a right eejit, standing there with my hair short on one side, and long on the other. Then she got bored and went to bed and left me there. I had to search high and low for the scissors and then when I found it I had to try to cut my hair short at the back and on the side that she hadn't chopped. I still look stupid, with my hair short at my ears and uneven. I can't even tie it up because it's not long enough. I wish Mammy were here, Caroline, so she could give me a hug and look after me and send Marion to her room. She's the only person who can get through to her when she gets her moods. And I'm tired of being the mammy here in the cottage. I want to go home.

May God be with you,

Lily

13

June 30th

Much to Martha's surprise, it was only just over a week before Rob's Land Rover crunched over the gravel driveway and he arrived to start work in Ruby's room. He and Martha hadn't spoken since the night of their so-called date and he had given no indication to her that he was arriving at all.

Martha was working in her study, Ruby at the crèche, when he arrived and let himself in the front door and up the stairs without a word. Martha heard the door unlock and open and froze at her desk, hearing the footsteps head upstairs. Nervously, she popped her head out the study door and crept down the hallway to peer up the stairs. On spotting the huge dusty footprints making a trail in the door and upward, however, she soon realised who it was in her house and quietly let herself back into the study without acknowledging him. She wasn't quite sure what to say to him.

On top of everything else, she was exhausted. Ruby's teething was keeping her awake for at least an hour every night on top of the numerous trips in and out of her room each night to replace her soother. Martha was deeply regretting ever giving her one in the first place. She hadn't seemed to need it half as much in London.

There was something that was puzzling Martha far more, however. Something odd was happening to the soothers she had taken to lining up on Ruby's bedside table at night-time so that they were easily to hand in the dark. What bothered Martha was where she was finding the discarded ones. In London, they had always fallen within a short radius of the cot, or rolled underneath to gather dust. Here, however, she kept finding them hidden behind the picture of the hare that she was using to hide the exposed brick of the chimney-breast. And last night, she was sure she'd only used three of the stash of five. When she'd gone in to tidy up that morning, however, she'd found only one left on the bedside table. Three were scattered around the cot and one behind the picture.

Martha gazed out her study window trying to figure out just what Ruby was doing that meant the soothers ended up behind the picture. She was also trying to remember going up to her a fourth time to give her the last soother. Her only theory was that there must be a slant on the floor near the cot, though it didn't look like it, and somehow the soothers sometimes rolled over to the chimney-breast. Well, it wasn't like Ruby was *putting* them there herself so that had to be the reason. In that case, however, she'd hear them on the monitor hitting the floor – then again she was so tired at the moment that when she did sleep, it was deep and dream-filled. Sometimes she was sure she heard Ruby crying in the night and would stumble out of bed, still asleep, and across the landing into the dim room to find her in a sound slumber, her stars and moons circling the walls silently.

The scratching in the wall hadn't abated either – if anything it was worse, and certainly more frequent. Ruby seemed to sleep right through it, but Martha lay awake, night after night, for hours, hearing it come over the monitor. It would start as a faint tapping noise, sounding more like scratching after a while – then it would die out, sometimes for hours on end, only to suddenly come back stronger than before.

Martha's skin felt tight with tiredness and her eyes were red and puffy. Truth be told, the house was starting to bring her down. It was bright and friendly in the daytime when she looked around her at the pale yellow walls of her study, decorated with photographs of Ruby and framed shots of places where Martha had been – a black and white shot of the Piazza Navona in Rome, and her favourite – a shot of the copy of Michelangelo's David outside the Medici Palace in Florence.

Since that night of the storm, however, she had found herself less comfortable in the cottage, aware of every creak and groan of a floorboard, tuned in to noises at night-time that wouldn't have bothered her previously. She realised that the house was beginning to make her feel *stressed* of all things, and that she was investing a lot of time and energy into reassuring herself that noises meant nothing.

She heard a thump from above her and flinched in her chair. Rob had clearly dropped something up there. Martha felt strangely reassured that yes, there was another person in the house, and yes, that thump had been caused by something actually falling and if she went upstairs and looked, there would be something that had physically landed on the floor. For the last three nights she had heard again the creaking in Ruby's room that sounded like footsteps. Martha knew that there was nothing there but couldn't help but be unnerved by what sounded *exactly* like another person entering the room and crossing over to roughly where the cot was situated. There was no doubt about it but Hawthorn Cottage – or Eyrie Farm as she found herself calling it more often – was a very different place at night to what it was during the day.

She had just made up her mind to go upstairs and offer Rob Mountford a cup of tea when she heard him thump back down the stairs and out the front door, slamming it as he went. Moments later, the Land Rover revved and she heard the crackle of gravel as he drove down the lane. He hadn't returned by the time she went to pick Ruby up from Lullabies after a fruitless morning. Nor by the time she drove back from the village, having picked up some shopping.

By seven, as she took Ruby's bottles from the steriliser,

Martha conceded that nothing more would be done that day on investigating the scratching or the replastering of the wall. She made up the bottles, gathered up the little collection of soothers for the night and made her way upstairs, leaving Ruby playing happily on her playmat.

Ruby's room was surprisingly untouched, despite the obligatory set of footprints, an open toolbox and a bag of plaster. Martha set things up for the night, pulled down the blackout blind and turned on the moon and stars lamp. She sighed at the mess and then left the room, pulling the door shut behind her. She stepped out into the gloom of the landing and then stopped dead as she heard a noise from behind her.

It was a series of light thumps as opposed to the usual creaks. It sounded for all the world like . . . no . . . that was impossible. Martha caught her breath. The sound she heard sounded like little *footsteps*. They went in quick succession – one, two, three, four, five of them – and then stopped for a moment before beginning again, sounding as though they were going in the opposite direction. Five again, and then they stopped. Martha was frozen. She kept listening, her hand still on the door-handle. It was the last noise that unnerved her most of all. She had heard Ruby drop her soother a thousand times, and there it was again. The unmistakable click as the plastic hit the floor.

Martha's stomach dropped and immediately intense goose-bumps sprang up all over her body, goose-bumps that were so hard they hurt. She was unable to move. Had she really just heard what she thought she'd heard? Her blood turned cold for a moment and then suddenly a huge rush of heat flooded through her entire body. She couldn't get it out of her head that what she had just heard was a small child run across the room and then back again, dropping the soother along the way.

Martha let go of the door-handle as if it were hot and walked with quick steps toward the stairs. She didn't want to run. To run would be almost to admit that she'd heard what she thought she'd heard, but she couldn't have. Martha knew that it couldn't have been the footsteps of a child, it wasn't possible. She couldn't get the image from her mind, however, and flew down the stairs and back to the brightness of the living room where Ruby played contentedly on her playmat. She lay there in her babygro, half an eye on the muted TV and half on a Paddington Bear she was chewing which really had too many detachable pieces for a seven-month-old.

Martha closed the living-room door firmly behind her and gathered her baby in her arms before sitting down on the armchair under the window where a patch of sun shone in. She craved the brightness after the gloom upstairs. She tried to think logically. What on earth had just happened? What had she heard? She took a deep breath. The soother hitting the ground was easily explained – she had been studying Rob Mountford's mess as she had put down the soothers on the small side table. One could have rolled, settled itself close to the edge of the table and teetered there before falling to the ground. All of that was logical. What she couldn't for the life of her figure out was the sound – the trotting *footsteps* over and back.

Martha held Ruby close to her as she heated her bedtime bottle and turned the TV to a repeat of *Open All Hours* as she fed her daughter. She forced herself to focus on the screen and block everything else out of her mind but time and again the sound played back in her head. Little footsteps, little feet . . . No. It couldn't be, and that was that.

Ruby slept in her arms through a couple of hours of mindless sitcoms that Martha barely watched. By the time they were over she realised the baby was sweating from her mother's body heat and knew it wasn't fair to hold on to her any longer, much as she didn't want to let her go.

She kept her eyes down as she climbed the stairs – partly to watch her footing, partly because she didn't want to look up. The landing above was dim and gloomy and Martha shivered as she reached the top of the stairs, keeping her eyes focused on the sleeping Ruby. She didn't admit it to herself but she was afraid to look around her, afraid of what she might see. She felt the goose-bumps return as she stopped outside the bedroom door and then took a deep breath as she nudged it open with her elbow and stepped in. She raised her head to look, finally.

The room was exactly as she had left it – the low lighting, the blanket pulled back in preparation for the sleeping child. Martha laid Ruby down gently and pulled a single layer of her blankets over her for comfort. Her daughter immediately began to snuffle and turn her head from side to side. Martha knew that she had come to the moment she had been dreading. She turned to the side table and went to pick up a soother. Her heart sank as she counted how many were there. Four.

She glanced at the ground nearby. There was no sign of the fifth soother at her feet, or under the cot, or anywhere within the vicinity of the small table. Steeling herself, she looked behind the hare picture. Nothing. *Where had it gone?* Martha took a deep breath and took the cover from the teat of a pink soother. She turned back to the cot and placed the soother in Ruby's mouth. The child immediately settled. Martha bent and kissed her clammy brow and then, as she raised herself, she froze. It was difficult to make anything out in the dimly lit room but, with her head turned slightly to the right, she could see it – the small blue plastic rim of the fifth soother, dropped right in the middle of Rob Mountford's tools, in front of the bricked-up fireplace.

14

Eyrie Farm,
Shipton Abbey,
Norfolk,
England

July 25th, 1953

Dear Caroline,

It has been a long time, I know, since last I wrote, but I find myself with barely a minute to myself as the time draws nearer for the baby to arrive. Of course I know I cannot send this to you but it's a comfort for me to write it and I can hope you will read it some day.

Marion is huge as a house – she'd kill me if she saw that so don't tell her, whatever you do! Her ankles are swollen as well and she is crippled with pains in her back so she finds it very hard to get up and around sometimes. Again, I find myself doing everything that needs to be done and all of her fetching and carrying as well. At least she seems not to get the fidgets any more in her legs. She'd be up all night pacing the house when *they struck and I'd have to be up with her, making sure she was all right. Mammy wrote to me and said that it's all normal and that it's my duty as her sister to make sure she's well and rested, for when the time comes there will be very little sleeping done.*

I am nervous for when the time comes. If it's sudden, then I'll be the only person here with Marion and I am no midwife nor matron. Mammy says that as soon as Marion starts to get pains, or when her waters break (she says I'll know it when it happens) that I am to cycle to the doctor straight away and he will come himself or send a midwife. I think Daddy has made arrangements with the doctor through Mr Mountford. He has sent me an envelope which is to be given to the doctor as soon as the baby is born. I think that it will tell the doctor that the baby is to be put up for adoption straight away. Again, that makes me sad but we cannot keep a baby, just us girls on our own in the countryside, and when the baby is born we can go home again.

Mr Mountford visited us last week, thank God. I thought that after Marion's shenanigans he would never call again. He brought the doctor with him and he examined Marion and said that all was well and the baby was a small one but once she could feel it kick that all was fine. Thank God Mr Mountford wasn't in the room for the examination because Marion made a show of herself. When he asked if she could feel the baby kick she shouted at him "I'll kick you!" and drew back her leg to do that very thing. She cried and wailed when he examined her, saying that he was molesting her and that she would tell our daddy what he had done and that he'd pay for the consequences. The examination ended soon after that. I hope that the doctor doesn't tell Mr Mountford what she said to him for we should be shamed again. God forgive me for my lack of charity but Marion seems to do nothing but bring shame on our family name, and these people being so kind and so generous.

Mr Mountford's son then came the following day with a box of old toys and baby clothes and blankets. It was very kind of him, of course, but we shall have no need of that when the baby is adopted. Maybe we will pass them on with the baby to its new mammy and daddy – Mr Mountford's son, Robert, says that they are no use to them any more and are cluttering up the attic. I asked if he would stay for a cup of tea but he had to be on his way. He seems a nice enough fellow.

I must go now for I hear Marion rousing and I know that she will want a bath.

May God be with you,

Lily

15

July 1st

Rob Mountford returned the following morning and with him was an assistant – a boy of about seventeen or eighteen years of age, carrying a radio. The lad rang the doorbell before Rob had a chance to let himself in this time, which gave Martha the opportunity to go to the hallway to meet him and say hello. He grunted in response and carried on upstairs, barking orders to the boy who Martha gathered was called Sam.

She shrugged her shoulders at the response and picked up Ruby's changing bag to drop her down to Lullabies for the morning. Strangely, considering the events of the night before, she'd had a good night's sleep, as had Ruby. There had been no scratching in the wall for a change and Martha felt optimistic that it would soon be a thing of the past once Rob had investigated what sort of animal or bird was resident in the chimney-breast.

When she drove back up the driveway, however, her optimism waned as she was greeted by a foul smell. She followed the sound of voices right around to the end of the garden where Rob and Sam were staring at a patch of ground.

"What's up?" she asked gingerly, walking toward the two men.

"Don't come any closer!" barked Rob and Martha stopped, but not before she felt a squelch underfoot and looked down to see muddy water rising up around her foot.

"Oh dear," she said, and took a step backwards.

"Bloody septic tank," said Rob, almost to himself. He then looked at Martha. "Gonna have to fix this before I can do the plastering. You're in danger of a flood."

Martha opened her eyes wide in alarm and she saw Rob's face soften slightly.

A note of reassurance entered his voice as he said, "Nothing to worry about. We've found it in time but I need to head off in a bit to get my tools. Should be back by the afternoon though."

Martha nodded and walked back toward the house as the two men bent again to the ground.

Once inside she left her soggy shoes in the utility room and went upstairs to wash her feet and fetch clean shoes. Back downstairs she put the kettle on, feeling very frustrated. Time was moving on and she hadn't written a word yet. This bloody house, she thought. If it wasn't inexplicable noises and creaks it was the waterworks, or the plastering, or the electrics. If she'd known that it was going to be like this she'd have just stayed in London. Maybe she should have anyway. Martha sighed as she made herself a coffee and headed to her study, determined at least to get some work done.

She heard the Land Rover pull away outside. She was on her own again and vowed to make use of the reprieve. As always, she found it easier to use pen and paper than the laptop and she settled down to begin the day, determined to have written at least twenty A4 pages before leaving to pick up Ruby. She bent her head over the pad and started to scribble furiously, finally feeling a flow that both the weather and her exhaustion seemed to have drained from her over the past while.

Martha wrote for about an hour, lost completely in her story. Rufus, her unicorn, had been captured by an evil enemy of the King of Faragad and, still unaware of his magical powers, he had no idea why. Martha placed him in a cell, tethered by his horn to a wall, feeling trapped and isolated, unsure of what was to come next. She closed her eyes and reached inside herself for some of the emotions she'd been having lately and wrote from the heart, passionate about the words. In his mind, Rufus wondered why on earth he'd put himself in the position which had led to his capture and wondered if things would ever be as they should again. Through the magical creature on the page Martha poured out her fear and frustration, almost subconsciously. She had reached half of her day's target when she was roused suddenly by the thump of footsteps from upstairs and the sudden blast of a radio.

"Jesus H!" she shouted in shock, and jumped to her feet to go and investigate. She had reached the door of the study when she calmed sufficiently to realise that it must be Sam upstairs. Only Rob needed to go get the tools so Sam must have stayed behind to make a start up there.

Martha paused and then sat back in her chair. She looked at the pad, filled with writing. She was caught in a flow and she decided to run with it. The radio was very loud but to go upstairs to ask Sam to turn it down would also mean making polite chit-chat with him and that would put her back to square one when she returned.

She picked up her pen again.

It was difficult to concentrate with the music blaring from upstairs. She recognised the station as one she never listened to – a local classic hits one. Sam seemed to have a particular fondness for very old songs, she noticed, as the volume rose for particular songs – Elvis Presley, Eddie Cochrane. She pressed ahead with her work, trying to ignore the music. She appreciated the fact that it sounded like he had taken his boots off and was padding around in stockinged feet. At least he wasn't treading septic tank overflow everywhere.

By a quarter to one she had reached the target of pages she had set herself and was feeling very chuffed with herself. She picked up the folded buggy from the utility room and decided to walk down to collect Ruby and then carry on for a stroll in the sunshine.

"See you later, Sam!" she called up the stairs as she went out the front door. There was no answer. Martha doubted he had heard her with the volume of the music.

Within the hour Martha was striding along the beautiful country lanes around Shipton Abbey. Ruby sat in her stroller, her feet perched on the safety bar across the front. She giggled in the breeze and Martha stopped at intervals to tilt the stroller back towards her to give her daughter upside-down kisses which made her squeal with delight. Being outdoors after such a productive morning made Martha feel refreshed and revitalised. The noises were nothing more than noises, the septic tank could be fixed. It was all fine. Her resolve to stay in Shipton Abbey, and at Hawthorn Cottage, was strengthened again.

She was five minutes from the centre of the village when she felt the first thick drops of rain on her head. She ignored them at first until a large splash landed on Ruby's nose and the little girl crinkled her face and looked upward, blinking into the light. Martha retrieved the plastic rain-cover from the tray under the buggy, glad that she left it there at all times but disappointed to spot that her own rain-jacket was missing. She realised that she hadn't actually needed it since moving.

The drops grew thicker and the sky was a block of dark grey above her as she moved quickly toward the village and beyond to the road home. She was soon soaked through, however, her black linen trousers and loose white smock beginning to stick to her skin. She decided to take shelter at the Abbot's Rest.

She reversed in through the door of the pub, taking care not to trip on the step down onto the pub floor and gently lowered the buggy after her. She peered inside to see that Ruby was fast asleep and breathed a sigh of relief that she wouldn't have to entertain her in the pub.

Martha negotiated the pushchair into a space between two empty tables. The pub was deserted as far as she could see. She went to the bar where she waited for a while until eventually a girl in her early twenties with a bored expression on her face came through and took her order for a coffee. There was no friendly 'I'll drop it down to you' and Martha had to wait at the bar for the mug of coffee and take it back to the table herself. She sank into her seat and watched as the girl went back through into the lounge where the TV was blaring.

Martha shook in two sugars and a little milk and sipped the hot drink, surveying her surroundings as she did so. The downpour outside made the room gloomy and the fireplace smelled strongly of soot dislodged by the rain. She felt uncomfortable but it really was too wet to head outside so she sipped her coffee again and leaned over the buggy, wiping the drops off the plastic to peer in at the sleeping Ruby.

As she leaned over her daughter, Martha became aware of a shape moving slowly toward her in the gloom. She froze, not wanting to look up and see what was approaching her out of the dark inner area of the pub. Out of the corner of her eye she made out a face and the flesh of two wrinkled hands. It was the old lady from the other night. Lil Flynn, Mary had called her. Martha forced herself to look up into the face of the old woman. In turn, Li Flynn was staring at the rain-soaked stroller.

There was silence for a moment. The old lady broke it by extending one of her knotty, misshapen hands and pointing at the baby, saying, "'R'you keeping her up at Eyrie Farm?"

Martha was completely taken aback. She looked at Lil Flynn, tried to figure out what to say. "Ummm, hello," she began. "This is my daughter, and yes, we're staying at the cottage for a while."

"Shouldn't take a baby up to Eyrie Farm," came the response.

The woman must have been drinking since early morning to slur her words so, thought Martha. She knew she should bring the conversation to an end but was intrigued.

"Why so?" she asked.

She shifted slightly as the old woman flopped down beside her. She smelled musty and unwashed and a faint tinge of alcohol fumes seeped from her as she leaned toward Martha.

"One up there already," she said. "There's a boy up at Eyrie Farm."

Her words chilled Martha, who leaned back and away from the woman. What she said next made Martha turn ice-cold.

"He's in the fire," said the old lady. "In the wall. There's a boy in the wall at Eyrie Farm." She fell silent, and turned her head, her vacant eyes having difficulty focusing as she stared into space. "*Immured*," she said, rolling the word across her tongue, closing her eyes as though savouring it, or daring herself to say it.

Martha stared at her in shock.

"Does he cry at night?" the old woman asked suddenly.

Martha recoiled in horror and tried to shuffle away along the bench where she sat. The old lady leaned after her, locking her eyes with Martha's.

Martha tried to change the subject. "It's Lil, isn't it?" she asked, trying to sound as bright as she could. "Lil Flynn?"

The crone leaned away from Martha as if she had been insulted. She regarded her with rheumy eyes, filled with disgust. "My name is Lily *Mountford*," she said, pronouncing the surname with pride, as though it made her titled.

Martha was taken aback again. "I'm sorry," she said but the old lady had stood up and was weaving her way back into the gloom in the direction from which she had come. Martha realised she had been holding her breath, and exhaled as the woman walked away. She gasped again as Lily turned one more time.

"Mother did it, you know," she said and shuffled away.

Martha couldn't get out of the pub fast enough. She slammed five pounds down under her undrunk coffee – it was all that she had in her purse but she didn't care that she had paid almost three times the price. She bumped and bashed the stroller off stools and tables as she manoeuvred it out the door, all the time peering behind her to make sure that Lil Flynn – Mountford – was nowhere near her.

She had made it back up the hill out of the village when she realised that the rain had actually stopped and a huge rainbow arched over the abbey and into the sky behind her. She was painfully out of breath – her throat burned from when she had almost flung herself up the hill. She paused for a moment and stared back at the village to catch her breath.

What on earth did that old woman mean? That there was a boy immured in a wall somewhere at Hawthorn Cottage? And what did she mean did he cry at night? A shiver ran down Martha's spine. Lately – those dreams of a baby crying, and what Alison Stockwell had said . . .

"Oh, cut it out!" said Martha out loud. What was she doing scaring herself when the old woman was clearly delusional with drink. What was more interesting was that she had said her name was Mountford. What did that mean?

Martha walked on toward home. As far as she knew there was only one family named Mountford in Shipton Abbey and that meant that if Lil Flynn – or Lily Mountford – was telling the truth then she was in some way related to Rob. Why then had he been so eager to get Martha away from the pub that night of the dinner? And why did Mary dismiss her so? Maybe the old woman was Rob's mum? No – too old, and hadn't Mary said that Rob's mum had died when he was young? His gran, then? She could understand why Rob would want to keep them apart in that case – it would never do that a relative of the great Rob Mountford was the village drunk. And was Mary playing along because she wanted to get Rob and Martha together after all? She *had* given him advice on taking Martha out in the first place . . .

Martha was very confused. Her earlier enthusiasm for life in Shipton Abbey had taken a knock – she felt very much like an outsider all of a sudden.

She noticed that she had actually reached her own driveway and turned in toward the cottage. She saw that the front door was open, but there was no sign of Rob's Land Rover. Sam must still be inside, she thought, and that meant that Rob would most likely have to come and pick him up later. She groaned inwardly – she couldn't face another awkward conversation and she didn't want to be on edge all afternoon waiting for him to tramp in on her.

Ruby was still asleep, she noticed, and she left her in the

stroller in the hallway where it was cool and quiet. It was quiet, too, upstairs. Martha crept up to Ruby's room to check on progress and to advise Sam that the baby was sleeping. She was surprised to find the place deserted – the only change from this morning was that the numbers on the clock radio that Sam had brought with him were flashing on and off. Other than that, he seemed to have replaced everything in the room exactly as it had been that morning. Martha was struck by the fact that this was quite unusual, particularly when he seemed so young, but she didn't complain. Poor Sam was probably scared of his boss as well.

While upstairs she peered into the other rooms and found them also empty. The display on her own clock radio was also blinking – she realised there must have been a power cut in her absence. Probably some lightning accompanying the thundery cloudburst.

Ruby was stirring as she returned downstairs and Martha unzipped her plastic covering and slid the beaming baby out into her arms. She jiggled her gently and asked her what she had dreamed about while asleep. The little girl tugged at the beads that Martha wore and popped them into her mouth to relieve her throbbing gums.

Martha made her way down the hall and toward the kitchen, her eyes focused on her daughter as she ran a finger around her mouth for any signs of new teeth. When she reached the kitchen she turned to look at the room before her and stopped dead in her tracks.

All around, the floor was littered with small white bundles. The sky had grown dark outside as another thundery shower approached and Martha strained her eyes to ascertain exactly what she was seeing. It was nappies. The lid was off her kitchen bin and strewn around the floor were five or six nappies which had been in the kitchen bin because the nappy bin upstairs was full.

Martha stared at the floor in disbelief. "That little *shit*!" she said out loud, making Ruby jump. "I can't believe him! Leaves his own tools neat as you like upstairs and then turns my kitchen into a bloody *landfill*!" She stepped over two of the bundles and slid Ruby into her high chair, strapping her in.

Martha made her way around the room picking up the nappies, rolled up and taped tightly as she always did with them. Had Sam lost something in the bin? Knocked it over and then didn't bother to pick up the nappies? Why not? And how had he scattered them so far around the room? Had he played *football* with them?

The nappies all firmly back in place in the bin, Martha stormed out to the hallway to get her mobile phone from the pocket in the buggy. She was seething – who did Sam think he was, making a mess like that and not cleaning it up? What had he even been doing in the kitchen? Surely if he'd made a cup of tea then there would be signs of that? Or had he cleaned away the sugar and milk, wiped up any telltale cup rings, washed and dried a mug and spoon and yet still managed to leave five or six dirty nappies all over the kitchen floor?

Deep in thought, she didn't notice the pushchair. The darkened hall made it difficult to see it in the gloom and before she could stop herself she had walked straight into it and was falling, taking it with her.

She landed awkwardly. Her arms, head and upper body were flat on the floor and the buggy had fallen over underneath her legs which meant that her lower body was elevated by the stroller underneath her, her legs in the air. Martha groaned as various handles and pulleys dug into her body. She crawled forward on her arms, her legs following, and she eventually cleared the buggy. She rolled onto her side and looked back. It suddenly struck her that she hadn't left it there in the first place. It had been *moved*.

She was certain she had left it beside the door. It made no sense to move it further down the passageway because that meant she couldn't get past. Near the door, the hallway was wider. What's more, she had left it parallel with the stairs – what she had just fallen over had to be *across* the hallway, at right angles to the stairs in order for her to walk into it. Still lying on her side, she peered above her head at the front door. It was ajar. Sam, she thought. It could only have been Sam. Had he been here after all when she came home? In the living room, maybe? How could she have missed him when she came in? He must have heard her calling him names when she saw the mess in the kitchen, and scarpered. But why ambush her with the buggy? She could have killed herself. What if she had Ruby in her arms? Not that Sam would probably even have noticed that there was a baby in the house. What kind of stupid, immature person would actually try to block someone's way in order to get out of their house unchallenged? Why had he been hiding in the first place? Was he having a nose around and didn't want to get caught?

Martha's mind was a jumble as she lay on the floor, becoming more and more aware by the minute of pains in her body where she knew she would be bruised. Ruby began to cry and Martha managed to struggle to her feet. She closed and locked the front door, righted the stroller and pushed it into the living room out of the way. She retrieved her mobile phone from the pocket and with a slight limp made her way back to her grizzling baby.

What the hell had just happened there, she wondered? Who was this Sam guy? None of it made any sense. In her earlier rage about the nappies, she had intended to ring Rob Mountford to find out exactly what the deal was with this Sam and let him know in no uncertain terms that she was not happy. After her fall, however, she felt vulnerable and a little scared. She rang Sue instead, desperate to hear a friendly voice.

"Well, Ms Clampett!" asked Sue as she answered the phone.

Martha felt immediately cheered at the corny old *Beverly Hillbillies* reference, and sank down onto a kitchen chair beside Ruby, stroking her foot as she chatted.

"I hate the bloody country," she said. She realised how despondent she sounded and that she was close to tears. "I've just nearly killed myself on the bloody buggy, having had to clean up a landfill of baby crap in my kitchen. Oh – and to top it all off my septic tank is busted!"

Sue laughed. Then Martha heard the click of her lighter as she lit herself a cigarette. "Tell Auntie Sue," she said then, and exhaled loudly.

"Are you in a hotel again?" asked Martha.

"Traveller's Inn, Edinburgh," came the reply. "Outside!"

Martha told her about her afternoon, starting with her fall and working backward. "Then earlier on I had to go into the pub . . ."

"Had to?" laughed Sue.

"It was bucketing down outside – and I had a coffee!" Martha giggled back. "But the old lady I told you about was in there again . . ."

"Li'l Kim?" asked Sue, a grin in her voice.

"Lil *Flynn*," retorted Martha with a laugh. "Though it transpires she thinks her name's Mountford."

"Like Man Mountain Mountford?"

"Are you on the sub-editor's desk this week or something with all of these catchy titles?" asked Martha, enjoying the relief of the banter.

"Nah," replied Sue, inhaling and blowing smoke out again. "A feature on unusual courses at universities. Anyway, what happened with the old lady?"

"Nothing much," said Martha. "Except she tried to convince me that there's a boy been chucked in a fire and bricked up in my house somewhere – 'Im-yoooooored'!" she wailed, imitating the old lady's voice from earlier. "I mean, come off it, the only thing that's in these walls is a rat – or a nest of the damn things, scratching at all hours of the night and keeping me awake!"

Sue was silent.

"Sue?"

"Are you sure it's a rat?" Sue said, her voice uneasy.

"No," replied Martha, somewhat taken aback. "Could be a bird, could be a mouse – could be a Superhero for all I know. Man Mountain is supposed to be sorting it out but he's too busy now having to clear up the shit that's slowly seeping up through my garden."

"That's not really what I meant," said Sue, all traces of humour gone from her voice. "How has the temperature been?"

"The temperature? Fine," said Martha, puzzled. "Heat wave pretty much. What's up with you? You're not going to start asking me if I'm *alright* all the time or telling me that if I need anything to shine the Sue-beam into the sky, or that there's a cow trapped under my attic insulation?"

"No," said Sue. "But . . ."

"But what?" exclaimed Martha, annoyance creeping into her voice. "My God, you're as bad as everyone here in Summertown!"

There was a silence before Sue broke it with a giggle. "*Summerisle*," she corrected. It was an old joke, referring to places that they found strange. Martha had hated *The Wicker Man* with a passion and could never get the reference correct.

"Whatever. And now Ruby-Doo is in on the weirdness as well by the way – chucking her soothers all over the place . . ." Martha was about to tell Sue about the strange sound of footsteps from Ruby's room when there was a commotion at the other end.

"Sorry, chuck, I have to go," came Sue's voice. "I was waiting for a cab and now it's arrived but he's got my name wrong and – look – I'll ring you tomorrow. In the meantime just take care of yourselves, okay? Love to Little Blondie – byeeee!"

Sue had rung off before Martha had even had time to say goodbye. She sighed and then realised it was past Ruby's dinnertime and jumped to her feet to heat her bottle and her food. She felt calmer after the chat with her friend. Best maybe to confront Rob Mountford about his choice of employee face to face.

16

Eyrie Farm,
Shipton Abbey,
Norfolk,
England

August 4th, 1953

Dear Caroline,

I write to you with a broken heart, Caroline, for three days ago Mammy passed to her eternal reward – I can scarcely write for the tears!

Mr Mountford came and told us himself. He said Daddy had telephoned him and asked him to pass word on to us girls. She took bad the other night at home and Daddy telephoned the doctor but it was too late – she took to her bed and lay down and died. Daddy thinks it was her heart.

My sorrow is the greatest I have ever felt – my beloved mother with her kindly smile and warm embrace. What am I to do without her, Caroline? I will not ever see her face again nor hear her voice, nor read her letters full of wisdom on how to deal with

93

my plight here on my own in England. To make matters worse, we are not even to go home to bury her – Daddy says that we are to stay where we are and pray together for the repose of her soul. I long to speak to him myself but we have no telephone here at the cottage and I could not dream of asking Mr Mountford if we could use his. I am sure that he will come in good time and let us know more.

Marion has been shattered by the news and has taken to her room and won't let me in sometimes and other times bangs on the floor so hard that I run to her thinking that the shock has brought the baby on early. Then she shouts and rants and cries and blames me for breaking my mother's heart by not looking after her properly. God forgive me, Caroline, but I think in my soul that it is she who broke my mother's heart by bringing such shame on our family and worrying my mother so.

Oh, Caroline, I am lost. Surely Daddy will have to bring us home now because he is alone and has no one to care for him? I can scarcely think of Marion and the baby now, even though her time is soon. I don't care, cannot care, about anything other than the fact that my mother is never to speak to me again.

Pray for us, alone here without a mother, and for my father alone at home. Pray that our reunion is swift and that we bear this grief like Our Lord bore His suffering.

God save us all,

Lily

17

July 2nd

Martha was watching for Rob's Land Rover from the living-room window first thing the following morning. She stood there, hoping that he'd arrive before she left to take Ruby to crèche so that she could just get what she had to say out of the way.

He arrived at eight, alone, which Martha felt was ideal. She had no idea how he was going to take being challenged about who he brought to her house – Martha didn't even know who Sam was – he could be a relative for all she knew. She was wary of offending Rob, partly because of his unpredictable temper and partly because she felt it was important to keep him sweet for the remainder of her tenure. And to get her septic tank fixed as soon as possible.

She met him at the front door before he even had the chance to take out his key.

"Rob, hi, how are you?" she said, in her best businesslike voice. "I'd like a word."

He looked bemused as he squeezed in the doorway past her and into the living room where she indicated he should take a seat. So far, so good, she thought. She was in control of the situation.

Martha cleared her throat. "First off, Rob, I'd like to ask that when you do arrive to work, you ring the doorbell first and then wait for an answer, rather than just letting yourself in. If I'm here then obviously I'll be able to let you in straight away. If not, then feel free to use the front door if necessary."

Rob's eyes widened. "It's my house –" he began, indignantly.

Shit, thought Martha, here we go . . .

"That's true," she said calmly. "But basic tenant rights indicate that you can't enter without my permission."

The big man looked chastened, and more than a little bewildered. Martha suspected that the idea that he might not be able to treat the house entirely as his own had not entered his mind, much less that there were laws governing it.

"Right then," she continued, "the second thing I want to address is Sam –"

He cut her short. "Yeah, you've heard then. Sorry about that."

It was Martha's turn to be bewildered. Heard what?

"Little bugger, sorry-for-swearing, met a buddy of his in town yesterday when we were getting a new spade and he disappeared off to the pub on me and never came back. Fellah drank his weight in ale and can't be roused for love nor money this morning."

Normally, Martha would take mental notes of how Rob spoke to tell Sue. Instead, she tried to figure out what he had just said. "You mean Sam was with *you* yesterday afternoon?" she asked.

"Well, up until four o'clock when he parked himself on a bar stool," replied Rob. "Brought him to help with the lifting but he's useless. Kid's the son of Pa's accountant, on his school holidays . . ."

Rob's words disappeared into the background as the colour drained from Martha's face. She had been alone in the house after Rob had left. Sam hadn't been here after all. So who the hell had been tramping round upstairs, turning the radio up and down? Who came in the front door and spread nappies all over the kitchen floor? Who had moved her pushchair so that she fell over it and nearly broke her neck? Martha's stomach sank.

Logic, Martha, she thought. Someone must have let themselves into her house while she had been gone, and had still been there when she got home. Doing what? Entry must have been through the front door after Rob and Sam left – maybe the door had swung open? Had it been open when she left to get Ruby and called to say goodbye to Sam? No wonder he hadn't answered . . . A chill ran down her spine as she thought about it. Someone upstairs for all that time, with the *radio* on?

Then what? They went upstairs, easy as that, and walked around in stockinged feet listening to classic hits? Then hadn't touched a thing all day until they decided to come downstairs and fling nappies around? And when she returned, they had hidden until it was safe to leave but not before setting up an ambush in the hallway. *Why?* What had they done all day long and what was the purpose of it? None of this made the slightest sense.

"You're absolutely sure that neither you nor Sam came back here at any stage of the day?" asked Martha. "Neither of you forgot anything upstairs for example?"

"Sure as eggs," replied Rob. "We left here yesterday morning, called back to the yard for a while, had a bite of lunch and then headed to Bickford for some bits. We were back in Shipton about half three and I was trying to teach the lad about tools when he did his vanishing act. Trouble is, I can't do the tank alone, nor the chimney – and all my other lads are up to their necks over at the Meadows."

Martha knew he was referring to the new Mountford Construction-built estate on the Bickford Road.

"Can't spare 'em," continued Rob. "So that's why I'm here, to tell you that I can't do any work till that blighter sleeps off the ale. He's lucky to still have a job, truth be told."

Martha didn't respond. She wondered if she should tell Rob that she'd had an intruder but decided quickly against it. If he knew, then he might insist she had a guard dog, or want to hang about day and night to make sure she was safe. And his property, of course. No. No need to get Rob Mountford involved just yet. She'd just have to make sure she was more vigilant about keeping things locked. After all, the intruder hadn't done any harm other than make a mess and the buggy ambush, which was a far cry from what could potentially happen if they were really dangerous. It still puzzled her as to who would do such a thing, however, or why.

"Sorry there's another delay on the work," mumbled Rob.

Martha looked at him and almost felt sorry for him. "Well, don't let it happen again," she said sternly, thinking it no harm to stay in control.

Sue rang just after Rob left, her tone upbeat, with no indication in her voice of the previous day's anxieties. Martha let her talk, trying in her head to put into words what had happened the previous day but not knowing where to begin. It was wonderful to hear Sue's voice but Martha was glad when she said she had an appointment and had to cut the call short. It gave her more time to get her head around what exactly had taken place.

Martha made full sure to check all of the locks and to put on the alarm when she left to take Ruby to Lullabies. Being inside the house was making her skittish and nervous, particularly since it had occurred to her that the 'prankster' might actually have been a potential burglar casing the joint. She decided to walk down to the village, even though the talk with Rob had made her late. She felt better the instant she stepped outside the cottage and took a breath of air. It struck her that her life currently seemed to revolve around every creak and groan of the old cottage and little else.

It was nice to see the warm smile of Mary Stockwell at the crèche door. Aneta, her Polish assistant, hadn't arrived yet, it seemed. Martha thought to herself that she was actually missing other people, much as she usually enjoyed her own company.

"Any sign of that ring and vicar yet?" joked Mary, leaning over the childproof gate to bend down to Ruby in her pushchair.

"Oh, very funny," said Martha.

Mary laughed at her own joke. "Here, what's with this global warming?" she said, pointing to a huge black cloud over the abbey while they were bathed in sunshine at Lullabies.

"Monsoon season alright," replied Martha. "But I'm prepared!" She took her rain-jacket from the tray under the buggy, then folded the buggy to leave it into the Lullabies cloakroom until collection time.

"Hey – what happened here?" Mary exclaimed. She held the buggy out for examination, having noticed that one side of the frame was bent out of shape.

Martha laughed. "Same thing that happened here," she replied, showing Mary the huge purple bruise on her elbow.

"Bloody hell," said Mary quietly so that the children inside wouldn't hear. "That's nasty."

Martha shook her head. "Long story. And I'd better be off. Actually, I'm going to head down to the village for a bit – I fancy breakfast in the tearooms."

"Mmmm . . . I'd love to join you . . . D'you think Ruby would mind helping Aneta keep an eye on these others for an hour or so?"

The two women peered in the door where two toddlers ambled around, examining their surroundings. Kai had a dummy firmly planted in his mouth. The plastic rim was in the design of a huge set of teeth which gave him the appearance of having a grisly grown-up grin. Ella was busy humming a tune to herself and swinging a bib round and round absent-mindedly, like a propeller.

"Aw bless," said Martha sweetly, followed by "Bye then!" and she pretended to scarper.

They both laughed and Mary turned with Ruby in her arms to head inside.

"Actually, Mary," said Martha, "how about some supper later, at the cottage? Nothing fancy – just some pasta and salad but I'd really like the company."

Mary smiled. "That sounds like bliss! An evening away from stroppy teenagers who are hot, bored and waiting for exam results? What time do you want me?"

"About sixish would be lovely," said Martha.

"See you then!" said Mary and then turned suddenly to make a grab for Kai who was swinging from the door handle.

Martha smiled and turned toward the village, feeling a flood of relief that she wouldn't be alone that evening.

Martha sipped a glass of wine as she prepared supper. She traced a finger down the condensation on her glass. It was yet another stifling evening after a day of thundery downpours. She felt a bead of sweat trickle down the back of her strapless sundress.

She was jumpy as she prepared the food and was trying her best not to let her mind wander. There was a strange feeling about the house. Logically, it could only be a combination of the humidity and the events of the previous day but that didn't stop her having to suddenly look over her shoulder more than once, sure that someone was watching her from the doorway. The trill of the doorbell made her jump out of her skin but the fright was followed by an immediate relief that company had arrived.

The two women ate in the kitchen. The grey skies outside were too grim to contemplate using the conservatory and she made the table cheery with tea-lights and a bunch of flowers from the garden.

Both of them cleared their plates, chatting about the weather, the news, current affairs. While Martha took a break to change and feed Ruby and get her to bed, Mary washed up and prepared a pot of coffee and two plates of brownies from the village bakery and ice cream from a local dairy. She served them up just as Martha returned, baby monitor in hand.

"Oh my God, Mary," she exclaimed, taking in the gleaming work surface and empty sink. "I don't think there's been a night in almost seven months when my washing-up's been done before ten – sometimes ten the following morning need I add!" It was a simple gesture but Martha was overwhelmed.

"Oh it's nothing! I know it's tough on your own and it's the least I could do after that grub – where did you learn to cook like that?"

"Oh, it was nothing special," Martha shrugged as she crossed the room to the fridge and took out a second bottle of wine. "Top up?"

Mary nodded enthusiastically and held out her glass for a refill.

"My dad taught me to cook," said Martha, raising her glass to her companion and staring into space. "He and my mum ran a little country pub."

Mary noticed the faraway stare. "You alright, love?" she asked.

Martha looked at her, as if coming back into the conversation. "Oh, I'm fine," she said and looked down. "My mum used to help my dad in the kitchens but she died when I was five."

"Oh, I'm so sorry, Martha . . . was it just you and your dad then?"

Martha nodded. "Till I met Dan – my husband. It wasn't a bad life really. Mum had been sick for years, wasn't ever able to look after me or anything, so it was almost a release for her, and for my dad to be honest. And he coped very well on his own, bless him. I learned from the best!"

Mary nodded. "I know what you mean. My husband has been gone for years. Didn't die of course, just . . . up and left us all." She looked into the distance. "I coped on my own. It was better than . . . well . . . what things were like before he went. Him cadging money we didn't have, being an awful example for the kids. Only one who remembers him really is Ryan – my eldest. The others don't really know much about him and that's for the best."

Martha thought she could discern a nervous look in Mary's eyes as she spoke about her husband. What had he done that was so bad, she wondered. She looked sympathetically at her friend. "At least you've given me hope that Ruby won't grow into a total disaster with her father off the scene," she said, the unmistakable tone of bitterness creeping again into her voice.

"You've got to try to let go of him for her sake," chided Mary softly. "Don't make *her* bitter about someone she doesn't even know."

Martha nodded. "You're right," she said, "but sometimes it's very hard."

The two sat in silence for a moment.

"Besides which," said Mary, "won't she have her new daddy, Rob, to take care of her?"

Martha threw back her head and laughed. "Dear heavens – *never*!" she cried out dramatically, thumping her fist on the table in mock determination.

Mary laughed. "I'll stop, I promise! But remember you're young and pretty, Martha – you'll meet someone new, for sure."

Martha blushed and shook her head. "Oh, speaking of Rob Mountford," she said, taking a swig of wine, "I met Lil Flynn in the Abbot's the other day again."

Mary sat up, her expression earnest.

"She said her name was Lil *Mountford*," Martha went on. "Have you any idea why?"

Mary looked genuinely baffled. "Not a clue. I've only ever known her as Lil Flynn – she used to run a little sewing business from her house out near the marshes. She never married – not as long as I've been here anyway."

"So you're not local?" queried Martha.

Mary shook her head. "Not a bit of it – I'm from Bickford originally. Duncan Stockwell was the local – Drunken Duncan as they used to call him in the day. I just never left Shipton Abbey after he did." She paused, stared into space. "Reckoned that it was the safest place to be as long as he wanted to be somewhere else."

"I didn't realise you weren't born and bred here," said Martha, refilling their glasses and feeling slightly tipsy. "So you don't know the history of this place at all then?"

"Only the stories," said Mary, raising her glass to her lips. She stopped midway, as if she realised she had said something she shouldn't have.

"What stories?" asked Martha, her heart beginning to beat a little faster.

Mary hesitated, looked around her. "Oh nothing. Just local yarns about it being haunted – you know the way these stories spread around when a place is deserted. There's bound to be tall tales." She looked distinctly uncomfortable.

"What kind of tales?" asked Martha again, sitting up straight in her chair.

Mary shook her head. "I'm not filling your head with stories made up by . . . kids . . . over the years, and then leaving you on your own with a small baby to be frightened. There's *nothing* in this house, and that's an end to it."

Martha was silenced by how forcefully the older woman had spoken.

"Now the abbey, on the other hand," said Mary, "*there's* somewhere you shouldn't go at night-time – all sorts of tales from there." She spoke quickly, as if changing the subject away from Hawthorn Cottage. "There was a team of archaeologists did a dig a few years back and they couldn't move for bones."

"Yuk!" said Martha, momentarily distracted.

"Oh yes," continued Mary. "Apparently the monks liked to immure folk as punishment at one stage."

Martha started. There was that word again: *immure*.

"Dear God," she said, "is that really true?"

"Apparently," nodded Mary.

Martha noticed that her eyes were a little glassy. "There was a bad lot in there once. They'd have their way with local boys and then blame *them* for the sin that they'd just committed. They bricked them up in walls as the punishment. Apparently the place was literally *insulated* with young lads – some of 'em barely more than babies."

Martha shuddered. "That's terrible," she said.

Mary shrugged. "Different times. All the lands as far as Bickford were owned by the abbey. No one dared say a thing when their children went missing – they'd been called by the monks in the first place and that was a great honour. No one realised their little boys were entombed in the abbey walls."

Martha shivered, feeling extremely disturbed. She felt the prickle of an unexpected tear and excused herself to go to the bathroom.

So, she thought, as she made her way up the gloomy stairs. The monks had invented the habit of bricking little boys up hereabouts. So it wasn't an entirely random concept – probably just a local legend that grew arms and legs over the centuries and was now the favoured method of the local drunk for scaring people.

Martha reached the landing at the top of the stairs and bent to click on the small lamp she kept on a table outside her bedroom door. It cast a low but warm glow over the wooden floor. She carried on into the bathroom. She looked in the mirror as she washed her hands. It stood to reason, she thought, that if this house or at least parts of it had been built about the same time as the abbey, then maybe that's what the tales were that Mary was talking about.

She actually found herself feeling a bit better as she dried her hands. Mary was right – it was just stories, nothing to get spooked about.

There was a lightness in her step as she left the bathroom and crept softly over to Ruby's room to check her. She felt better again when she saw that none of her soothers had gone missing and the one that Ruby had used to get herself to sleep was now firmly embedded in her cheek. Martha smiled and gently wrestled it out. Ruby gave a long, sleepy sigh and turned her head to reveal a large red mark where the pacifier had been. Martha bent to leave a lingering kiss on her forehead.

She hadn't realised before now how much her meeting with Lil Flynn had stayed with her, how much the old woman had creeped her out. And yes – it was scary to have someone break into her house – she had yet to figure out how to deal with that – but at least it was something *physical*, and careful locking of doors and keeping the alarm set would sort that one out. She was new in the village after all. It had probably just been kids in her house, larking about on their summer holidays. Even Mary had said hers were bored and that usually led to mischief. Surely if anyone wanted to harm her, they had ample opportunity to do so. No, it wasn't the physical presence of an intruder that had unnerved her so much that she had stayed in the village all morning. It was a creepy old woman who had tall tales mixed up with whiskey in her head.

Martha stole from Ruby's room and, as she turned away from her bedroom door, she saw a glimpse of something black lurch into the bathroom. Martha grinned again – Mary was certainly showing the effects of the wine. Come to think of it, she wasn't feeling too clever herself. Time for a fresh pot of coffee, she thought and headed downstairs. She'd have it ready for Mary when she returned from the bathroom.

Martha made her way down the stairs, feeling her skirt generate a light breeze around her legs as she walked which was nice in the humidity of the evening. It was still uncomfortably sticky, even though it was nearly ten o'clock. She pushed open the kitchen door and stepped in, eyes focused on the coffee-maker, and jumped as she registered a shape at the kitchen table. She gasped and turned sharply, only to see Mary with her back to her, sitting exactly where she had left her earlier.

"Mary!" she exclaimed, shocked.

The older woman turned to face her, a sheepish expression on her face. "I hope you don't mind, Martha," she said, "but I've phoned for Ryan to come and get me. I'm a little woozy on my feet after all this wine and it's a school night."

Martha watched as Mary got to her feet unsteadily.

"I'll just use your bathroom," Mary whispered, and stepped carefully out into the corridor, her black skirt floating behind her.

Martha gazed after her. If Mary was just going to the bathroom now, then who the hell had she just seen going into it? The sense of unease that the house gave her, that had lifted earlier when she heard about the tales of the monks, suddenly descended again. What was going on here? Had she seen . . . ? Oh, cut it out, Martha, she said to herself. Just snap out of it. It was dark upstairs, the landing dimly lit, and she'd had her own fair share of wine. All she had seen was a trick of the light as they called it, just a distortion of her vision from the corner of her eye. "Get over yourself," she whispered and made her way toward the coffee pot.

She was too tired to stay up after Ryan arrived in his souped-up car and carted his mother off with a roar from the exhaust. Martha went immediately up to bed and fell into a deep sleep. Her mind reeled from the events of the past couple of days but she couldn't think about it, couldn't reason any longer with herself. She just needed to sleep it all away, to be oblivious. She fell into a deep sleep, unmoving except to cast off her duvet in the humidity.

Late into the night she stirred, checked her clock, saw that it was three thirty, then found a cool spot on the pillow and fell straight back to sleep. She sighed as she felt the duvet lift beside

105

her. Dan's late again, she thought. But it's nice to have him here. She settled her body against the weight in the bed beside her, felt the hairs on his legs as she touched against him. Maybe tomorrow they could talk, sort all this mess out, she thought, and fell further into sleep.

18

July 3rd

Martha didn't remember her dream the following morning – she was too intrigued by a postcard waiting for her in the tree at the end of the driveway. The postcard was from Sue – a picture of Loch Ness, postmarked Edinburgh. Martha smiled and turned the card over. It was years since anyone had sent her a postcard – trust Sue. '*Sending you a wee pressie from Scotland,*' it said. Martha pondered over what it might be. Sue favoured the more unusual gift and Martha reckoned that it could be anything from a stick of rock to the actual Loch Ness monster.

Rob Mountford returned that day also, bringing a pale and sheepish Sam with him. They got to work immediately on the septic tank. Martha listened to the hum of their voices in the distance as she sat in the study, working hard to make up for her previous day off. Only Aneta had been there to greet her at Lullabies that morning so she assumed that Mary was having a lie-in after the excesses of the night before and felt guilty.

The routine stayed like that for the next few days. The men continued to work in the garden and Martha worked in her study in the mornings and in the afternoons took advantage of the return of finer, fresher weather to take Ruby on trips in the car to the surrounding area. Sue had taken to texting her daily, enquiring if she was okay, as if checking in to see what new disaster had befallen Martha and Ruby in the wilds of Norfolk. Martha was touched but also somewhat exasperated. Sue never once mentioned the Scottish gift, which left Martha feeling very intrigued.

On Friday afternoon, Martha placed Ruby in her buggy and went to explore the abbey properly for the first time since she had moved to the country. It was difficult, however, to negotiate the buggy over the uneven ground and Martha gave up eventually as a group of tourists stared at her efforts.

Dressed in a light sundress and flip-flops, she rested on the wide grassy area at the side of the abbey, overlooking the estuary. It had once been a massive cemetery but was now a picnic area. Martha looked around her, feeling that it was inappropriate to picnic on the site where so many bodies had found their final resting place. She found herself wondering if the bodies of the young boys were underneath her also, and suppressed a shudder.

She sat Ruby on the ground between her legs and gave her a toy to play with but the little girl returned to one of her favourite pursuits of trying to eat as much grass as possible which Martha had to dust from her hands and occasionally retrieve from her mouth.

Martha sighed and closed her eyes for a moment. She suddenly felt very much in need of a rest. True, she had been desperate to get out of the city and away to her new life but, now that she was here, she felt like it was an awful lot of work. She was responsible not only for herself but exclusively for Ruby too – everything her little girl ate, wore, learned. She had to be there too if anything went wrong . . . Suddenly, sitting on the grass in glorious sunshine, the magnitude of caring for her daughter hit Martha and she felt overwhelmed. What if an emergency happened? What if she needed to get her to hospital? Worse – what if something happened to Martha and Ruby was left alone? They could be alone in that house for days before anyone found them. If something happened at a weekend then no one would know anything was wrong until Monday or Tuesday if Ruby didn't turn up at crèche . . .

Her head began to throb with the sudden worry. This time two years ago she would have been finishing for the weekend, sitting outside a pub in London maybe, enjoying a drink with colleagues before heading home to Dan and a barbeque in the garden . . . she had really only herself to worry about. She wouldn't change Ruby for the world, of course, but what a huge task being a mother on her own was. Martha wondered if this was how her father had felt when her mother died . . .

Maybe having another person around might help, she thought. She could look into tidying out the boxroom, taking a lodger perhaps? Another girl who maybe worked locally? Just another presence at Hawthorn Cottage. Surely Rob Mountford couldn't complain about extra rent?

She gazed upward at the majesty of the ruined abbey and her thoughts turned to how incredibly huge the monastery as a whole must once have been – a small city of its time, she supposed – with lands as far as Bickford and other neighbouring towns – lands as far as Eyrie Farm . . .

She couldn't get the house from her mind, what had happened there, how it made her feel. She remembered at first how it had been a haven. How carefree it had all felt, just a month ago, like the first few days of being on holiday. But now that holiday was well and truly over and she had a lot of work to do, a small child to care for and Eyrie Farm to deal with. It bothered Martha to feel that the house should be 'dealt with'. She should just be able to live there, for heaven's sake. Instead she never knew what was going to happen next with the noises and the shadows, the constant feeling of unease. A thought struck Martha that had been floating around the back of her mind for some time now but that she hadn't acknowledged. She never felt alone at the cottage, always felt like she was working around someone else . . . always a guest . . . but never a welcome one . . .

A cloud passed over the sun and the shaded area where Martha sat grew gloomy. She shivered, and noticed that Ruby had stopped playing with the grass and was looking up, trying to see where the sun had gone. Time to go home, thought Martha.

But where was that? Not in London any more, not with her father and stepmother . . . but Hawthorn Cottage or Eyrie Farm. And that certainly didn't feel like the home it should be.

Maybe Sue had been right. Martha stood up and gathered Ruby to her. Maybe this was all wrong for her. Maybe it was time to return to the city and her so-called friends. A wave of sadness washed over her and unexpected tears pricked her eyes as she bent to lower Ruby back into pushchair. One landed on the baby's leg with a plop.

Martha sniffed and wiped her eyes with the back of her hand. "Sorry, love," she said, as Ruby stared at her, puzzled. "Mummy's fine, and she'll take care of you no matter what."

19

Eyrie Farm,
Shipton Abbey,
Norfolk,
England

August 8th, 1953

Dear Caroline,

Praise be to God for he has sent us a light in our suffering! The baby is here – Henry Joseph Flynn, named after our great patriot Henry Grattan and our own dear father. He is a tiny bundle of beauty, with our mother's dark eyes, God rest her soul, that seem to look everywhere for something new to learn when he is awake, and tiny pink lips that I cannot help but kiss.

Marion's pains started early in the morning and she came to my room and told me to fetch the doctor immediately. I got dressed and rushed to get him, and he drove me back in his motor car, which was a great thrill, my bike in the boot! When we got back, Marion's waters had broken – Mammy, Lord rest her, had been right – I knew exactly what had happened. I had never seen Marion so terrified, but even in the throes of her pains she managed to make a holy show of us by kicking out at the doctor and telling him to get out, and then to get rid of the pains, and then to make the baby go away. And the doctor would tell her to walk around, that the pains would get worse before they got better and she'd shout swear words at him till she was gripped with another pain and then she'd bend over and hold the bars of the chairs till it passed. The doctor said he would leave us then, and said he'd send for Mrs Collins, the midwife, to come to Marion in a few hours. I couldn't imagine how she could sustain the pains any longer, for by the way she was acting it was as if the devil himself were killing her. The doctor said that all was well and that the baby would probably be born some time the following day. At that, I thought Marion would kill him stone dead, such was the look of fury in her eyes but she was gripped by another pain then and the doctor made his escape!

Such a night we put in then, with Marion roaring and screaming, saying things like she was being broken in two and that she didn't care if the baby died so long as the pains would stop. Mrs Collins came later in the day and took Marion to her bedroom and didn't allow me in, except to bring water for a cloth for Marion's brow. When it came close to the time, Mrs Collins called me to the room and bade me hold Marion's hand as hard as I could, and to mop her brow with a cool flannel when she needed it. Marion was hysterical with the pains, and one minute wanted to push and the next minute didn't want to push and then she was swearing and cursing and telling me all sorts of curse words and saying evil about the baby and our poor dead mother. All I could do was pray that this would pass but I feared that Marion would die.

And then with one great push he was with us, little baby Henry. Mrs Collins held him upside down and smacked him on the bottom, would you believe, and he let a great roar of a cry from his little body and I couldn't keep from crying myself that he was alive and all right because he was a funny colour. Mrs Collins swaddled him then in a blanket that had belonged to the

Mountfords and tried to hand him to Marion but she wanted none of it, so little Henry was placed in my arms with his little face all wrinkled up and his nose squashed to one side, but Mammy said that I had come out the same way, Lord rest her, and not to expect any baby to be beautiful. But he is, Caroline, he is the most beautiful thing I have ever seen. He opens his eyes and looks at me like I am a thing of wonder and he makes my heart melt.

Marion refused to feed him with her own milk, but Mrs Collins has given us some powdered formula, they call it, which is better for babies by all accounts. She has shown me how to make it up and then how to give Henry his bottle and wind him and settle him to sleep. He sleeps a lot and scarcely cries, bless him. I am sad for Marion for it is such a joy to hold him but she refuses to take him from me and I am left to look after him. I don't mind, but I will find it very hard to hand him away when the time comes but I must remember that he is not my baby, and perhaps Marion is too afraid to become attached to him for it must only be a matter of time before someone comes to take him to his new home.

Henry sleeps in a cot by my bed now. Marion is very tired after her labours and needs all her sleep. I then have to get up in the night to give Henry his bottle but it is a wonderful thing to have him so near, and to hear his tiny breathing in the silence of my room at night. Mrs Collins says that she will come back in a day or so to check him and to show me how to bathe him. She says also that she will share the news with Mr Mountford who will telephone Daddy. I pray the news that both Marion and the child are safe and well will provide him with some light in his darkness. I haven't heard a word from him since my mother's passing and I worry so, and fret, that he is all right. Surely he will be in touch soon to tell us when we are to return home. What an adventure this has been!

I must go now – little Henry has roused from his nap and will need another bottle. He is a small baby so I pray that he will grow big and strong. I have something else to confess to you,

Caroline. I baptised Henry myself! I hope I remembered how to do it properly, the way the nuns taught us at school. I know lay people are only supposed to do it in an emergency, but what if he died unexpectedly, Caroline, as babies sometimes do, and his little soul was condemned to stay in Limbo for all eternity? Isn't that an emergency, surely? Anyway, I did it. I tried to make it special with a candle and Henry in a white gown that was in the box of things the Mountfords sent for him. So now, I hope, if he dies, he can join Mammy in heaven.

Please pray, Caroline, that a loving mammy and daddy will be his new parents and look after him, for he is surely a little angel on earth.

May God be with you,

Lily

20

July 11th

Martha breathed a silent prayer that there would be no thunder and lightning that night.

Another week had passed. The septic-tank job remained uncompleted as Rob was continually tied up with administrative problems at the Meadows. One of his workers had uncovered a coin on the site and it seemed that any more work had to be suspended until it was investigated further. As a result, Rob was in a foul humour and told Martha when he called her to explain that he didn't have time for "sodding archaeologists and their bloody digging". Rumour had it that the coin was Roman and a full dig would be warranted at the site. Martha stayed well out of Rob's way.

Her own mood remained black. She was worried about Ruby – irrational fears of what would happen if she herself was hurt or injured. This in turn caused her crippling writer's block. She sat each morning at her desk, growing steadily more uneasy about her ability to finish the book she so desperately wanted to write, but Rufus refused to be his usual magical self. Then she would be a complete failure, she thought – as a wife, as a writer – Ruby would never respect her.

Martha also worried that she had no friends here in Shipton

Abbey other than Mary Stockwell, that her main source of human contact was dropping Ruby to crèche each morning. The other mothers remained complete strangers to her. Kai's mum was eighteen and waiting for exam results. Ella's mum closer to Martha in age but each morning she literally handed the toddler over to Mary or Aneta and swept back out to her Range Rover with a brusque "Hi". She was a solicitor in Bickford, Mary told her, and her sharp suits and dresses made Martha feel a little intimidated.

Martha's melancholy wasn't helped by a series of power cuts at the cottage. Plugging in the kettle was liable to trip the main power switch and Martha developed the habit of keeping a torch, a candle and matches beside her as the evenings grew dark. She never knew when an investigation of the fusebox might be required, or simply just a couple of hours in the dark waiting for the mains to come back on. Martha grew to dread bedtimes. She hated to admit it but she slept with the light on most nights and feared waking in the dark to another power cut. It was also so stiflingly hot all the time that she slept on top of her covers which made her feel uneasy and exposed. Sometimes she read by candlelight, a nervous feeling in the pit of her stomach as she waited for the first rumble of thunder.

Martha hated thunder, had an abject fear of being alone in a storm. It took her back to the night that her mother died, when a stern baby-sitter left her alone in the dark in pyjamas that were too warm – the terror she had experienced, too frightened to get out of bed, stiflingly hot under the covers where she was hiding from the storm. It was a time in her life that Martha couldn't bring herself to think about, but lying in her bed in Hawthorn Cottage, the five-year-old child that she had been that night was there again – sweating and terrified of the dark.

What woke her at three thirty wasn't a storm, but the cold. She was freezing. In her dream, she had been outside on a cold, damp day and woke to find that her mind had simply created this because of the drop in temperature in her room. At first she tried to stay asleep and reached for the covers that she had pushed aside earlier and pulled them back over her body. She turned on her stomach, her head to one side and snuggled down to try to regain her body heat. Her eyes flickered, she registered that the room was dark – there must be another power cut as she had gone to sleep with her bedside light on. At the same time, she heard Ruby's cries coming from the monitor and realised she had to go settle her daughter.

She flung back the covers, pushed herself slightly off the pillow and went to bend her right leg to turn herself over but found that she couldn't. She tried again, fully awake now, registering that all was not well in the room around her. She couldn't move her left leg either.

Ruby's screams were increasing in intensity and Martha felt a surge of panic run from her gut through to her throat. At first, her brain couldn't process what was happening – it was too unlikely, *impossible* even – but it was clear what was happening. She could move neither leg to turn over because someone was holding her ankles.

Ruby screamed even louder, a panic to her cry, gasping now for breath between the screams. Martha was flooded with terror and instinctively scrabbled wildly with her feet but whoever was holding them down wouldn't let go. In fact the grip was getting stronger. Martha pushed herself up on her elbows and tried to turn her upper body to see who her assailant was, to make out some shape in the pitch darkness. As she did, however, her elbows gave way from underneath her. Whoever was holding her had started to pull and Martha slid down the bed in a sudden and rapid movement.

"*No!*" she shouted, and grabbed at the sheet, her whole body struggling. She had to get free to go to Ruby – she knew that, but why *couldn't* she? Who was stopping her?

The baby's cries were unbearable – great gasps for air and screams of abject terror which to Martha, her brain on high alert, sounded muffled. Someone's hurting my baby, screamed her mind as she was pulled further down the bed by hands she couldn't see.

Helpless, Martha tried her hardest to kick out with her legs but succeeded only in kicking at the air. Suddenly, as quickly as it had begun, the attack stopped and Martha came to an abrupt halt, her ankles flailing around wildly as she found herself resisting a grip that was no longer there. She felt rage rather than terror bubble through her body as she was finally able to flip herself over.

"Who *are* you?" she roared as she turned.

It was dark but she could see enough to make out that whoever had been there was gone. Martha blinked, turned her head rapidly from side to side – she could make out no unusual shapes in the room.

Ruby was still screaming, the sound more muffled than before but the panic still clearly there. If someone had been hurting Ruby from the start, she thought, then who had been in *her* room – were there *two* of them? It struck her that even though what she could hear was horrific, it meant that Ruby was still there – no one had taken her away – and she was still alive.

She scrambled from the bed and fled for her daughter's bedroom. In the blink of an eye, thoughts flashed through her head. She should have armed herself, she knew, but the primal urge to have her daughter in her arms was too strong. If she could just *touch* her, then Ruby would be okay. She knew her attacker might be in the darkness of the landing, waiting for her as she ran across, but the urge to get to Ruby was so strong that she couldn't have stopped herself if she tried.

She flung herself inside Ruby's room, screaming from the bottom of her gut for them to leave her baby alone. The crying continued, the sound of a child in pain and terror. As soon as Martha screamed, however, the screaming was joined by a second low whimper. Martha stopped in her tracks and surveyed the room before her. She felt like she was being elevated from her own body for a moment, and as though the floor had started to rotate around her. The desperate screaming and crying continued but there was no attacker or abductor in the room. The moons and stars circled the walls, casting a dim glow around the room – how was that happening in a power cut? – and Ruby was just starting to grizzle at being woken unexpectedly.

Martha gasped. It wasn't her daughter screaming and crying – *it was the wall.*

She took a step backward in complete shock, gazing at the chimney-breast from where the sound seemed to come, the exposed brick still slightly visible under the picture of the hare. The crying filled her head – she longed to clap her hands over her ears and run, to do anything so that the terrible wailing and gasping would stop – so that the *suffering* that she could hear would come to an end. What kind of an animal could make such a *human* noise?

She willed herself to the light switch. If the nightlight was working, there had to be power. She flicked the switch up and down a number of times. Nothing. There was a power cut, but a small electric light was still working – *how?* Panic engulfed her and a small cry escaped from her lips. Yet again, nothing made sense. She looked around the room, not knowing what it was she sought.

Ruby, she thought. Must get Ruby out of here. She rushed to the cot where her daughter lay – silent but with arms outstretched, looking to be picked up, her face contorted in fear at the sound that surrounded her.

The dreadful crying had lessened a little – sobs now – horrible, sad, pathetic little sobs and gasps for air. Martha could now make out the scrabbling noise that she was so used to hearing. It flashed across her mind – *what if it's not an animal?*

She picked Ruby into her arms and held her head close to her, trying to block the sound from her ears, still scanning the room uncertainly. She bent and picked up Ruby's blanket, popped her pacifier back in her mouth, took Hugo and turned to leave. She stepped toward the door.

A wrenching sob came from the wall and something in her snapped.

"For the love of God, *stop it*!" she cried at the top of her voice, close to tears herself. "Just shut up, *shut up*!" she roared.

Immediately the room fell silent. The only crying now came from Ruby – a gentle, tired whimper of confusion and fear at her mother's loud voice. Martha stopped for a moment to focus, her heart pounding so hard that her eyes swam with little stars.

She gathered herself together and moved toward the door, stepping into the corridor, back out into the pitch darkness. She scanned the landing, tried to make out what she could from the dim glow that Ruby's nightlight cast from her room – *how is that working?* She could see nothing, but then again the light was next to useless. Gingerly she edged toward the stairs in the black darkness, trying to move as quickly as she could in her bare feet. She kept moving, virtually blind in the dark, peering over Ruby's shoulder to see what little she could. Her arms were full with the child, the blanket, the teddy bear, making it awkward to move, knocking her off balance.

Frustration and terror coursed through her and she squeezed back hot tears of panic. She extended her foot and tried to feel in front of her for the top step of the stairs. She had to be careful – she couldn't stumble or trip or both she and Ruby would fall down.

Where had her attacker gone? Was he – or *they* – in hiding somewhere, getting ready to pounce on them both? Was it their intention to snatch Ruby? Where had they *gone*?

Martha looked behind her without thinking and yelped as she took the next three steps too quickly, trying to catch up with herself. Her heart pounded and she came down hard on one foot and felt her balance go. She instinctively reached out to the banisters and felt Ruby slide down against her body. As she grabbed her, the pacifier fell from the baby's mouth. Martha heard it bounce off the banister and hit the floor below. A sharp shot of fear ran through her. She hadn't thought it possible to feel any more terror but it kept coming in waves. She gasped and steadied herself, her foot smarting from where she had come down hard, her temples pounding, her cheeks wet from tears.

The house was now completely silent, save for Ruby's whimpers and her own ragged breath. It was pitch black in the hallway below her. She would have sold her soul for even the slightest hint of orange glare from a street lamp but, as it was, the dark almost appeared solid. Above her, she heard a small tap, followed by a scratch, then faster – the scrabbling had started again. Martha moaned, took a breath and focused her concentration on getting herself and Ruby down the stairs. She tried her best to move slowly and carefully, all the time petrified that her attacker would come shooting out of the darkness behind her. Or below her.

Ruby was starting to cry harder now, aware of the loss of her soother. Martha cursed it. She knew by the cries that she needed to find it or Ruby would grow hysterical and it was essential to keep her calm if they were to get out of this. The other four soothers were still in her room – and there was no way Martha was going back up for them. Terrified, she made her way awkwardly down the stairs, her pace frustratingly slow, constantly aware that there must still be someone – or more than one person – in her house. At last she felt the change in texture beneath her feet as she stepped from the bottom stair and felt the parquet tiling of the hallway.

Martha had her eyes open but the dark was such that she wondered were they actually closed and blinked to figure out which. It didn't help that she had closed all of the doors downstairs leading onto the hallway before she went to bed, and blinds and curtains were firmly closed in each room. There was no chink of light from the front door – the intruder must have entered through a back way.

She was bathed in sweat again, despite the fact that the whole house was permeated with the cold that had woken her up initially. Her hands were getting slippery now and she struggled to hoist Ruby back onto her hip as the baby squirmed and kicked.

"Shush, darling," whispered Martha, her voice trembling.

She sank to her knees by the bottom step, her hand reaching around in the darkness to try to find the dropped pacifier. Ruby struggled in her arms and cried angrily at the added inconvenience. With each movement of her hand Martha felt sure it would be there, under her fingers, that she would feel the plastic rim and then she could pick it up and run – run where? She decided that the study was the safest place – she could lock the door and decide on their next move. The soother remained out of reach each time and Martha grew angry every time her hand touched bare floor.

She felt blind as she groped around. She knew she was outside the dining-room door – could feel the saddle-board and the bottom of the closed door against her hand. Then she felt the door give way – it hadn't been fully shut. It swung back gently and, terrified, she peered into the dark room. Nothing. No movement.

There was no light to spill from the room but in a strange way the darkness was brighter. Or perhaps Martha's eyes were finally accustomed to it. Either way she made out the shape of the soother on the ground just beside her thigh. She gasped with relief and reached toward it, her fingers hovering above it, ready to pick it up.

Then she froze. From above the dining room she heard another noise that she'd heard before. One step, two steps, three steps . . . the heavy creaks that sounded like someone walking to the cot. Her stomach tightened and a cold sensation shot down her back as she grabbed the soother from the floor. She stood up rapidly, staggering a little as her balance went. Regaining it, she scurried as quickly as she could, panting and emitting small cries of panic, down to the study door where she fumbled to open the handle with her elbow and forced her way in, slamming the door behind her and managing to hold Ruby with one hand while she locked it with the other.

She felt no relief in the study, but paused for a moment and took a deep breath. First things first, she had to put Ruby down before she dropped her so she felt her way in the dark toward the small sofa that was set against the wall on her right-hand side. As carefully as she could, she lay Ruby down and sucked the soother herself for a moment to take away the floor germs before giving it, and her blanket, to the little girl. Ruby settled quickly, pulled her blanket to her face and snuggled Hugo beside her.

Martha knelt on the floor alongside the sofa and exhaled, realising that her chest hurt from holding her breath. She glanced around her. The room was small and it was easier in here to make out shapes in the dark. She was fearful of opening the blind, however, in case whoever had been in her house was outside. She needed to try as much as possible not to give her location away.

There was no phone in the study. She used her mobile phone always and, ironically, that was upstairs beside her bed in case of emergencies. Beside her torch in case of blackouts. Martha almost sniggered.

Making sure that Ruby was as near the back of the sofa as she could be, Martha tiptoed to the door and pressed her ear against it. It was completely silent in the hallway. Did that mean the intruders had gone? Or were they still lurking somewhere in the house? She reached out her hand and found the golf umbrella that she kept beside her desk. She slid it out and took it in both hands, leaning up against the door.

The house remained silent. Martha felt herself relax a little – it seemed that whoever had been up there was gone. She only had to lie low now and make it to her car at first light which couldn't be far off. The car keys were in her handbag – finally a stroke of luck – which was slung over the back of her writing chair. This idea gave her hope and she allowed herself a moment to think, sliding down against the door and sitting on the floor.

How had someone got in, she wondered. The front door was definitely closed, and she was sure she had locked it before bedtime – her previous intruder ensured that she was vigilant about that. Was this the same one? She thought of the footsteps upstairs and the number of times she had heard them. Was it just school kids playing pranks or was it something more sinister? They must have got in through the back somewhere, maybe broke a window or forced the conservatory door – but *why* did they want to get in? If they were burglars, everything of value was downstairs – even her handbag. And why would a burglar go anywhere near the occupants of a house, still less grapple with one by the ankles? Was their intent rape? She shuddered. If so, why didn't they go ahead? Or did they want to snatch Ruby? Then why hadn't they just taken her? Why would one of them hold Martha down while the other made Ruby cry?

Blood rushed to Martha's face. It hadn't been Ruby crying. It was Martha herself who had made Ruby cry. The crying noise had come from the wall. But that was impossible. Wasn't it? Martha froze as Lil Flynn's words echoed in her ears . . . *'There's a little boy in the wall at Eyrie Farm . . .'*

21

July 12th

Martha woke with a jolt, completely unable to figure out where she was for a moment. Her back felt stretched and her neck ached where her head had fallen forward. She saw the golf umbrella in front of her on the ground and realised that it was the sound of it falling that had woken her. She was instantly alert, feeling guilty for having allowed herself to drop off. There had been intruders – what if they were still in the house? They could have forced the door behind her, broken the window, taken Ruby from her.

Sunlight flooded in through the slats of the wooden blinds and Martha realised that she must have been asleep for hours.

She glanced at the sofa where she had laid her daughter the previous night, to see her two little eyes open and searching the walls inquisitively but without fear. The movement of chubby hands followed as they gently reached to her blanket and pulled it up to her chin. Her soother slipped out and she stuffed the end of the cellular blanket into her mouth in its place. Her legs kicked as she grew more alert, she made a little noise. Martha loved to watch her daughter wake, but not today. It meant that she was going to have to move, to leave the sanctuary of her study. They needed to leave, and Martha was suddenly terrified that whatever had been there the night before was still there, waiting for her.

What on earth had she been thinking, bringing Ruby down the stairs in the dark like that with an intruder in the house? Why hadn't she just locked them both in safely upstairs? Of course – the noise coming from the wall. In the daylight Martha realised that it could only logically have been whatever was there all the time, whatever animal or bird was nesting in the chimney, perhaps disturbed in some way by the intruder. It couldn't be anything else.

Martha blocked from her mind the thought that the intruder had seemingly disturbed something *inside* the blocked-up fireplace, while not disturbing her daughter *outside* it in her room. She didn't want to think about that.

She stood slowly, sliding back up the door the way she had slid down. Her back throbbed as she stood and she gave a little cry as her knees clicked loudly. Ruby turned at the noise and beamed immediately at her mother, as though on a great adventure. Martha smiled back weakly – her heart filled with love for her daughter and also terror at how close she had come to not being able to protect her. That was her worst nightmare come true.

"Hello, petal," she whispered gently and dared to step away from the door. She paused. Nothing burst through or rattled the handle. Martha walked slowly and stiffly across the room and knelt to give her daughter a kiss. She stroked her face, held the chubby fingers that stretched out to grab her hair and kissed the little open mouth over and over. How on earth could she keep her safe?

A familiar smell made Martha wrinkle her nose and she leaned in to check more closely. Sure enough, it seemed that Ruby had made the decision for them to leave the room. "Pooh!" whispered Martha and Ruby giggled. Martha lifted her gently into her arms and pushed herself upwards, the weight of the baby causing a drag on her back and making her wince.

Martha held her breath as she turned the key of the study. She gingerly pulled the door toward her and peered out into the hallway. It was completely empty, the pushchair left by the front door, folded and propped against the wall. The dining-room door was open, as she had left it, and all the other doors were still firmly closed.

She hesitated, then took the key from the lock and slid it into the pocket of her pyjama bottoms for safe keeping. Squatting down, she picked up the golf umbrella. She knew it would be useless as a means of defence, particularly with a seven-month-old baby in her other arm but it gave her some comfort.

The hallway seemed so much smaller and straightforward in the light of day – last night it had felt cavernous, full of hidden nooks and crannies where anyone might hide. She assumed it must be about seven o'clock, judging by the strength of the sunlight coming in through closed blinds. She felt much braver being able to see at least and she cautiously crept upwards, her bare feet padding silently, while Ruby played with a strand of her hair. She stopped and peered upwards. The landing appeared to be empty. She made her way slowly up the rest of the stairs – her own room was also empty but she shivered as she saw in daylight the evidence of the night's events. Her duvet was flung aside and the undersheet was pulled halfway down the bed where she had pulled it with her as she was dragged. She stepped into the room and lay Ruby down on the bed and then tugged the sheet back upward and smoothed it down before replacing her pillow at the top of the bed. She didn't want to have to be reminded of the night before any more than she had to.

Ruby, safe in the middle of the bed, was starting to grizzle with both hunger and the sensation of the soiled nappy. Martha did a quick sweep of the room – under the bed, in the wardrobe, behind the curtains and door – to make sure it was empty –and then decided it was safe to leave Ruby to go across the landing.

Emboldened by the daylight, she padded across the room and tried to think logically. The chances of someone still being in the house were slim. Why would they stay silently lurking all those hours?

Armed with the golf umbrella she did a quick check of the bathroom, the boxroom, the linen cupboard – nothing. There was only Ruby's room remaining. Her heart began to pound again. She was afraid also of disturbing again whatever had made that terrible noise last night – that was the last thing she wanted to hear.

Martha raised the golf umbrella and gently pushed the door open as wide as she could. She knew that she had left it wide open last night when she had fled but there were those footsteps – undeniably footsteps this time.

The room was as dark as it had been in the middle of the night, the moons and stars still circling. Martha crossed quickly to the window and pulled up the blackout blind, allowing sunlight to flood in. Still she felt no relief. She could see no one in the room but still felt uneasy. She whipped her head around, sure that there was someone at the door, watching her. Nothing.

It struck Martha as strange that there was no disruption in the room – the little pile of soothers was still on the changing unit, the cot untouched other than the creases where Ruby had lain the night before. It disturbed her to see that the room appeared completely as though no one had been in there, but there had been – *had to have been*. She felt her panic return – she didn't know why, there was clearly no one there but all the same she moved as quickly as she could to gather clothes, nappies, talc and cream as well as the soothers and a couple of toys. She balanced the lot on the changing mat and gathered it up in her arms to run across the corridor. Once back in her own room she dumped it all on her bed and ran back a second time, this time giving the baby's room a final appraisal and then pulling the door tight behind her.

Martha changed and dressed Ruby quickly, then herself in jeans, trainers, a T-shirt and a hoodie top. Then she sat down beside an increasingly cranky Ruby for a moment. She needed a plan. Her primary urge was to get out of the house. She knew it was daylight and that she was probably safe but she still felt a desperate urge to get out of there and speak to another human being face to face. She'd have to go to the police, of course. She could ring them, but then they'd tell her to wait for them there which she didn't want to do. Best to drive to the police station at Bickford and talk to someone there.

Ruby grew increasingly agitated beside her. Martha picked

her up. "Right then, Ruby-Doo, come on with Mum – we're going to have an adventure in the car!" Her gentle tone did nothing to soothe the baby – in fact it had the complete opposite effect and Ruby suddenly opened her mouth wide and bawled. It dawned on Martha that she was going to have to feed her. She'd been so intent on getting them prepared to leave that it hadn't occurred to her to do it. She felt uneasy, but she knew she'd have to stay in the house long enough to get her child fed.

Martha picked the screaming Ruby up, took her phone from her bedside table and hurried downstairs. She walked along the hallway and reached the door to the kitchen, stopping as she did. Surely if the intruder were in there she'd know about it by now? Her blood ran cold for a moment but she pushed the kitchen door open and hurried in, closing it behind her.

The kitchen was bright and glowing warm in the sunshine as she walked in and Martha was comforted by the bright surroundings but still aware that she had to hurry to get out of there. She slid Ruby into her high chair and placed a plastic toy in her hand which alleviated the screeching for a moment, but it was clear that there would be no let up until she was fed. Martha hurriedly busied herself preparing porridge and fruit and preparing a bag with further food for later in the day. She had thought no further than going to the police in Bickford but she didn't know how long that would take and better to be safe than sorry with a hungry baby. Besides which, completing the normal, everyday chore would calm her.

A thought struck her. The conservatory door. Had that been the means of entry for the intruders the previous night? It must have been. She hurried across the kitchen and down the step into the sunroom, expecting to feel a cool morning breeze greet her from the open door. But it was closed. She went to it and checked. It was locked.

Ruby's wails redoubled and Martha rushed back to the kitchen, checking that the conservatory key was in its usual place on the hook inside the kitchen door as she went.

Tears were streaming down her daughter's face. "I'm so sorry, Ruby," she said and made shushing noises as she slid the high chair over to the kitchen table, making a space for it between the two chairs already there, shunting one out of the way. She fetched the bottle and food, set it up on the table to keep it clear of little hands and sat down herself in the chair beside Ruby as she took the lid off the bottle and slid it into her mouth. Ruby began to suck hungrily, her eyes closed.

After a few moments Martha took the bottle from her mouth, hoping that the edge was off her hunger, and held out a spoonful of porridge and fruit. Ruby usually responded like a little bird, her mouth wide open, but this morning her face wrinkled in disgust and she turned her head away as far as she could from the proffered spoon and once again burst into tears. "Okay, okay," said Martha and returned the bottle to her mouth.

Martha looked at the clock – almost eight in the morning. They'd slept longer than she'd thought. She turned back to Ruby and tried again with the spoon, with the same reaction. "Oh, Ruby," said Martha, exasperated and panicky. "Ruby Doo, you have to eat your porridge if you want to grow up to be big and strong!" She was almost reluctant to speak just in case her voice alerted someone to their presence. She offered Ruby the bottle again and she drank eagerly, ignoring her mother and focusing entirely on the formula.

The room darkened slightly as a cloud went across the sun and Martha shivered as it grew chilly, looking around her in trepidation. More than ever she wanted to leave. There was a sucking noise as Ruby drained the bottle and Martha tutted. "Right then, Rubes, you drank your bottle all up so let's eat your porridge, eh? *Please* eat up and we'll go on our adventure." She stirred the mixture together and held up a fresh spoonful. There were no tears this time, just a point-blank refusal. Ruby turned her head to the right and leaned away from Martha. "Come *on*, Ruby," said Martha, growing even more panicky and impatient. "Just one spoonful!" She held the spoon gently against Ruby's lips but she refused to part them.

Martha decided to try a new tack. "Are you ready for the aeroplane?" she asked and waved the spoon in the air to catch Ruby's attention. "Are you ready . . . one . . . two . . ."

Martha didn't know which happened first. She thought it was the spoon – as she held it aloft ready to swoop the food down toward Ruby, it was slapped from her hand, and she saw it fly in an arc through the air and land on the floor, scattering porridge and pear where it fell. At the same time, or just before, or just after – she didn't know – the chair that she had moved to make way for the high chair at the table slid rapidly backward across the floor.

Martha stared in disbelief. There was no one else in the room. Her brain struggled to rationalise what she had just seen. It was for all the world as if someone had stood up rapidly and pushed the chair back as they did so. The same someone who had smacked a spoon out of her hand.

"Oh Jesus," she said, panic rising in her voice and tears pricking the backs of her eyes. Her eyes grew wide, searching for some explanation of what had just happened. "Oh Jesus, oh Jesus, oh Jesus," she said as she stood up slowly and dropped the tub of food from her hand.

She was barely aware of what she was doing. She unclipped Ruby from the highchair with fumbling fingers and grabbed the changing bag from the worktop. Her breathing was rapid as she moved and she realised that the room was absolutely freezing cold. So cold that she could see her breath in little clouds of vapour coming from her mouth.

She felt as though she were in a dream as she flung open the kitchen door into the hallway. A fleeting thought ran across her mind that she shouldn't, in case something she didn't want to see was on the other side, but it was too late – the door was open. The hallway was empty. Martha dived into the study for her handbag, scrabbling to pick the leather handle from the back of the chair where she had slung it. She whimpered with panic as her fingers failed to grasp it once, twice – she had it.

She ran out into the hallway, moving awkwardly, weighed down by Ruby and the two bags. Something made her look behind her as she ran. Still nothing there. She reached the front door. Her hands trembled as she undid the chain, turned the key in the mortise lock – she wanted to scream with frustration, felt she wasn't moving as fast as she needed to at all – and undid the latch. With the door finally open, Martha flung herself outside as if over the finishing line of a race and out into the sunshine.

Somehow she managed to get Ruby secured in her rear-facing car seat. She ran around the car without a look back at the house and sat into the driver's seat, locking the doors after her. She turned the key badly in the ignition and released a squeal of panic when the engine coughed but didn't catch. She tried again, the engine thankfully hummed into life and she set the car in gear, reversing clumsily and at speed into the hedge, scratching the boot. Her eyes were now fixed firmly on the open door of the cottage, petrified of what might emerge.

She stared at it all the way down the drive in the rearview mirror and barely glanced left or right as she turned out onto the main road. It was only when she drove too far out into the centre of the road and had to swerve dangerously on a corner to avoid a head-on with a truck that she finally realised they were both fine, but wouldn't be for much longer if she kept driving like that. She pulled into a farm gateway, completely off the road, and took a deep breath.

As she sat there, she couldn't stop herself continually checking the rearview mirror, as if whatever had knocked the food from her hand was suddenly going to appear, something shuffling down a busy country road on a Saturday morning in July. She shook her head and looked again in the mirror but this time to check Ruby's reflection in her Kermit the Frog mirror on the headrest of the back seat. She seemed fine and was tugging at a small book attached to the handle of her car seat.

Martha leaned her head back, gave a silent prayer of thanks that Ruby was so placid, and that she was fine. At the same time she felt despair. What on earth had she got them into? What had just happened to her at the cottage? Was she hallucinating? Was the local nonsense true and was Hawthorn Cottage – Eyrie Farm – really *haunted*? Martha didn't really have an opinion on such things – ghosts, spooks, spectres – they were just something that had never crossed her frame of reference. But this – physical objects flying about the place? Spoons knocked from her hand?

Chairs moving of their own accord? Martha grew pale as she began to think over her time in the house. What about all those footsteps that she first thought were floorboards creaking? Assailants getting in through locked doors . . .

She shook her head. There had to be a logical explanation for all of this. Someone had physically dragged her down her bed after all – she had felt hands around her ankles. There must just be some other means of entry. Could something magnetic have happened to cause the spoon and the chair to move? But what about the scratching upstairs?

"Come *on*, Martha!" she said aloud and hit the steering wheel with her hands. She put the car into gear and cautiously edged out onto the road. She built up speed slowly, her trembling legs making it difficult to clutch down and accelerate smoothly. She gingerly drove down the hill into Shipton Abbey and past the Abbot's Rest and up Middle Hill, turning right into the village car park which was deserted so early on a weekend morning. It was only eight forty-five. A few moments ago she had been feeding Ruby, nervous that there was an intruder hiding in her house, planning what she would say to the police. And here she was now, in her car, unsure of what was real and what wasn't.

She stepped from the car, afraid her legs wouldn't hold her. They felt like jelly, alright, but they supported her weight and she went to the boot to get the buggy. At the very least it would be something to lean on when she tried to walk with legs that felt like pipe-cleaners. She opened the boot and groaned. It wasn't there – of course it wasn't – she'd seen it propped up against the wall beside the front door earlier. She resignedly slung her handbag over her shoulder and took the changing bag from the back seat, hanging it across her chest. She unclipped Ruby from the car seat and lifted her gently on to her hip, then locked the door with her key fob. "Let's go for a walk to clear our heads, eh, chuck?" she said to the little girl. Ruby gave a jiggle and gasped as fresh air hit her face. Martha pressed her own face against her daughter's cheek and breathed in her sweet, innocent scent. How normal it felt to do that! Weighed down with bags and baby, she then turned and began her descent into the village.

She was tiring already when she reached the bottom of Middle Hill. She had no real idea where she was going; she simply wanted to see other people around her, sense normality. She hadn't walked far along the cobbled main street when she heard her name being called.

"Martha! Ruby! Over here!"

She searched for the voice. It was Mary Stockwell from a table outside the village café and bakery.

"Mary!" she called gratefully. "Thank God it's you!" As she crossed the street to the café she heard the reassuring clink of cups, the gushing of the coffee-machine inside. A warm smell of baking hung over the pavement in the summer morning air and Martha had never felt so relieved in her life.

Mary stood up and reached to take Ruby across the burgundy canvas that separated the outdoor area of the café and the pedestrianised street. She glanced at Martha and a look of concern crossed her face. "Whatever's the matter, Martha?" she asked, and sat down with Ruby while Martha made her way to the table.

"Oh Mary, I don't know where to begin!" Martha stopped as she caught sight of herself in the café window, which by a trick of the light showed her reflection clearly.

She looked white, washed-out, with huge grey circles under her puffy eyes. She noticed some spots on her chin were bloody where she had absentmindedly picked at them during the long night in the study, or perhaps in the car on the way into the village – she had no recollection of doing it. Her hair was unwashed and sticking up. "Oh my God, look at me," she said, horrified. She hunched down in the chair and fumbled in Ruby's changing bag for a baby wipe which she used to swipe across her eyes and then dab the bloodied spots. She then rummaged in her own handbag and to her surprise found a hair band that she used to keep her hair back when applying make-up. She was grateful it was there and slid it onto her head. It wasn't a huge improvement but she felt that at least she'd tried. She breathed a sigh of relief.

"Sorry, Mary," she said, more calmly than before. "We've had a hell of a night."

"I can see that," replied Mary, straightening Ruby's dishevelled clothes and warming her chilly feet with her work-worn hands. She was reaching down for the changing bag to search for socks when a shadow fell across the table.

Both women looked up, expecting to see Rosemary, the owner, ready to take their order.

Instead, a tall man stood there with his hand outstretched. "Martha?" he asked. "Is it Martha Armstrong?"

Mary looked at Martha, thinking that she perhaps knew him. Martha looked at the man and then back at Mary again.

"Yes, I'm Martha Armstrong," she said warily.

"Great," said the man. "I'm Will Peterson." He withdrew his hand as Martha didn't offer hers in return. "I was told to say I'm your present from Scotland – does that make sense?"

Martha stared blankly up at him for a while and then remembered Sue's postcard. What the hell was she up to? Who was this guy?

The man continued to speak. "Your friend Sue Brice told me there was a bit of trouble at your house. She thought we might be able to help one another."

Twenty minutes later Martha was sitting alone with Will Peterson outside the café. She felt distinctly better than earlier, with two freshly baked croissants and two cappuccinos inside her.

Ruby had gone home with Mary for a nap. She had grown grizzly and unsettled, clearly exhausted after her night's adventures. Mary had watched as Martha made no effort to take her home as she normally would, saw this strange man who claimed to be a 'gift from Scotland' and felt vaguely uneasy. She couldn't bear to see an unhappy child, however, so she took the baby and her changing bag and strolled the short distance to her house, on a lane parallel to the High Street.

"She's lovely," said Will Peterson, gazing after the little girl and giving her a little wave. Ruby watched from the safety of Mary's shoulder, more than ready for her nap.

"You called her Ruby-Doo," observed Martha. "Did you hear Sue calling her that?"

Will looked surprised. "Not at all. It just seemed like a logical thing to call her."

Martha eyed him suspiciously. "Why did Sue tell you to come down here?" she asked, finally able to focus on the problem now that Mary and Ruby had gone.

Will sat forward, a serious expression on his face. "She told you that she's doing a feature about university courses, didn't she?"

Martha nodded.

"Well, I was one of her interviewees. I'm a student of parapsychology."

Martha looked at him blankly.

Will saw that she didn't understand and shifted in his seat. "This makes some people nervous but parapsychology is about the study of things like the causes of psychic abilities and so on. And uses scientific methods to explore things like . . . life after death."

A chill ran through Martha. "You mean ghosts?"

Will shrugged and nodded. "Yes, if that's what you want to call them – among other things of course. Anyway, Sue told me about her experience at your cottage –"

"What experience?" snapped Martha.

Will looked sheepish. "Shit, she told me she was going to fill you in before I got here . . ."

"She didn't tell me anything," said Martha coldly, then remembered a couple of missed calls from Sue the previous evening. She had meant to ring her back but had forgotten. Martha's mind was racing. What experience? Had something happened to Sue like what had happened to her with the spoon and the chair? Surely it couldn't have. Anyway, all of this had some sort of logical explanation. It couldn't be *ghosts*, for heaven's sake!

"Okay," said Will and began to explain what had happened to Sue in Ruby's room. He started with the scratching and scrabbling that Sue had heard.

Immediately Martha felt relief. "Oh, that happens all the time," she said. "There's some sort of an animal – a rat or a bird or something – nesting in the chimney-breast and they start doing their thing when everything goes quiet at night-time." She blocked out the memory of the previous night's horrific gasps and cries. "My landlord's going to fix it soon. Is that why Sue sent you up here?"

Will was listening intently. "That's what I thought it was too," he said. "But what interested me about Sue's story was the fact that the noises were accompanied by an extreme and sudden drop in temperature. She said it got so cold in the room that she could see her own breath, like on a frosty day."

Martha's face fell. The same thing had happened to her not an hour before. She wasn't, however, going to tell this guy that. She just wanted to get rid of him. Who was he anyway?

Will continued. "Sue said also that you seemed unsettled and a little unhappy here?"

Martha snorted. "With all due respect, Will, I'm recently divorced and have had to sell my house in London and move here with my seven-month-old daughter. It's tiring and stressful and I think anyone would be bloody unhappy sometimes under the circumstances." Her voice had dropped to an angry whisper. She wanted this guy to just go away so she could plan what to do next, try to figure out in her head what had happened to her. Her house had been broken into, nightmare noises had come from her chimney, and, to top all that off, stuff had started moving around her kitchen by itself. The last thing she needed was to analyse all that with one of Sue's 'finds'.

Will remained calm. "Oh – I understood it from Sue that you moved here voluntarily? That you saw the house on the internet and decided it was time to make a life change by moving here with Ruby?"

His face was blank but Martha reddened at being caught out in her exaggeration. She didn't know why she'd told the story as if she'd been forced to move here. Damn Sue for having blabbed her life story to some random stranger.

"Look," said Will, placing his hands on the table, "I hope you don't think that I'm taking a liberty when I say that you look a little anxious and tired. Your friend – who took Ruby – she seemed very concerned about you. Also, looking at it logically, you're wandering around on a Saturday morning with two bags and a baby in your arms and no pushchair for her. Maybe I'm putting two and two together and making five but you look like someone who left your house in a hurry this morning?"

Martha looked at him across the table. Who the hell did this guy think he was? Had he been *following* her? Was he her intruder? She felt rage bubble up inside her. "Teach you that in parapsychology school, then, do they?" she hissed. "A special class in Jumping to Conclusions? Along with a course on Reading Into Things That Aren't There? That's what you people specialise in, isn't it? Pretending to find things that aren't there and scaring the life out of folk?" Her hands were beginning to tremble again, a combination of rage and caffeine.

Will turned and gathered his jacket off the seat behind him. "I'm really genuinely sorry to have bothered you, Martha. As it happens, my remit in researching stuff like this is usually to disprove and debunk what's presented to me as so-called paranormal evidence, if that's what you want to call it. It's my job to be a sceptic, to prove that things that aren't there, as you put it, actually *aren't* there at all. I can see I've upset you, landing on you out of the blue like this, and I'm really sorry. I'll leave you to it."

He stood to go but paused as Martha spoke.

"I think I had an intruder last night," she said quietly.

Will sat down, looked at her with kind eyes. "You *think* you had?"

"I *know* I had," Martha corrected herself. This heebie-jeebie talk of ghosts was obviously rattling her brain. "I know that Sue has meant the best in asking you to come down here," she continued, "but I was physically held down by someone. It couldn't have been supernatural or whatever you call it."

Will nodded. "Look, why don't we have another coffee?" he said gently. "At the very least you can tell me all about it – you look like you need to get it off your chest."

Martha paused for a moment. Suddenly the temptation was strong to pour the story of the night's events out to this complete stranger. She had to talk about what had happened to someone –

make some sense of it by hashing it out with another human. And it didn't feel right talking to Mary for some reason. The villagers here were very good at making Martha feel like an outsider, like they knew something that she didn't, and she wanted to think things out a little longer. Obviously, there was something about this guy that Sue trusted and, after all, she trusted Sue completely. Another half an hour in the sunshine wouldn't do her any harm and then this stranger could just go back to Edinburgh and Martha could go to the police like she'd planned and then . . . Maybe it was time to think about going back to the city?

"Alright," she said. "But make mine a decaff. I think I'm cranky enough as it is."

Will smiled and hung his jacket back on the chair.

Martha studied him while he tried to catch the attention of a waitress. Early 30's, she thought – roughly the same age as herself probably. He was slightly over six feet tall, with dark, slightly shaggy hair that came down below his ears. He had a day's stubble on his chin, looked tired. He was dressed in jeans, a T-shirt and a pair of tatty canvas runners, with a small bangle made of wooden beads on his arm. He was handsome in a dishevelled way, with kind, brown eyes. There was something that disarmed Martha about him, made her relax in his company. She sat up straight as she thought this. Steady on, she told herself. She knew nothing about this guy after all.

Will ordered the decaff cappuccino for her and a pot of herbal tea for himself and Martha found herself telling him about the night's events, rationalising the story in her head as she went. It had to have been an intruder, a physical presence who disturbed whatever animal or bird was trapped in the chimney. Will listened patiently, interrupting only occasionally to clarify a point. Martha finished her story at the point where she and Ruby had reached the safety of the study. She couldn't tell him about the incident with the chair and the spoon, or the drop in temperature. That would make it real, and mean that something sinister had happened to Sue like he said, and she needed to work that one out a bit more. Besides which, he'd likely think she was nuts.

"So, you see that there's nothing of interest to you really," she finished. "I'm going to report the intruder to the police – that's where I'm off to now – and then . . . well . . . I suppose I'll get a guard dog or something!" She pretended to laugh and took a sip of cold coffee, looking past Will to the street, hoping that he would agree and say that her story wasn't of any relevance to him whatsoever. She found herself growing tired and wanting to be alone to get on with what needed to be done.

Will looked at her looking past him and then spoke. "I'd very much like to investigate your house, Martha," he said.

Her heart sank. "What? Why?"

"There are a couple of things in your story . . . look, you'd be doing me a massive favour. I need an investigation to complete a paper I'm doing and this sounds like it could be a suitable case study."

"A case study?" exclaimed Martha, a little louder than she had meant to. "But there's nothing para . . . psychological *about* it? I told you – it was a person!"

"I know," said Will, reassuringly. "Remember, I need to disprove stuff and with all of the info that I have from the locals –"

"What info?" demanded Martha. "And when did you talk to locals? How long have you been here? Have you been following me?"

Will shook his head, raised his hands to try to get her to calm down. "I've been here since yesterday morning," he explained. "I didn't want to just roll out to your house – Sue said you'd be working on your unicorn book, so I went to the pub at lunchtime and got chatting to a few people. I didn't leave till after closing time. I was going to call out to your house this morning – it's just a complete coincidence that I came in here for breakfast and I heard your friend call you – I took a stab that an attractive woman called Martha with a baby about Ruby's age might be Sue's friend and I was right."

"What did the locals tell you?" demanded Martha, her heart starting to beat, a curiosity rising in her chest. This was more of what Mary Stockwell had been talking about – or not talking about actually, as she had refused to say anything. "Was it some old blather about ghosts and monks and stuff?"

Will looked confused. "Umm, yes," he said. "Look, let me put something on the table here – a deal so to speak. You look like a woman who could do with a night's sleep after your ordeal. Actually, you need a tissue as well." He handed Martha a napkin and looked away.

She looked at him, surprised, until she realised that one of the spots had started to bleed again where she was absentmindedly picking at it. She slapped the tissue to her chin, mortified.

"I have a room booked in the brand new shiny Breakaway Inn near Bickford and –"

"Oh, I don't *think* so!" said Martha sternly. Was this seriously his game? Was he some sort of sleaze trying to get her to his hotel room?

It was Will's turn to be mortified as he realised what Martha thought he was saying. "Oh my God, *no!*" he exclaimed. "What I want to suggest is that we do a swap – why don't you and Ruby take the hotel room for tonight and I hang out at your house? I get an investigation for my paper and you and Ruby-Doo get an uninterrupted night in a safe, secure, completely unatmospheric environment. And to top matters off, if your – intruder decides to come back then I'll be waiting – and he'll be caught on camera into the bargain. How does that sound?"

Martha softened. What a fool she was making of herself – a clearly nonsense tale about intruders which he could see through like a window, and then jumping down this man's throat every five seconds. Not to mention the spot-picking. That was a seriously disgusting habit she had to stop, but it was a nervous response she'd had since she was a teenager and most of the time she didn't even realise she was doing it.

She certainly needed sleep. And a bath. Her limbs ached from her sleeping position the night before. A brand-new hotel certainly sounded appealing rather than listening to every creak and groan from Hawthorn Cottage. And she really couldn't face going back there at night-time. She certainly hadn't thought about somewhere to spend the night, not to mention the intruder having another try. What was to stop them now that they'd got in once?

"Why should I trust you?" she asked Will outright.

He smiled. "I really don't blame you if you don't. Sue said you'd be suspicious and you're absolutely right to be." He held his hands up. "I have nothing on me to prove that I'm not a serial killer but Sue said to ring her if you wanted to check me out – and I've also written this down." He handed her a sheet of paper covered in names and numbers. "These are all genuine people at the university who can vouch for me. I've given you their direct lines but if you want to ring the main switch – get it from Directory Enquiries rather than me – you'll get put through as well. Oh – and Sue said to give you this." He fished another piece of paper from his jacket pocket.

It was a note in Sue's handwriting: "*Use wisely, Grasshopper,*" it said. "*If only as protection from the Man Mountain.*"

Martha couldn't help but grin. "Typical," she said.

"I confess that I read it," said Will. "But it means absolutely nothing to me. She also said that she'd sent me to save you from 'Summerton'. I assume you both communicate in code all the time."

Martha giggled. "Fine then, I'll ring Sue but take it that we can do the swap."

"Great," said Will. "You ring Sue. She'll reassure you."

Martha warmed to him. He seemed to have gone to a lot of bother to prove that he was trustworthy. Most serial killers did, however, she countered. She pressed Sue's number on her phone and held it to her ear in front of him. She could sense nothing shifty about this guy. And there were a lot of witnesses around – if he were a serial killer, then so far his stay in Shipton Abbey had made him foolishly recognisable to a very large number of people between the pub and the café.

Sue's phone rang out, went to her message minder. Martha listened to the default answer message from the manufacturers and asked Sue to call her back as soon as possible.

"Look, let's shake on the deal," she said. "I'm sure you're okay, but if Sue says otherwise . . ."

"She won't," said Will confidently, "but if you're unsure at *any* point then just tell me and the deal's off. We'll do this on your terms."

Martha eyed him again. "Done," she said.

Will smiled. "Excellent. Now you just have to show me the house."

Martha's face fell. She hadn't planned on returning there today, much less with a total stranger, but she supposed she'd have to. For starters, she'd left the front door wide open. Way to keep an intruder out. On top of that her laptop, the TV and her jewellery were in there. Secondly, she'd need a change of clothes and some toiletries and nightgear for herself if she were going to stay away that night. Maybe if Will were with her . . . well, he'd either murder her horribly or act as a sort of guard.

"Fine," she said reluctantly. "Just let me ring Mary."

Mary was concerned about Martha and this stranger, but Martha reassured her he was a friend of a friend who was going to house-sit for her while she and Ruby went on a short, last-minute break. What she didn't tell her was that the break was five miles away and that, while house-sitting, Will was going to check for ghosts. Put like that, it all seemed too ridiculous.

Will instructed Martha to meet him at the car park of the Abbot's Rest where he'd left his car overnight. He'd paid a fortune for a cab to Bickford after his all-day liquid lunch in the pub the previous day and had cadged a lift back to Shipton Abbey that morning from a porter who was coming off night duty at the hotel. If nothing else, thought Martha, there was another person who could potentially identify him.

She was nervous about going back to the cottage but as she walked to her car and set off the short distance to their meeting point, a plan formulated in her mind. Stay the night in the hotel, let Will do what he had to do, then tomorrow morning get into the car and head back for London. It was that simple. She couldn't stay in that house again, put Ruby in danger. She pushed the events of that morning in the kitchen to the back of her mind. Let Rob Mountford deal with whatever bizarre stuff was happening at that house.

Will pulled out of the pub car park in a battered Volvo estate and Martha pulled ahead to let him follow her. She had a sinking feeling in the pit of her stomach as they drove the short distance to the cottage, despite the fact that having a plan was making her feel a little better. She felt sick as she turned into the driveway, dark with overhanging branches. She parked alongside the conservatory and Will pulled in outside the front door, stepping excitedly from the car and gazing at the cottage, taking it all in.

"This place is really lovely," he observed as he strolled around to the boot and unlocked it.

"Well, that's what I thought too," said Martha, coming around the side of the house to join him.

"I think your intruder might have come back though . . ." Will's voice was concerned as he pointed at the open front door.

Martha reddened slightly. "No, that was me. I'm, eh, terrible for not locking it properly and it blows open in the wind."

Will glanced round him. It was a calm day and even the bushes weren't moving. "You sure it's not because you left in a hurry?" he grinned.

Martha reddened and looked away. "We should get going if you want to get your casework started," she said.

"I'll go first then, just in case," said Will kindly.

Martha was careful to look nonchalant but couldn't have been more grateful that she didn't have to lead the way.

Will bounded in the front door, completely without trepidation. Martha stepped cagily in behind him, noting with relief that the stroller was still folded up against the wall. She picked it up and turned to head to her car with it. No harm having it ready to go in case she needed to make another hasty exit. "Won't be a minute!" she called.

She returned to find Will peering into the living room. She felt a longing to just leave the house at once. She wanted to go upstairs, get her things and go, but she was too afraid to actually do it and didn't want to admit to Will that she was. She stayed where she was, behind him.

Will peered into the study and then crossed the hall, striding into the kitchen and skidding on the spoon that had earlier been knocked from Martha's hand. Her heart gave a thud as she saw it. Such an ordinary little thing – an orange, plastic spoon. How had it flown out of her hand like it did? Will yelped and grabbed at the chair beside him to halt the skid. The chair. Just something else that had moved by itself, she thought.

"Someone didn't like breakfast?" asked Will, bending to pick up the spoon and place it on the table.

Martha stared at it, as though she expected it to fly through the air again. "Something like that," she said.

Will watched her stare at the spoon, studied her expression. "Let's check for signs of forced entry then," he said gently. "You say you left everything as it was?"

"Yes, I did. Apart from the front door."

Will did a tour of the downstairs rooms, finally crossing the kitchen into the conservatory to check the door. It was as Martha had found earlier – still firmly locked with no signs of anyone having tried to open it.

"No one got in here," said Will, scanning the panes of glass around him, turning his head upward to scrutinise the sloping glass ceiling. "No one's been in through here at all. All your downstairs windows are locked as well – I couldn't see any signs of tampering or breakages."

Martha began to panic. "But there must be – there was a *person* in my room!"

Will gave a shrug. "What about upstairs? Could someone have used a ladder maybe? Stood on something?"

Martha thought for a moment, running through the possibilities in her mind. "I haven't got a ladder. They'd have had to drive here with one and then drive away with it again – and park either here or out on the road, with a huge risk of being seen in either case. And I didn't hear any car. Besides, the windows are very small upstairs and leaded – I don't think anyone could actually fit through the openings." She was growing more baffled by the second. How had they got in?

"What about keys?" said Will. "Have you lost any recently?"

"No. They're all present and correct."

"Well, is there anyone else with a key?"

It was the obvious answer. "Just my landlord," she said and stopped in her tracks. What if Rob Mountford had done it? Had let himself in, not with the intention of harming Ruby but . . . Martha shook her head. Surely he wouldn't have done that? She knew that he was attracted to her, but was he so warped as to do *that*? He was an odd man, though, and she didn't know him at all come to think of it. Could he have let himself in the conservatory door, maybe? Her mind was racing, as it dawned on her that Rob Mountford must have been her attacker. It couldn't be anything else. But what had stopped him if that was the case? Had he been spooked by the animal in the chimney? Was that what had saved her from a worse attack?

"I think I know what happened," she said in a small voice and related her theory to Will.

He didn't look too convinced. "Possibly. But of course there may have been another key – he surely made some copies in case of one going astray. Anybody else working with him that he could have given a key to?"

Martha remembered Sam with a jolt. "Last time he came he had a young guy with him – a schoolboy really – but he was only helping him out – there would have been no reason he'd give him a key . . ."

"Still, it's a possibility."

"I suppose it is," Martha said unwillingly.

"Let's have a look upstairs then," Will said kindly.

Martha nodded. She was anxious walking up the stairs, and amazed that the room was exactly as she had left it that morning. She'd expected it to have changed in some way while she'd been out. Such a short time since she had been here but it felt like a different day – like it had happened to a different person.

She stepped into her bedroom behind Will and reached the end of the bed where she had left Ruby's dirty nappy rolled up and taped closed. She reddened as she realised that the room smelled faintly of it, and grew even more embarrassed to see the underwear she had worn the day before peeking out of her pyjama bottoms where she had flung them on the bed. She cursed herself silently and edged toward them. How was she to know that three hours after she'd thrown them there that she'd be back in the room with some random stranger? It struck her how foolhardy she was being – in a deserted house in the countryside with a man she'd met that morning. How trusting she was being. And she'd trusted Rob Mountford too. And look how that had turned out . . .

Martha turned her back to Will and bent to roll the underwear into the dirty pyjamas. She then dropped the bundle into the wicker laundry basket in the corner. When she turned to face him again, he was lying face down on the bed.

"What are you doing?" she asked nervously.

"Show me exactly what happened," said Will. "You were lying on your stomach like so, am I right?"

She nodded. "Yes – my head was facing that wall over there – and I'd just thrown back the covers to go to tend to Ruby. Then he grabbed my ankles . . ."

"Show me. Do to me exactly what happened to you."

Martha reluctantly placed her hands on Will's ankles.

"Was the pressure only that light?" he asked immediately.

Martha realised she was barely touching him. "No," she said hesitantly.

"Put all your weight into it and do exactly as your attacker did," urged Will.

She did as he asked, grabbing his ankles and bearing down with all her weight.

"That's better," said Will, propping himself on his elbows and turning his head and shoulders toward her. "Did you not just do this, though?"

"Of course I did, it's instinctive, but at that point he started to drag me off the bed and my elbows went from under me. The next thing I knew he'd let go of my ankles and when I turned he was gone."

Will lay face down again. "Okay, drag me down the bed and

then let go of my ankles and leave – just show me exactly what happened."

Martha pulled his ankles as hard as she could, leaning back with the effort of trying to drag him down the bed. He moved about a foot and she then let go and turned to run. She had taken a single step when Will shouted, "I see you!" and she turned to find him lying on his side, looking at her.

"Did you get tangled up in the sheets or the duvet or anything as the attacker left?" he asked.

She thought for a moment. "No. I turned over really quickly but he was gone."

"Didn't you catch even a glimpse of him as he left?"

She thought again. "No. Definitely not – he was too quick. I didn't see anyone."

Will sat up. "You say this Mountford is a big guy?"

"Yes, he is."

"About my height and build, say?"

Martha shook her head. "He's a bit taller than you, I reckon, and definitely build-wise he's much bigger."

"So a bit of a 'Man Mountain' then?" said Will with a slight grin.

"How did you . . . ?" Martha stopped and blushed again as she realised that Will had figured out Sue's message. She'd kill her when she saw her. Did he think now that something had gone on between her and Rob?

Will grinned and stood up off the bed. "We need to do this experiment again. But –"

"With me in the bed and you pulling my ankles?" she said in alarm.

Will nodded. "I can understand that you might not be comfy with that idea, but it's kind of key to my investigation and it would really be a huge help."

Martha was taken aback. She had thought he was just helping her out, trying to figure out what had happened to her, not plunging into his investigation already.

"I'll understand completely if you don't want to do this," said Will.

Martha thought for a moment, looked at his expectant face and gave in. She raised her knee to climb onto the bed. "If you were going to murder me you'd probably have done it by now, wouldn't you?" she said. "We do this once, though, and once only."

"Understood," said Will.

She felt vulnerable and stupid as she lay on her stomach in her habitual sleeping position. What the hell was she doing this for?

"You ready?" said Will.

In the event, they tried four times in total to recreate the events of the previous night. Martha was intrigued by the fact that no matter how quickly Will ran toward the door she saw him every single time when she turned. "I don't understand," she said. "I definitely didn't see anyone."

Will offered no opinion. "There's something else you haven't done either," he said, standing by the open door, giving Martha space to get up from the bed.

"What's that?"

Will responded by pointing his foot and pushing down gently on the floorboards underneath him. They gave a small creak of resistance. "You haven't mentioned actually *hearing* your attacker at all," he said.

Martha thought for a moment. She couldn't shake the feeling of unease that was growing by the minute as she realised that any attacker couldn't have left the room unseen. What had happened to her was impossible unless she'd dreamed it and she knew that it had been real.

"Listen to what happens when I walk out," said Will.

The floorboards creaked quietly but there was no mistaking the sound of footsteps on the wooden floor of her bedroom and out onto the landing.

"If I go down the stairs you'd hear this," he called and she clearly made out the sound of descending feet and the occasional creak. "This is coming up!"

She heard the footsteps ascend again.

"This is if I go into Ruby's room!" He demonstrated the sounds of entry into all the upstairs rooms as Martha sat on her bed listening, and feeling sick.

Will returned to the bedroom door. "Did you hear any of that last night?"

Martha shook her head, unable to unravel why, when she could hear Will so clearly even when he tiptoed, she hadn't heard her assailant the previous night.

"This Mountford was really big," said Will, enthused by the activity. "Probably would have made even more noise than me, even with his shoes off – hey, let's try that."

Martha looked up to ask him to stop but he already had his trainers off and was leaving the room. She realised she could still tell exactly where he was by the sounds of the floor.

"Will!" she called. "Yes, I can hear you!"

He returned, sliding his left foot into his trainer and then the right one, tugging them at the back with his hand to get his heels in.

"I did hear *some* footsteps," she said suddenly, her mind flashing back to the definite creaks she'd heard from above when she was on her knees in the hallway, searching for the soother. She explained to him how she'd heard similar noises from the wood settling before but that last night it had sounded exactly like someone upstairs.

"Okay," he said. "That's enough for now. Let's get your bag packed and you off for a night of sumptuous splendour in Bickford's finest budget hotel!"

Martha was still reeling with confusion, wracking her brains to figure out the gaps in the basic logic of what had happened to her. Will smiled warmly, though, and she couldn't help but smile back. For a moment she contemplated telling him everything – about what had happened in the kitchen, the temperature drops, the fact that the screaming in the chimney hadn't sounded remotely like a bird or an animal. That it had sounded like a trapped child . . . but she stopped herself in time. Don't get any more involved in this than you have to, she thought. Just keep quiet and get out of here quickly.

Will was hauling bags of equipment into the house from the boot of the Volvo as Martha took her final pieces of luggage from the study.

"Bit foolish of me to leave all this in the boot outside the pub overnight," he said. "Some of it belongs to the university and technically shouldn't be here!"

Martha smiled. She had turned the corner of the house when a thought struck her and she went back into the cottage.

"Will," she asked, "when you were in the pub was there an old lady there called Lil Flynn?"

"Funny you should mention her. She wasn't there – the landlord said she was sick and that it was just as well as we were talking about this place here. Apparently she's responsible for all sorts of stories about it – she just hangs round the pub staring at people, asking about it. By all accounts her talk over the years has stopped people coming near it – postmen, delivery men – have you found that?"

Martha was surprised that Will had gleaned more information from the locals in a single night than she had managed since she'd been here. So distance wasn't the difficulty in having things delivered here – Lil Flynn was no doubt why the postman left her mail in a tree like it was some sort of enchanted forest or something. This bloody place, she thought. She turned to her car, preoccupied, leaving Will staring after her.

She left Will unzipping bags of what looked like cameras and battery chargers and drove off toward the village. She felt foolishly excited about spending the night in a hotel and her heart lifted as the thought struck her that she wouldn't have to spend another night at the cottage. Her heart grew lighter the further away she drove. The cottage was all someone else's problem now.

Ruby was awake and gave a squeal of joy as Martha took her from Mary.

Mary eyed her, concerned. "Are you sure you're alright, love?"

"I'm absolutely fine. I'm just looking forward to getting away and having a good night's sleep. I've, eh, been really stressing myself out with my work."

Mary nodded, but looked as if she knew she wasn't getting the truth. "That man – from this morning – is he up at the cottage?"

"Will? Yes, he is. Look, Mary, to be honest, I think I had a break-in last night – nothing to worry about! – and he's going to just watch the place for me while he's in the area."

Mary grew wide-eyed. "You *think* you had a break-in?"

Martha nodded. "I mean, I definitely had a break-in but, really, it's nothing to worry about – he or they were disturbed before they had the chance to take anything. Actually – I need to tell Rob Mountford about it – didn't you say he lived on the Bickford Road?" Martha was feeling brave. It might just be the time to call to Rob Mountford, at the weekend, in his father's house, and see what he had to say for himself. He could have the nice little reward of her notice on the cottage as well, effective immediately.

"He does," said Mary, handing Martha Ruby's changing-bag. "But there's no point in calling to him – he's away at a trade thing in France with his dad at the moment. He's been gone since Thursday – Alison found out from his sister. I thought to myself – that means Martha won't be getting her wall fixed any time soon."

Martha barely heard the end of the sentence. Rob Mountford was in France? Had been since Thursday? That meant that he couldn't have been her intruder on Friday night . . . What if he'd flown back especially – used France as a cover to come back and do what he wanted with her? Flown back and then what? Driven fifty miles from the nearest airport to let himself into his own property and ravish a woman he'd been alone with dozens of times before and had made no actual sexual approaches to at all? And, if he had been trying to rape her, why had he then just let her go?

Martha felt logic slipping away from her. It was now highly unlikely that Rob had been her attacker. He was her only logical explanation and now that was gone. Except for Sam . . .

"Mary," she asked, "is Sam around? You know, the young guy who was helping Rob?"

"Oh, no, love, he'd be no good to you," said Mary, thinking

Martha was wondering if Sam could complete the work on the house. "He hasn't a clue – he's only a gofer really."

Martha longed to ask more questions – like whether Sam had a police record, whether he had ever been accused of anything – even as she thought of this, she felt it didn't ring true – he had seemed so shy, so diffident . . . She was roused from her thoughts by Ruby tugging her hair. "Ow!" she said playfully, remembering that Mary was watching her. She had to stay calm, stay as normal as possible. "Right, madam," she said, a little too cheerfully. "Let's get you in the car and get gone! Thanks again, Mary, for everything. I'll be in touch."

With that, she turned and walked away hurriedly before Mary could ask her anything more. She needed to be away. From Shipton Abbey, Eyrie Farm and most of all her own thoughts.

22

Eyrie Farm,
Shipton Abbey,
Norfolk,
England

February 1st 1954

Dear Caroline,

Here we are again, another St Brigid's Day and another birthday for me. I can scarcely believe that I am eighteen today and that a full year has passed since first we arrived at Shipton Abbey, for we are still here.

So much has changed, and so much has not changed since last I wrote down our tale. Not only are Marion and I still here in the countryside, but little baby Henry, now six months old, is still with us. We are still sure that he is to go to a loving home. Mrs Collins said that he is not too old to be adopted yet but that we should continue to take care of him.

We would be lost without the advice of Mrs Collins. She has taken the place of Mammy, Lord rest her, in being the person to tell us what to do. I say us, but Marion, to be truthful, isn't as interested in Henry as she should be.

Now, Henry eats little bits of the food that we eat – I mash potatoes and carrots together for him and he eats it and smacks his lips. And if I am stewing apples for myself and Marion, I give him a little as well and he smiles at me and holds his mouth open wide for more! It won't be long before he asks for a knife and fork, I think!

He still sleeps in my room with me. I put him on his tummy every night with a little bear the Mountfords gave him, which I have called Ted, for company, and I sing him a little lullaby before he drifts off to sleep. He is very good and only cries once or twice in the night and once I rub his little back and sing a little song to him he settles off back to sleep, to be ready for another day's adventures.

We still have not heard from Daddy, but that is only to be expected, I suppose, with my mother's loss so recent. There isn't a day goes by, Caroline, that I don't think of her and wish that she could just see Henry – Daddy too, for he would fall in love with him in an instant and bring us all home to be together as a family.

Mr Mountford calls to us every now and again which is good. He always brings us a little gift, some butter, or some fresh eggs from the hens at his farm. The extra food is helpful for us now that Henry is eating more than just his bottles.

I know that rationing must be nearly over, thank God, but sometimes Daddy hasn't remembered to send us money and I have to keep a very tight fist on our budget. I have to hide what little money we have because Marion would have it spent on stockings or material to make dresses – or sweets. She is a devil for the sweets all the same and has got very fat since Henry came along. I have had to let out her skirts and I fear I will have to ask Daddy for money soon to make her some new ones.

Of course with no word of Henry's adoption, there is also no word of us going home so I fear we are living day to day here in England. We had Christmas here of course, just the three of us.

Mr Mountford very kindly made us a present of a chicken which I cooked here for us, and we had some of the vegetables that I sowed last spring – to think that I thought we would never be here to harvest them!

I managed to put enough money by to give Marion a gift of some hair-ribbons, and I made Henry a rattle toy with some buttons and a little box that Mrs Collins brought me. Marion didn't have gifts for us but, after all that she went through to have Henry and her long and difficult recovery, I don't suppose she had the time to sort something out for us. She did buy herself some pretty hairpins though, when she went to the village after New Year's. I suppose she deserved to treat herself after months in Granny Flynn's cast-offs.

Of course, New Year! I almost forgot to tell you that Marion and I went to a party for New Year – my first one ever! Robert Mountford came to call one day before Christmas in a brand-new motor car (it seems all the Mountford children have their own, save for Charles who will get one at his next birthday, Robert tells me) with proper invitations for us. Of course I said first that I could not go but that Marion should go and I would stay behind to take care of Henry. When I showed him to the door, however, Robert said that he was especially concerned that I should attend the party and that he had already arranged that Mrs Collins should watch little Henry so that we could celebrate 1954. Well, I was shocked and pleased, Caroline, I can tell you. And what's more, Robert then handed me an envelope of money that he said Daddy had sent to Mr Mountford so that we could have new party dresses. I thought this odd, I must confess, that Daddy had not sent the money direct to us as he does with our housekeeping, but I didn't question it. I also put a little aside for a rainy day for there was an awful lot of money there, but I didn't tell Marion of course.

To make it even better, Robert then promised to come back in his motor car for us the very next day to take us to Bickford, which is a big town nearby, so that we could buy our dresses. I then did a very devious thing and didn't tell Marion where I was going. If she had come with us, then she would have spent every penny and more on herself and I was determined to have a new party dress – is that wrong of me? – for my first ever proper party. Instead of waiting at the door for Robert, I wrapped Henry up warm and left Marion with strict instructions to feed him and change his nappy, and then I went out onto the road to meet Robert where she could not see me. Oh, Caroline, what a lovely day we had! I bought two bolts of cloth for us, one in red for Marion and one in green for me, with matching ribbons, and there was even enough money for us to get some new shoes. I have become better at sewing, I must admit, and with Mrs Collins' help I was sure I could make us beautiful party dresses in time for New Year's Eve!

Then Robert took me to a little café for tea and cakes – I could scarcely contain my excitement at the delicious cream tea that we shared – that's what you call tea and scones with jam and cream in England, it would appear. I ate so much that I was stuffed and Robert thought it very funny that for such a skinny thing as I am, I could manage three scones to myself, and four cups of tea. It was dark when he dropped me back at Eyrie Farm but what a wonderful day it had been – what laughs we had – I hadn't laughed so much since you and I were together, Caroline, a lifetime ago.

I asked Robert to drop me in the lane outside – did I mention I had hidden the bike in some bushes so that Marion would think I was gone to the village on it? I have grown devious living with my sister! I also wanted to make sure that she didn't forget about Henry and get up on the bike and cycle off to Shipton Abbey or anywhere else as she is wont to do. Anyway, Robert dropped me at the lane, and helped me take the bike from the bushes. I was embarrassed at first admitting my deceit but he roared with laughter and said I was a rock of sense, if a devious one at that, and then he looked me right in the eye and said that he couldn't wait until New Year's Eve. I, too, was very excited about the party. I told Marion that the bolts of cloth had been sent from Daddy in Dublin and she didn't question me. She never writes to Daddy, I do all that, so she will never mention it to him till it is too late and then my defence for my deception is purely one of sound housekeeping which is something my father admires.

Of course when I arrived home, poor Henry hadn't been fed and had dirtied his nappy. The poor little mite was screaming blue murder and Marion had put him in his cot and shut the door of my room so as to read her book in peace. I despair of her sometimes and wonder if her lack of interest in her son is purely as a defence so that she isn't too sad when he is taken away. It must be an awful burden for a mother to bear, but sometimes I see a coldness in her eyes when she sees me feed him or play with him that leads me to believe she doesn't care. Is that possible? God knows I thought that she would get sense the minute he arrived but I think I was wrong on that front as well – she spends so much time on that bike, gallivanting and disappearing for hours. Then she won't tell me where she's been . . .

Mrs Collins helped me no end with the dresses and I gave Marion hers the day of the party itself (I was afraid she'd wear it if I gave it to her beforehand and she'd be sure to spill something on it or snag it). We both looked beautiful in the end. Of course Marion thought that her dress was too big for her when she saw it and she gave out to me for half an hour solid, saying that I thought her fat and who did I think I was, being a skinny bag of bones that no man would ever marry. I thought of her disgrace and wanted to say that no one would want to marry her either if they knew she was soiled goods but I held my tongue for fear of what she might do.

Mrs Collins came at seven o'clock and bade us enjoy ourselves but to be home by one o'clock at the very latest. I was shocked. Daddy would never have let us stay out so late, but Mrs Collins said that it was New Year's Eve and what good was it if we didn't see in the New Year and have a little dance for ourselves after the clock chimed midnight? Mr Mountford sent a driver for us then – can you believe it? Marion and Lily Flynn being chauffeured to a party on New Year's Eve! I felt like Audrey Hepburn!

The party was the best time I have ever had in my life, without comparison. There was punch which I didn't drink, as I think there was wine in it and I didn't want to break my Confirmation Pledge.

There was party food – delicious little pastry cases filled with a sort of mushroom soup – I have never tasted anything like it in my life. And how we danced – it was just young people at the party, Caroline, no Mr and Mrs Mountford at all, although they did pop their heads in at one point to make sure we weren't doing anything wrong! The room was decorated with balloons and a banner that said 'Welcome 1954' and we danced to records by Eddie Cochrane and Tony Bennett and Frank Sinatra – my feet scarcely left the dance floor all night. And then they played a Doris Day song – 'Secret Love' – Robert tells me it's from a film where she's a cowgirl called Calamity Jane and that he'll bring me to the pictures in Bickford some time soon – and he danced with me in front of everyone. Marion made a show of herself as usual by trying to butt in and get him to dance with her. Then she disappeared for a while in a temper when Robert wouldn't dance with her. He wouldn't let me go find her though and made me finish the dance with him all the way through. It was wonderful!

I save the best till last though, Caroline. Robert drove us home at half past midnight exactly, after we had sung 'Auld Lang Syne' and had a final dance to a very funny song about Constantinople. He made Marion sit in the back seat which didn't suit her at all until he said that movie stars and princesses always sat in the back seat and sure then you couldn't stop her getting in there at all!

That meant that I could sit in the front seat with him and wasn't it like a long leather couch – all the one seat, all the way across. Anyway, we were driving through the village when Robert reached out and took my bag off my knee and dropped it on the ground. I had no idea what he was doing and had opened my mouth to give out to him, when he made a face at me to shush, so I did. Sure didn't he have a plan all along? When we got to Eyrie Farm he pulled up outside and when I bent to pick up my bag he stopped me and made a face that I should go on inside. It was like a spy film, Caroline. Anyway, myself and Marion made to go into the house, and wasn't Mrs Collins at the front door waiting for us. And then I heard Robert start up the car, and just when I was about to go into the house, he stepped out of the car and shouted at me to come back and waved my bag at me. I did what he wanted and went back to him and whispered what was he doing at all but he bade me shush again and then said, "Lily, you are as beautiful as a real lily and the most beautiful girl at that party tonight and I think I love you and will you marry me?" as quick as that! Sure all I could do was laugh and I went red from my toes to my cheeks. And Robert looked awful hurt and said he was serious and for me to think about it, and then do you know what he did? He kissed me, Caroline. Square on the lips, when Mrs Collins wasn't looking! And then he got into his motor car and drove away and me looking after him. I was floating on air, Caroline, for he's handsome and kind and wonderful, as I have got to know in the months since New Year's Eve.

And yes, we are in love, Robert and I. It is a secret and we have to meet in secret when and where we can, for he cannot be seen to drive here too often and I dare not leave Henry with Marion for too long so I am tied to the house. Mr Mountford has also said that we should try to keep Henry up at the farm because if the villagers saw him then they might put two and two together and realise what our shameful secret is. I don't know how long it can last between Robert and me, if I am to go home to Dublin any day soon, but he says he would follow me to the ends of the earth so I try not to think about parting and enjoy it while I can. He is wonderful, Caroline, and between him and Henry, my days are happy for the most part.

My one unhappiness, I fear, is my sister. I try to remain charitable and kind to her but sometimes she does things that are cruel beyond belief. Like after New Year's she seemed to know that I had some new secret to hide and she spent her days taunting me and ridiculing me and pestering to find out what it was. I would never tell her about Robert for she would tell Daddy in an instant and then do her best to break us up and most likely have him for herself, for she has no shame any more.

She couldn't pass me by but she would pinch me or pull my hair and one day she went wild on me and without a word of warning she slapped my face when Henry was in my arms having his bottle. She set about beating me, Caroline, knocked me to the floor and the little man was screaming and crying in my arms for it was all I could do to hold on to him so he didn't fall and hurt himself. She called me names, all sorts of awful names, and told me that if I didn't tell her my secret she would take her son from me – her son, after all this time denying him! – and take him by his feet and smash his skull in against the wall of the outhouse. She was slapping me all this time, and trying to grab Henry, and I lay on him to keep her away which upset him more but what else could I do to keep him safe?

She grew tired then of beating me and walked away while I watched her. Then she picked up the kitchen knife off the table and without a word of warning she slashed her arm with it and said she was going to kill herself and then I'd be sorry for they'd take Henry from me for sure. And I'm sure it was evil of me but I didn't care. I just took Henry and ran away and put him in his cot and locked the door to keep her away from him. And when I returned, the poor little boy crying his heart out upstairs, she had cut her arm five or six times and there were trails of blood everywhere. I knew the cuts weren't deep enough to kill her and I went to get a bandage for her. Then nothing would do her but to take her bloody arm and smear it all along the wall of the kitchen. I fear I am living with a madwoman, Caroline. She has these episodes and then she seems to forget about them and goes off and does something else that she fancies like reading a book or eating sweets and I am left to clean up after her. I dare not tell Robert about her madness for I am sure he would leave me and tell his father and that would be the end of us here in Shipton Abbey.

How I wish you could write to me, Caroline! It helps so much to write to you even if I can't send the letters – I fear I should go mad myself otherwise.

Your ever loving friend,

Lily

23

Will had been right – the Breakaway Inn just outside Bickford was completely without character, just four bright clean walls and brand-new furniture and carpets and wood and chrome like every other budget hotel in the world. Martha didn't think she had ever felt so reassured.

Once settled in – she made a ritual of making up the travel cot, unpacking their clothes and toiletries – she drove to Bickford and she and Ruby mooched around the shops for a while. They even went to a fast food joint for the first time since she could remember. The food was bad and it was completely out of character for her. It felt wonderful.

She passed the police station as she wandered about and thought about doing what she had actually come to Bickford to do. But why bother? She knew it was the right thing to do, to try to prevent this person breaking into other people's houses but, much as she told herself that, she couldn't bring herself to go inside. It would mean having to go back to the house, fill out forms, answer questions – long hours wasted in the police station when she could just go home. Plus, there was the delay between being broken into last night and what she had done until now. Why had she left it so long? Why not ring them immediately she was sure that the intruder was gone? Why hadn't she gone straight there? The questions could get awkward, she thought. She pushed the stroller on past the building. They were safe now, she reasoned, and that was all that mattered.

Back at the hotel she enjoyed a long bath while Ruby played in her cot and, once she was asleep, Martha lay on the bed in her pyjamas with the TV on low and watched a romantic comedy while enjoying a hot chocolate she ordered from room service.

This was exactly what she needed, she thought. No spooky old house, weird landlord, creaky floors, flying spoons . . . then she blocked the thoughts of the cottage from her mind and read a few pages of her book before dropping off into a deep, blissful sleep.

24

July 13th

The following morning Ruby woke early and Martha lifted her into bed beside her where the two of them dozed, heads together, Ruby's leg entwined around Martha's right arm. Then Martha was awoken fully by her phone vibrating on the bedside table. It was a text from Will – she groaned when she saw his name at the top of the screen. It brought reality into her temporary wonderland and she realised that soon enough she was going to have to get up and sort out her complicated situation.

"Gtng sm kip. Meet u @ htl @ 1," the text read.

Martha snuggled back into Ruby. At least she could block it all out for another short while. As she lay there feeling totally relaxed for the first time in ages, she decided to go ahead and book herself in for another night. It wasn't the Ritz, but one more night would help her to regroup, formulate a plan, move on to the next stage. One thing had become abundantly clear to her and that was that she had no intention of spending any more time at the cottage. As of tomorrow, she was gone back to London. It had beaten her, for sure, exactly what she hadn't wanted to happen, but she didn't care. Better be defeated in London than assaulted – or worse – in the creepy countryside.

She booked the room under her own name for that night and

she and Ruby enjoyed breakfast in the bustling dining area, overlooking reception. By one she was back there, dressed and made up and feeling a sight better than she had the day before. She could scarcely believe that it was roughly twenty-four hours only since she arrived at the hotel. Will arrived bang on time, carrying a laptop. He paused in reception and caught sight of Martha who had positioned herself so that she could see the entrance doors, Ruby in a high chair beside her. She noticed he had changed his T-shirt but his hair was tousled and another day's stubble was added to that which already covered his chin.

"Hello, Ruby Dooby Doo!" he said and tickled Ruby's bare foot.

She gave a beam of delight which surprised Martha. Usually it took the baby a while to fully check out new faces before they were deemed worthy of smiles. Will beamed back.

"You ladies look refreshed," he said, sitting down opposite Martha.

She noticed his eyes were slightly bloodshot. "You don't," she said and immediately wished she hadn't. It implied she was interested in how Will had got on, and she wasn't. One more night in the hotel and she was gone forever. She could hire packers, she thought, who could just come and sort out her stuff. She need never even set foot inside Eyrie Farm again.

"Oh, I'm fine. Got a couple of hours sleep this morning and had a change of clothes. I'll be right as rain after a toasted sandwich and some coffee." He caught the eye of a waitress who indicated that she'd be with him in a minute. He turned his attention back to Ruby and stuck his tongue out at her. She responded by reaching out a chubby paw to grab at it.

"You're popular today," smiled Martha. Will couldn't be a totally bad guy, she thought, if he was prepared to allow yoghurt-covered hands up to his face.

Will grinned. "She's cool," he said, shaking his head from side to side and laughing as Ruby adopted a serious face and did the same.

"Did you sleep okay?" asked Martha. "The spare bed didn't feel damp or anything, did it?"

"I didn't sleep in the cottage. Oh, your keys – I locked up everything once I'd tidied the equipment away – here you go." He handed Martha back her keys.

She took them, surprised. "Where did you sleep then?"

Will nodded at the window and Martha looked out to see the dark blue Volvo parked outside.

"You slept in your car?" she said in disbelief.

Will nodded. "Wouldn't dream of sleeping in your house without asking. Investigating it is one thing . . . oh, hi, yes, I'd like a toasted cheese and ham, please, and a black coffee." He gave the waitress a dazzling smile as he placed his order.

Martha took the keys and put them in her handbag which was slung over the back of her chair, bewildered that a man who was willing to drag her around the place by her ankles one day wouldn't doze on her spare bed without permission the next.

"Aren't you having anything?" asked Will.

Martha realised that he and the waitress were staring at her. "Just a sparkling mineral water. Thanks."

Once the waitress had gone, Will went back to playing the head-shaking game with Ruby.

Martha leaned across the table. "You know, I assumed sleeping at the house was part of the deal," she said awkwardly.

"Don't worry about it," Will shrugged. "In any case, it's sometimes useful to give the ghosts a free gaff and then spy on what they get up to!"

"And did they get up to anything?" she asked.

"You're very keen to know for a woman who doesn't believe there's anything paranormal going on," he observed.

Martha sat back. He was right. She didn't want to know. She just wanted to get gone.

"As it happens, no, nothing happened at all, at least while I was in the house," said Will, playing with a sachet of sugar. "I was up all night monitoring everything, cameras in all the rooms, a couple of controlled experiments, trigger objects, heat sensors

– not a thing. Not even high EMF readings which could lead to feelings of unease and paranoia."

Martha didn't understand a lot of what he was saying but she realised that she almost felt disappointed. That was rubbish – it was good that he hadn't found anything. It meant she could get under the radar and leave without a fuss.

"That's when I was there," said Will. "I have to go back through the footage and recordings in case something registered when I was out in the car but I'm fairly confident it's all quiet. Oh – there was one thing. An EVP – do you know what that is?"

Martha shook her head, trying to hide her natural curiosity.

"Electronic Voice Phenomenon," explained Will. "Basically I use digital recorders to pick up anything that can't be heard by the human ear. There was one in Ruby's room but it's very difficult to make out so I've mailed it to a buddy of mine to try to sharpen it up for me." Will noted Martha's worried face. "It's probably nothing," he said reassuringly and sat back as the waitress returned with his food and set it in front of him.

Will took a large bite of his sandwich and studied Martha's face as he ate. "You *have* told me everything, Martha, haven't you?" he asked.

Martha blinked and busied herself adjusting Ruby's socks. "Of course," she said. Part of her thought about telling him what had happened in the kitchen the previous morning. She decided against it. Let's just let this whole thing go away, she thought. She unclipped a placid Ruby from the high chair and sat her on her knee. She saw Will study the action with interest. "I'm sure I've told you everything about the intruder," she said. That, at least, was the truth.

"Okay," Will said quietly.

"Listen, Will, the thing is, I'm actually moving out this week so I'm really not all that bothered with this investigation business. I mean I'm happy to let you put up your cameras and your voice thingies and what not, but the results aren't really any of my concern. It's not my house after all."

Will continued to look at her as he ate his sandwich. "You

never mentioned you were moving out before," he said.

Martha turned Ruby's sleeves up. "Well, I didn't think things were going to get so . . . *involved*," she said awkwardly. "It's all gone a bit . . . too far. And it's really none of my concern."

"Sue said you were determined to last six months here," said Will bluntly, finishing off half of the sandwich.

Damn him, thought Martha. Why can't he just bloody drop it? "Well, I've had an unexpected opportunity come up back in London," she lied.

"That's good," said Will.

She could hear disbelief in his voice.

"I suppose then I should get in touch with your landlord about any results," said Will. "Of course, you believe he was your intruder, don't you?"

"Oh. On that, it turns out he's abroad so he couldn't have let himself in. It's best to just leave it to the police, I think."

"What did they say? When you went to them yesterday?"

Martha couldn't think what to say. "Well, I . . ." she began, running out of words then.

Will was relentless. "Only, if it's a police matter, then you won't really be able to leave the area for a while and I assume if you have to stick around you'll stay at the cottage. And if you're staying there then it might be worth your while knowing the results of my investigation once I've had a chance to go through all the evidence."

Martha was growing frustrated. Why couldn't he just leave it, say goodbye, go back to Edinburgh and just leave her alone? Why was he so intent on quizzing her? It wasn't any of his business if she stayed or went. "Look, Will," she said in a gentle voice, "I really don't know what you want from me. You say you found nothing at the cottage so hanging about here isn't going to get you a very interesting case for your paper, now is it? Like I said, there's nothing paranormal as you call it up at Eyrie Farm and I'll be able to deal with the police from London. It's very kind of you but, really, there's no need for you to hang around. I do appreciate you taking an interest though – and the hotel swap was a great idea. You're a student, though, so what say I pay for the room for last night and we're all done and dusted here then."

Martha smiled sweetly and Will mirrored the smile. Result, she thought.

"Really," he said, "there's no need for that. I can well afford the room – consider it a gift." He turned his attention to the crisps on his plate and popped one in his mouth. "You see, Martha, I think there's *every* need for you to stick around." He looked directly in Martha's face, the smile gone. "You say you had an intruder. But this intruder managed to get in and out through locked doors and appears to have floated soundlessly around your house faster than the speed of light and had the strength to drag a grown woman half out of bed. Not to mention our prime suspect is overseas. It may not be *para*normal but it doesn't sound normal to me." He returned his attention to the plate. "On top of all that, I think you're lying. I think this isn't the first funny thing that's happened to you at that house and I think you're getting out of it because you're scared."

Martha was speechless for a moment. "You shouldn't believe local gossip," she said and began to gather up the toys Ruby had been playing with and put them in her changing-bag.

"I didn't get that from the locals. I'm getting it from you."

Martha stopped what she was doing and looked at him.

"Before I studied parapsychology, I did a degree in psychology," he went on. "However, even a fifteen-year-old with a book on the subject could spot a mile off that you're lying. Sitting Ruby on your knee to use as a physical shield against me? Hardly fair because she's only wee." He leaned over and rubbed Ruby's cheek, running his hand under her chin across to the other cheek. Ruby scrunched up her face and batted at Will's hand. "I won't go into the details – but your body language alone is telling me there's something fishy going on. Not to mention all the signs you left at that house – what did you call it, Eyrie Farm? – the signs of someone who scarpered at speed. I think you're really scared, Martha, and I'd like to help."

Martha began to rearrange the items in the bag furiously. "I'm moving out, remember?" she snapped. "So I don't need help but it's clear that you need your paper done and I'm the lemon you're going to try to build your case around with your ghostly nonsense, is that it? I have a little girl here who needs a snooze and I've got a lot to do to get moved – I have to get back to the cottage and pack for starters . . ." She just wanted to get back to the hotel room to hide. She had no intention of going anywhere near the cottage but she was determined to make Will believe she wasn't scared. Hopefully then he'd take his psychology and leave her alone.

"So you're heading back to the house?" said Will.

Martha nodded. Surely she could lose him now.

Will glanced under the table. "Did you leave your bags at reception or are they in your car already? I could have helped you carry them, you know."

Martha looked blankly at him. "What bags?" she asked, as if Will had said something ridiculous. Too late she realised that she had walked herself into having to make another explanation.

"Checkout time was twelve," said Will. "I assume, if you're heading home again, that you checked out?"

Martha could have kicked herself. "I've actually booked in for tonight as well," she said, trying to make it look as though it were the most natural thing in the world to do. To have a two-night break in a budget hotel five and a half miles from where she lived.

"Oh really?"

"Really."

"Because you're not scared to go back to the cottage," continued Will, signalling for the bill.

"Not at all," said Martha, affecting nonchalance.

"So you're staying another night but you're going back to the cottage now?" he continued. "In that case, would you mind awfully if I popped back with you? I think I've left a notebook behind me."

"No!" said Martha, too quickly.

Will was regarding her with a supercilious grin.

Dammit, she thought. "Oh, okay, no problem," she said. "Let's go then." He could pick up his damned notebook and then surely he'd go back to Edinburgh. There was no need for him to stay here, was there?

Will waited in reception while Martha picked up some toys for Ruby from her room. She reluctantly admitted to herself that a trip back to the cottage might be a good idea. She could actually pick up some purées for Ruby instead of buying jars. And she could do with some more clothes for both of them.

This time Martha followed Will in her car and pulled in behind him outside the front door of the cottage. She felt detachment when she looked at it – as though with her decision made to return to London she had cut any connection whatsoever with this building. It was sad in one way, considering the haven this had once been but Martha's overwhelming emotion was relief at never having to sit there anticipating creaky floorboards or strange scratchings ever again.

She opened the front door with her key but, instead of going first, stood back to let Will go before her. Ruby was grizzling with tiredness in her arms, but Martha had no intention of letting her sleep while they were there. She went into the study and laid her down on the sofa, wedging her in with some cushions. Then she went to the kitchen to take some purées from the freezer.

Will went upstairs, to get his notebook, she presumed. She noticed that he must have cleared up the mess on the kitchen floor and all the chairs were neatly in place at the table. She was grateful for that. The kitchen felt almost normal again.

She was busy chipping cubes of frozen mango out of an ice-cube tray when her doorbell rang. It made her jump – she didn't think that anyone, save for Rob Mountford eventually and Sam, had ever rung her doorbell. "Dammit," she said. She didn't want to be there any longer than she had to, but she knew that Will was upstairs and if she left the door unanswered he'd probably think she was a right antisocial cow. Although why should she care what he thought?

She hurriedly popped another frozen cube into a Tupperware container and slid the tray back into the freezer. The bell rang again as Martha scurried down the hall, wondering who on earth it could be. After all, it seemed none of the locals would come near the place and Rob was still away. Sam, maybe? She hoped so . . . she had a few questions for *him*.

She opened the door to find a big man standing outside. He had thinning reddish hair, gelled into carefully feathered spikes, and wore a peach-coloured silk shirt loose over black linen trousers and Birkenstock sandals. He had his back to her but turned as she opened the door. She spotted at least two rings on each hand and a shiny gold chain around his neck. His features were small, his face slightly pudgy, and he had the beginnings of a reddish beard.

"I'm looking for Will," he said in a strong Scottish accent with a slightly camp affectation.

Martha was about to ask him for his name when Will came cantering down the stairs behind her.

"Gabriel! You found your way here."

The huge man stepped into the hallway, brushing past Martha as though she wasn't there. "Got a taxi," he said. "Bloody bugger wouldn't come up the driveway and I had to walk. In this heat – can you imagine?"

"This is Martha," said Will.

The man called Gabriel looked around him until he saw Martha, as if he were discovering her under his foot. "Charmed," he said, insincerely, and turned back to Will. "This place is pretty godforsaken, isn't it?"

The two men made their way down the hall leaving Martha at the open door, wondering what was going on.

"Excuse me," she said. They ignored her and kept walking. "Ex*cuse* me," she repeated, more loudly this time. Will turned back toward her, beckoning her toward the study. Gabriel carried on into the kitchen, studying the walls and floor.

Martha was irked. What the hell was this guy up to now? She closed the kitchen door, and followed Will into the study. "Can you explain to me what's going on?" she said loudly.

Will indicated that she should be quiet and closed the study door over behind her. "I hope you don't mind," he said in a low voice. "Gabriel's done some work with me in Edinburgh and I

171

asked him to pop down and take a look around."

"Why? You said yourself that you didn't find anything – why do you need a second opinion?"

"It's not so much a second opinion as a different opinion. Gabriel's a sensitive."

Martha snorted. "He doesn't seem very sensitive to me!"

Will put his finger in front of his lips and made a shushing sound. "He's a medium. A spirit medium."

"Someone who pretends to communicate with dead people?" Martha couldn't believe what she was hearing. What on earth was Will playing at? "How bloody long is this going to take?" she hissed.

"He doesn't pretend, Martha. At least I don't think he does. We've had a very high hit rate on some other cases we've looked at and I wanted to see how he'd do here. He's actually part of my casework."

"On a case where there's nothing there?"

Will looked at her. "Now you know, and I know, that I don't believe that and neither do you. It won't take long and, besides which, it would be a shame to disturb Her Majesty over there." He pointed at the sofa where Ruby had fallen asleep.

"Oh dammit!" said Martha. "I hadn't intended being here long enough for that to bloody well happen."

Will sensed a note of panic in her voice. "I won't leave till you're ready to go," he offered. "How about that?"

The two made their way quietly out of the room into the hall. "Why would you stay with me when there's nothing here?" she snarled, desperate for Will and his psychic friend to just drop it.

"Oh, there's something bloody here alright," a voiced boomed behind her.

Martha jumped for the second time in the space of five minutes.

"A whole lot of something, in fact," said Gabriel. "William – will you accompany me upstairs? I think there's a whole *world* of surprise up there." He swept past Martha and stood at the bottom of the stairs, a worried expression on his face.

Will looked at Martha and then followed him silently. Slowly, the two men began their ascent, leaving Martha watching from the hall, the familiar sinking feeling in the pit of her stomach.

She sat in the study, absentmindedly stroking Ruby's foot as she slept, listening to the progress of the two men upstairs. The room was bright and comforting in the sunshine and Martha found it difficult to believe that the last time she had been in this room she had been crouched against the door, in abject terror.

She heard Will and Gabriel make their way around the upper floor. They were mostly silent – only occasional muffled words came down through the floorboards. They visited Martha's room, then the bathroom, stopped for a while on the landing, then the box-room and finally Ruby's room where what sounded like a heated exchange took place in hushed tones, followed by a very long silence.

The quietness ended abruptly as a heavy pair of feet stamped from the room and down the stairs and then she heard the opening and slamming shut of the front door. She heard the gravel outside crunch and then a car door slam. Ruby stirred and her eyelids flickered but she simply turned her head toward the back of the sofa and returned to sleep. Martha suddenly felt very tired.

A second pair of feet, quieter, came down the stairs and along the hall. Will poked his head around the door. "Sorry about that," he said quietly. "Gabriel wants to go for a drink – he can be a bit drained after a walkabout like that."

Martha smiled weakly. "It's okay. He didn't wake her up. Does that mean you're leaving?" She was aware that there was a tinge of desperation and panic to her voice but she didn't care. Half an hour ago she'd felt fine, couldn't wait to get rid of Will. Now the arrival of a *medium* made things a little different. She realised that the prospect of Will leaving her alone was making her very anxious.

"I'll wait until you're ready to leave," said Will kindly, no trace showing of the man who had tried to catch her out when they spoke earlier.

"What about Gabriel?"

"Don't worry about him. He can wait in the car and cool off a little – he's, um, a little miffed with me about something."

"I should be too," said Martha. "You set me up to be here this afternoon, didn't you? So that you could meet Gabriel? It's not a coincidence that he arrived when we were here."

"I'm sorry. Again," said Will, looking genuinely remorseful. "I didn't want to bring him here without you knowing but I knew you'd never agree to meet him so I kind of decided to – well – serve him up, as it were. I phoned him from reception when you went to get Ruby's things. He'd come down from Edinburgh this morning."

"It's alright. I feel too bloody tired to care and if this casework is so important to you then you can bring whoever you like in here so long as it really doesn't involve me."

"Come with us to the pub," suggested Will. "Let me buy you a drink to say sorry."

Martha shook her head. "No, ta. You and Gabriel carry on there without me."

"Please," begged Will. "He's awfully cross with me actually and I could really do with a bit of moral support. Call it repayment for the hotel room – which I have no intention of letting you pay for, by the way. Just the one. You'd really be giving me a dig-out . . ."

Martha looked at her watch. It was nearly Ruby's dinnertime. Poor child, she thought. Being fed on the trot again. "Alright," she said. "I have to feed Ruby anyway. She shouldn't sleep for too much longer. Tell you what – give me a hand gathering up a few bits and we can go then, alright?"

Will beamed. "Deal! Now what do you want me to do?"

Martha mainly wanted Will to be in the same room as her while she gathered up Ruby's food into a small portable cooler and packed a bag with more clothes for both of them. She felt fine in the study but nervy at being alone in all the other rooms.

By the time she had finished, the baby had woken and Martha settled her into her car seat while Will locked the house and waited for her to drive onto the road first.

She was very grateful for his consideration. Even though she'd been trying to show him she wasn't frightened, she was. Very much so. But this time he hadn't tried to get her to admit anything which made her even more grateful.

The two cars parked side by side at the Abbot's Rest. The car park was beginning to empty out as the busy Sunday lunch trade dried up. Martha watched as families drifted out to their cars – mums, dads, grandparents, babies, toddlers. All normal people going to their normal homes, able to protect and provide for their children, happily married.

Will helped her take the stroller from the boot and she thought that they must look like another happy family heading to the pub on a Sunday afternoon. Apart, of course, from the really big, cross psychic medium, that is. Gabriel had stormed out of Will's car and across the car park into the pub. Will saw her watch him go and caught her eye, pretending to quake in terror and then rolling his eyes heavenward. Martha smiled.

Gabriel had secured a table in a dark corner of the pub and when Martha and Will walked in he was frantically trying to attract the attention of a waitress.

Martha looked around at the setting. "Can we not sit outside? It's a lovely –"

"*No!*" bellowed Gabriel, and she sat down on a stool, shocked. "Look at my skin, woman! Do you think I can take *that* outside in that sun?" He swung his head around, desperately seeking service. "Besides, what I have to say can *not* be shared with all and sundry in a beer garden."

"Hang on," Martha interjected. "If you boys are going to talk about whatever you did at the cottage then I'm going outside to sit by myself. I'm moving out of there – none of it concerns me." She stood up to leave.

"Sit *down*!" commanded Gabriel.

She obeyed again out of shock.

"That's where you're very wrong, dearie," said Gabriel. "Very wrong indeed. This concerns you bigtime. You *and* your bairn."

Martha looked from Gabriel to Will and back again. Will shrugged as he caught her eye – obviously Gabriel had shared nothing with him on the drive from the cottage.

Gabriel at last caught the eye of a waitress. "I want the biggest glass of sauv-blanc you can come up with," he said, pronouncing it 'sov-blonk'. "And whatever these two *nellies* are having." He pointed a disdainful finger at Martha and Will and sat back in the armed chair that he had commandeered, rubbing his temples with his beringed hands.

Will ordered a bottle of beer and Martha a mineral water. She would have given anything to join Gabriel in a glass of wine but she knew she had to drive back to Bickford. And possibly as far away from this place as she could.

"Right," said Gabriel in a low voice. He sat forward and leaned on the table, his bulky frame almost making it topple over. "As you well know, William, I don't do bairns." He pointed at Ruby and Martha frowned. "You have never seen me take a case where there was a bairn involved and I am *ripping* with you that you never told me there was one here."

Martha immediately felt defensive. She leaned forward and took the finger that Gabriel pointed at her daughter and pushed it back in line with the others clenched to his palm. Will went from looking apologetic to alarmed but Martha didn't notice.

"Her name is Ruby," she said firmly. "And she's my daughter."

Gabriel turned to her in an exaggerated move and sneered. "I don't care if her name is Shirley-Bloody-Bassey-the-Third and she *shits* rubies in her nappy. *I. Don't. Do. Bairns.*"

Martha was again taken back at his rudeness and Will cringed in his seat.

"However," continued Gabriel, "I am unfortunately 'in' now, as you so like to put it, William, so I'll tolerate it." He re-extended his finger and pointed it from Will to Martha and back again. "But! Do not expect there to be a moment when it tugs on my beard or my heartstrings and all of a sudden I'm running round looking for an eager surrogate and snivelling."

Martha was fuming. How *dare* this man be so rude! She understood that people didn't like children but did he have to *point*? Refer to Ruby as '*it*'? She opened her mouth to defend her daughter but the waitress arrived with their order and the moment was lost in the dropping of beer mats, the counting of change and Gabriel taking an enormous gulp from his glass.

"Right," he continued, "what do you know about the history of that house?"

"Not much," replied Martha timidly. She knew she should stand up for herself – his bulk and tone made him a very intimidating presence, however, and instead of getting up and walking out like she should, she somehow felt an inexplicable urge to please him. "It belongs to my landlord, Rob Mountford. Used to be called Eyrie Farm but he changed it to Hawthorn Cottage to improve its chances of being let – that's 'eyrie' as in nests, not Halloween. It belonged to his family for years apparently, and he was made a gift of it a while ago and did it up single-handedly. At least that's what I've been told. Though my childminder tells me one thing and he tells me another. Apparently, some bits of it could go back to the twelfth century when the abbey was built."

Gabriel snorted. "Pfff! Twelfth century, my arse – there's more concrete in that place than Wembley Stadium."

"The Romans used concrete," said Will suddenly. "You can see it in the Colosseum."

Gabriel gave him a withering look and turned back to Martha. "You say Mountford is the name. Do you know who actually lived there?"

Martha shook her head. "As far as I know it was derelict until a few years ago. There's stories about it maybe being connected to the monastery. That's all I know."

Gabriel looked thoughtful. "No," he said. "It wasn't a monk."

Martha looked at him, alarmed. Was this guy trying to tell her that someone or something had come through to him at the cottage?

Just then she caught sight of the clock and realised it was time to feed Ruby. Good. A distraction. She busied herself getting pots of hot water from the bar, heating up the bottle and food. The small party remained silent as she fed her daughter. She was glad of it in one way because it gave her a while to collect herself. In another way, it was intimidating. She was pleased that Ruby didn't make a fuss and emptied the tub of food enthusiastically. With her fed, Will ordered another round of drinks, switching to a coffee for himself.

"Okay," said Gabriel, taking a swig from his fresh glass of wine. "There's an entity up there – its name begins with 'M'."

Martha felt panic rise in her. An entity? A ghost? But there was no such thing – was there? Had they been living all that time with something that was *dead*? It didn't help her panic how matter-of-fact Gabriel was being, as if describing an actual resident. Someone who had been there all along . . . Her eyes widened as he continued.

"That's why it's interesting that it's owned by people called Mountford but I don't think it's exactly right," continued Gabriel.

Martha's eyes swivelled round to Will who had taken out a notebook and was scribbling notes with a pencil, like he was taking dictation. It seemed so – *ordinary*, what they were doing. "Hang on," she said. "Are you being serious? Are you saying there's a ghost up at my cottage?"

"Oh, well you know it, missy," Gabriel retorted. "I got the impression it even let itself be seen by you. And maybe you'd like to tell me about breakfast-time yesterday?"

Will's head shot up from his notebook and Martha felt herself redden from the chest up. Why had he brought this stupid psychic here, complicating things? She was going to have to tell them what had happened. Was she ever going to get away?

"Martha, is it true that something happened? That you've seen something?" said Will, his voice both stern and eager.

Martha nodded.

"What?" demanded Will, leaning toward her.

"I didn't want to tell you," she said quietly, taking a sip from her glass. "It sort of made it . . . well . . . *real* or something. I just want to leave . . ." She stared at her lap. Taking another sip, she began to explain quietly what had happened with the chair and the spoon, glancing around from time to time to make sure that no one else was listening. They'd think she was nuts if they heard.

Will's face grew hard and he shook his head as he scribbled in his notebook. "This could really have helped me, Martha," he chided. "I knew you weren't telling me everything, knew there had to be a bloody good reason why you didn't want to be here and why you got out in such a hurry."

Martha was surprised to find her eyes welling up with tears. "I just didn't want it to be true," she said with a sob. "I just wanted to get Ruby out of there and I knew if I told you, of all people, it would turn into something huge and I'd never be able to get away."

Will covered her hand with his for a moment.

Gabriel rolled his eyes. "'M', for want of another name, is very active up there. And not in a good way. It blocked me at every turn as I was trying find out who or what it is and why it's there. All it wanted to do was tell me how much it doesn't like you."

Martha could feel the blood drain from her face. "How do you mean?" she asked, in a very low voice.

"I should explain that my skills involve being able to see, feel and hear spirit," said Gabriel calmly. "The Scottish term for me is 'fey' – probably in more ways than one, but I prefer to think of myself as sensitive or intuitive. I could actually hear the voice of this entity in my head, giving me messages – does that make sense to you?"

Martha shook her head. "Not really. Sort of. What did it say?"

"It said it tried to get you with the pram," said Gabriel and looked at her for an explanation.

It didn't make sense to Martha for a moment but she gave a small cry as she remembered coming back to the empty house when she assumed that Sam had remained behind. "There were nappies all over the kitchen – and music upstairs and the buggy had been moved across the hall so that I fell over it," she recalled, turning over her arm to see the remains of the bruise on her elbow and showing it to Will and Gabriel.

Will wrote furiously. "Explain to us from the start, Martha," he said.

Fighting back tears, she told them exactly what she had seen and heard.

Gabriel nodded in agreement to much of the story. "It mentioned the music alright. It said that it doesn't like that modern muck that you listen to and wanted to hear something good. The nappies thing makes sense too – it said you should wash the damn things once in a while."

Martha was baffled. Why on earth would she wash them? Then it struck her. "Does . . . *it* . . . think that they're cloth nappies?" she asked, unable to believe that she was asking a question which acknowledged the presence of a ghost. That a spirit or a poltergeist had scattered nappies all over her kitchen floor. She felt as though she were having an out-of-the-body experience.

"Must do," said Will. "That helps with a rough timeline, to know that it's not familiar with disposables. We must find out when they were invented . . ."

Gabriel continued. "It would also lead me to surmise that it's a man perhaps – you know, the little lady should be doing her job around the house sort of thing? It says you nearly saw it upstairs as well but it hid on time. This entity is very strong, I have to say – its presence hit me the second I walked in the door."

Martha shook her head, unable to believe she was playing along, but still wracking her brains to think when she could have seen what Gabriel was referring to.

"There was someone else there at the time, apparently?" he prompted. "There was wine?"

Martha's mind flashed back to when Sue was there – no, she had seen nothing then. The only other person she'd had wine with at the house was Mary Stockwell. The shadow. Going into the bathroom. The one that she thought was Mary. Martha's heart sank. This was all too close for comfort.

"I did see a shape once," she said. "It was going into my bathroom. I thought it was my friend but then I went downstairs and she was there all along. I thought it was just a shadow, and we'd had a lot to drink . . ."

"Anything else, Gabriel," asked Will, as though asking him to add an item to a shopping list. He turned a page in his notebook and looked at Gabriel who nodded, his face taking on a serious look.

Martha had no doubt that Gabriel believed one hundred per cent in what he was saying and, looking at Will, he did too. As for herself, Gabriel seemed to know too much about recent events for her to totally disbelieve him, and this scared her more than anything. Could this be true?

"It was cross with you about the feeding, it said," stated Gabriel. "Lost its patience with you as much as the child because the little brat wouldn't eat and it wanted you out. Those are its words, not mine."

Martha's face grew black with anger at the reference to Ruby as 'the little brat'. She went from wishing he wasn't telling the truth to thinking he had better be.

"That's why it lost its temper and smacked the spoon from your hand – again, a very masculine action," said Gabriel.

A thought struck Martha. "When the chair skidded back it was like someone standing up in a hurry. Was . . . it . . . in the room with me? Watching me feed Ruby?" Martha reached out and grabbed her daughter's hand in her pushchair. Ruby had again fallen into a deep sleep and didn't flinch.

Gabriel nodded. "Sitting right beside you most likely. Look, I know it's scary but all I can do is report the facts. As much as it dislikes you – and, I'm sorry, Ruby too –"

Martha gasped with fear.

"I sense that it's also fascinated with you – the concept of you being a mother. Like, it can't understand how you can actually *care* about a baby. I also sense that it's been in Ruby's room quite a few times as well. Sort of . . . studying her."

Martha was horrified. If he was to be believed, then all this time a dead person who hated her and wanted to do her harm had been spying on her – and Ruby.

"Why doesn't it like us?" she demanded urgently. The more scared she felt, the more she treated this as real.

"I couldn't quite get that," said Gabriel shaking his head. "It blocked me. My theory would be that it's because you're living in its house. I've seen this numerous times – quite often if a spirit manifests or engages in poltergeist activity then it's because it's trying to get what it considers trespassers out of its home, and by trespassers I mean the living."

Martha shuddered. She looked around her for some perspective, to see familiar surroundings in the midst of this outrageous conversation. She saw that the pub was almost empty.

"What I can't get over," said Gabriel, "is how strong it is. It has to be getting that energy from somewhere. Have you been feeling miserable up there?"

Martha pondered the question. "A little, I suppose. A bit melancholy – sort of negative, I guess."

"That makes sense," said Will. "An entity needs to get energy from somewhere to enable it to be active. Sounds like it's been draining this energy from you. Have you had power cuts as a matter of interest?"

Martha turned to Will. "So you believe all of this, do you?" she asked.

"I do and I don't. Technically science doesn't accept any of this – clairvoyance, life after death etcetera. But speaking for myself, I'm always on the lookout for irrefutable evidence and, if I can find it, then maybe that will change and gradually science will come round. Gabriel is able to match so much of what he's saying to actual events that he couldn't possibly know about, and that it makes it very hard for me to believe it's wrong."

Martha sighed and turned back to Gabriel. "Was this *thing* actually what I thought was my intruder the other night?" There was no point in trying to avoid it any longer. There was too much weirdness going on and she had to know.

Gabriel nodded. "It wanted to give you a right old fright but it said the little brat wouldn't shut up and it nearly drove it mad." He looked at Ruby.

So did Martha, frightened by the prospect that this thing wanted to shut her up. Except of course Ruby had barely cried that night . . .

"I've more information," said Gabriel, "but I'm exhausted." He did look tired and Martha had noticed that there had been a distinct lack of sarcasm for a while. "Why don't we go back to that godforsaken cube of a hotel and meet up for dinner or something? Doing a house like that always makes me feel a bit seasick and you know how it is – you're always ravenous once you get onto dry land." He stood up and wandered off in the direction of the gents.

"I won't be able to leave Ruby later," said Martha.

"Why don't you see if the hotel could send someone to watch her?" suggested Will. "And you could have a break for a few hours – would you be comfortable with that?"

Martha hadn't thought of it. Her face was pale as she gathered up her belongings to leave. "That's actually a good idea," she said. "I could really use a drink or ten!"

Will smiled at her attempt to joke. "Good. I'd suggest driving back with you but I can't leave my car here again with all the gear in it. Nor Gabriel, unfortunately, and not only has he had about a half-bottle of wine but he can't drive. If you like, he could go with you? Keep you company?"

"No!" said Martha, too quickly. "I appreciate the offer," she added hastily, "but I'll be fine, really. It'll only take us ten minutes to get back."

"Right then, William – take me to paradise," announced a voice behind Martha's ear as Gabriel returned from the toilet.

Will looked at Martha. "You're sure then?"

She nodded. "Yeah, I am."

"Okay," said Will. "I'll ring the hotel for you and see if we can't rustle you up a couple of free hours before bedtime."

Martha was about to thank him again when Gabriel made a loud snoring noise and tutted loudly.

"Come on then," smiled Will, and the small party made their way out into unexpected sunshine.

The hotel baby-sitter was unavailable but a pregnant receptionist jumped at the chance of a couple of hours off her feet. She arrived at Martha's room dead on eight o'clock and Martha left her to relax, giving Ruby a lingering kiss as she slept in her travel cot. She was exhausted, Martha thought. All that sleeping today and now no problems in getting her off. Again, she thanked her lucky stars for such a dream baby.

On returning to the hotel she had showered, changed and reapplied her make-up and, while unnerved by the earlier revelations, she felt she was ready for what Gabriel had to say.

He and Will were seated in the dining area before her, Gabriel in a turquoise version of his earlier silk shirt with a huge matching ring on his right hand, Will in a black shirt and jeans with his sleeves rolled up.

"That's better," said Gabriel, giving her a once-over as she arrived at the table.

Martha opened her mouth to respond but she saw the big man smirk at her playfully and tried not to look surprised. She sat down, trying also not to laugh.

They ordered a main course each and a bottle of wine between them and chatted informally about Shipton Abbey and its surrounding areas with Gabriel concluding that "The seasidey bit's alright but that pub's just a great hole of despair".

"There's a Michelin-recommended restaurant at the back of the pub, you know," remarked Martha innocently.

Gabriel almost spluttered his food onto the table. "There *is,* is there?" he exclaimed. "And we're eating tinned ravioli in a roadside caff? William?" He looked at Will in disgust.

"Learn to drive and we can go to any amount of Michelin-starred restaurants you like," said Will, popping a spiral of pasta into his mouth. "But I fancied a drink and Martha very much needs one so for tonight we're eating where our beds are."

Gabriel looked dismayed. "There's taxis!" he wailed, outraged.

Martha snorted. "How long have you two been married!" she laughed, feeling comfortable enough to join in the banter. She took a mouthful of wine and looked up to see the two men staring at her, not moving.

Gabriel, of course, was first to speak. "*We. Are. Not. A Couple.* Do you understand?" he said in his booming voice.

Martha swallowed hard, feeling the redness of her embarrassment start from her chest and run all the way around to her shoulders and upper back.

"Even if he were of the correct persuasion," continued Gabriel haughtily, "I wouldn't be interested. But *that*," he pointed at Will, "is a *breeder* – and I wouldn't touch him if he was lilacs, sunshine and the cure for the common cold all rolled into one."

Will's expression went from mildly amused to a look of outrage. "What's wrong with me?" he demanded indignantly.

Gabriel dropped his fork in his half-eaten pasta. "I'm not even going to answer that, you hairy bloody hippy," he said dismissively. "It wouldn't be worth the seconds of my life I'd never get back. Now you've made me lose my appetite!"

Martha put her fork down. "I'm really sorry, I didn't mean to offend anyone. Not that it's offensive to be . . . ummm . . . gay. Or to be . . . umm . . . *you*, Will . . . it's just . . ." She reddened deeper as she spoke, wishing she'd never opened her mouth.

"Oh shut up, both of you!" said Gabriel. "As none of us appear to be eating, shall we retire to that feeble excuse for a bar and get to the bloody point?"

Once settled on armchairs at the far end of the modern bar area, Martha was amazed to see Gabriel almost undergo a transformation from the moody spoiled child of dinner to the deathly serious man she'd spent the afternoon with in the pub. Within moments of him starting to relay his information, she wished herself back at the dining table, embarrassing herself all over again.

"I had a very unnerving experience in the bairn's room," said Gabriel.

Will again took out his notebook and started to scribble. "Martha, tell me first about the noises that you hear from the chimney-breast."

Martha didn't want to think about them. It had to be an

185

animal, unlikely as that seemed. There was no other possible explanation.

"It's just scratching sometimes," she shrugged.

The two men remained silent and looked at her.

"Please, Martha," urged Will, "please tell us exactly what you've heard."

Gabriel placed the tips of his fingers together and nodded attentively as Martha reluctantly described what she'd heard coming from the blocked-up fireplace on a regular basis. She then relayed to them what Alison Stockwell had told her on the night she had gone out with Rob Mountford.

"You say there was heavy rain that night?" asked Will.

Martha nodded, wondering what that had to do with anything. "And thunder and lightning," she added.

"Perfect conditions," muttered Will. "However, we're looking at an impressionable teenage girl left alone in a strange house with a young baby."

"Forget that," said Gabriel, his face suddenly lighting up. "What about impressionable young mum goes on romantic date with landlord, eh? Spill!"

"Nothing happened," Martha protested before being interrupted by Will.

"Gabriel!" he said, annoyance in his tone.

Gabriel leaned over toward Will's chair and spoke into his face. "In a Michelin-recommended restaurant," he said accusingly.

Will looked away from him in annoyance and back to Martha. Triumphant at staring the longest, albeit in a one-sided competition, Gabriel flopped back in his seat.

Martha couldn't help but smile but it fell from her face as Gabriel resumed his serious tone.

"It's consistent with what I was picking up from Ruby's room," he said gravely. "I don't really know how to put this, Martha, but by my reckoning there's a second spirit at the house. It's a wee boy, and from what I can tell he was bricked up in the fireplace. Before he passed."

Martha gazed at Gabriel in horror. That was what Lil Flynn

had said. What she thought was a tale grown from the stories about monks walling up their victims. It had to be nonsense. No one could do that. To a child?

"No!" she found herself saying. "This is going too far now. You've been listening to the stories from the village. Walling people up! Rubbish!"

"Immurement is a historical fact!" growled Gabriel. "As a form of execution, torture or punishment for sin. Virgins were immured in the foundations of buildings as a form of protective sacrifice. Anchorites – sort of extreme hermits, if you like – voluntarily had themselves walled up as the ultimate act of withdrawal from the world – except in their case they lived on, with food passed through the wall to them daily. It's fact not fiction. Oh, hark at me! I'm as bad as Will and his Interesting Facts about Concrete!"

"This isn't the Dark Ages," said Martha, flushing, "and all those horrors have nothing to do with my house. What's in the chimney-breast is an animal. Sometimes they can . . . they can sound human – like cats and foxes . . ." She realised she was sounding slightly hysterical and allowed her voice to tail off.

"Martha," said Will, "it ties in with what I heard at the pub – the rumour's been around for years . . ."

"No!" Martha shouted. "It's just an animal! My landlord's going to take care of it!"

"Oh for God's sake, woman," said Gabriel suddenly. "How? How in the name of all that's holy could it be an animal? That's survived in a chimney for well over a month at least? Do you see low-flying aircraft round these parts flinging foxes and kittens round willy-nilly? Do you think *Santa* left it there? I know what I felt – there's a person's spirit in there – and it's trapped!"

Martha and Will stared at Gabriel, seeing that there were tears forming in his eyes.

"This is why I don't do poxy bairns," said Gabriel, clearly upset and wiping tears as they began to roll down his cheeks. "They can't defend themselves – living or dead – and I can't defend them either and time after time awful stuff happens to

187

them. I've seen it and I can't take it. That's why I don't do bairns." His voice had fallen to a whisper by the time he finished.

"I didn't know that's why you felt that strongly, mate," Will said, and searched in his pockets for a napkin or a tissue, ostensibly to comfort Gabriel but in reality to give him himself something to do with his hands during the awkward moment.

Martha stared at Gabriel in shock. She hadn't expected him to be so – *sincere*, especially as a child was involved. Her heart warmed a little to the giant man, but it couldn't counter the sense of dread she felt.

Gabriel took a moment before he spoke again in a soft voice. "He's petrified in there," he said, blinking more tears down his face. "He woke up in the dark and he didn't know where he was. His head hurt – he couldn't find a way out and he started to call out, to try to . . . escape." His voice fell to a whisper as the horror of what he was trying to explain became too much for him.

Martha could feel her own tears beginning to form at the backs of her eyes as she absorbed what the medium was describing.

"He tried until he passed, bless him." Gabriel had composed himself.

"How long?" asked Martha, glad that Gabriel had spared them the details.

"Too long," answered Gabriel, shaking his head. "He was very weak when he went in there. He was hungry. And terribly thirsty. "

Martha's eyes flooded with tears at this small detail. How could this have happened? She squeezed her eyes shut to try to stop the tears but it only forced them down her face.

"He couldn't breathe," continued Gabriel. "There was no room for him to move . . . he was crying out for help, trying to scratch his way out . . . no one came for him. No one until you, Martha."

Martha sobbed as she thought over all the nights of the scratching noises and the annoyance she felt at them. Was this true? Had she been sharing her home with the soul of a little boy that someone had done this to? Was it really the cause of the crying and the scraping? A sob escaped her and she raised her hand to her mouth as she remembered how awful the noises had been on the night when she thought she had her intruder.

"I shouted at him!" she whispered, aghast. "Told him to shut up . . . I just couldn't bear the noise . . ."

"Since you've been there he's found some comfort," said Gabriel. "I felt that he likes it when you sing to the baby – he thinks you're singing to him. Oh – and he likes the moons and stars – does that make sense?"

Martha nodded. "Ruby's nightlight," she explained. She couldn't get the picture of herself happily dancing and laughing with Ruby, while she changed and dressed and played with her – with a little boy there as well.

"The funny thing about him, Will," said Gabriel, "is that now he can actually get out of the wall if he wants to, but he's so scared of whoever put him there that he never – or rarely – does it." He turned back to Martha. "He said he sometimes gets the comfort and brings it back in with him – does that make any sense to you, Martha?"

Martha wiped tears from her cheeks, again confused by what Gabriel was saying. It suddenly hit her. "The soothers! Ruby's pacifiers – they keep going missing and I keep finding them over by the chimney-breast – could that be *him*?"

Gabriel nodded. "That's it. Sometimes he says he can't reach them and that makes him cry."

It made sense to Martha. "They only go missing when I put them on the bedside table, which is low. If I put them on the changing unit then they stay put but that's higher up. I never realised that before now."

Will coughed. "Gabriel, I can understand how an alleged entity can supposedly move a physical object but how are these soothers actually giving him comfort? He can't bring them through a brick wall." His voice was calm and rational in the midst of the high emotion.

"You'll probably think this is wishy-washy," said Gabriel, "but I sensed from him that while the plastic bits obviously can't go through a wall, the comfort attached to them can. He picks up what Ruby gets from them – they soothe her – and he can take that with him. I know it doesn't make sense but . . ."

Will shook his head. "I believe you because it's you, Gabriel," he said.

"But this isn't enough evidence." Martha was amazed that Will could profess belief so easily. She had found herself impressed by his professionalism, envious of his detachment. A thought struck her and she swung her head around to Will. "I've heard him actually," she said, recalling suddenly the little footsteps that she'd tried to ignore, the plop as the pacifier hit the floor near the wall. "I've heard his little feet run across the room and pick up a dummy and then it drops on the floor by the chimney-breast. Is that evidence?" Suddenly, remembering those little footsteps, Martha realised that she couldn't fight it any longer. She believed.

Will jotted the information down but didn't make eye contact. "Do we think he's connected with 'M' in any way?"

Martha turned to Gabriel – she had all but forgotten the other spirit as she heard about the poor little boy.

Gabriel nodded. "It blocked me when I was trying to connect with the boy, so I feel *it* can connect with him as well. They're on the same plane – I don't think I'd be putting two and two together and making ten to say that M had something to do with putting him there in the first place. Again, it all leads me to his being a man . . . physically bricking up his body . . . and, I mean, it's not usual for women to murder children."

"But not unheard of," said Will. "Myra Hindley, Rose West . . ."

Martha felt a sudden jolt through her body. The words of Lil Flynn again: "*Mother did it.*" Everything tied up with what she had said . . .

"Right," said Will, putting down the notebook. "I think we've got a lot here. Is there anything else that's important, Gabriel?"

The medium nodded and looked down at his feet. "Just a couple of things," he said. "The boy's name is Henry. And he's nearly four."

There was complete silence for a good three or four minutes. None of them knew what to say. Gabriel eventually broke it by standing up and walking off to the lift. He was crying too hard to even say goodnight and the others watched him go sympathetically.

"He feels a lot of what they feel, apparently," Will said once the lift doors had closed.

Martha lifted her tear-stained face from her hands and sniffed. She nodded in response, drained, unable to think of anything to say.

"I think I'll head to bed myself," she said eventually, her voice thick with tears.

Will nodded. "I'm going to stay up a while. Have a stiff drink."

"Goodnight then," said Martha. There was no point in even trying to talk about what Gabriel had just told them. It was too huge. She stood up and walked a couple of yards, then hesitated and turned back to Will. "I'm sorry," she said.

Will's BlackBerry which he had placed on the table earlier beeped and he was momentarily distracted. "For what?" he asked, picking it up and checking the message.

"For lying. For trying to pretend there was nothing going on. I've felt weird in that place for ages, but I just wanted to ignore it and get away. I guess I was in denial . . . especially about the . . . noises I heard from the chimney . . ."

Will nodded acknowledgement. "I understand why you wanted to stay out of it," he said. "It sounds like some pretty scary stuff was going on up there."

Martha stared into the distance and nodded slightly herself. "And thanks, Will," she continued, looking back at him. "For going through doors first, and waiting for me – and stuff . . ." Her voice trailed off and she felt a little silly.

Will smiled. "That's nothing. Just what I do. Now I have to figure out what to do next."

Martha nodded and turned for the lift. She silently wished him well with what he had to do. For her, however, it was over. She couldn't bear to know any more.

25

Eyrie Farm,
Shipton Abbey,
Norfolk,
England

February 1st, 1955

Dear Caroline,

"May Brigid bless the house wherein you dwell." Do you still sing that hymn in the convent on this special day? The first day of spring?

I am nineteen today, as I am sure you know, and my life continues here at Shipton Abbey, sometimes with great happiness but more often with sadness and a sense of longing. I will tell of our last year here in this letter, and explain why.

As I have said, we are still here in Norfolk, and there is no sign of us ever going back to Dublin. That makes a part of my heart sing, more of which later, but another part of it aches for our familiar places which I haven't seen in so long. To walk on the strand at Dollymount, sit in the sun in St Stephen's Green, take a picnic to the Hill of Howth for a day out. I am now old enough to do all of these things for myself but instead I am trapped here in a tiny village in an alien land. I know nothing of England, just this tiny piece of land where this cottage and this village are. I am in a sort of prison but with enough freedom to make me long for more, and even as I am a prisoner I am a keeper of sorts as I am still Marion's keeper.

Daddy no longer writes, or telephones the Mountfords. I fear he has forgotten us, which makes me fear for him, wondering just how badly the shock of Mammy's death has affected him. I write to him every Monday without fail and tell him of our progress, but there is never an answer.

To my joy, Henry is still with us, now a boy of eighteen months, walking and talking a little and bringing such happiness to my heart but also such a dread that he should be taken from us now. I am, to all intents and purposes, his mother. Marion has never shown interest in him and couldn't care if the boy were dressed or naked, fed or starving, indeed, alive or dead, God forgive me. But, to me, Henry is the sun, moon and stars, my greatest joy. To see the sunlight reflected in his brown hair as he potters about outside (when I can risk letting him out), the curiosity in the eyes so like my mother's, his little winter coat that Robert gave him, from a chest at his house, buttoned up to his neck and the little red scarf and gloves that I knitted him keeping him warm.

He is a slight small child, skinny for his age, Mrs Collins tells me, but he has plenty to eat and an abundance of love from me. He is still a good sleeper and nowadays I put him in his little crib – he will soon have to sleep in the bed with me, I fear! – and tell him a story. I tell him about Brer Rabbit and Brer Fox, and about Snow White and the Seven Dwarves and such tales as I can remember from when I was little and my mother, Lord rest her, did the same.

Henry is such a loving child. He is generous with hugs and little kisses and when he smiles it's as if the heavens have opened up their glory, such is the effect he has on me. And Robert loves him as well – last summer when he was smaller we took him as far as the seaside on an excursion, Henry hidden on the floor of Robert's motor car while we drove through the village. We are in a Limbo of sorts. Henry must remain a secret until he is taken away but there is no talk of that yet. How cruel can my father be to leave him with me so long, the threat of losing him always hanging over me like a curse? Every night I say goodnight as though it is the last night I will do so, every kiss may be our last, every game perhaps our final one. I live still from day to day, totally in love with this child and fearful to the core that I will lose him.

And what of his mother? The woman who carried and bore him? I fear she is a lost cause, Caroline. She gads about day and night, most of the time I don't know where she is. I fear she may bring more shame upon us for sometimes she is gone all night and returns in the morning looking the worse for wear. She smokes cigarettes and drinks whiskey, she tells me, and goes gambling and dancing with boys.

I don't know how much of it is true but I fear for her life as well as her soul. She treats this house like a doss house, and me as her servant. I am expected always to cook and clean and most of the time is it easier to obey as her rages have grown more violent in nature. Last August for instance, I was late back from meeting Robert and I came home to find her hiding in a doorway. She jumped out at me before I saw her and punched my face as hard as she could with her fist, like a cowboy might in the pictures. I was stunned and bleeding and with that she grabbed my hair and drove me into the kitchen. I was fearful for my life and for that of Henry, for I knew that she would harm him but still I left him with her for just half an hour. She had tied him to a chair, Caroline, and I don't know what else she did to him but he was crying his little heart out and had soiled himself all over and she had bruised his face and pinched his little cheeks. Indeed she cannot walk past him without inflicting some tiny little punishment upon him – a pinch here, a smack there, a tug of his darling curly hair. If I told her off for doing so then she would just scream at me that she is his mother after all. Some mother she is! I pray sometimes that God will just take him away to some lovely people who crave the comfort of a child and who have a warm home with plenty to eat and shiny toys. And then no sooner have I wished this happiness for him than I clutch him to my chest and cry and pray that no one will ever separate me from this darling, darling boy.

There is one advantage to Marion's carefree lifestyle and that is that Robert is free to come visit me at the cottage and spend time with myself and Henry, like a proper little family. Oh, you should see how Robert is with him, Caroline, dandling him on his knee, bringing him little presents like the little carved train and the spinning top he gave him for his first birthday last August. I had to tell him to stop bringing so many gifts for when Marion sees them she flies into a rage and has already smashed some of them – a little wooden soldier and skittles that Robert gave him so he would learn to knock them down with a ball. She hates for Henry to have new things and her not.

The love between Robert and me has grown more over the year, and not less. I can scarce believe that I should be so fortunate as to experience the love of this good man. Our 'Secret Love' as we call it, for he doesn't tell his father about me any more than I tell Marion. His father still visits from time to time and I have heard him express his disappointment that Robert has chosen to remain at home to learn the family business of building rather than go to Oxford or Cambridge, and how he wishes for Robert and Charles to make matches like Iris has, with wealthy people who can extend their family fortunes but that at nineteen Robert is still too young. Iris was married last year to one Frederick Forbes – Freddie, Robert calls him – and Robert told me such tales of the wedding.

Robert has said that he is serious about me and that he wishes to love no one else and that when we are both twenty-one, in two years' time, then come hell or high water we will be married. He says he will talk his father round to realising what a good match we are, and it is not as if I am without a penny or two to bring to the family from Daddy's business, and sure aren't Daddy and

Mr Mountford friends these many years? Robert feels it isn't the right time now and I agree. Best for us to wait until we are old enough to do as we see fit and no one else. In the meantime we content ourselves with our snatched visits, and I listen over and over to our song, 'Secret Love', on the record player that Robert gave us for Christmas. Marion complained and said to Mr Mountford himself that she should prefer a transistor radio. I saw him smile when she did that, and she pouted her lips as is her latest habit. I think he finds her funny.

If only he knew. If only he saw the scars on her arms under her cardigan where she cuts herself time and time again and threatens to cut Henry and me too. If only he saw the state of her room when she refuses to clean the sheets that she has soiled in many ways. To the village, for she spends much of her time there now, and Bickford too, Marion Flynn is the fun-loving Irish girl of mystery – she tells the villagers nothing. I am too shy to make friends and know only Mrs Collins, Dr Baker and the grocer to say hello to. Daddy said we should keep our heads low and so I must continue to do that, even if Marion won't, and by doing so we have the village wondering about the girls up at Eyrie Farm. If only they knew that it was three of us and not two, for we have done such a good job of hiding my little Henry with the help of Mrs Collins. Were it up to me I would shout Henry's name to the world and my love for him also.

And so another year has passed, Caroline. I wonder by my birthday and St Brigid's Feast Day next year what life will bring us all in our sorry tale?

Your friend,

Lily

26

July 14th

Will and Gabriel were already seated at a table, deep in conversation, when Martha entered the dining area the following morning. It was considerably emptier than it had been the previous morning, the weekend trade over for another four or five days. Just another ordinary Monday morning.

Martha busied herself by thinking about what she might do when she returned to London later that day. She knew that Sue would put her up for a while until she could find a place of her own. She could continue with her writing back in the city. Of course things would be much more expensive there so her nest egg mightn't stretch as far. There would be higher rent, a higher cost of living, more expensive childcare. Worrying as these financial thoughts were, however, Martha was excited to be thinking them. Things were going to return to normal.

"Good morning," she said quietly as she reached the table.

Will and Gabriel looked up in surprise – they had been so engrossed in something on Will's BlackBerry that they hadn't seen her approach.

"Oh, morning," said Will. Gabriel nodded at her.

A waiter appeared out of nowhere carrying a high chair for Ruby and Martha smiled gratefully and lowered her into the seat.

"How did everyone sleep?" she asked. She was aware that her imminent escape was filling her with optimism but she couldn't forget the subdued atmosphere of the night before. She glanced at the white faces and puffy eyes of both men and realised that she didn't need to wait for an answer to her question. She began to sort out Ruby's breakfast.

"Looks like another scorcher out," said Will, playing with Ruby's hand as Martha fed her some bottle.

She glanced out into the car park where already a heat haze rose off the parked cars. "Mmm," she agreed. She looked at Will and Gabriel who were not speaking and felt uncomfortable, like she had interrupted something. She itched to get away. Not long now and she'd be relaxing in Sue's apartment which was bright and modern, safe, imagining across the miles to where dark, scary Eyrie Farm would be once again deserted. Good riddance, she thought.

A waitress arrived with scrambled eggs for both Will and Gabriel and they ate in silence. Martha decided to have some fruit from the buffet once Ruby was fed. With any luck, the others might have finished by then and she would be left in peace. She wanted to find out what the other two had planned for the day – when she could reasonably expect to get on the road – so she could give Sue a ring with an ETA. There was still a lingering atmosphere of the night before in the air, however, and she didn't really know how to bring it up. The three sat in silence until the men had finished eating and Ruby had turned her face away from the last spoonful of porridge and fruit. Martha knew someone would have to speak so she broached the subject casually.

"So, Will, what time did you finish up last night?"

"Hmm? Oh, not long after you," he said, still preoccupied with his BlackBerry.

Martha sighed and stood up to head to the buffet for her breakfast.

When she returned she caught Gabriel making a face at Will as though urging him to do something. Will, in turn, glared at

Gabriel and Martha detected a barely discernible shake of his head. She continued to look at them both as she began to eat, aware now that she had definitely interrupted something.

"Spit it out," she said eventually, growing annoyed at the awkward silence and how the two men were avoiding eye contact.

Will sighed. "We've got the –" he began, but was cut off by Gabriel.

"You and the bairn need to spend another night at the cottage," he blurted out.

Martha swung her head from Will to Gabriel and her mouth opened in disbelief. "What?" she demanded, outraged.

Will looked at Gabriel in exasperation while the big man continued to avoid eye contact with either of them.

"Are you out of your mind?" said Martha. "No! I will most certainly not be spending another night at that place. Tell him, Will."

He looked down at the table to avoid her gaze.

Martha went red. "So, this big idea is down to both of you?" she said, staring at Will. "Why on earth would you think I'd even want to set foot in that place, much less stay a night in it?"

"Look, Martha," he began in a calm voice. "In order for us to investigate properly –"

"Us?" interrupted Martha, her breakfast forgotten. "Us? You mean *you*, don't you, Will? You alone and your bloody paper or whatever it is you're working on for Spooky School! This isn't about 'us' at all – it's about *you!*"

Gabriel butted in. "In all fairness, Martha –"

It was her turn to look ferocious. She spun around in her seat to look at him and stopped him in his tracks. "Oh, you're poking an oar in now, are you?"

Gabriel made to speak again but he was silenced by Martha snapping at him, "Why should you help him out? He lied to you about there being a child involved. And he's investigating you as well, or didn't you know that? Probably trying to prove you're a total fraud like all these scientists. Can't you see it, Gabriel? There's no point in being on his side – he's using us both for his studies. Freaks like us with the haunted house and the ability to see dead people!"

"Steady on, Martha," said Will, sternly. "I'm not using *anyone* and if you remember correctly you weren't entirely honest with me from the start which is why the investigation has to take place again."

"So it's *my* fault?" Martha's voice grew high-pitched with incredulity. "You're telling me that somehow it's my – my – *obligation* to go back in there when I didn't even want to be involved in the first place! You've a bloody cheek, asking me to do that. I owe you nothing – absolutely nothing – and I think you've a nerve asking me to go back in there for your own ends. The answer's no."

She made to stand up but was stopped in her tracks by a hiss from Gabriel.

"Sit *down*," he snarled, looking her directly in the eye with a face more ferocious than her own.

Despite herself, she sank back slowly onto her chair.

"That's better," continued Gabriel. "Now you listen to me, madam, and put that temper of yours back in its box. You're like an alley cat and all we want to do is explain. For starters – I am *perfectly* aware that I am a case study of Will's. Do you think I answer his call just because I love and adore him? Will's investigation – or case study of my gift, if you will – is as much for my benefit, and that of mediumship in general, as his own – but that is not any of your business."

Martha felt uncomfortable. She couldn't understand why this man intimidated her so much. But he was right. She was wrong to assume that Will was investigating Gabriel in secret. And it *was* none of her business.

"Secondly," continued Gabriel, "I think you're forgetting that, investigation or not, there's the spirit of a wee child in that house who needs help. That, ultimately, is what I do. It is for that reason – for him – that I am *telling* you, not asking you, that you need to spend one night of your tiny life in that house in order to put an end to an *eternity* of misery for a small boy."

Martha snorted, anger flooding over her again. The situation was ridiculous. This guy, who didn't know her from Adam, ordering her about, telling her to be somewhere she didn't want to be and somewhere that she had no obligation to be. Here he was talking about spirits and spooks and outside the sun was blazing and she had a real life to get back to at the other end of a motorway. She leaned toward Gabriel.

"You don't *tell* me anything, do you get that?" she said calmly. "What you and he –" she indicated an uneasy-looking Will, "want to do is between yourselves. You want to go up there and move in – feel free." She rummaged in her bag, then slammed the housekeys down on the table. "But for the millionth time this is *nothing* to do with me. In fact, if this haunting palaver is true, then I am putting myself and my daughter in danger by merely sticking a key in the door, it would seem, so I'll pass, thank you very much. I'm going back to London as soon as I can get my car packed up but you two – well –" she indicated the keys on the table, "knock yourselves out!"

Martha turned to the high chair and began loading the feeding equipment from Ruby's high chair into her bag.

"You selfish *bitch!*" hissed Gabriel. "Imagine if that were your wee girl up there trapped in that fireplace? Wouldn't you want someone to help her? Or do you only care about yourself and to hell with everyone else? That poor kiddie – that four-year-old boy – was *alive* once, just like your child there. With all the cutesy-pie little gestures and faces, all the promise for the future and some – some *bastard* put an end to that by *sealing him up with bricks!* How can you call yourself a mother?"

Martha was stunned into silence. She stared at Gabriel, frozen in the act of filling the bag with the empty bottle and spoons. The air crackled with tension. Will held his breath as Gabriel's eyes burned into Martha's, his face red, his breathing laboured.

Martha responded by taking the changing bag and flinging it onto the table. She then stood up and stormed away from the table. Cups clattered as they fell, a stream of coffee poured over the edge of the table causing Will to slide his chair back suddenly to avoid a soaking. Martha's own bowl was upended, the contents draining slowly out onto the tablecloth. A pile of salt was forming where the bag had knocked over the cellar.

Ruby watched her mother storm across reception and push the swinging door open to the car park before disappearing out of sight. The little girl's lower lip began to wobble and she let out a long wail of anguish.

Martha was blinded by the sunshine as she stepped outside, her heart pounding, her hands and legs trembling. How dare he say that to her? A total stranger speaking to her that way? She was livid – who on earth did he think he was? She was doing just fine as a mum – what right had he to question something he had no knowledge of? And as for his demands? Telling her to do things she had no intention of doing? Calling her names? Who *was* this person?

She closed her eyes and took a deep breath. She stood in the middle of the car park, her hands on her hips, her face turned toward the sky. Against her better nature she knew that part of what Gabriel had said was right. She couldn't pretend there was nothing there at the cottage. All the logic in the world couldn't explain what she had felt and seen and heard. Again in her head she replayed the little footsteps padding across the floor of Ruby's room, heard the little clatter as the soother hit the floor. A vision formed, unbidden, in her head of the skinny bare legs of a child climbing *into* the wall and vanishing. Martha shook her head to get it out. Is that what it must look like? It was too much to take in.

She had thought ahead a thousand times to what Ruby might look like at four years old, what it might sound like when her little legs ran across floorboards. How would she cope if someone hurt her? Martha's heart contracted – if anything were to happen to Ruby she'd die herself. It was unthinkable that harm should come to her – surely every mother felt that way?

She was roused by the sound of someone approaching and her stomach tightened as she turned, expecting another tongue-lashing from Gabriel. Instead, she saw the tear-streaked face of her own daughter holding out her chubby arms as Will carried her toward her.

"Oh Ruby, I'm so sorry," said Martha, sweeping her into her arms and pulling her tight against her body. What a hypocrite she was, standing here worrying about how she'd feel if someone else hurt Ruby at the very same time as storming off and deserting her with two completely strange men. A sudden jolt of guilt hit Martha so strongly that she felt her knees might buckle underneath her. She pressed her baby tighter to her. "I'm sorry, little girl," she whispered into her hair and stroked the back of her head.

Will looked down and shuffled his feet awkwardly. "Look, I'm sorry about Gabriel," he began.

Martha turned her back on him and walked a few steps away.

Will was about to turn and walk back into the hotel when Martha spoke.

"What would I have to do?" she asked.

"Oh, Martha!"

She swung around as he walked toward her, his face alight.

"I'm not promising a damn thing," she said, wiping tear trails from Ruby's face.

Will stopped. "I understand. All we'd need you to do is to stay one night – just do exactly what you'd normally do – put Ruby to bed, watch TV, go to bed yourself."

"But I'd be alone?"

Will shook his head. "Yes and no. I'd be outside monitoring everything that happens. The house would be rigged up with cameras and audio equipment and I'd be with you in a couple of seconds if needs be."

Martha thought about it for a moment. "And what about *him*," she said, a contemptuous tone to her voice as she nodded toward the big glass frontage of the hotel.

"Gabriel will stay nearby but he couldn't be in the house all night."

"Why not?"

"The 'M' entity is what we'd call an intelligent haunting. We need to record evidence of it doing just that . . ."

"Intelligent haunting?" said Martha.

Will nodded. "It can interact with people if it wants to, move objects around and block Gabriel from finding out anything about it. Similarly, we've seen that if I'm there on my own then it doesn't seem interested in responding, if my own investigation is anything to go by. That's why we need things to go back to exactly how they were the last time we had activity."

"You keep saying 'we' again, Will. *I'm* the one who's being terrorised by this so-called ghost, and an unfriendly one at that. *You* are the one who is benefiting from the experience with evidence to put in your paper. There isn't a 'we' here."

Will looked at his feet. "I know," he admitted. "This is the case I've been the most excited about since starting my course – I'll be honest, this paper is very important to me – as is everything I've learned about Gabriel. I won't deny that it will benefit me."

Martha shifted Ruby to her other hip. "And what about Gabriel – what's in it for him?"

"He wants to help the spirits. Like I said, he'd be nearby – we'd move operations to the B&B at the Abbot's Rest so he'd be moments away if he's needed. If there's activity, or a manifestation, or if both spirits are strong, then he might be able to help them move on. That's all he's concerned about."

"You've certainly got this all planned out – logistics and everything. Just waiting for me to obediently fall into line and get these spirits all nicely riled up for your cameras. What exactly is in it for *me*, Will?"

He looked directly at her, seeing that she was physically uncomfortable as she moved the heavy baby back to her original hip. "It's a word I'm reluctant to use, but I think what's in it for you is *closure*."

Martha snorted. "Closure!"

"Think about it. You can get in your car and drive back to London today – I can't stop you. But you know what you've experienced at that house better than anyone – and don't say it hasn't disturbed you. You know what you've seen and heard, and all the stuff that you thought you could explain but you couldn't. If you

just go and never come back, you'll always be thinking about it –
wondering was it real, or were you going mad. Wondering what the
whole story was. Like why didn't the spirit like you?" Will held out
his arms to take Ruby from an increasingly tired Martha. She slid
her into his arms, glad of the relief on her back and hips. "And I'm
not trying to tug on your heartstrings here but if Gabriel's to be
believed then something awful happened to a child up there.
Someone didn't just wake up one day and brick him into a fireplace
– there had to have been more to that little boy's story, more to his
little life – don't you want to know what happened? And could you
spend your life thinking that you could have helped but you didn't?
I don't think you could – I don't think you're that sort of person deep
down. And even if you don't believe a word of all this, it surely
couldn't do any harm."

She hadn't thought about anything that Will had said – hadn't
thought beyond just getting back to London and sinking into
Sue's spare bed. Will had a point. She was haunted literally in
Shipton Abbey but he was right – she'd be haunted forever more
if she didn't see this through. Still, the thought of being alone in
that house – particularly now that she *knew* what was there –
terrified her to the core.

"You'd be outside?" she asked.

He nodded. "In my car, directly outside the front door."

"If this haunting is so intelligent, as you call it, won't it know
you're there though? Know we're setting it up, as it were?"

Will shrugged, dancing absentmindedly from side to side to
keep Ruby amused in his arms. "It could well do. We don't really
know. All we can *really* do is try to recreate as best we can the
normal circumstances in the house and take it from there."

Martha watched as her daughter smiled contentedly at the
constant motion. "Surely I could leave Ruby with Mary overnight,
where she's safe," she said, her heart aching with love and terror
simultaneously.

Will shook his head. "I'm really sorry, Martha, but Gabriel
feels that Ruby's somehow key to all of this. I swear to you that
she'll be my main priority and I'll keep her monitored literally

every second of the way. Look at it this way – think of all the nights and days in that house that absolutely nothing has happened. Tonight might be no different and, whatever the outcome, I promise I'll pack up my things and help you pack up yours if you like and we'll head away from Eyrie Farm tomorrow regardless."

Martha reached out and stroked her daughter's cheek. "Why night-time though? A lot of stuff has happened during the day."

"Fair point. Evidence suggests, however, that there is a greater chance of paranormal activity at night-time. Ghosts seem to prefer the dark!" He gave a weak smile at his simplistic explanation. He simply couldn't think of another way to put it. "And if we had a thunderstorm like your baby-sitter – then ding dong! That would be even better!" He grinned, noticing that Martha's face was beginning to soften.

"Let's not have a thunderstorm, eh?" she smiled.

She looked up at the cloudless sky and back at her daughter, by now contentedly playing with a button on Will's shirt pocket. She was obviously completely relaxed in his company and trusted him. Martha decided that maybe she should, too.

"Alright," she said. "One night only and for my peace of mind, like you say." She looked Will in the eye, almost passing her trust over to him.

"Good," he said simply. "And don't worry, I'll keep you both safe."

Martha nodded and began to walk back to the hotel door. "You'd better," she said.

They walked back toward reception side by side, Martha unusually calm about what she had just agreed to do, emboldened by the heat of the sun on her bones. When they reached their table, Gabriel was gone and the table uncleared, but Ruby's changing bag was neatly packed with her breakfast things, cups and bowls were straightened and a napkin lay in the centre having been used to wipe yogurt from the side of the bag.

"Gabriel must have done this," observed Will. "He's full of surprises. He's really upset by this case for some reason. That's no excuse for calling you names, by the way."

"Oh, we both lost our tempers," said Martha, feeling embarrassed about the way she had stormed out of the restaurant. "It's obviously something he feels passionate about – if the shoe were on the other foot I'm sure I could bandy some insults around as well."

"Still though, it wasn't called for, how he spoke to you."

Martha shrugged and picked Will's BlackBerry out of the side pocket of the changing bag. "Don't forget this. He must have put it there for safe keeping."

"Oh God, yes, I nearly forgot! My friend sent back the cleaned-up EVP – have a listen." There were headphones attached to the device and Will held them out to Martha.

"No thanks," she said, shaking her head.

Will looked crestfallen. "Oh. Okay. I was hoping you would, though. I'd be interested in hearing what you think."

Martha looked at his disappointed face and felt guilty again. "Oh, give it here," she said and took the headphones, placing them in her ears.

Will smiled and held the BlackBerry out of Ruby's reach while he called up the email with the audio file. When it began to play, Martha's ears were filled with a loud crackle and she jumped at the unexpected noise, but then realised it was just the crackle that silence made when recorded.

For a few seconds there was nothing and then she was sure that she heard it. A tiny voice saying something briefly. Martha gave a start and looked at Will as it fell silent again. She took the earphones out. "I couldn't make it out," she said.

"Listen again," he replied.

This time, Martha was ready for the little voice. This time, she made out two distinct words: "*Go 'way . . .*". The exact way that a child would say it. Martha felt her blood run cold. This wasn't just a sound in the silence. This was an actual voice. A child's voice. A *dead* child's voice. She thought she'd be terrified but instead found herself intrigued. There was a third word and she wanted to find out what it was. "Again," she mouthed to Will. She made him play it three more times before removing the headphones. "I can make out the first two words, I think," she said.

Will looked at her, excited. "What do you think they are?"

"*Go 'way*?" she said, hesitantly.

Will nodded.

"Like a child would say it," added Martha.

He nodded again. "What about the last one?"

Martha shook her head. "That one I'm not so sure of."

"Have a go," urged Will.

Martha could see that her response was of urgent interest to him. "Well, it sounds a bit like '*Manny-un*'," she said, realising how stupid it sounded when spoken out loud.

"Exactly!" cried Will, making both Martha and Ruby jump. "That's what we thought as well – 'Mannion'. It's a name."

Martha nodded.

"It gives us something to go on," said Will. "We don't know the gender but it's usual that a surname alone would be used to refer to a man rather than a woman. We think that Mannion is the 'M' that Gabriel's been picking up. I think we've got our man!"

"Oh good," said Martha, taking Ruby back from Will, filled with renewed dread at what the night held for her.

27

Eyrie Farm. Martha had all but given up using the name Hawthorn Cottage. It was just wrong for the place – too twee, too sanitised. The original name was more suited to a place where some unspeakable act seemed to have happened.

The place had started to look different too, she thought. She tried to remember what it felt like to look at the house and long to go inside, to be embraced by the cosy building and feel safe within its walls.

Will was there already when she arrived back in the afternoon, the front door open, cables trailing from the rear of the Volvo through to the hallway. Martha was glad of his presence and the bustle of activity.

"Welcome home," he said ironically as she stepped out of her driver's seat and looked up the house as if seeing it for the first time.

Martha gave a weak grin and rolled her eyes before stepping around the car to retrieve Ruby from her car seat.

Will helped her to carry her cases into the hallway and Martha stepped in behind him, slowly and deliberately. The place felt different now, as though it were alive. The interior was completely unchanged from the last time Martha had seen it.

Why shouldn't it be, she thought. What did she expect? That the ghost liked *Changing Rooms* and would have rearranged everything while she'd been away?

She peered in each door along the hallway and finally reached the kitchen and placed Ruby on her playmat. Will was working in there, fixing small cameras to the fridge and the top of the cupboards. She felt safest where he was.

"Now before you get a shock," he said – Martha noticed that he didn't say 'fright' – "Gabriel's upstairs just giving me a hand. He's going to go back to the B&B shortly and let us get on with things."

"Oh," replied Martha, surprised. "I thought he wasn't coming over today?"

"He helped me set up some of the equipment just now and then said he had one little thing to do before calling a cab and heading back," said Will, struggling with some masking tape as the small camera slipped sideways.

The floorboards upstairs gave a familiar creak and Martha had never been so grateful to Will that he had warned her of Gabriel's presence. It was bad enough being here, without thinking that things were going to kick off within five minutes of her walking in the door. She decided that now was as good a time as any to bring her case upstairs, with another person up there, even if it *was* Gabriel.

"You alright if I leave Ruby here for a minute?" she asked Will.

He grunted in assent, a screwdriver between his teeth.

Martha made her way cautiously up the stairs, not sure what to expect. Knowing that there were two other adults in the house made her feel braver and gave the cottage something of a less-threatening feel than normal. She thought about how long she'd lived in her house in London – it had never made her feel nervous or edgy. When she was in a room she was *in* it – not thinking about being in it, not thinking about the other rooms and what might be happening in them, not anticipating noises of any sort. She realised that she'd been living on edge for the past month, almost without realising it.

As she mounted the stairs she heard Gabriel cough from Ruby's room and wondered had he done it deliberately to let her know he was there. She was grateful that he did, and that Will had warned her of his presence, because when she reached the top of the stairs she caught the shape of his huge bulk, dressed in black, leaning over Ruby's cot. Had she not known he was there she might have died of fright.

She coughed herself and Gabriel looked up to see her standing in the doorway.

"Gabriel," she said.

"Hello, Martha," he replied quietly. "I'm just finishing up a couple of things and I promise then I'll be out of your hair."

Martha watched him and thought she saw him slip something under Ruby's mattress. She'd ask him about that later. "No rush," she said. "Just leaving my cases in my room." She turned to cross the corridor, hesitated, and then turned back. "I'm sorry about earlier, Gabriel."

The big man shook his head. "*I* was totally out of line. I had no right to say what I did at all. I just get – very – worked up sometimes . . ."

"Enough said." Martha held up a hand to stop his apology. "Let's just forget about it and move on, eh?" She smiled at Gabriel's sheepish face.

"Gladly," he said and smiled gratefully in return. He took a final look at Ruby's cot and smoothed the sheet down with his hand. "Right," he said. "That's me done. Have you got the number of a taxi firm handy by any chance? So they can make me walk all the way out to that road again?"

"Let me take you – it's just the Abbott's, isn't it?"

Gabriel nodded. "Unfortunately," he groaned.

Martha grinned. He just couldn't help himself.

"Room there hasn't seen a lick of paint since Diana was wearing see-through skirts," he continued, rolling his eyes to heaven.

"Come on. You'll just have to drown your sorrows in the cheery bar to get over it!"

Gabriel groaned and followed her out of the room, pausing

for a second to look toward the chimney-breast as he left. Martha looked away. She didn't want to have to think about all that yet.

Having ascertained that Will wouldn't let Ruby out of his sight while she was gone, Martha led the way to her car and unlocked it, allowing Gabriel to fold himself into the passenger seat.

"My God!" he exclaimed, searching awkwardly for the handle to move the seat backwards. "Where did you get your bloody car – Toytown Motors?" He grunted as the seat shot backward and jolted to a halt.

"Only half a mile thataway, Gabriel!" grinned Martha, engaging reverse and turning the wheel to manoeuvre the car around.

"Point taken," he said and tugged at the seatbelt.

Martha made her way down the drive and turned right for the village. As she picked up speed, she settled back in her seat and glanced across at her companion. "Just out of curiosity, what exactly were you doing in Ruby's room?" she asked.

Gabriel searched for the button to close the window as he felt his carefully-styled hair ruffling in the wind. "Just a few words of protection for the wee thing," he said.

Martha was taken aback to hear this, and hugely touched. "Oh," she said, aware that she hadn't kept the tone of surprise from her voice.

Gabriel smirked. "You didn't think I'd care enough, did you?"

Martha tried to backtrack. "No, it's not that . . . it's just . . . well, Ruby doesn't sort of seem on your *radar*, I guess."

Gabriel stared out of the window in silence for a moment. "Both of you are very much on my radar, Martha. When there's a child involved . . ." The big man sighed. "I had a wee brother. Well, I say he's my wee brother but he was actually older than me. Died before I was born."

"Oh, I'm sorry, Gabriel!"

The medium shook his head. "First I knew of him was when I met his spirit on the landing of my parents' house."

A chill ran through Martha.

"I was twenty-eight and in the army," he went on.

Martha swerved slightly as she turned to look at his face, to see if he were joking.

Gabriel grinned. "Steady there – don't be fooled – I can be very butch when I need to be!"

"Blimey! I wasn't expecting that!"

"Anyway, there he was – this wee boy in short trousers and a side parting, on the landing looking as real as you or me, and he just said 'Hello Gabriel, I'm your big brother', and vanished on me. Scared the living wits out of me, I can tell you. Anyhow, I said nothing for a while – trying to take it all in. I didn't know if I was seeing things, never mind if I'd actually *had* a brother. I started to see him every time I was on leave. Sometimes he'd just smile and vanish, other times I'd spot him watching me and he'd actually *run* away. Bit pointless, I always thought – why run when you can vanish? Eventually I asked my mother if I'd had a brother and the colour her face went told me everything I needed to know. His name was Laurence and he was drowned when he was nine. He just used to come back to see his baby brother."

Martha was fascinated. She couldn't believe how matter-of-fact Gabriel was being. "And what happened?" she asked, eager to know the rest. "Did you help him pass on or whatever the correct terminology is?"

"Och, no. I see him all the time – he's my spirit guide. In fact he's sitting in the back seat right now."

"Fucking hell!" exclaimed Martha and jammed on the brakes in shock, fixing her eyes to the rearview mirror, expecting to see a nine-year-old boy in the back seat. Luckily there were no cars behind her as she ground to a halt in the middle of the road. There was nothing reflected in the mirror.

Gabriel roared with laughter.

"Jesus, Gabriel! Don't say stuff like that!"

He continued to laugh and Martha couldn't help but join in as she put the car into first and set off again.

"Oh, your face was priceless!" he giggled, wiping the corner of his eyes with the backs of his hands. "He's not there now but please don't be scared when I tell you he was there a while back."

Martha's eyes grew wide and she glanced again in the rearview mirror. She found herself unable to stop swearing. "Fuck *off*, Gabriel, you're kidding me! There's been a real live ghost in my car?"

"Language, missy," he chided. "Probably not the first time either! You see, the dead are all around us, just getting on with things, and most folk can't see them. Some of them are aware of us and they try to interact, some are just carrying on doing their thing with no idea they've passed over and some of them are troubled and need our help. That's what I try to do."

They had reached the entrance to the Abbot's Rest car park and Martha pulled into a spot and switched off the ignition.

She turned to face Gabriel, riveted by what he had to say. "So they're in a whole different parallel existence then?"

Gabriel thought for a moment. "Sort of. Some of them are on different planes to each other but what they all have in common is that they were once alive. They were people with jobs and relationships and worries and they needed to pay the bills and they fell in love and out of love and had families and – and – hobbies! They were accountants and knights and postmen," Gabriel nodded toward the pub, "and monks."

"Did you just see one?" asked Martha, staring at the exterior of the building.

Gabriel shook his head. "I don't see one every time I open my eyes and look out the window, you know," he said with a smile. "Laurence was my first one and after him I began seeing others occasionally. The first bad experience I had was a colleague who was blown up in Northern Ireland. He was presenting as he looked when he died – not pretty – and he was as confused to see me as I was to see him. He didn't actually know he was dead. I hadn't a clue what to do of course, so I couldn't help him but he made me want to work on my – skills, I suppose you'd call them. I did some training – started going to a spiritualist church. Did a lot of practice."

Martha was again gobsmacked. "You make it sound like Grade Five Piano."

"Well, no one's just given a skill that they're instantly brilliant at, are they?" retorted Gabriel. "You have to work at it – which I did – still do. I left the army a year later. I couldn't focus on it because my gift was getting stronger but I couldn't really figure out what to do with it. I kept getting bombarded at inopportune moments with old dears who wanted to say goodbye, and worse still, more soldiers but from all points in history – and let me tell you, people do *horrible* things to each other in war. And out of it, I guess." Gabriel trailed off, looking pensive. "The army was just the wrong place to be till I knew what to do with myself so I just worked on the gift, I suppose. Went on the dole for a few years while I learned how to handle it all."

"So is Laurence the reason that you don't do children?" asked Martha.

"Oh no – Laurence is the reason I do this in the first place. It's just that since I learned how to use this gift better – I'll never use the word 'mastered', mind – I've seen a lot and because children are defenceless, awful things happen to them sometimes. People treat them as though they're not human – they often treat their animals better. I've seen dreadful things, Martha. I'm not going to tell you about them because I don't want to burden you but where I can I try to avoid cases with children. I don't walk away if they come to me – it's just that I'm not very strong around wee ones. But I'm trying."

Gabriel's eyes were sincere and tinged with pain. Martha was more sure now than ever that he was genuine, that he wasn't making any of this up. And still unnerved that a ghost had been in her car. Funnily, she didn't feel frightened, but almost honoured. Weird, she thought, for someone who hadn't been entirely sure ghosts existed at all until the last day or two.

"You've got your own spirits, you know," said Gabriel. "With you all the time, looking out for you."

"What?"

"Oh yes. They're like arseholes and mobile phones."

Martha furrowed her brow – had Gabriel finally lost it?

He tutted. "Oh keep up, woman – everybody's got one is what I mean."

"Oh," replied Martha, only slightly the wiser.

"Your Ruby, for example – she's got a host of grannies. There's a skinny old thing with wonky glasses – connected to your . . . *husband*?"

"Oh God, Granny Goodwin!" exclaimed Martha nervously. "My husband's grandmother."

"You have a *husband*?" It was Gabriel's turn to be taken aback.

Martha rolled her eyes. "Ex. Very much ex. Trust Ruby to have a minder from his bloody side after he ran out on her."

Gabriel's eyes widened. "Bloody hell, you have a history?"

"Another time," said Martha.

Gabriel nodded, seeing her reluctance to speak, her face carrying an expression like she had just tasted something unpleasant. "Fair enough," he said. "But fear not – there's a second one – a tubby lady, beautiful face and shiny black hair – wasn't too old when she passed. Was her name Ruby as well?"

Martha felt tears at the back of her eyes. "That's my own grandmother. I never knew her because – you're right – she died young, but she was an amazing woman."

"Well, there you go. She looks after you as well sometimes. There's another woman too – thin and small but she's not very well from what I can tell?"

Martha knew instantly that he meant her own mother but she couldn't go there with him. "I know who that is," she said, the tone of her voice suggesting that it was all that needed to be said.

Gabriel barely took any notice. "Right then. So now you know. When it comes to spirits, you have to remember that they're just people. Sometimes it's startling when they try to communicate but look at it from the point of view that they're just doing what they can to get their point across – like we might in a country where they speak a different language. But maybe we'd do it with less flinging stuff and moaning!"

Martha smiled. "That's for sure!"

"I know it's not that simple, nor that cut and dried, but tonight – when you're . . . on your own –"

A shadow flickered across Martha's face.

"Just maybe remember what I've told you and remember there's folk looking out for you."

Martha nodded, processing the words, but distracted by the thought that the evening was wearing on. "Thanks, Gabriel."

"No worries. Now let's get this done and dusted, eh?" he said, searching for the door handle to no avail. "This bloody car!" he roared in frustration and Martha leaned across and gently pulled on the handle to open the door.

"How did you spend time in the army without being able to drive, by the way?" she asked.

Gabriel leaned toward her and spoke in a low voice. "Big difference between 'can't drive' and 'won't drive', my darling. But don't tell William – he'd have me carting equipment round for him from John O'Groats etcetera. And besides which, it would interfere with the pleasures in life . . ." He mimed drinking a glass of something and rubbed his belly.

Martha burst out laughing. "*Gabriel!* You're such a liar!"

She shook her head and turned on the ignition, putting the car into reverse. Gabriel began to climb out but then she stopped him.

"By the way again – what did you put under Ruby's mattress when you were up there?"

Gabriel smiled. "Contrary to popular belief that I am the spawn of the devil, I am, in fact, by birth and baptism a . . ." He made the sign of the cross across his chest and mouthed the word 'Catholic'.

Martha opened her mouth wide in surprise, only half in jest.

"Proper Catholics, of course, think I am the antichrist itself," continued Gabriel, "but when you're brought up Holy Roman then it's very difficult to shake so I've just left the babe a loan of some extra protection – a trinket of mine if you will. It can't do any harm anyway, no matter what God, if any, you choose to worship. If all else fails, my sweet, then do as St George of Michael bids us and have a little faith. Now begone, woman! And good luck!"

Gabriel stepped from the car with little ceremony and without a look back, and flounced into the doorway of the Abbot's Rest, leaving the car door wide open so that Martha had to get out and close it before clambering back in and reversing out of the parking spot.

She arrived back at the cottage to find Will on his hands and knees in the hallway taping cables to the floor while Ruby lay beside him, red-faced and fascinated. The smell from her nappy hit Martha the second she reached the doorway.

"Oh Ruby!" she exclaimed in disgust, stepping around Will as he reversed toward her, and picking her up. "Sorry, Will!" she said, wrinkling her nose at feeling a damp stain on the baby's jeans.

"S'alright. Happened a while ago though so I can't smell it any more. I was going to have a go at changing it once I'd finished this." He sat back on his ankles. "How did it go with Gabriel?"

"Oh, we got chatting," replied Martha.

"So you've kissed and made up then?"

"Something like that. I'm amazed he used to be in the army!"

Will shuddered in mock horror. "I've seen the photos! Here, if you hang on two minutes I'll go with you upstairs. To change Ruby."

"Oh, I'm fine to go on my own," said Martha, suddenly realising that she was – she didn't feel at all nervous about going upstairs by herself.

"You sure?"

Martha figured that Gabriel's pep talk had worked. "Yeah – I'll be fine. If I need you I'll shout."

Ruby's room felt cool with the window open but otherwise just like any other room. This is fine, thought Martha as she changed her daughter and selected some clean clothes for her. She dropped the used nappy into the nappy bin and rotated the dial on the lid to seal it inside in plastic. Better empty that before we leave, she thought, reminded suddenly that tomorrow she'd be leaving for good. The thought cheered her immensely.

Strapping Ruby onto her changing mat, Martha turned to the

cot and reached in under the mattress where she had earlier seen Gabriel do the same thing. Her fingers instantly found what they sought and she took the object out to have a better look. She smiled as the delicate silver rosary beads glinted in the sunlight coming from the window. You old softie, Gabriel, she thought. She was touched that he had left an object so beautiful and probably personal here to give Ruby the extra protection that he believed she might need.

Martha slid the beads back under the mattress and turned to retrieve her daughter. She must make sure to get them back to him tomorrow. Chances were, anyway, that everything would be fine. She kissed her daughter's chubby cheek and went downstairs to rejoin Will.

28

Eyrie Farm,
Shipton Abbey,
Norfolk,
England

February 1st, 1956

Dear Caroline,

"Through her holy intercession with our Father in Heaven, may St Brigid bless you and make you generous in your giving, pleasant in your greeting, honest in your speaking, loyal in your loving, clear in your thinking, strong in your working, and joyful in your living. And when it's time for your homecoming, may there be peace in your passing and a warm welcome in heaven."

Isn't that a lovely blessing all the same? I got it from a book of the saints' blessings that Mrs Collins gave us, would you believe? She had a distant cousin from Cork visit her last year and this cousin brought a book about saints to Mrs Collins and she a staunch Protestant. How she laughed when she received it but then she thought of us and imagined that I might like it. I was pleased to receive a gift but, to be honest, Caroline, as I haven't been to Mass nor received Communion since we arrived in Shipton Abbey three years ago I am sure that I am no longer part of the Holy Catholic Church. And indeed I think God is angry with me, he must be, for despite my regular prayers, and my teaching them to Henry, this past year has brought us nothing but sorrows.

It began in the springtime last year when finally a letter from Daddy arrived. I was sure it would have details of all the arrangements for our homecoming and my heart sank when I saw it for now that Henry is almost three years old I could no more be without him than without my own two legs and there's no lie in that. I feared beyond fear itself that this letter contained news that someone should come to take him away to the loving home that I so wanted for him once. The letter said no such thing, however, and all it contained was a letter saying that Daddy was very sorry but there was nothing left for us, that his business had been lost to creditors and that the house where we grew up had been sold to try to raise funds to clear debt. We are penniless, Caroline, our father having lost everything he worked for since he came back from the war.

In the letter he told us that there was no point to our coming home because there is nothing there and that he himself could now be reached only by sending post to Granny Flynn's old address where I assume he must have moved to stay with Uncle Thomas who inherited her house when she passed. I am glad in a way for the first time that my mother is gone, Lord rest her soul, for she could never have lived through this. Although I feel somehow that if she were still here everything would have turned out differently.

There was no mention of Henry in the letter, my one consolation, for I can take it that my father has arranged no adoption and that my darling boy is to stay with us. The letter made Marion very angry indeed but for the first time she didn't fly into a rage but very quietly went outside for a long walk. I fear it has hit her hard that our inheritance, indeed our dowries, should we ever be lucky enough to marry, is gone and that we are *paupers with no hope of a return to our childhood home nor even Dublin.*

Gone too from me is Robert, my one true love. At first I was angry beyond belief. I wanted to kill Marion with my bare hands for it was she who ruined everything, but now that we are to stay here forever what is the point? All I can do is get on with my life as I am destined to be alone. At least I have Henry and if I will never be a wife at least I can know some of the joy of being a mother.

It was Marion who found out about Robert and me when she spied on me one day leaving the house. I had taken to leaving Henry with Mrs Collins in secret rather than with Marion because I feared that the child would be hurt if left in her care. She saw me leave the house and hid in the bushes and saw Robert pull up in his motor car on the road outside and worst of all she saw him kiss me hello. Of course this drove her into a fury and when I returned she told me that she had gone straight to Mr Mountford and told him of the unsuitable match that his son was making. She slapped my face, and began acting the older sister for a change, and told me that I was impertinent and who did I think I was, in a romance when I had Henry to look after and a house to keep and us ruined with no money and no dowries.

The next day word came from Robert, a letter, to say that he was forbidden from seeing me, that his father felt we were an unsuitable match and that he was to go to university in the autumn as his father wished for him and it was imperative that he obey his father's wishes. I cried as though my heart should break, Caroline, for though the letter was in Roberts's handwriting, the words not his own, but his father's. What have I become, I ask myself? Penniless, living on the charity of others, with no prospects and a small child, though I would not be away from Henry for the world. And hanging over us forever is the shame that my sister has brought on our name.

When we had money there was some hope of banishing that shame but now we are cast adrift, our father uncaring, left to our own devices in a strange land that has never felt like home. It's like being a prisoner on Devil's Island, Caroline. For sure, a paradise with the trees and the estuary and the simple changing of the seasons, but we are prisoners here. Where do we go? What do we do? My prospect of marriage seemed to be a future for us but thanks to Marion that is never now to happen.

I thought my heart would break in those weeks after Robert's letter. How I craved his warm kisses and embrace, to hear his voice reassure me and tell me that we should be together forever, how he couldn't wait to, like the song, shout our love from the highest hills. I have since realised that there is no point in even thinking about it, let alone long for it, so I have shut the part of my heart that is too painful to open. He will never come back to me. I have not seen him since. I take it just that he is at university where he will meet new friends and rise high above my humble station. I am sure he has forgotten me already.

The strangest part of our fortunes in this most desperate of years is on the part of who but Lady Marion herself. You'll remember that I mentioned that Iris Mountford had married a Frederick Forbes? Well, Frederick has a brother called Albert, or Albie as he is known, and by some twist of fate he and Marion are courting. She met him at a party that she had managed to attend – Marion has never lost her desire to gad about and at the time spent more nights away from this cottage and her son than she spent in it. I have no notion how she inveigled an invite to this particular party but it seems that her ways caught the eye of Albie Forbes and she has been stepping out with him steadily since last Halloween, an appropriate time of the year for such a horror as Marion!

You wouldn't believe the change in her, Caroline, since this all started. She paints herself to Albie as some picture of virtue and indeed in some ways she lives up to that – she has stopped being flighty and hanging about with whoever will keep her company or show her a good time. Albie picks her up in his motor car when they go out together. Like the Mountfords he is very rich and lives over near Bickford. She makes sure that he waits outside and also that Henry is hidden away when he calls. If Henry so much as tugs at a curtain she comes home in a rage and once she beat him soundly with her shoe so that the poor little boy was bruised for days on his back and legs and little bottom. Now, when Albie is coming, I make sure that Henry is safely up the stairs in the little back room so that he can't be seen from the front of the house.

Marion has completely denied him and what else did I expect? She has always wanted the finest things in life and now, she says, she has her chance because Albie is truly besotted and if she is attentive and virtuous and all the other things that a fiancée should be, then she and Albie will be married and she will never have to want again. Albie must never know that she has a son and she has managed in some way to ensure that Mr Mountford will also keep her secret, he being the only other person other than Robert and Mrs Collins who is aware of Henry's existence. I dread to think what she has done to ensure Mr Mountford's silence but silent he is, and Marion now goes to respectable parties and on days out and to Bickford dancing. She has even been to Norwich to a dance, which is further than either of us have been in our three years here.

Albie has given her a small gold ring with a single ruby set on top of the band. She says it's not an engagement ring, but as good as. Needless to say, while Marion is now a street angel, she is still the house devil she always was. She loves to wave her ring in my face and flaunt her romance at me, knowing that my heart is broken for the love that she spoiled on me. She still does unexpected things as well. For instance, once she just flung out her hand and hit me on my temple with the ring and made me bleed. She never apologised, as always, just said I was lucky to still have my eye and it's all I deserve having brought shame on us by seeing Robert behind her back. I don't know if she loves Albie as I love, loved, Robert. He is a funny looking fellow, skinny with sandy hair slicked back with brilliantine as it is curly. He is ten years older than Marion, pale with beady green eyes but she talks of him as if he were James Dean!

He went to Cambridge and I am unsure now what he does, other than that he is very rich indeed which is what I think Marion loves more than poor Albie himself. She will not allow *me to meet him of course, although at least he knows I exist. She has told him we are orphans under the wardship of Mr Mountford, which is a risky strategy as Mr Mountford is his brother's father-in-law, but so far Marion remains undiscovered.*

I am happy for her – it would be selfish of me to be any other way and if one of us at least makes our fortune then that is at least a blessing in itself. She has used her relationship with Albie to be even more horrible to Henry though, if that is possible. He is only three, a little fellow for his age and slow to speak because every time he opens his mouth to talk she shouts at him to shut up. The poor little boy is terrified of her, and has taken to hiding behind my skirts if she so much as walks into a room where he is. This infuriates her more than ever and she has taken to grabbing his little head at the temples on either side and lifting him by it while he screams and wriggles to be free. I am terrified that she will break his neck and I have to run to try to hold up his legs, as though he were being hanged. If she manages to get him up by his head she swings him from side to side and he screams even louder because all the while she is shouting in his face to shut up, and telling him that he is nothing but a bastard and it's his fault that we live here in the countryside, alone.

She screams at him every time she sees him, that he killed his grandmother, that he will be the ruination of us and that if Albie ever sees him or hears him that she will kill him stone dead with her bare hands. Poor Henry can scarce understand what she is saying but she would spend all of her days and nights frightening him if she could. She has clearly told him that when she marries Albie she will not take him to live with her in her new big house but leave him here in Eyrie Farm with me.

That does not make me entirely unhappy because I know I can keep Henry safe. On the other hand it makes me a prisoner for life because who will want a girl with a small child? Who will believe that he is my sister's child and that the shame of his birth wasn't all down to me? Next year he will be due to start school and I am worried already what to do. Should I try to teach him myself at home? Or do as Mrs Collins has suggested and up and leave Eyrie Farm and go somewhere that no one knows us and live a life of pretence, wearing a wedding ring and telling people that I am a widow and that Henry is my son?

The thought of the future, if I am to be Henry's carer, make me nervous and worried. Our fiscal situation is precarious. Obviously Daddy doesn't send us our allowance any more as he has nothing left, so I am glad that I have squirreled some money away from the amounts that he used to send. I have also started to take in some sewing and repairs, using Mrs Collins as a 'front' as they say in the pictures! That earns me a few shillings and I try to hide as much of that as I can from Marion who is a huge drain on our resources with her new lifestyle.

By some miracle, Mr Mountford lets us stay in Eyrie Farm. After my romance with Robert was discovered I was sure that it was curtains then and we would be out on the streets of England, homeless and destitute, but it seems that Marion has some special hold over Mr Mountford and we still have a roof over our heads, so I suppose I must be thankful to her, whatever she has done. I know that I haven't enough money saved to start a new life elsewhere though, and if Marion leaves to marry Albie then where does that leave me and Henry? As with Robert, I try to put it to the back of my mind, but as another year is closed for me on another St Brigid's Day and my twentieth birthday, the worry creeps more and more to the forefront of my mind.

Pray to God that He will look after us, Caroline. I haven't been the best servant to Him but if ever there was a soul who needed His help, it is I.

Your friend,

Lily

29

Martha found Will rifling through the kitchen cupboards and then crossing to the fridge and rummaging through there. He turned his head when he saw her.

"Do you ever eat anything?" he said.

Martha smiled. "Sorry, it's all a bit Mother Hubbard at the moment – I haven't had a chance to do a proper shop with . . . everything. Unless you'd like me to defrost some puréed sweet potato for you? I'm sure I've some with broccoli in it somewhere?"

"Mmm . . . sounds delicious!" said Will, making a face at Ruby. "Actually, I think we're okay." He took a jar of pesto from the fridge.

"Oh, let me," said Martha, realising that he intended to cook.

He put his hands up to stop her. "Not at all, I insist! You hungry?"

Martha was starving. She had eaten nothing since half a bowl of fruit in the hotel that morning and she realised that it was now approaching six o'clock.

"Actually I'm ravenous," she said and smiled. No one had cooked for her in a long time – 'chick stuff', Dan had called cooking. It didn't stop him barbequing in front of guests though.

And taking the credit when Martha was the one who had spent hours making salads and marinades.

Martha kept jumping up to help Will as he cooked but he commanded her to sit down so often and so fiercely that she eventually obeyed and sat at the kitchen table, half an eye on the cooking and half on Ruby who was fascinated with a plastic bowl that Will had given her.

Will beavered around the kitchen, opening a packet of pasta, chopping olives and cherry tomatoes and toasting stale ciabatta bread in the oven which he slathered with garlic butter that he had mixed himself. Fifteen minutes later he served Martha a steaming bowl of pasta and a plate of crispy bread.

"For madam," he said, "a serving of my finest linguine with basil pesto." He swooped the dish down in front of her with a flourish. "Or as I like to call it – Lin-greeny."

Martha burst out laughing. The joke wasn't that funny but it was so long since anyone had said anything that stupid and lighthearted to her that she couldn't stop herself. Will beamed, thinking his joke was hilarious, and retreated to the worktop to serve his own food, chuckling to himself. The sight of him, so proud at his own ridiculous wordplay, made Martha laugh even harder and she had to calm herself down before she could eat a bite.

Will was still chuffed with himself as he plonked a huge glass of red wine down in front of her. "You like my joke?" he said in a stupid accent and set her off again.

She composed herself with a long sigh and took a mouthful of food. "Not so much," she replied. "But, genuinely, I'm enjoying the company and being cooked for is a real novelty for me." She wound more pasta around her fork, skewered a piece of olive and popped the lot in her mouth.

It was the normality she was enjoying, she realised. She had usually been tense in this house on her own, even without knowing it sometimes, but she felt relaxed with Will here and with Gabriel's encouraging words still in the back of her mind. Suddenly, the incongruity of the situation hit her – she had earlier been reassured by someone telling her that dead people had jobs and here she was sitting in a house that was apparently full of ghosts, rigged throughout with cameras and microphones. And yet she was enjoying pasta and a joke. Shouldn't this be more . . . momentous, she thought. More serious? More solemn?

A small twinge of panic hit her and she pushed all thoughts from her mind. Deal with it later, she thought. She remembered that Sue used to address her as 'The Procrastinator' after they had seen *Terminator* in college. She was right. Martha was queen of blocking out stuff she didn't want to think about and for once she was glad of the skill. She took a gulp of wine to wash down some food which had lodged in her throat. She gave a small cough and shifted in her seat.

"Are you not having wine?" she asked Will, noticing the glass of water in front of him.

He shook his head, his mouth full. A tiny piece of pasta jutted out from the corner of his mouth, as though waiting until there was room for it to fit in. Will reached up with his hand and pushed it in, like a child might. Martha found the gesture endearing and smiled.

"Not tonight, ta," he said. "I have to keep a clear head for later."

Martha pushed her own glass away. "Then I'd better not either."

Will gently pushed it back toward her. "I don't want to say that you might need it but . . . well . . . you might need it. Dutch courage." He grinned almost sympathetically.

Again, Martha coughed and looked around her nervously, her earlier burst of courage waning.

Will saw the shadow that crossed her face. "So," he said, scooping up more food. "Am I allowed to ask for Martha Armstrong in a nutshell?" He instantly furrowed his brows and looked puzzled. "That didn't sound right, did it?"

Martha smiled. "Not really," she replied with a grin. "Not much to tell – born in a small town, parents ran a pub, Mum died when I was young so Dad brought me up – hence very awkward adolescence with *exceptionally* bad clothes. That was followed by the slightly Goth phase in school . . ."

Will's eyes widened. "You were a Goth?"

Martha rolled her eyes in embarrassment. "A very half-hearted one! I think it was because I hadn't a clue how to be a proper teenager and let's face it – it solved the bad-clothes problem. I think I liked the whole clearly defined group thing as well – I had something to belong to, something I could be sure of almost. It only lasted six months anyway and then I just reverted to relatively dull and boring. I think I had a lucky escape – could have died from hairspray poisoning otherwise." She paused for a bite of bread. "Studied journalism in college – I met Sue there. Thought it was a good choice because I'm good at writing but that's only ten per cent of being a journalist – unfortunately I was absolutely crap at the other ninety per cent of stuff like asking people awkward questions and getting within a ten-mile radius of conflict. I didn't do a very good job at it. Sue, on the other hand, is brilliant. Not only does she have the balls, but her mind works in a totally different way to most people's and she thinks of the most brilliant questions. One time she was interviewing Pierce Brosnan –"

Will coughed to interrupt her. "Martha Armstrong in a nutshell, please – not Sue Brice, nice and all as she is!"

Martha giggled. "Sue Brice – yes, remember that name! You'll be seeing lots of it in the future, believe you me! Anyway, I ended up becoming an advertising copywriter in the long run and met my husband – well, ex-husband – Dan, while working in an agency. He was a sales rep who worked his way up to Chief Account Director, and I slogged away coming up with captions and concepts for ten years." Martha paused for a mouthful of wine and more pasta. "Loving the Lin-greeny by the way," she grinned.

Will smiled back. "Would I know any of your advertising work then?"

Martha thought for a moment. "Do you remember the Albert Hitchcock commercials for ketchup?"

It was Will's turn to think. "Oh yes! The guy in the tank top who looked like he was getting attacked by birds and it was all dramatic and everything and then the camera pulls out and it turns out it's just one sparrow and it's done its business on his head?"

Martha nodded. "There was a series of them based on Alfred Hitchcock's movies – *Psycho*, *Strangers on a Train* – and at the end of each poor Albert Hitchcock would turn sideways . . ."

"And the outline of his profile would appear – like on the TV show!"

Martha nodded. "That's right – looking *nothing* like Alfred Hitchcock but the music was similar and then the tagline would come in: 'The Real One's Better'. Simple, really."

Will looked at her in amazement. "That was *you*? My God – those commercials are classics! They've been in those Top 100 Commercial Countdowns for years!"

"Number seventy-eight," grinned Martha, embarrassed but flushed at the unexpected praise.

Will raised his eyebrows at Ruby who was turning a small Humpty Dumpty over and over in her hands. "Your mother's a *genius*, Ruby-Doo!" Ruby looked at him quizzically and then beamed, delighted with the attention, like her mother. Will turned back. "So, how did an award-winning advertising copywriter end up in the back end of nowhere by herself?"

"Well, for starters, the ads never won any awards, Fact Fans!" said Martha.

Will looked shocked but continued to eat, expectantly watching Martha for the rest of the story.

"The whole advertising thing wasn't as satisfying or as exciting as people seem to think – you bust your guts coming up with a concept that you think a client will love and that's right for their brand and then they positively hate it and want to do something really banal and rubbish. You're just torn all the time between your creativity and trying to make the money guys happy, and then the sales guys are on your back all the time because their commission depends on you coming up with something amazing in thirty seconds flat – oh, it could just all be very stressful a lot of the time."

"But surely you must have been really well-respected after Albert Hitchcock?"

Martha shook her head. "Where I worked, the creatives are

always the underlings. All a successful commercial does is raise the bar higher. They actually used me to sell the agency for a while – the sales execs used to wheel me out at meetings like a Victorian Freak to try to win accounts. Dan even had a line where he introduced me as 'The Bird Behind Hitchcock' – it was funny three times max but it wore very thin after a thousand outings! To be honest, we were married by then so I was 'My wife! The Bird Behind Hitchcock!'"

Will grimaced and shook his head.

"I was getting really sick of the job at that stage," she went on. "I mean, people were expecting me to come up with stuff that was exactly right for them at the drop of a hat and I couldn't do that – I mean it's not like being an electrician or a plumber for example. Go in, see problem, search mental skill bank and toolbox and job done. There's only a finite number of things that can go wrong so electricians and plumbers have a pretty good chance of getting things right – and people love them! I bloody *wish* I was an electrician or a plumber!"

"You'd look rubbish in overalls," said Will, smiling.

Martha smiled back. "Good point. Anyway, my heart just wasn't in advertising any more – the constant expectation just put me under pressure I couldn't live up to and I've always wanted to be a writer – children's books – so I had a plan all formulated. I wanted to resign and have Dan support me for a little while to see if I could make a go of it at writing. Bear in mind we were absolutely loaded at this stage. Dan was on a massive salary – and all his bonuses were going into a special savings account for the future – or so I thought."

They had finished eating and Will had pushed his chair back and stretched his legs. "So he didn't have the savings?"

Martha sipped her wine and shook her head. "He had the savings alright – it's just that they were for a different future than the one I had planned. I got pregnant around then so I decided to stay in work for a while until I had the baby, save up as much as we could, it was all rosy in the garden. I was just about to have Ruby when I found out that Dan's future was with one of the other account directors. He'd been seeing her for a couple of years apparently – they had this whole life set up together. So that was the end of that. We split up, I had Ruby and we sold our house and with my share I decided to just do what I wanted to do and this is it." Martha indicated the house around her. "A total break away, new life, new career – I just needed to get away from things in London."

"Was it a messy divorce?" asked Will sympathetically.

"The divorce itself wasn't. But the mess was in my head – and my heart, to be honest. Realising that he'd been cheating on me for years, that he had this whole other life with this woman. All the business trips, golfing holidays abroad – he was essentially living two lives. Of course you torture yourself – picturing them together – ugh! And all that money. I'm not materialistic but we had worked so hard and saved so hard and I just had this vision of the future . . . I don't even want to think about it!"

Will shook his head. "What about Ruby then?" He bent down to pick her up and sat her on his knee, wrapping his arms around her and snuggling into her face.

Martha watched these gestures of affection from a man she'd known for what – two or three days? It hit her that Ruby's own father had never done that.

"He's seen her once," she smirked, coldly. "Came to the hospital after she was born. Sue held my hand during the birth actually. Drew the line at holding my leg though! Dan waded in when Ruby was a day old with an enormous teddy bear and tried to come over all fatherly and hold her up to the window – do you know that scene in *Only Fools and Horses* when Del Boy has Damien for the first time? Yeah – Dan tried to do that, showing her the lights of the city, blithering on about destiny. I just bloody lost it when he started mouthing off about 'bearing his name' and I chucked him out – and his bloody giant bear with him. I was quite proud of myself, actually!"

Will laughed quietly.

"Our subsequent communication was through our lawyers," said Martha. "And Ruby's name is Armstrong – not Smith – isn't that right, petal?" She leaned across the table to stroke Ruby's chubby cheek and Ruby jiggled in Will's arms, contentedly playing with the wooden beads around his wrist.

"He was a very stupid man to let you go," said Will. "I wouldn't."

There was silence. Martha looked at Will, expecting him to explain the remark, to observe that it hadn't come out right. He didn't.

Martha blushed. "We just wanted different things, I suppose. When I was 'The Bird Behind Hitchcock' he thought I was great – ambitious, all fired up by work like he was, but he had me all wrong. We had loads of money and a lovely house but I just wanted to fill it with more babies and write my books. I lost the fire for the sort of work he wanted me to do. We were going in completely different directions – the whole thing should have ended years ago. I was too young and probably too needy to spot that."

"Should have stuck with your Goths," offered Will.

Martha laughed. "Anyway – he's with Paula now – Queen Bitch as they call her in the agency. She's his chief rival on the sales team and has all the drive and career ambition and ruthlessness that he could ever want, so he's happy. And do you know what? Good luck to him. I've got Ruby and because of her I wouldn't change a thing. Onwards and upwards, eh, Rubes?"

They fell silent for a while, Martha sipping her wine, Will rubbing Ruby's hand. Ruby gave a long yawn and Will laughed at the effort that she put into it.

There was a sudden bang from upstairs as Martha's bedroom door slammed shut in a gust of wind. She knew what the sound was, knew why it had happened – because of the open windows upstairs. They both jumped nevertheless.

Don't get sleepy, Ruby, thought Martha, knowing that her bedtime was coming very soon and with that, darkness. "What about Will Peterson in a nutshell?" she asked. She was genuinely interested to know more about this relative stranger. She also wanted to keep the conversation going, to stave off bedtime, to avoid ever having to stand up from the table and face what was next.

"Oh blimey," said Will. "Let's see. Dad was in the army so we moved house a lot when I was small – just me and my twin sister Lucy. Have you any siblings by the way?"

Martha shook her head.

"So, yeah, me and Lucy and my mum who is a lovely little housewife. She and my dad have settled in the countryside, in Cornwall. She's in the WI – all flower-arranging and baking considerably bigger buns and all that. Lucy's still at university – we're not big on proper jobs in our family! She's studying archaeology so she's been at it for years, more power to her. Goes off on digs all over the place . . ."

Martha coughed. "Will Peterson in a nutshell, please!"

He grinned and nodded apologetically. "Played rugby in school, never a Goth, liked 80's electro pop – Depeche Mode, Kraftwerk, Gary Numan . . ."

Martha looked at him in shock. "You are kidding!"

Will looked indignant. "I'll have you know that OMD, for example, have provided us with some of the most symphonic pop music this side of Bach and Abba!"

Martha threw her head back and laughed.

Will carried on, looking at her in mock disdain. "I won't apologise for it either! My taste as a twelve-year-old was impeccable. Anyway, it developed into a love of dance music – trance, house, all that kind of thing. I lived on Ibiza for a year which was fairly nuts. Came home via Barcelona, Amsterdam, Dublin – just dossed round for a while, I guess."

"Quite the traveller," said Martha.

"Well, sort of. Dublin's great but it's hardly a kibbutz in Israel, is it? Actually, I've been to China – that was pretty adventurous. I didn't like it though. There's a lot of spitting." He shuddered at the thought.

"What were you working at that you could travel so much?"

Will looked almost embarrassed. "I, eh, dabbled in property in the late 90's."

"What's wrong with that?"

Will shrugged. "I dunno. With the economy the way it is I just don't go on about it much."

"Everyone who could, did it. There's nothing to feel sleazy about unless you screwed people over, I guess."

"No, nothing like that." Will shook his head. "My gran left me a house – that was when I was travelling first, doing bar work and stuff, so I went home with the intention of living in it. It was in London, actually. Islington. I stayed there for a while but I hated the city so I gave the house a lick of paint and stuck some clean carpet in it and dammit if it didn't sell for a small fortune. It hadn't really occurred to me to make a living out of it but Lucy's got this mad business head for a bone-digger and she gave me a talking to and I tried it. Bought two houses in the same area for what I'd made on Gran's and it just grew from there."

"So how on earth did you end up doing what you're doing?" asked a baffled Martha, draining her wineglass.

"Well, I was studying psychology at night-time – at this stage I'd moved to Edinburgh and I was living in this old flat near the Royal Mile. It was a spooky old place and I kept seeing this old man on the stairs."

A chill ran down Martha's spine.

"I got chatting to him one day."

"So he was *alive?*" said Martha in amazement.

Will spluttered with laughter. "Oh lord, yes! But he used to tell me all these things his wife used to tell him. I never saw her, assumed she was an invalid maybe. Turns out *she'd* been dead for a couple of years! He got me interested in the psychology of his situation – why couldn't he let her go, what comfort did he get from thinking she spoke to him and so on. So I used to visit him – bring him cakes and stuff. He was a dear old thing. Used to chat to her while I was there so it was like there were three of us."

Martha's eyes grew wide. "Like how exactly?"

"Oh, just small stuff. I'd be doing the whole 'bit nippy today, Bernard, shouldn't you have a warmer jumper on?' sort of stuff and he'd laugh and say 'Norah asked the very same thing earlier! What's that, darling? Forecast's for rain? Oh dear, better get to the shops early' and so on. I thought it was just his way of communicating with me, some little habit he'd retreated into after she'd gone, but one day he said the oddest thing to me. 'Will', he said, 'Norah tells me you've got a lot of property round the city.'"

"What was odd about that? You did, didn't you?"

"I did. But I'd never told Bernard. I didn't want him to think that I was some sort of sleazy shark, making friends with him because I wanted to buy him out or anything. I still wasn't entirely comfortable with how I made my money so I'd told him I was a student."

"Surely someone you knew in common could have told him?"

Will shook his head again. "Genuinely, we didn't know a single person in common. The only person he communicated with was his dead wife and I'd only lived there a month or so and knew two people – one was Canadian and one was Chinese and neither knew him."

"Could he have been in your flat maybe, had a look around?"

"Not to my knowledge. And not likely. He was crippled with arthritis in his legs and hands. He only used to come out as far as the landing for a cigarette because Norah hated him smoking in their flat. I lived three flights up from him and there was no lift."

"Maybe you let it slip to him some day and then forgot you had?"

"Possibly. Well, it was just a little thing, really, but I couldn't figure out how on earth he knew. It turns out he wanted to – sorry, *Norah* wanted him to sell his flat and go into a retirement home where he could be properly looked after, but the poor old thing didn't have a clue how to go about it. They'd lived there for sixty years, can you believe? Apparently Norah thought I was a lovely young man and just the sort of person who'd give Bernard good advice."

"And did you?"

Will nodded. "I got him a great price and sold the one I was in as well. Bernard was thrilled – he moved into a lovely place near their daughter and grandchildren. I went to China then and when I got back I heard he'd passed on. He went and left me money as well, the silly old thing."

"Aw bless," said Martha.

"They wouldn't give me his daughter's details to give it back so I donated it to cancer research in the long run. That's how he lost Norah."

"Oh, Will, that was a lovely thing to do," said Martha, impressed.

Ruby was beginning to grizzle in Will's arms. Martha glanced at her watch. Seven thirty already; bedtime. She felt panicky at the thought of having to go upstairs to change her. Ruby threw her head back and squirmed. Suddenly, Martha spotted her changing bag. Clean nappies, she thought, and her babygro from the previous night were in there as well. Reprieve. She wouldn't have to go upstairs just yet after all.

"Bottle time for someone, I think," she said, standing and taking Ruby from Will.

"Let me," he said and busied himself heating up the bedtime bottle while Martha set about changing Ruby for bed on the playmat, kicking the kitchen door shut behind her before she knelt down.

"What happened then?" she asked, eager to hear the rest of his story.

"I just couldn't get the thought of this man out of my head," he continued. "Norah's presence had begun to seem natural and convincing to me." He crossed back from the worktop to the table and poured Martha a second glass of wine.

She didn't really want it, but if it meant putting off whatever they were going to have to do later then she'd take it.

"I went to China with Bai, my girlfriend at the time, and while I was there she was chatting in Chinese with her family a lot so I had plenty of time to think about Bernard and Norah. Being with a Chinese person also meant that I saw a lot of local culture and customs. Honouring the dead was a huge thing for

Bai's family, and ghosts and spirits are really important to the Chinese. You just don't make light of what we call the paranormal over there. It just dawned on me one day – what if Norah really *was* talking to Bernard? If she could see stuff and know stuff that he couldn't and she was busy filling him in about it? It was like a light bulb going off in my brain – the simplest solution. Cancer had taken her before she was ready to go but her passing was merely an end to her physical body. We're not just made up of our bodies – what if her *consciousness*, free now from all the drugs and the pain and the disease, was able to rise up and just carry on living with the man she loved?"

"You old romantic!" said Martha, fastening Ruby's bib around her neck. She rose and sat back down at the table. Taking the bottle Will handed to her, she popped it in Ruby's mouth.

"I just stopped thinking 'Why?'," said Will, "and opened myself up to 'Why not?' Then I met Gabriel at my dad's retirement party of all places. He was on a date with one of his old army buddies – well, it was complicated – but he spent the whole evening talking to me which was the end of his date and the start of a few worries for my mum for a while! Anyway, he intrigued me. Did he tell you about Laurence?"

Martha nodded. "How awful to lose your brother in an accident when you didn't even know you had one."

Will's brow furrowed momentarily. "Laurence didn't die by accident," he said.

"But Gabriel told me he drowned!"

"He was drowned alright," said Will gravely. "But by someone else. Laurence was murdered by a guy called Martin Pine who it later emerged was a known paedophile. That's why his parents never told Gabriel he had an older brother – they just didn't know how."

Martha was stunned. Gabriel had shown no signs that something this horrific had happened to his brother. Her heart went out to him – he was probably so used to hiding the truth that it came like second nature to him. "So Laurence *is* actually the real reason he doesn't do 'bairns' then?"

"It has to be a large part of it," agreed Will.

They fell silent for a while and watched Ruby drain her bottle, her eyes closed tight. Martha eased the empty bottle from her lips and replaced it with a soother from her pocket to allow the baby to drift off to sleep, to avoid having to take her upstairs. Martha's earlier positivity was almost gone.

"I take it that's why you decided to study parapsychology then?" said Martha, eager to keep the conversation going.

"Gabriel told me about it. He almost challenged me to come and do it and to get back to him when I was done – defying me not to believe – you know what he's like!"

"Now listen here, William . . ." said Martha in a deep voice, with a bad Scottish accent.

Will guffawed at the terrible impersonation and Ruby jumped in her sleep. "Oh shit, sorry!" He chuckled again. "I only started the course last year so I'm a bit of a rank amateur really. Parallel to the course is the study I'm doing on Gabriel himself. He fascinates me. I just follow him round as he does his thing sometimes. I go to his spiritualist church occasionally as well – my fellow parapsychology students would frown on me for having a shred of belief but I think a little differently about the . . . supernatural, as it were, than them."

"How's that?"

Will thought carefully for a moment. "Anything supernatural or paranormal is supposed not to be scientific. But if it's real – and I think it is – then it's a law of science, just one we haven't discovered or pinned down yet. If it exists, then it's all science. The question is proving it exists and that's where I am coming from. I don't want to prove it *doesn't* exist and deep down I think a lot of people like me want that too. To prove it exists, I try to get as much experience of so-called paranormal activity as I can, so I just hang about with Gabriel. He likes to help people – he doesn't advertise, but word gets round. He visits people in their homes who are having problems of a paranormal nature and he tries to help. I help him out sometimes – check for things like high EMF, add a scientific perspective to things. We're quite the team!"

"And that's how Gabriel earns his living then?"

"Oh no," replied Will. "He refuses to take payment for helping people out. He won't do private readings either. He wants folk to believe his skill is *real* and not something he's using to make a fast buck."

"So how does he live?"

Will grinned. "He'll kill you if he finds out I told you this but he's a tour guide on the Edinburgh Bus Tours!"

Martha's face creased and her shoulders shook with silent laughter.

Will joined in. "He's only here with us because his bus is broken down and they don't need him for a few days!"

That made Martha laugh harder. "I'm not laughing at what he does," she said eventually, wiping away tears of laughter from her eyes. "It's just that it's *Gabriel* doing it! I thought he owned an art gallery, or a restaurant or something!"

"I know. He's such a grand old dame and the tourists love him! He makes a fortune on tips! Brilliant at his job, he is!"

"He's just one surprise after another, isn't he?" said Martha, shaking her head.

"A gift that keeps on giving," giggled Will.

They sat in silence again for a while.

"I think someone should go to bed," said Will eventually, nodding at Ruby.

Martha had to agree. The baby was beginning to sweat in her mother's arms and had an expression of discomfort on her tiny features. It was time, thought Martha, and glanced for the first time at the cameras dotted around the room, the cable taped to the floor. While they chatted she had completely forgotten that they existed. A feeling of dread filled her stomach.

"What do I have to do, Will?"

Will sat forward and placed his hands, palms down, on the table in front of her. "Nothing," he said. "Just put Ruby down and then do whatever you'd have done before all of this started – watch TV, work, knit, read a book – whatever."

Martha gave a weak smile.

"I'll be outside keeping an eye on everything," he assured her. "In the meantime, keep an ear and an eye out in here and tell me about anything unusual that you notice – anything that you see or hear or feel – chances are there won't be a single thing. In the vast majority of cases that I've investigated, nothing physical happens."

Martha nodded, noting carefully what he was saying.

"Just think back to whatever Gabriel said to you earlier," continued Will. "You seemed to feel a lot better after you spoke to him."

"I did," said Martha, almost reassuring herself as she stood up and walked slowly toward the kitchen door.

"We'll put Ruby down together, will we?" suggested Will quietly, as though encouraging a child.

Martha smiled, then nodded and faced down the hallway as Will held the kitchen door open for her.

The hallway felt different, cooler. Martha knew this had to be because of the open bedroom windows and the contrasting warmth of the kitchen where they had been for a long time. She stood at the bottom of the stairs and watched Will go ahead of her.

When they reached Ruby's room, they set about making the room ready for her. Will closed the window and blackout blind, pulling together the cream curtains with their lemon trim. Martha carefully placed her daughter in her cot and arranged the cover over her, and Hugo alongside her head to snuggle into. She switched on the nightlight and turned to survey the room. Everything was as it should be.

She turned to walk away, her hip brushing against the bars of the cot as she did so and she heard a familiar noise – a plastic clicking in her pocket. She took the small collection of soothers out and placed them on the changing mat, high up on the changing unit. She looked at them, hesitated, and then picked them up again, putting them instead on the night table lower down.

She glanced at the chimney-breast and thought for the first time since returning to Eyrie Farm about the small voice on Will's recording. Had something genuinely awful been done here to a little boy by some man? Was this Mannion his dad, maybe? A grandfather? An uncle? Just some stranger? She still couldn't quite believe it. What if this Mannion came back and tried to hurt Ruby? Mistook her for the other child perhaps . . .

Martha turned suddenly to Will who was checking a small camera on the night table, training it on the soothers, separating them out individually. She grabbed his arm.

"Please, Will, let me put her in my bed with me," she pleaded, panicking at the idea of not being with Ruby.

Will straightened and gently grasped Martha's hand. "It'll be fine," he said, gently rubbing her fingers. "It's really important that everything's as normal."

"But –"

"Come with me for a minute. Let me show you something." He guided Martha gently from the room.

She took a long look at her daughter with a worried face, but allowed herself to be led.

Once on the landing, Will produced the parent unit of her baby monitor from a clip on his belt and pressed the switch. He must have brought it with him from the kitchen, thought Martha. All the little lights across the top of the unit suddenly came on at once, as they did when the unit was first switched on.

Martha's mind flashed back suddenly to the night in the conservatory with Sue. That growling noise, she recalled. Was that the start of all of this? She didn't have time to think any further because Will was steering her down the stairs. She glanced behind her once, then they carried on downstairs, through the front door, and out to the open boot of Will's car. Wires trailed from the boot through the letterbox. The boot was packed with equipment boxes and Will opened one to show Martha a laptop within. He lifted the screen, blank at first, and then it flashed into life. Martha leaned in further to see that the screen was split into four different sections. She recognised her kitchen in one, the dining room in another and the two top screens were her room and Ruby's. She saw the sleeping form of her daughter in night vision, unmoving in her cot.

"That screen doesn't change," said Will, tapping the image of the baby's room. "Once you've gone to bed, then the screen showing your room won't change either. I'll be watching you both at all times, but I can only do that from out here and you can see how close I am if you need me."

Martha nodded. "What about the other rooms?"

Will ran his fingers over the mouse pad and the two lower quarters of the screen flicked to the bathroom, the conservatory, the living room and then the dining area. "I can keep an eye on them from here – every room is monitored and I'm recording it all as well."

Martha noted three cables similar to the laptop cable stretching toward the house and assumed that there were more computers in other storage boxes.

"I can analyse it afterwards," said Will, "but for the time being I can watch you and Ruby constantly all night – if you want me to, that is?"

"Of course! But Ruby's the most important person here," she said forcefully. She thought for a moment. "How will I . . ." she started and trailed off.

"What?"

"Well, how will I manage – I mean, you'll look away . . . ?"

"When you're changing?" said Will, almost shyly.

Martha flushed bright pink. "Umm, yes."

Will smiled. "Tell you what, when you go upstairs, go right up to the camera and give me the thumbs-up. I promise I'll blank your screen and when you're tucked up in bed just text me and I'll get you back online right away. No funny business, I promise!"

Martha smiled. "I don't want to end up on Youtube in my jammies or anything," she grinned.

"Heaven forbid," said Will and squeezed her arm. "Are you okay?"

Martha looked back at the house. The summer dusk was falling. It was that time of evening where it was much brighter outside than in. The hallway looked dark and forbidding. She thought about her conversation with Gabriel earlier, tried to summon strength again from his words. She took a deep breath.

"Not really," she replied. "But Gabriel thinks that this is the right thing to do to help that little . . . boy." It felt strange to talk about it after such a normal evening. "So I can't *not* do it, can I?"

Will smiled. "Good girl," he said and gave her arm another reassuring squeeze. He unclipped the monitor from his belt and handed it to her. "With the knowledge of what you've experienced, I'm much more prepared now. Let's do it then?"

Martha breathed deeply and nodded.

"Mind yourself," said Will.

"No, *you* mind me!" she replied and immediately felt foolish.

Will looked at her, saw that she was tiny and vulnerable and impulsively wrapped her in a hug. She was crushed in his arms and breathed in his smell which was new and comforting at the same time. "I'll mind you," he said, and she felt momentarily safe. He released her from the hug. "I'll mind you both."

Martha stepped back and turned to the front door, facing it head on. She stepped inside the hallway carefully and closed it behind her, alone again in the darkening hallway, with whatever, or whoever was sharing her home.

She stood with her back to the front door and looked up the stairs and down the passage to the kitchen. She was aware that she was literally a few feet away from Will, but with the door closed behind her it felt like a million miles. She became aware that she could hear her breathing and, once aware of it, couldn't block it out. In-out-in-out – she took a deep breath to try to calm herself.

She didn't want to move. Maybe if she stayed in this spot, close to safety, she would hear nothing. She then remembered the cameras and felt foolish knowing that there was a possibility that Will could see her. She took another deep breath and began to walk toward the kitchen. Act normal, she said to herself, glancing sideways into the open doorways along the passage, unable not to look yet terrified by the prospect of seeing anything.

What would I normally do? she thought, keeping Will's words in mind. Bottles, she thought. I'd normally do the bottles. She set to work at the sink, washing out dirty bottles and placing them in the steriliser. Then she washed up the dinner things while the bottles steam-sterilised in the microwave and boiled the kettle to make fresh ones.

She left the steriliser to cool for a few moments before lifting the lid. When she did, a huge cloud of steam wafted out in her face and she stepped back a little to let it dissipate in the air. Suddenly, she froze. Out of the corner of her eye she saw a white shape float past her. Instinctively she spun around. Nothing. Of course it was just steam playing with her overactive imagination.

Martha held her breath and scanned the room. Again, nothing. She glanced at the camera on the fridge, her heart pounding, and turned back toward the bottles. She knew that she had seen absolutely nothing but she couldn't shake a feeling that there had been someone right behind her as she opened the steriliser. She carefully concentrated on the task at hand – measuring out the hot water into each bottle, assembling the various components that made them up – teat, collar, lid. When four of them were filled she left them neatly on the worktop to cool.

Her next task was to tidy Ruby's toys. She began to pick up various plastic bricks, teddies, books . . . She jumped again as a shadow moved across the wall beside her, but it was merely light reflected from a mirror attached to the tummy of a colourful stuffed duckling. Martha straightened her back and stretched it, willing herself to get a grip, aware that her movements were being recorded.

She glanced around the kitchen. There were no other jobs left to do there. Normally she'd check the locks on the doors before retiring to the living room or her study but Will had triple-checked them earlier to make sure there was no access from outside.

What to do next, Martha thought. She poured herself another glass of wine, contemplated taking the bottle through to the living room with her and decided against it to keep her wits about her. She placed the cork back in the neck of the bottle, wedged it down, and made her way to the living room.

Once inside, she turned on the big overhead light rather than one of her lamps and closed the curtains in the bay window, smiling in the general direction she thought that Will might be. With the light on, all she could see in the window was the reflection of the room behind her.

Martha turned on the TV set and then sat down on the couch with the remote control in her hand. So far, so good, she thought, feeling the earlier glasses of wine begin to give her the Dutch courage she needed. She flicked through channels for a while, decided on the news and then couldn't fully concentrate so she found an episode of *Desperate Housewives* and settled on that instead. She lost herself in back to back episodes, muting the TV occasionally to listen for noise in the rest of the house, constantly checking the monitor to make sure it was working properly. All was silent. There weren't even the usual creaks that the cottage made as it settled for the night. Ruby too was calm, making Martha grateful that she was getting a peaceful night's sleep.

After a while watching TV, she found herself growing tired and lay down on the couch to stretch herself out, realising that all that time she had been virtually folded into a fixed position on the very corner of the couch, legs underneath her and arms folded across her chest. She was glad that Will had encouraged her to drink the wine – it certainly made her a lot calmer than she thought she would have been. Normally, she might have enjoyed a hot shower before bed but she was acutely aware that there was a camera trained on the bathroom and she didn't entirely trust Will's thumbs-up system. He had instructed her to act normally but the night was anything but.

Martha yawned deeply. All the stress and effort was telling on her now. It was no good – she was going to have to go to bed. She would have loved to stay where she was, to doze on the sofa with the reassuring hum of the TV in the background but she knew she had to do what she normally did. She decided to do it quickly, like ripping off a plaster. She turned off the TV and left the room without a second glance.

Her bedroom was freezing, the window still open, letting in the night air. She shut it quickly and pulled her curtains. Looking around her room, she was satisfied that nothing untoward had happened – so far anyway. She spotted the camera secured to the wall high up in the corner by the door and as agreed went right up to it and gave an enthusiastic thumbs-up. She wondered if Will had seen her and when he would blank out her screen – if at all. To give it more time, she crossed the landing, switching on the small lamp on the low table outside her room, and peered in at Ruby. To her relief, everything was fine. Nothing had been touched in the room – including the soothers on the small night table. That gave her the most relief, Martha realised. She retreated to her own room, undressing cautiously, like she might in a changing room at the gym – just in case – and climbed into bed.

Martha thought about what to text Will. 'In bed now, as if you don't know' was her first thought but she rejected it. The jokey tone in her head wouldn't translate well into text and Will would think she was accusing him of being a pervert. Eventually she decided on 'Ready' and put the phone down on her bedside table before turning her back to the camera and lying down. She left her lamp on, certainly not brave enough to commit herself to the dark.

The phone buzzed on the night table and Martha jumped. "Jesus, Will," she muttered under her breath and then regretted it, remembering too late that the house was wired to record sound as well. She checked the text: "Try 2 gt sm sleep. Will. X" She noted the 'X' and smiled to herself. The text was brief. Was that just Will's way, or was there perhaps something going on that she didn't know about, that it would be best she slept through? Immediately her mind began to race. She thought about texting Will back to ask but didn't. Why on earth would she want to risk getting an answer that told her anything other than that things were fine?

She rolled onto her side again and stared at the wardrobe, and it was in this position that, despite herself, she fell asleep fifteen minutes later.

30

July 15th

In her dream, Martha was lying on her side in her bed in London. Dan had been out but she'd heard the bedroom door creak open, had heard his footsteps gingerly cross the room. She had a feeling of dread as he lifted the covers and climbed in beside her.

The movement of the duvet was what woke her and she rushed back into herself from the dream. Her eyes flew open and she tried to focus on what was in front of her. It should have been the wardrobe.

On the pillow, facing her directly, was a woman's face. Martha could clearly make out short black hair, pudgy cheeks and the beginnings of a double chin. The duvet was spread across the two of them, causing it to be elevated in the centre and Martha was vaguely aware of being able to *feel* the length of a body in the bed beside her. She was completely confused. She blinked, lifted her head off the pillow and scrunched up her eyes. She opened them again. The face was still there, if anything closer to her own face, almost nose to nose.

Martha jerked her head back, got a clearer look at the pasty, doughy skin, almost grey in colour and the deep-set dark eyes glaring back at her from under bushy brows.

Then it dawned on Martha that although she could see and

feel the clear physical shape of a person beside her, she could also see *through* the woman, could clearly make out the wardrobe and the wall behind her.

Martha screamed – more of a yell than a scream – and propelled herself from the bed, throwing herself into a standing position. She turned back to face the bed. It was empty, but the figure was now standing beside it, facing Martha, mirroring her posture. Its mouth was now moving, but no sound emerged. Martha yelled again and made a dash for the door. Instantly the figure was in front of her again. Martha couldn't fathom how it had moved – a black shadowy streak across the room from the bed to between Martha and the door handle.

Martha could see what the woman was wearing – a plain, round-necked sweater over an old-fashioned pencil skirt, ruffled around the hem. Black shoes with thick heels about an inch high. At the same time she could clearly make out the door through her. In a split second it crossed her mind to wonder if she could put her hand through the woman as well.

The woman's mouth moved again. Panic rose higher and higher in Martha as the grey, pasty face drew nearer and nearer to her. She took a step back and the face remained as close as ever. Martha opened her mouth to scream again but stopped as she finally heard what the figure was saying in a low, rasping whisper.

"*Shut the brat up!*" it hissed, the words not in synch with the movement of the mouth like a badly dubbed movie. "*Shut it up! He won't take me back if he hears the brat.*" There was a vile stench from the figure, like rotten vegetables.

Martha stepped back again, her breath shallow and coming so fast she thought her heart might explode. "Let me *out!*" she roared, her mind a jumble.

The figure vanished instantly. Martha stared at the spot where it had been. She swivelled around and scanned the room. Nothing. All of a sudden she heard a squeal from Ruby's room and then she heard her daughter start to cry.

She lunged for the door handle, her mind again registering the rotten smell as she moved through where the figure had been.

Ruby's screams grew louder, the same cry that she made when she hurt herself, a terrible squeal followed by silence as she drew in a huge breath followed by a scream as she exhaled and the crying grew more pitiful.

Martha's hand slipped on the door-handle – she was lathered in sweat underneath her pyjamas. "*Come on!*" she roared in desperation and tried the handle again. The door opened and she dashed across the landing, tripping as she went over the small table where the lamp stood. It had moved – been moved – from its position in the corner to the middle of the corridor floor. Like the buggy, thought Martha, as she caught it with her foot and spread her arms out to try to recover her balance. She didn't fall, but the table did, clattering to the ground and bringing with it the lamp, the ceramic base shattering in pieces as it hit the floor. There was a loud bang as the light-bulb blew, followed by darkness.

Martha reached out for the wall to steady herself. With her free arm she pushed the door of Ruby's room wide open and managed to propel herself in. The moons and stars circled silently, as always, calm and restful, but Ruby lay in her cot, her arms and legs rigid and trembling. She was screaming now, rather than crying, and staring at the chimney-breast.

Martha gathered her up in her arms, frantically shushing her and turning toward the doorway. Ruby remained rigid. It was then that Martha realised she could hear a scratching noise, not as loud as usual and not as fast but growing in speed and intensity. A loud crash from behind her made her turn suddenly in the direction that so fixated Ruby. The huge painting of the hare had tipped over and there was the figure again, at the chimney-breast, beating with its fists against the wall.

Martha could clearly see the exposed brick through what still managed to look like a solid body. She was frozen to the spot, unable to take her eyes off the spectre pounding the wall, its hands moving so quickly they were a shady blur. Then the screaming started again, the same as she had heard it before – sobbing, gasping, squealing.

"Go '*way*, Mannion!" it screamed this time, a child's muffled voice as though coming from another room.

Martha knew finally, for sure, that it wasn't from another room. She knew exactly where it was coming from, knew that what Gabriel had said was irrefutably true.

The child's screaming grew more wretched and Ruby's own wails louder. Martha was almost deafened by the cries of the children and the scrabbling from the wall. She couldn't bear it.

"*Leave him alone!*" she screamed at the shape.

The figure was immediately still, its hands still raised to the wall as if frozen in mid-action. Suddenly it was facing Martha. She hadn't seen it move but it was instantly in the new position. Its hands were by its sides and Martha stared at it again, registering the hideous, emotionless eyes, breathing in the terrible stench.

She realised suddenly that the figure wasn't stationary, but drifting toward her, floating with barely any discernible movement. It was getting closer and closer. "*What have you done?*" it bellowed – the mouth again out of synch with the words, the voice loud and booming this time. It sounded like it had an echo to Martha, or worse still, like it was made up of two voices at once, coming from inside a tunnel. Martha had never heard anything like it. All she could do was stare, seeing for the first time the inside of the phantom's mouth with dirty, broken and rotted teeth, the tongue black as though it had eaten coal, or liquorice.

Ruby screamed again and it brought Martha back to her senses. She pressed Ruby's head into her shoulder and turned and ran from the room, feeling the presence of the entity behind her, just an arm's reach away. Panic rose in Martha, her breath coming in gasps.

The landing was flooded with light from her bedroom which reached the first three or four steps of the stairs but she knew that once she got past the turn in the stair that she would be descending into pitch blackness. She forged ahead, terrified by the prospect of the darkness, even more terrified by the thing that she could feel gaining ground behind her.

An involuntary shudder ran up her back. It's going to touch me, she thought. She screamed again, a proper scream from the base of her throat, couldn't dare to look back for fear of tripping on the stair yet aware with a million senses that she was about to be touched . . .

Suddenly the light in the hallway came on. Martha stopped on the stairs, momentarily blinded and confused . . .

Will! In her blind panic she had completely forgotten that he was there. The feeling that she would be grabbed was gone with the light, the child upstairs stopped crying and Ruby finally relaxed in her arms, her screams reduced to whimpers of incomprehension. Martha turned and looked up the stairs. It was all gone – the stench, the noise, the atmosphere – as if it had been *sucked* upward and away. She stood still and stared at the landing.

Will made a thump as he tripped on the bottom step in his panic to reach her. "Martha, what's going on?" he demanded, his breaths short, his voice urgent.

She was transfixed by the landing, unable to tear her gaze away from where, seconds before, that awful thing had been. She was terrified it would suddenly reappear but couldn't move except to point. "She . . . she . . ." Her words were barely audible.

"What?" barked Will.

Martha blinked and looked at him, as though trying to ascertain if he were real. "She was upstairs," she said, her voice growing stronger and her brain trying to make sense of language to tell Will what had happened. "I think it was Mannion – it's a woman. She spoke to me . . ."

Will didn't reply. He dashed past Martha and up the stairs, pulling his BlackBerry out of his pocket as he did so. Martha watched him disappear into Ruby's room and turned to make her way down the stairs.

"Gabriel?" she heard him say. "Can you make your way out here? I think it's time."

Martha made her way to the study, her sanctuary, and sank down onto the couch. Ruby sobbed quietly and Martha held her close, stroking her downy hair and muttering words of comfort.

253

The little girl didn't fall back to sleep but sat on Martha's knee, wide-eyed and curious.

At last she heard Will clatter down the stairs and tread down the hallway toward her. Relief flooded through her body when she saw his reassuring face. He came to sit beside her on the sofa.

"Are you okay?" He placed his arm around Martha and gave her a squeeze, then leaned toward Ruby and lifted her face to his with a gentle finger under her chin. The baby studied him with her huge blue eyes and solemn face.

"We're fine," said Martha, realising that her voice was trembling and that her legs felt like jelly.

"What happened up there?"

"Is she gone?" said Martha.

"There was nothing up there that I could see," replied Will gently.

She told him as accurately as she could, the process slow as she sought the right words to describe what she had seen. Will listened without comment, nodding in encouragement when Martha struggled for words.

"I could even *smell* her, Will. Couldn't you see anything?"

Will shook his head. "The screen to your room went completely blank on me. I thought it was technical but it seems now that it wasn't. One minute you were there asleep and the next the screen went blank. The first I knew there was anything wrong was when I heard that lamp break and then you showed up in Ruby's room, shouting at the wall. I'll need to review the footage very carefully of course but nothing of what you've described has shown up on camera, just your reaction to it."

Martha closed her eyes, exhausted, and leant her head against Will's comforting arm. They sat like this, barely speaking, for what could have been ten or fifteen minutes until there was a voice from the hallway, a heavy tread of footsteps.

"Hallooo?" it called.

Martha jumped.

Will squeezed her arm. "It's just Gabriel," he said.

Martha closed her eyes with gratitude. The more the merrier, she thought. As long as they have a pulse.

"We're in here, Gabriel," replied Will and the heavy tread came down the corridor.

Gabriel appeared at the door. "What's happened here? You all look like you've seen a . . . not funny?"

Will frowned at him. "How did you get here so fast?" he asked.

"Taxi driver at the door was dropping off as I came out. Had to walk up from the road again, of course."

Gabriel sat and Martha ran through her story for a second time and Will his, adding in some phrases that she didn't fully understand: references to 'thermals' and 'K2s'. She did gather that the only thing that Will had noticed was that the temperature in the house as a whole had dropped dramatically just before all of this began.

"What time is it?" she suddenly asked, aware that she hadn't a clue.

"It's four in the morning, love," said Gabriel kindly.

Sure enough she could see a lightening in the sky and as Gabriel and Will chatted quietly between them she heard the first chirrup of the dawn chorus. She couldn't wait for daylight.

"Right then," said Gabriel, standing up straight. "Time for me to see what I can do. Martha, I'll need a hand from you."

A look of fear flashed across her face. "What do I have to do?" She didn't want to see that *thing* again, or worse still, hear the screaming of the little boy.

"Just hold my hand, that's all," said Gabriel.

"What about Ruby," said Martha. "Will – you'll watch her, won't you?"

Will shook his head. "I can't, I've got to monitor closely what Gabriel's about to do."

"She'll be safe in here," said Gabriel. "William can assign one of his magic screens to her and we can make a wee nest for her on the floor out of cushions."

Gabriel reached out and rubbed Ruby's hand. Ruby, in turn,

grabbed his finger and studied his face intently. Martha found herself almost as shocked by this as by the rest of the night's events.

"Will, can't you take her out to your car and watch her out there?" she pleaded.

"It's too cold out there, Martha," he replied. "I can't close the boot with the cables and it's a hatchback. It might be July but it's the middle of the night – it wouldn't be fair on her."

"But what if –"

"She won't come in here," interrupted Gabriel. "I'm pretty sure this room didn't exist when she lived here so it doesn't exist for her now. I've picked up nothing from it – from her – any time I've been in here."

So that was why she always felt safe in here! Do you swear you'll keep her on screen, Will?" begged Martha. "And if the screen goes blank you'll go straight to her, no matter what?"

"Cross my heart," replied Will.

Martha built Ruby a soft nest on the floor out of the cushions and the throw from the sofa. Gabriel retrieved some of her toys from the kitchen and even found a soother beside the steriliser which she rattled in her pudgy hand, watching the grown-ups fuss over her so intently. Martha was eventually satisfied that she couldn't come to any harm – physically, at least, and laid her down on her back.

"They can't fall any further than the floor," remarked Gabriel.

Martha supposed it made sense and Ruby promptly waved her legs in the air and started to play with her feet through her babygro.

"Come on," urged Gabriel. "The sooner we get started, the sooner we get this over with."

Much as Will had led her reluctantly from Ruby's room earlier, Gabriel led her from the study now and Martha shut the door behind her, unwillingly leaving her daughter for the second time that night.

Once in the hallway, the door closed behind them, Gabriel took Martha by her hand and led her back upstairs. Once again she heard the front door close as Will slipped out to begin whatever it was he was going to do.

Gabriel switched off the downstairs lights as they climbed, and Martha felt her anxiety build again. She allowed herself to be led to Ruby's room and they stepped inside, Gabriel closing the door behind him and switching off the overhead light which Will must have switched on. Once again, the nightlight was the only illumination.

Gabriel saw Martha glance at the shapes as they rotated around the walls. "I normally use a candle," he said, "but these will do fine. Now hold my hands."

Martha nervously did as she was bidden, unsure exactly what she was doing.

Gabriel stepped towards the bricked-up fireplace, guiding Martha with him. He grasped her hands firmly. "I want you to imagine a white light around you," he said, bowing his head and squeezing his eyes shut.

Martha looked at him as he did so and followed suit, imagining the white light protecting her, enclosing her body in a protective bubble as he instructed. She tried her hardest to focus but found it difficult to keep her thoughts in one place, distracted by the fact that Ruby was alone downstairs.

Gabriel sensed this. "Try to concentrate, Martha," he urged. "I know it's difficult but do your best."

Martha shut her eyes, a pit of fear in her stomach, and concentrated on Gabriel's hands squeezing hers. He continued to mutter some words that Martha could neither hear nor understand. She assumed it was an incantation of protection of some sort and trusted in Gabriel's abilities to keep her safe.

Finally, he fell silent and after a moment, cleared his throat and began to speak.

"I would like to speak with Mrs Mannion, please," he said clearly and concisely, as though communicating with someone who had a poor grasp of English.

Martha almost giggled aloud with nerves at how strange it sounded.

"Or is it Miss Mannion?" asked Gabriel.

Martha jumped as a loud bang came from downstairs somewhere. Gabriel flinched as well and his eyes flickered open for a moment.

"Is it . . .?" whispered Martha.

"*Ssssh!*" he replied fiercely.

Martha closed her eyes again and concentrated hard. Please don't let that have been near Ruby, she prayed silently, fighting the instinctive urge to run.

"Is that you making noise, Miss Mannion?" asked Gabriel again in his loud voice. "This isn't your house any more, you know. Are you aware that you've passed over, Miss Mannion?"

There was another loud bang, from upstairs this time, just outside the bedroom door. Martha jumped again, her eyes opening in panic to check the door to the room. There was nothing there.

"You don't belong here any more, Miss Mannion," said Gabriel. "It's time for you to move on, to cross over."

Martha felt the room go cold in an instant, the temperature dropping as it had downstairs in the kitchen before the spoon was knocked from her hand. She glanced around, terrified that she might see the awful spectre again but still there was nothing, just the room as it always was. She shivered involuntarily as it grew colder.

"She's here," she whispered to Gabriel.

He nodded, deep in concentration.

"Henry, you're here too, aren't you, wee man?" he said in a gentler voice.

Martha's eyes grew wide in alarm. She was almost prepared to see again what she had seen earlier – at least she knew what to expect. But to see yet another spirit? And that of a child?

"It's alright, Henry, we're here to help you," said Gabriel. "Now can you think of someone that you want to see again the most? Your mummy, maybe?"

Martha opened her mouth to speak to Gabriel. Why hadn't she told him before what Lil Flynn had said, of her suspicion that this Mannion *was* his mother.

Suddenly she became aware of a strange sensation behind her. There was a feeling of heat behind her legs, as though she were standing in front of a low heater. Then a slight tug on the hem of her pyjama top. She turned her head to look but there was nothing there that she could see in the dim light. She turned back to Gabriel, willing him to open his eyes and look at her so she didn't feel so alone. She also wanted to see if he could see something behind her legs because she was suddenly sure that the warm feeling was Henry. She had an urge to turn and touch him, comfort him in some way. Her eyes filled with tears for him. If what she felt was Henry it reached only halfway up her thigh. She was a small woman – would that make him a very small child for nearly four?

"You also, Miss Mannion," said Gabriel. "I think you have done some evil in your time to this child, am I right? But there must be someone who has passed who will come for you?" Gabriel fell silent, waiting for a response.

Martha was still aware of the strange sensation against her legs.

Gabriel gripped her hands tighter. "Both of you, Henry and Miss Mannion, should see a light over by the door. That light is for you both. It's growing now, ready to receive you – don't be afraid of it. Henry, whoever you want to see the most will be there in that light for you and you'll be safe and happy. No one will hurt you any more, wee pet. Now walk toward that light and don't be scared."

Martha wondered if Gabriel could see the little soul because no sooner had he urged him to walk to the light than she felt the heat separate itself from her legs, felt no more the gentle tug on the back of her pyjamas. The sensation was sudden, and she turned, instinctively. "Henry . . ." she said, but realised it was too late. He was gone.

"And you, Miss Mannion," said Gabriel, "you must follow the boy. I pray that our Lord Jesus Christ, and God His Father can forgive you for what you have done in this life. I pray that you are truly sorry. Now don't be afraid of the light –"

He was cut short by the same feeling that Martha had

experienced on the stairs, that they both now felt again. It was a feeling of everything being sucked from the room, out through the doorway. Into the light, Martha assumed.

Gabriel looked up and scanned the room. "Oh," he said, quietly and thoughtfully.

"What's up?"

He still held her hands and looked all around him. "That didn't feel . . . it was different, that's all," he said, his eyes continuing to scan the room, a puzzled expression on his face.

"Are they gone?" whispered Martha.

Gabriel turned back to face her. "I suppose they are. There's nothing here any more so they must have crossed."

Martha could feel the temperature rising around her, except at the back of her legs where they were strangely chilly.

Gabriel sighed, then took a deep breath and closed his eyes again. He bowed his head and Martha felt that she should do the same. They stood there for a few moments, heads lowered, until Gabriel released Martha's hands gently.

"All is done," he said.

Martha noticed him scanning the room again, as though checking for something. All of a sudden an overwhelming urge to cry came over her and she began to sob. Gabriel said nothing, just put his arms around her.

Martha had no idea where the outburst of emotion came from. She didn't think she had ever felt so sad – that poor little boy, snuggling into her legs. Had she imagined it? She didn't think so. Suddenly she wanted to know what had happened to him there, what the story of his short life was and that of the dumpy woman dressed in black. What on earth had happened here that their spirits remained? Until now?

Finally she forced the tears to stop and sniffed loudly before extricating herself from Gabriel's embrace. "I'd better go to Ruby," she said, her voice thick with tears.

Gabriel nodded and she walked from the room, leaving him again looking around him.

The sky had turned to full daylight as Martha made her way

down the stairs. She walked down the hallway, opened the study door gently and her heart filled with relief and joy as she saw her daughter, safe and sound asleep in the nest that they had made for her. She padded over to the sofa and sat down on the cushionless base and stared at Ruby, her smooth brow, her pink cheeks flushed with sleep. At her fingers spread wide in a star shape, at her tiny blonde curls. She was overwhelmed with love and couldn't tear her eyes away from the sleeping form of her child.

Martha heard Gabriel tread down the stairs, and the front door open as Will let himself back in. They spoke to each other briefly in muffled voices and she heard them step lightly by and into the kitchen. One of them filled the kettle and Martha heard it click and gently start to boil. Just another morning, she thought, and was gripped with sudden tiredness. She leaned back and closed her eyes for a moment but opened them soon after, sensing another person in the room.

Will stood quietly at the door, watching her. He smiled when she looked up and she took in his face – his dark brown eyes, tousled hair, kind expression. Martha smiled back and they looked at each other for a moment or two before Will extended a hand to her and indicated that she should follow him.

Martha pushed herself up off the sofa, took a look at Ruby who remained asleep and reached out for Will's hand. He clasped it gently but firmly, stroking it with his thumb as they walked to the kitchen where Gabriel was pouring boiling water into three cups. Martha sank onto one of the kitchen chairs and Will squeezed her hand before letting it fall and crossing to the worktop where she saw his laptop was booting up.

Gabriel passed him and plonked a steaming cup of tea in front of Martha. She smiled her thanks, too exhausted to speak, and stared at the mug – a brown pottery mug with a ceramic sheep forming the handle. What an ordinary thing, she thought. And to follow what they had just done with a cup of tea at five o'clock on a summer's morning. It was surreal.

"Gabriel, I want your opinion on this," said Will, pointing to the laptop screen.

Martha could make out Ruby's room on the screen and in the centre herself and Gabriel holding hands. She picked up her tea and walked out to the conservatory – whatever it was, she didn't want to see it. For her, this was all over, her part played, the dead at rest. What was Will's word? Closure – that was it. She had closure.

Martha sank down onto her wicker chair and drank in the sight of the brightening garden. Dew sparkled on the grass and a lazy bee hovered around the lavender. She had closure, she thought. Except she didn't, did she? She couldn't kid herself that this was the end and that she was now free to walk away. What had gone on here? What was real and what wasn't? When had this happened? How had Henry ended up bricked into a *fireplace?*

Martha shuddered. How had the small little thing she was sure she had felt hiding behind her half an hour beforehand spent his last moments? Had he been gasping for air in that soot-filled atmosphere, bricked up in a tiny space – the fireplace in her own room had just enough room for a single log in the grate, and the chimneys were narrow and tight. Had he suffocated? Had he died of hunger and thirst? Of fear? Who had put him there – that woman? Who had done the actual *brickwork*, for heaven's sake? What had the spirit meant when she had said that someone wouldn't come if he didn't shut up?

Her mind raced. She remembered when she hadn't cared – when her sole focus had been getting away, which she still wanted to do. It had been easier then, not knowing, *choosing* not to know. But now she had to know. She couldn't pack her car and go back to begin again in London without getting to the bottom of all this. There was someone she had to speak to.

31

Eyrie Farm,
Shipton Abbey,
Norfolk,
England

February 1st, 1957

Dear Caroline,

Oh, what joy is in my heart as I write on this fine spring day. There is sunshine and snowdrops and at last a little warmth in that sun and I am a different girl from the one who wrote to you this day last year from the depths of misery.

That misery is lifted from my shoulders, Caroline. What a year it has been, a complete turnaround in my fortunes and only good to come, please God, as we gather pace into 1957 and as I come of age today.

I shall start with Marion – it is scarcely to be believed but her love affair with Albie continues to flourish and last month he finally proposed marriage to her and gave her the most beautiful ring I have ever seen – a single milky perfect pearl rising up out

263

of a nest of no less than ten round cut diamonds on a platinum band. He had it made especially for her in London and presented it to her on New Year's Day, going down on one knee and asking her to be his bride. She has been too elated to be cruel to myself and Henry and is soon to move to live at the house that she and Albie will share once married. She will live there with Albie's grandmother until the wedding, would you believe! She leaves us in two glorious months to move to Bickford, her fortune made, and her secret here in Eyrie Farm intact. I don't care. She will no longer be my responsibility but that of Albie Forbes and that makes my heart cheer with the weight that's lifted from it.

She has me driven mad with the talk of her wedding. Who would have thought it but the Forbes family is Catholic so there is no need of conversion, and as the parish priest in Bickford is a friend of the family (I fear he may be one of the family) they are sorting the paperwork for her so there is no need for a letter of release from Clontarf Parish and therefore no chance of her secret being discovered – the secret that her father is still alive, that is, not the secret of her son who has never been recognised by any church, much less officially baptised. Again, I care not, because she is lost in a swirl of magazines that she has ordered especially and books of flowers, trying to plan their marriage for this summer.

The humour in the house has improved all around. Henry is even managing more little words although when he speaks it sounds funny as he can't pronounce his letter 'r'. And the little rogue insists on calling me Mammy and Marion by her Christian name, except he cannot pronounce it properly so it sounds like 'Mannion'. It sounds very sweet but I try to stop him saying it because there is no guarantee that she won't fly into a rage and it makes her very angry altogether that he doesn't call her 'Mammy', despite the fact that she has spent his short life denying his existence and now aims to enter into a marriage where her husband-to-be has no knowledge of him. When she moves to Bickford I fear that will be it – Henry will be cut out of her life forever because this secret is such that she must never tell. She will never appoint me officially his guardian but to all intents and purposes he is my boy now and I will love him and protect him double what Marion could ever have done. As long as I am alive, Henry will never want for love or care.

He still takes my breath away, Caroline, with his dark brown hair that has lost all his baby curls. I have started to cut it using a pudding bowl as a guide and he looks quite the little man with his big toothy smile. He is still small and thin but that is merely his build – maybe he takes after his father, whoever that scourge may be. He runs around the garden at great speed – he loves to run! I say he will be an athlete when he grows up and then he pelts back across the garden at me and throws his arms around my legs and almost knocks me over and my heart floods with love for him again.

The only sad note in the whole thing is that there is still no word from Daddy, nor from Uncle Thomas, so I have no idea how he is bearing up. I continue to write to him, although not as often as I used to. It is so disheartening to write so often and not hear anything in return.

Things are even looking up here at Eyrie Farm. Mr Mountford is still happy to have us here as his tenants. Well, I say tenants but we pay no rent and I am sure that my father doesn't. I should really talk to him to formalise the arrangements for when Marion moves out but I keep putting it off. Mr Mountford is not my greatest friend since the business of Robert before. On the other hand, he is currently having an extension built for us at the back – a small room downstairs to be used for whatever we wish – a sewing room, or study or another bedroom. And atop that will be a small indoor bathroom – oh, the luxury of it all! All sorts of improvements are being carried out and every day some of Mr Mountford's lads come to the house and work through until teatime. Oh, the life that's around the place with the workmen here! Last year, Albie gave Marion a gift of a transistor radio and miracle of miracles, she lets me share it, so there is always music playing – hits by Elvis Presley, Dean Martin, The Platters. The young men here are always polite and, although Henry has to be hidden upstairs, he too hears the music and dances by wiggling his little bottom around and shuffling his feet. I spend much of my day upstairs with him because it is not fair to lock him away by himself all the day but he seems content, the poor child who has never yet played with another child his own age and has been outside Eyrie Farm only twice and both those times had to be smuggled away in Robert's car.

Marion loves to flirt with the workmen. She feels there is no harm in sitting outside on their piles of bricks, swinging her legs and flashing them smiles. She knows they daren't respond because she flaunts her engagement ring so and makes no secret of telling them that she is to be Mrs Forbes before the year is out. If Albie saw her though I'm sure he'd be none too pleased, for he is a serious chap underneath it all and is very possessive of his Maid Marion as he calls her.

Of course Marion likes nothing better than to play with the boys when they are here and before Christmas, when they had just started, nothing would do her but to challenge one of them that she could build a section of wall faster than he could. Of course the boy, Terry, scoffed at her and said what nonsense she was talking, that women couldn't build walls, so she let him go first, allocated him a section to build and timed him before stepping up herself.

At first of course she made mistakes and made sure to drop some bricks and get some mortar on herself so all the boys laughed. They had gathered in a circle to watch her make a fool of herself, they thought. But don't you remember, Caroline, that when Marion was small, Daddy used to take her sometimes to his jobs and he showed her how to build a wall with the bricks and the mortar and to make sure it was even with a spirit level and all the tricks of the trade. Daddy's little shadow, Mammy used to call her. And how to everyone's surprise, young Marion became very good at building. Mammy used to give out to Daddy, saying what sort of a skill was that to teach a little girl but he used to laugh at her and take Marion off with him all over the place.

Well, she certainly hasn't lost her skill because she beat Terry hands down by a full five minutes in building her section of the wall on the new room. The boys weren't so smart after that I can tell you, and how Marion and I laughed, the first time in years that we have shared something as sisters. It seems silly of me after all that we have been through, after all that she has done to me and to little Henry, but that day gave me a memory to cherish with my big sister, like no other from before.

And now to the best news of all, my oldest friend. You must keep this a secret, but Marion is not the only one in the family with an engagement ring and a promise of marriage. I have my own, hidden in a box in my room, not with ten diamonds in it but a simple gold band with a single diamond in the centre, given to me by my own darling Robert.

Yes, he is back, Caroline. A chance meeting last summer was the happiest of my life. I was cycling back from Shipton Abbey, dropping some clothes I had repaired to Mrs Collins to return them to their owners and collect my fee for me, when of all things I had a puncture. I carry a repair kit everywhere with me but, would you believe, when I looked it was gone, most likely thanks to Madame Marion who had been off on one of her marathon cycles the day before. I fairly cursed her there on the road from the village. It's a short enough walk, Caroline, but the day was a hot one and I had to wheel the bike with the punctured wheel alongside me after being up at the crack of dawn to finish the sewing. I thought I'd never get home when around the bend came a motor car. I stood in the ditch and kept my head down, waiting for it to pass, but it didn't. It stopped beside me and, when I looked up to see why, who was standing in front of me but Robert!

I thought I would flee into the field when confronted with him! My knees felt as though they would buckle, my heart started to race and I felt such a blush come to my cheeks. All the stuff that you read in romances is true, Caroline. I felt as though a great wave had hit me and knocked me for six. "Robert," was all I could say. And the darndest thing was that the same look was in his eyes as was in mine. "Lily," he said and he bent to look at my puncture. I thought I would die, to have him so close to *me and not to be able to touch him. He talked as he fixed my tyre, told me that he was home for the summer from university where he was studying English and History but that he was unhappy there and longed to be back here in Shipton, near the estuary and near to me. I couldn't believe it. Could he really still have feelings for me?*

Yes, he had, Caroline. Like me, like the feelings that I had buried away, Robert was still as in love with me as he had been the day our secret love was revealed to his father. He brought me back to Eyrie Farm that day and we could scarcely take our eyes off each other. We met in secret a few times before the end of the summer and then he went back to university in October and we have written ever since. Such happiness I have never known. It is like the love I had for him before has grown tenfold with our separation and he the same. He proposed formally to me at Christmas time, when he was home for his holidays, and we snatched some time alone together at the farm when Marion was with Albie. He gave me my beautiful solitaire ring and promised that as soon as today, my twenty-first birthday should arrive, soon after would come another ring of plain gold and we should be husband and wife.

Of course it was difficult for me when Marion made her big announcement and flounced off to her fancy engagement party and me not invited. But I had a party of my own here at Eyrie Farm! Myself and Henry danced to 'Secret Love', a song I haven't been able to bear to hear since Robert and I were separated at first. Now our love is secret again, but not for much longer because he has promised me that he has a plan in place for us to be together, and Henry too, before the year is out. I have no idea what that plan is but I can scarcely keep myself from grinning with glee every time I think of it.

Please be happy for me, Caroline. I know that this will involve deceit but my life has been so filled with it, surrounded by it, for so long, that I fear I shall never be able to escape it. Once Robert and Henry and I are together, however, then the love we have will make up for the deceit and maybe some day we will be able to be honest and truthful and we won't be judged like we are now, or like I would be back in Ireland.

Pray to God and to your Saint Agnes, Patron Saint of Couples, that by the time I write to you on my twenty-second birthday all will be well.

Your friend,

Lily

32

Mary Stockwell was surprised to see the silver Audi parked in the community-centre car park – even more surprised to see the small figure sitting on the wall outside the door of Lullabies.

"Martha!" she exclaimed. "Are you okay? I didn't know whether to call you – whether Ruby was coming back or not . . ."

Martha was holding Ruby in her arms. It was only eight o'clock in the morning but the little girl was bare-limbed in a summer T-shirt. Martha herself was dressed in jeans and a light top, a cardigan discarded in the car. The heat had hit her like a brick wall when she had opened the front door to leave the house. It was sticky and oppressive, yet there was no sun breaking through the slate-grey cloud. It was clear that a storm was approaching.

She had left Will and Gabriel starting to roll up the yards of cable around the house, removing the cameras from every room. They were hot and exhausted but Will wanted the house cleared before they went back to the B&B for a few hours' rest.

Martha knew she should sleep herself, should leave Ruby with Mary and have a good four or five hours' rest – but she couldn't. She couldn't think of anything but finding out exactly what had happened at Eyrie Farm.

Mary held her arms out to take Ruby but Martha kept a firm grip. "I need to talk to you, Mary," she said. "And I need honest replies – not like before."

Mary looked puzzled, and hurt at Martha's refusal to hand over Ruby. "What have I done, Martha?" she asked, a genuine note of upset in her voice.

"What do you really know about Eyrie Farm, Mary? The truth – not the local folklore, the tales about monks to throw me off the scent. What do you know that you're not telling me?"

Mary sat down on the wall beside Martha. "Is that why you've been missing these last few days? Why those men have been around? Has something happened?"

Martha nodded, staring at Mary's face for signs. "Yes, Mary. Something has happened."

The older woman's face registered shock. "Is it true?" she asked in a whisper.

"I don't know, Mary. Is what true? What is there to be true? Everyone's been fobbing me off since I got here when I've asked about that house and I don't know what's true and what's not. That's why I need honesty this time, Mary. I swear that whatever you tell me won't shock me or scare me any more than I've already been shocked and scared."

Mary looked at Martha with a worried face and then looked down. She sighed. "Come inside," she said. "It's too hot to sit out here, and besides which, the others will be here soon."

Martha followed Mary inside the crèche, glad to step into the coolness of the room. She settled Ruby on the infants' mat with some toys while Mary opened the blinds and windows, turned on the small fans in opposite corners of the room and set about making two cups of coffee. After a few moments she thought better of it and instead took two bottles of water from the small fridge and handed one to Martha.

They sat and Martha looked at Mary challengingly.

Mary sighed. "I know I probably haven't been entirely honest with you," she said. "But it was for your own good, I thought. Maybe I was wrong."

"Maybe you were," said Martha, her voice hard at the admission of dishonesty. She had lived through too many lies in her marriage to tolerate them from people who were supposed to be her friends.

"I don't know for sure what the history of the place is – there are so many rumours that it was connected to the monastery, of bits being added on and taken off, of all the land surrounding making up the farm and it all being lost through gambling. The first proper fact that I ever knew was that there was a family living there – a couple and two small children – and the father gambled away the land bit by bit. They were left with nothing and then Charles Mountford – Rob's grandfather – stepped in and bought the place for a pittance. The farmer took the money and he and his family fled his debts. They were very unhappy by all accounts."

Martha felt her interest rise. This had to be them – the Mannions. Was Henry one of the children? Had they left him behind? Tried to kill him because they were poor?

"What was their name?" she barked at Mary and Ruby turned her head, startled, and stared at her mother.

"There's a good girl," said Mary soothingly to the little girl, while Martha resisted the impulse to go to her. Ruby's attention switched back to chewing the toy in her hand and Mary continued quietly. "I haven't the faintest what their name was, Martha, I'm sorry. This was way back during the war and I'm old but not *that* old!" She attempted a smile but Martha remained impassive. "And not from the area anyway. I only know what Duncan told me and Lord knows he was rarely sober enough to make any sense once he'd been to that place."

Martha's eyes opened a little wider. So Duncan Stockwell had some sort of connection with Eyrie Farm?

"Apparently," Mary continued, taking a sip from her water, "after Charles Mountford bought it, it lay idle for a while, got overgrown and a little shabby. Then two women moved in after the war, lived there for a few years and then – to my knowledge – just vanished. Both of them. After they left, the house was left too – to run to ruin until Rob Mountford took to doing it up and then you moved in."

Martha stared at Mary who was slugging back her water. "That's it?" she said. "*That's* the history of the farm that everyone's been hiding from me? Why keep all of that secret?" She could feel her anger rising. Mary must be still lying to her.

"Look, Martha, my knowledge of the history is sketchy but I only came here in the 80's from Bickford when Duncan and I got married. By that stage there were all sorts of local legends about the place – 'don't go near Eyrie Farm or the witch'll get you' type of tales. Local kids used to dare each other to go up there at night-time and over the years a few of 'em came back none the better for it with tales of shadowy figures and screaming babies and awful scratching noises like someone being buried alive. Of course no one with any sense believed them but then the tales grew arms and legs and next thing there were ghostly monks eating children and phantom ponies and all sorts."

Martha took a drink from her water, feeling the condensation from the plastic bottle trickle down her fingers in drops. "I had an idea that the stories would be something like that. Again, how does all this mean it has to be such a secret?"

Mary fanned her face with a laminated sheet of paper she had picked up. "Because . . . oh, *rats!*" she muttered.

Martha turned to see Kai waddle in the door with his mum. It had completely slipped her mind that Mary was simply arriving to do a day's work when she ambushed her. Martha was irrationally furious at the interruption. She knew it was a combination of heat and tiredness mostly but that didn't stop her staring at Kai's mum who scarpered within minutes of arriving, furious that the rich writer from London should look down on her like that.

With Kai settled with some toy cars, Mary returned to Martha and opened her mouth to begin again. The attempt was further frustrated by the arrival of Ella and her smartly-dressed mother. Martha wanted to scream but held back when she saw Aneta arrive. At least now she would have Mary's undivided attention for a few moments.

Mary ushered Aneta outside to the little garden play area with Ruby and the two toddlers, even though the Polish girl objected that this wasn't the normal routine. After what seemed like an age, Mary settled herself back beside Martha and resumed.

"I never believed all the village stories," she said. "When you start hearing about ghostly puppies it renders them a little invalid. Or so I thought at the time. Duncan never believed them either, and the 80's were hard on us with Ryan after arriving and Claire on the way so that's why he took the job up at the farm when Charlie Mountford – Rob's dad – offered it to him."

"What job was that?" asked Martha.

"Security, of all things. In the summer of '87 there was a bunch of travellers arrived in the village. They set themselves up on the abbey grounds – tents and campfires and whatnot. They were peaceable enough – didn't mean to cause any harm but you can imagine the fuss. Anyway, as it happens, Geoff Cooper from the service station had some huge bust-up with Charlie Mountford over some land when he was building his house. Geoff threatened to tell the travellers about Eyrie Farm being vacant and of course Charlie didn't trust him. And one thing that drives Charlie Mountford nuts is thinking that someone has something belonging to him that they shouldn't so he decided to put a security guard up at the house and offered Duncan the job after he got laid off. We were penniless, so he took it till something better came along, but night after night he'd come back, terrified, telling me about all this stuff that used to go on at the place." Mary looked into space pensively. "He started drinking heavily. He never had a problem with drink until then – the odd pint of ale, glass of wine at Christmas, but he never drank seriously. That place seemed to drive him to it. Alone up there night after night, stuck in that little room at the back where your study is now – it was the only one that was liveable in, even though it was just four walls and a plastic sheet over the window. He'd sit in there with a torch and a book keeping an eye out for the travellers, but they never came. She did though, he said – a woman. Is that what you saw?"

Martha didn't want to answer, didn't want to have to tell Mary what had happened. Not yet. "What else did he experience, Mary?" she asked, her voice gentler than it had been.

Mary sniffed. Martha noticed that there were tears forming in her eyes. "Scratching mostly," she said. "From that room where Ruby sleeps. Occasionally he'd hear a child crying, or footsteps upstairs and he'd go up there to find no one. He started having a little tipple to calm his nerves after he heard the growling – he said it was like a rabid dog – but he couldn't see dogs anywhere. Then he must have started taking a bottle with him when he went up there at night. He changed in himself – he was miserable and quiet, not interested in anything – he wasn't even there when Claire was born. His moods just got worse and worse and he'd come home stinking of whiskey and white as a sheet. Then he didn't come home one night – I had to ring Charlie Mountford to go up there to see if he was dead or alive. He was passed out on the floor of that room when Charlie found him. He sacked him on the spot for being drunk."

"I suppose it was to be expected, really, wasn't it?" said Martha. It was the only thing she could think of to say but she regretted instantly how hard it sounded.

"Irony of the whole damn thing is that was the first night he'd been up there sober in a month!" said Mary grimly. "We literally didn't have a penny – I made him late because I needed money for nappies and we had a huge argument. He couldn't get tick anywhere in the village and, besides which, he was seen cycling up by Eyrie Farm twenty minutes after he left home so he didn't have *time* to even go looking for booze. True, he could have had a stash up there but not very much if he was so desperate for my last fiver that he nearly hit me for it. And anyway, I doubt at that stage if he was capable of leaving anything behind him."

"So why was he unconscious?"

"That woman. He said he saw a woman up there. A woman with black clothes and rotten teeth, appearing in front of him everywhere he went, pounding at the wall. He passed out from *fear* because she wouldn't leave him alone – knocked his torch from his hand, slammed the door and locked it. He said she was screaming at him, and screaming at the child and the child was screaming too and then she was screaming at him to get out –"

"Stop!" said Martha, shaken.

They stared at each other silently.

"Yes," Martha said at last. "I've seen her too but she's gone now . . . and the boy."

Mary's eyes widened. "So it's *true* then?"

"You know it is! All that stuff you just said – you knew all of this and you kept it from me! How could you do that? Why?"

For the first time, Martha noticed that Mary's knuckles were white, her nails dug deep into her palms.

"I thought . . . I thought you'd tell me I was talking rubbish. I was testing you – you see, I never fully believed Duncan – he told me so many lies. As time went on and I hated him so much, I figured he was making it all up to get out of doing the job. I didn't believe a word that came out of his mouth – told him that I was a fool to listen to him and that it was all lies. Told him that if there was a single shred of truth to it, that it was nothing but pink elephants – he left because he couldn't take me calling him a *liar.*"

The realisation that her husband had been telling the truth seemed to shock Mary to the core. Martha instinctively held out her hand and grasped that of the older woman.

"That damn place has haunted me for over twenty years, Martha," said Mary in a whisper. "All the time I was blaming it for Duncan leaving when it was my fault for not believing him."

"It wasn't you, Mary," said Martha gently. "That house is so pretty on the outside but when you're alone there it's enough to drive you mad. Those feelings of sadness and melancholy that Duncan had – that's what that woman does – did. Sucking out energy from people to give herself power. She did it to me, but help arrived in time . . ."

Mary wasn't listening. "That's why I was so eager to see the place – to prove that it was just a house and that I'd been right to kick him out, right that he was a liar and a drunk. Then I thought Alison was trying to upset me when she came out with the same stuff after being there. She's going through a rebellious phase – I thought maybe someone had told her the stories about her dad – it's not hard to hear them around Shipton. We had a huge fight – her screaming it was true and me refusing to listen to her. I marched up there right afterwards to see for myself."

"Mary," said Martha firmly. "Mary!"

The childminder ignored her. Martha had to grasp her friend by her shoulders to get her to look in her eyes.

"Yes, Duncan and Alison were telling the truth," she said, "but it's not your fault that Duncan left you. That house – whatever was in that house – was evil. But it's gone now. My friends took care of that."

Mary looked at Martha with sadness in her eyes. "That's not much use to me now, love. I loved the bones of that man till he went to that house. Did everything I could to make it work afterward – had Alison and Oliver to try and bring us back to where we were. And I've been on my own ever since."

Martha nodded. "I know. But you have four wonderful children and this place –"

She was interrupted by the back door opening and the clumping footsteps of two hot and bothered toddlers and a red-faced Aneta with an equally red-faced Ruby. "It is too hot, Mrs Stockwell, for the little ones," she said.

Mary looked away and wiped the corners of her eyes. "That's fine, Aneta," she said as her assistant proceeded to take the children's cups from their shelves to give them drinks. She gestured to Martha that she should follow her to the front door. "Can you make sure Ruby gets a drink too, Aneta?" she said, before stepping outside into the thick heat.

They sat on the low wall outside.

"What is with this weather?" Mary asked out of the blue.

There was silence between them for a while.

"Martha, I don't want to know what happened to you at that house," said Mary, shuddering slightly. "But I do want to know that you and Ruby are alright."

Martha was relieved. She didn't know if she could tell her, could tell anyone in fact. "We're going back to London," she replied.

Mary looked down at her hands. "I thought you might. I suppose you want to be sure that Ruby's safe. When are you going?"

"Today," said Martha.

Mary was taken aback.

"My friends are leaving today," said Martha, although when she thought about it she hadn't discussed with Gabriel and Will what they planned to do beyond having a sleep at the B&B for a few hours. "I can't stay at the cottage any more. I know that whatever was there is gone, but too much has happened for me to feel easy there, especially now that I know what happened to you and Duncan."

"I'll miss you both to bits," said Mary warmly. "But you're right. Get as far as you can from that farmhouse. But, by the way, is there something I should know about that very dishy man from the café?"

Martha looked at her friend and saw a mischievous glint in her eye. "Good God, Mary! All you've told me and you're *still* trying to pair me off? Is it all you ever think about? First Rob Mountford, and now Will!"

"Will, is it? Where there's a Will . . ." said Mary, grinning. "I know which one of them I'd prefer for sure!"

Martha rolled her eyes. "Do me a favour and never take up comedy, do you hear me?"

Martha was glad to see Mary laugh. She'd arrived there, angry with her for the lies, and was leaving feeling only guilt and sadness that she had upset such a kind person. Upset to learn that Eyrie Farm had spread its poison to another family.

"Can I leave Ruby here for a couple of hours?" she asked. "I'll pay for all the days she missed, of course – and up to the end of the month."

"Don't be so silly," Mary dismissed the thought with a wave of her hand. "You'll need every penny you can moving back to the city. Leave her here as long as you like – in fact, I'd rather you never took her back to that place."

Martha suddenly felt a compulsion to hug her friend and threw her arms around her. It was an awkward hug, Mary taken by surprise and unaccustomed to the affection, but she returned it as warmly as she could. As Martha released her, she saw Mary wipe another tear from her eye.

"I should only be a couple of hours, absolute max," said Martha. "And I'll see you when I come to get her."

Mary watched her step over the wall into the neighbouring car park and climb into her car which she had reversed into a parking space. Martha waved as she engaged the car in first gear and gently rolled down the slight incline to the car park entrance. Mary was surprised to see her turn not right toward Eyrie Farm, but left into the village.

Martha had one more person to see.

Martha opened both the driver and passenger side windows all the way down as she drove out of the car park of the Abbot's Rest. John Farnley himself had opened the B&B door where he was still serving breakfasts. He was puzzled as to why Martha wanted that particular address but he gave it nonetheless. There was something weird going on up at Eyrie Farm these days what with those fellows from Scotland and the car full of equipment, asking questions.

Martha skirted the village, unable to get up enough speed to create the crosswind she required. Once past the Bickford roundabout she hoped to be able to speed up but she found herself crawling along behind a tractor, unable to overtake on the winding country roads. Martha sighed in frustration.

Eventually the tractor slowed practically to a halt and negotiated an awkward turn into a field where hay was being cut and she stepped up the pace a little. She thought about Eyrie Farm as she drove, how lucky she actually was, in a way, that all of this had come to a head and that she could finally get away. Her country dream was over, she knew, but she felt no disappointment, just relief. Sue was right. Martha was a city girl and always had been. Even as a child she longed to get away from the village and into the anonymity of the city. She had been kidding herself to think that she could start again in the country, alone, with no support for herself and Ruby. The more she thought about it, the more foolish she felt for ever thinking it could work.

Martha spotted the crossroads and knew that she was on the right road, close at last to her destination. She turned left, and drove inland, on a small road, bordered either side by reeds and marshy ground. She rounded a bend, and there it was, the cottage, just as John Farnley had described it. Outside was parked an old, white Ford Fiesta. It was filthy, but she could see fresh tyre tracks behind it. Odd, she thought.

She pulled in behind the Ford Fiesta and looked around her. This place was even more bleak and desolate that Eyrie Farm. She surveyed the rundown house. It was a one-storey building, more of a bungalow than a cottage. The exterior had never been painted and Martha could see long cracks running their way down the render. The flatness of the surrounding land meant that the cottage would be clearly exposed to winds from the estuary in bad weather. From where she was parked, Martha could see that the guttering was overgrown with weeds and that moss was growing between some of the roof tiles. The roof itself sagged in the centre, as though it hadn't long before a storm blew it right in. A porch ran along the front of the house, the window frames originally painted black but the paint dried and peeling to reveal wood turned grey by the weather underneath. It looked rotten in parts. A dead plant stood in a pot on the sill inside, and the glass itself was filthy. In each window along the front of the building, grey net curtains hung, some of them with holes ripped in them. Had Martha not been sure of John Farnley's directions she would never have believed that the house was inhabited.

The grass beneath her feet was flattened by being driven over, but weeds grew everywhere, a huge bank of them forming a border between the area in front of the house and the marshy land around. Dandelions licked the edge of the house itself, in the way that other houses might have rosebushes. Martha stepped gingerly through the greenery and made her way to the front door where the grass thinned out and a dry patch of dirt formed a welcome mat. She peered through the grimy porch door while trying the handle – it was locked. Inside she could see a brown door with a dirty fanlight above it, paint cracked and peeling, and the brasses green with lack of maintenance. It looked as though no one had been here to help this woman out in a very long time, if ever.

Martha tried the doorbell but it produced no sound. She knocked on the glass and waited, wondering if the old woman would even talk to her but she had to try. Lil Flynn knew something about Eyrie Farm and she needed to know what.

There was no sound from the cottage. Martha turned her back to the front door while she waited, gazing out over the flat marsh around her, toward the hills in the distance. She imagined this being the view that she would see every day and pictured the pretty scene from the window of Eyrie Farm – the recently cultivated garden, the trees and surrounding fields. How grim this all seemed, she thought, and turned back to the house to see if anyone was coming.

The sight that greeted her made her jump. It was a ghostly vision, the woman's face thin and lined, her rheumy pale eyes standing out in the wrinkles. Her skin was grey and pasty, the body skeletal. Martha breathed in sharply – the woman peering at her through the brown door was, for a second, reminiscent of the other woman – the one at Eyrie Farm. *Miss Mannion.*

Lil Flynn stared at Martha as she slowly shuffled around the door, hanging on to the handle for support as she stepped down into the tiled porch and then standing there for a moment, as if waiting for a pain to subside. She lurched toward the porch door and covered the space in one step but it was a clumsy one and Martha feared that she might fall over at any minute. The woman looked as if she was in agony, thought Martha, seeing her face scrunch up as she paused again, then opened the lock from the inside slowly and carefully before turning the handle and peering out at Martha.

"What d'you want?" she croaked, her voice thin and reedy.

"Lil, isn't it? Lil Flynn – I mean Mountford." She remembered how the old woman had been so indignant about her name when she had met her that day in the pub.

It seemed to work. The posture of the elderly woman seemed to relax a little and she looked Martha up and down.

"And to whom am I speaking?" she asked in her rasping voice, her accent affected, like someone trying to talk posh.

"My name is Martha Armstrong. I've been living for a while up at Eyrie Farm."

"What do you want me for?"

Martha stepped toward the door of the house. "I'd like to talk to you for a while if I could – emm – Lil." She had hoped to address her using the Mountford name for further success but, realising she didn't know if it was Miss or Mrs, she decided against it and hoped using the Christian name didn't sound disrespectful.

Lil Flynn turned her back rather abruptly on Martha and shuffled back across the porch and into the house, negotiating the step with great difficulty. She made no move to close the door behind her and Martha hoped it was an indication to follow. She stepped into the porch which smelled vaguely of onions and noticed two strings of them hanging on hooks under the window to her left. They were dried up and unused, Martha wondered if the old lady had perhaps grown them herself – but where was there to grow vegetables on this marsh, she wondered.

Lil disappeared into the house and Martha took a hesitant step after her. The brown door led immediately into a surprisingly large kitchen which was stiflingly warm and smelled of must and old cooking smells. There was a vague odour of fish in the air and Martha wrinkled her nose involuntarily. There was a filthy window draped with net curtains so dirty they were almost black, over a sink and draining-board piled high with pots, dishes and utensils. The cupboards had been painted a salmon colour once but, like all the other paintwork she had seen, it was cracked and peeling in places, under layers of grime in others. The worktop was covered in dust – Martha could tell that some of it had been there so long it was sticky – that was in the places that she could actually see the surface. The cupboard tops were covered in the woman's belongings – she could see stacks of bowls and cups, plates, cutlery and other kitchen equipment. Alongside these items were old handbags, stacks of kitchen towels, an ancient typewriter. It looked as though the old lady had been having some sort of cleanout and had stacked belongings from her whole life through on the surfaces. A table in the centre of the kitchen area was also covered with papers, boxes, and plastic bags full of God knows what.

Martha scanned the area in front of her – the whole floor was covered in ancient linoleum, riddled with holes where she could see grey concrete underneath. There was a pattern on the lino but it was so old and faint and filthy that she could barely make it out. Directly opposite her was another door, made of plywood. There was a gap about an inch thick at the base of the door where Martha could make out daylight. It must be freezing here in wintertime, she thought. She could see that the wood frames in the kitchen windows were rotten in here as well.

To her left, an old-fashioned solid fuel cooker was set into a recess in the wall. It was a faded orange colour, the dials grimy and cracked, the top black and dirty. Above it, a metal shelf for airing clothes jutted out from the wall, the length of the cooker surface. A wooden-framed chair sat in the middle of the room and Martha noticed it was facing an old TV set with a pair of old-fashioned rabbit ears perched on top. The TV stood on a unit set into the corner of the room by the other door. The shelves of the unit were also covered in all sorts of old stuff – yellowed books and papers, old notebooks.

Still standing in the doorway, Martha looked at the old lady, who was lowering herself onto a chair at the filthy and crowded table. None of the chairs around the table matched each other, as though they had been donated by various different sources, or found discarded over the years. Along the wall to Martha's right stood a dresser unit, another surface covered in pottery, bits of broken jewellery, cups with no handles. The place was like a tip, she thought, and looking at its owner she realised that it had taken a very long time to get into this state and that, if left to her, there was no way that Lil Flynn would be capable at lifting half the stuff, never mind doing a full clearout.

"Close the door," snapped Lil as she sat down. "You're letting all the heat out."

The room was stifling, thought Martha. It needed airing, for all of the windows and both doors to be opened and fresh air allowed to blow through, especially with the heat today. She looked at her hostess and saw her shiver, pulling her cardigan tight around her shoulders. Martha did as she was bidden and closed the brown door into the kitchen behind her.

"Haven't heard it called that in a while," said Lil Flynn, leaning her elbow on the table beside her. She nodded her head to indicate that Martha should sit down at the table with her and Martha hesitantly crossed the room, feeling the heat and the smell become overbearing. This would need to be fast, she thought.

"What's that, then?" asked Martha, lowering herself onto the dusty chair facing Lil.

"Eyrie Farm," said the old lady. "Thought the new name was Hawthorn Cottage. Bit fancy for that place, I think, but sure I suppose I haven't seen it since Little Robbie did it up."

Martha noticed that the old lady slurred her words. It was only half past nine in the morning – how could she drink so early? And where had she the booze hidden? For all the clutter on every surface save that of the solid fuel cooker Martha could see no bottles or cans of any sort. At least she wasn't rambling like she had been the two times she'd met her in the pub. She was right to come here early, to get to her while she might still be able to speak some sort of sense.

"In fact," continued Lil, "Little Robbie *told* me to only ever call it Hawthorn Cottage. Told me I was never to breathe a word to the girl up at the farm with the baby." She looked directly at Martha. "That's you, isn't it?" The she suddenly gasped, and arched her back with pain, taking a sharp intake of breath which made a hissing noise.

Martha was alarmed. "Are you alright? Can I get you anything? Some water? I think I have some painkillers in my bag . . ."

The old woman made a 'pff' sound at the mention of the pain-killers. "Sure I've enough of them to cure an army," she scoffed. "None of them bloody work. I do be in cloud-cuckoo-land with them half of the time but the pain still kills me."

Martha settled back in her chair, unsure what to do next. Should she continue to ask what she needed to ask? Was it fair on a sick old lady?

"Would you like a drink?" she asked in her kindest voice. "Do you have any whiskey?" Maybe just the one would warm the old lady up sufficiently to talk to her. Martha assumed that one wouldn't do any harm to a habitual boozer, might even help take the pain away. She looked around again, searching for a bottle.

Lil glared at her across the table. "Are you suggesting that I take alcohol?" she asked, clearly outraged.

Martha sat back in her seat, feeling sheepish. She knew she shouldn't have asked. "Not at all, Lil – it's just that I know you sometimes like a little tipple and I wondered if it – might – help with your pain maybe. No harm in a small one!" Martha grinned sheepishly, hoping to backpedal her way out of the faux pas with a little charm.

Instead of agreeing or even refusing, Lil Flynn pushed herself up from the chair and stood over Martha, pointing a finger furiously at her. "I am a proud Pioneer, madam! And I have been since I was twelve years of age. I took the pledge before my confirmation and I have *never* broken it!" she said fiercely, jabbing her finger at Martha. She turned suddenly and shuffled around to one of the handbags on the nearby countertop, using the table for support as she did so. She rummaged in the bag for a few moments before turning back, as quickly as she could, and slammed something down on the table in front of Martha. It was a small pin in the shape of a heart, surrounded by a circle of metal. Inside the heart was a picture of another heart, topped by a cross and with what looked like rays of some sort coming from them both. Martha studied it and looked back up at Lil, not understanding what she was trying to demonstrate.

Lil looked from the pin back to Martha and was clearly

frustrated that the younger woman didn't understand what she was trying to say. "Pioneer Total Abstinence Association," she said, lowering herself back onto the chair where she had been sitting previously, grimacing with the pain as she did so. "In Ireland we join the Pioneers to vow that we will abstain from alcoholic drink until we are a certain age, or for life in my case. I have *never* broken my pledge in all my years, and never will."

"I don't understand . . ." said Martha. "When I've seen you before you've been in the pub . . . and . . ." She couldn't think of a polite way to bring up the way Lil slurred her words, nor the hint of alcohol from her breath the last time they met.

Lil interrupted her. "This is young Robbie Mountford and his bastard of a father. I never use curses, but that man is the devil's own. He's a troublemaker and he has the young fellah at it as well." She was clearly agitated and gripped her hands together, her knuckles white.

"I'm sorry, Lil, but I really don't understand," said Martha, alarmed that she had caused the woman such stress when she hadn't been there five minutes.

Lil looked at Martha, her watery eyes even more moist than when Martha had seen her before. "You may have seen me in the pub because I sometimes go there for a glass of orange. It's lonely living out here and I go there for company now and again. It's not entirely suitable for a woman to go alone but no one takes any notice of me and sometimes the village folk will talk to me. I've no one, so what choice do I have when no one ever comes all the way out here to see me? Except that Community Nurse once in a blue moon, but I talk to her at the door – never let her in, interfering busybody that she is. I can't drive any more though, so I've no way to get to the pub unless I go down to the road and manage to get a lift from a neighbour."

Martha opened her mouth to say something but Lil continued.

"Young Charlie Mountford turned the village folk against me over the years, telling them stories about me that are all lies. He says I talk funny because I've taken drink, but I've talked funny since I was in hospital that time. And like I said, them tablets the doctor does have me take, they send me to the moon sometimes, so I've stopped taking them." The old lady folded her arms, like a petulant child.

Martha was unsure what to do at her outburst. "I'm sorry, Lil. I only knew what I assumed, but I was wrong and I'm really very sorry."

Lil shrugged. "Sure I'd probably think it meself," she said, looking away from Martha. "Folk find it hard to understand me sometimes with the accent and the damage."

"What damage was that, Lil?" asked Martha gently, genuinely intrigued by the fact that the woman was vehemently denying everything she had assumed about her. She had to admit that she had never actually seen the woman with a drink in her hand, but all the evidence pointed to what people in the village had said.

Lil sighed, stared into space for a moment and then looked at Martha. "Will you make me a cup of tea like a good girl?"

"Of course," said Martha and stood up to fill the rusted kettle. She extracted a cup and saucer from the pile of dishes in the sink which she now saw were encrusted with old food – clearly Lily hadn't eaten a proper meal in days if not weeks. She rinsed the cup thoroughly with boiling water before adding a teabag. The necessary items for making tea were all open beside the kettle, including the milk and Martha recoiled as she smelled the carton. She spotted a small fridge set in under the worktop beside her and opened it. Thankfully there was an unopened carton in the door. It was out of date but, once opened, smelled considerably better than the one on the worktop so Martha set it, the tea and the sugar on the table in front of Lil and sat back down again.

"Are you not having one?" said Lil in surprise, as she gingerly poured in a small drop of milk to the cup.

Martha balked at the thought. "No thanks, Lil, I had one just before I came out here," she lied.

It seemed to satisfy the old woman and she carried on with her own ritual, stirring the cup loudly for what seemed like an eternity and then setting the spoon down. Her hands returned to her lap.

"I was in hospital because I was *assaulted*," she said, pronouncing the word *assaulted* as though it were a new one that she had just learned. "At Eyrie Farm, in fact."

Martha was gripped. Another bad thing happening at that place. It must be cursed, she thought, to ruin so many lives.

"Tell me," said Lil. "Is there any sign of my boy up there like all those stories say?"

Martha couldn't have been more stunned. *Her* boy? Lil Flynn was Henry's mother? "What do you mean, Lil?" she asked nervously.

Lil continued to stare at her, her eyes watery but fixed, the rant about the Mountfords completely forgotten.

"My boy," said Lil, her face growing suddenly soft at a memory. "My little Henry."

Martha leaned forward in her seat toward Lil, studying her face. "Henry was your son?" she whispered. Then what had she meant when she had told her "the mother did it"? Was Lil Flynn admitting to murdering her own son?

The old woman didn't respond immediately. She looked alert all of a sudden, as if coming to after being temporarily stunned. She turned in her chair and scanned the room, her eyes eventually settling on the dresser. With great difficulty she stood, pausing again to let the pain subside, and shuffling unsteadily she went to the dresser and began to rummage in one of the boxes over there. She withdrew a bundle of envelopes and shuffled back slowly to the table.

Martha had remained silent, unsure what to say. To let on that she knew about Henry's existence? To tell her that that very morning Henry's spirit had nestled into her legs? Who then was this Mannion woman? Martha was even more confused than ever. She watched the old woman sit down, waiting patiently for her to continue with what she was about to tell her, at the same time fearful that none of it would make any sense.

Lil tossed the bundle of envelopes over to Martha. They weren't bound in any way and the top few slid off the sides. "Tie them up with a bit of string when you can," said Lil, matter of factly. "And when you read them, make sure you read them in order."

The first thing that Martha noticed was that the letters weren't addressed to Lil herself and they were unstamped, with no postmark on them. Instead they were all addressed to a Sr M Agnes Devlin at the Brigidine Convent, Marino, Dublin.

Lil saw Martha reading the envelopes. "They're all to my friend Caroline," she said, pointing a bony finger at the pile.

Martha was struck by how thin the hand was, with protruding veins and liver spots. The hand, more than anything, made her wonder what sort of life this woman had.

"She joined a convent the same year I came here to Shipton Abbey – we were pals though she was a year older than me and in a class ahead of me at school. She got the calling from God and I got sent here to look after my sister. At first I used to address them to her as Caroline Devlin but they started to come back to me. I realised that the Mother Superior wouldn't give them to her with her 'maiden' name on them as it were, so I changed it to Sr Agnes – that was the name she chose when she went in there, after St Agnes. Eventually she wrote to me and asked me to stop sending them to her. I guessed that her superiors had instructed her to do that. In any case, I stopped. Didn't stop writing the oul' things though. 'Twas lonely up at the farm, with Marion out gallivanting and sure I'd not much else to do."

Lil stared again into space, her tea untouched. Martha wondered why she'd asked her to make it if she wasn't going to taste it.

"I can't drink it any more," said Lil, noticing the direction of Martha's gaze. "But I love the smell of it." She smiled faintly. "I had Henry for company though. He was the light of my life, that boy. I loved him like he was my own, and God above knows he needed someone to love him like a mother should because Marion surely didn't. I'd spend every hour that God sent with him if I could. He was only just four the last time I saw him. Small for his age . . ."

A shudder ran through Martha. Exactly what she had thought when she had felt his tiny spirit beside her. She couldn't believe that she was actually talking to someone who *knew* Henry, that he had been at Eyrie Farm in living memory. She wondered for the first time if she actually wanted to know what had really happened.

"But he was wiry and strong and he'd run from here to Dublin if you let him." Lil smiled softly, lost in her memories. "He had a funny way of talking – used to call me Mammy, the little divil, instead of Auntie Lily, and Marion he'd call Marion, only he couldn't pronounce his 'r's' the right way. He'd say an 'n' instead. He was 'Henny', rabbits were 'nabbits' and his mother was –"

"Mannion," said Martha. The room around her felt like it was spinning. The spirit that Gabriel had banished wasn't a Mrs Mannion, it was Marion. The name of Henry's mother. Lil Flynn's sister. They must have been the two women that Mary had said lived at Eyrie Farm. The start of the mystery, and the hauntings.

Lil seemed not to notice the shock in Martha's voice and continued to reminisce. "That's right. 'Mannion' he called her. Used to get right up her nose and she'd get very cross, God love the little mite." A tinge of sadness entered Lily's voice. "She got cross with him an awful lot toward the end, when Albie finished with her."

Another name. "Who was Albie, Lil?" asked Martha softly. No sooner was one mystery solved than another opened.

Lil ignored her. "It was her that caused the damage that time. She went mad – I couldn't stop her rampaging through the house, knocking things over, breaking things, shouting that he'd ruined it all. I tried to hide him upstairs in his bedroom, to protect him from her, but she was like a madwoman." Panic entered into Lil's voice as she grew more agitated. "She barged in after us and pushed me outside the door and locked it – she was in there shouting at Henry, curse words and everything at him, and he was crying and screaming and I couldn't get in to him. I was banging on the door and shouting at her to leave him alone. I thought it worked – he went quiet all of a sudden and she came out to me. Had a pillow in her hand. I tried to talk to her but she started punching me and telling me to shut up, shouting about how Albie had found out and wanted nothing to do with her and if she couldn't have Albie I couldn't have Henry, or Robert for that matter."

Martha was totally confused now. She had no idea who Lil was talking about but the old lady didn't seem to realise she was even there. Martha knew that all of this was important but could scarcely keep up. Lil's speech grew more slurred as she spoke as well and it took every bit of concentration that Martha had to keep up in the stifling heat of the kitchen.

"I nearly had her out of the way and then I was going to go in to Henry and lock the door on her, keep him safe until she just calmed down but I saw over her shoulder into the room and Henry was lying on the bed, all still. I knew she'd hurt him, that she'd used the pillow on him – I couldn't believe it. At that moment, while I was off guard, she pushed me to the stairs and down the first couple of steps. I tried so hard but she was too strong for me. I lost my step on the stairs and went down like a sack of coal. I didn't remember any more until I woke up in the hospital. Robert had found me at the farm and brought me there.

That was the end of all of it – they never let me go to Eyrie Farm again and when I got out Marion was gone and there was no sign of Henry at all. I never saw her again, never heard from her even. And my boy was gone. My lovely little boy – she'd taken him and she didn't even love him.

Then the stories started. Charles Mountford wouldn't let me up near Eyrie Farm, said we were a disgrace and that I wasn't to go near the place. I tried telling folk what I'd seen – that she'd hurt Henry – but no one believed there was a boy up there in the first place, we'd hid him so well. I wondered why my friend Mrs Collins didn't speak out and support what I was saying – but sure she never came near me at all and later I came to understand why. Of course, after my time in hospital I couldn't talk right so Mountford started spreading it that I'd taken to the drink and that was why Marion had left, to go back home away from me.

And Robert told me that we couldn't be together. He was my last hope but not only his father but Charles Junior turned him against me then. It wouldn't have done for a Mountford to marry the likes of me after what had happened. Albie agreed not to tell anyone about Henry so it stayed a secret but that was the worst – because no one knew about him, no one believed me, what she'd done to him. And I could never find out if he was dead or not – if my own sister had killed him. He'd looked dead as a doornail when I saw him on that bed but it was only for a second and he might just have been knocked out, maybe. I've hoped all my life to see him again but instead I got this – banished, too ashamed to go home, too afraid that I might miss Henry or Marion if they came back. This house was a so-called present from the Mountfords. They didn't want me at Eyrie Farm so they fixed it that I got a mortgage for this place – imagine, a woman by herself paying a mortgage in that day and age. It wouldn't have happened at home, I tell you."

"You never found out what happened to Marion, did you?" said Martha, understanding now why she had seen a similarity between this skeletal woman and the ghostly apparition at the cottage, if only for a brief second. Lil looked as though she would blow away on a gust of wind. The vision at the cottage was someone who enjoyed a healthy appetite by the looks of things.

"I saw Robert one more time – when he came back from Australia."

Martha began to feel irritated that she didn't know who this Robert was. Obviously he and Albie were key to the story. She itched to look at the letters, to see what they would reveal. This was like hearing the story in reverse, having to memorise tiny details of the ending before going back to the beginning.

"It was about twenty years ago. He was outside my door one day, looking just like he used to, handsome and clean and healthy. I was ashamed. Sure what did I have to take care of myself for? This place has always been wild. It was a battle when I was a younger woman – my only joy the little patch out the back. I haven't been able to look after it for a while and the

Mountfords never helped me. Anyway, there was Robert, telling me he was sorry about Marion and sure I hadn't a clue what he was talking about. Turns out young Charlie had kept tabs on her for years. He was a sly one, never bloody told me either. She died young. Got hit by a train in London apparently and died instantly. Too good for her. She should have died roaring if she did away with Henry as I think she did."

Martha thought about telling her about what she knew from the events at the cottage and decided against it. It wasn't that she would never tell her, but she needed to think about it first.

"All the oul' stories started then from fellahs going up to the house in the night, about the noises folk hear and all. That chap that Mountford put up there as a security guard, the year of the travellers, was talking about scratching and screaming and all sorts. That's when I started going into that public house, to hear what he had to say. Couldn't stop meself. The more I heard, the more I knew in my heart what she'd done with him."

"What was that, do you think?" asked Martha, intrigued by the fact that Duncan Stockwell's stories fuelled Lil's suspicions, that the tales of a drunk were all the proof that this woman had of what had happened to a boy she evidently adored like a son.

"Marion knew how to lay a brick as well as any man," said Lil.

The words chilled Martha to the core.

"She spent all her time as a girl with my father and he taught her – and in any case, when the fellahs were there building on to the back, sure how could she not have learned anything with the time she spent out there batting her eyelids, Albie or no Albie, like a hussy?"

Martha had to be sure. "What do you mean, Lil? That she knew how to lay a brick?"

Lil Flynn sighed, as though tired of telling the tale. "When Robert brought me here, to the marsh, after I came out of the hospital, all our stuff was here. My clothes, Marion's clothes, Henry's clothes God save us. He'd brought it all here from Eyrie Farm. It was weeks before I went near it, sure I was half crazy with my head the way it was. That fall did me terrible damage altogether. When I got here first he handed me a necklace of Marion's, said he'd found it near the bricked-up fireplace in the bedroom. My mind was so confused it didn't dawn on me for a while that sure all the fireplaces in that house were open – didn't we light them in the wintertime? Although at the end of that last winter the chimney in my room got blocked somehow and, if I lit it, the smoke would just pour out into the room so I stopped using it. I meant to ask Mr Mountford to call a chimney-sweep but then . . ." Lil lapsed into a long silence.

"Lil?" prompted Martha gently.

The old woman sighed. "Then a long time after, I found the courage to sort out Marion and Henry's things – I knew she wasn't coming back and my lovely boy gone with her. I remembered the dress that Marion wore the day it all happened – it was her best one, red of course, but I remember it because she'd made such a fuss about getting dressed to go see Albie, to beg him to take her back. There it was in the pile along with all the other stuff, and it covered in mortar. And what's more I couldn't find what Henry had been wearing that day at all. I could remember it then and I still can – his little shorts and a blue shirt. He thought it was a big man's shirt and he used to stomp around the house in it pretending to be a builder, like the fellahs doing the extension. Now I suppose she could have just changed her dress and taken him in what he was wearing but then why would her dress be covered in mortar? I thought about what Robert had said about the necklace and one part of me put two and two together and another has never believed she could do it. Except I know she could. Marion would do anything to suit herself. Anything at all."

Lil looked pale and exhausted when she finished speaking. She closed her eyes and took a deep breath, grimacing with pain as she exhaled.

"I'd better let you get some rest," said Martha, unwilling to move but knowing that as long as she stayed, the old woman would sit with her and she looked very unwell. Martha wondered if she shouldn't get a doctor for her.

"You didn't answer my question?" said Lil suddenly, her eyes still shut.

"What question was that?" asked Martha, genuinely unable to remember what the old woman had asked.

"Do you ever see him up there?" She opened her eyes. "Henry. With all the stories that the Stockwell fellah told me, I thought maybe . . ."

Martha was amazed to see a note of hope in her eyes and felt her heart go out to her. She looked at Lil and thought about telling her everything, then shook her head. "No, Lil. I've never seen Henry," she said truthfully. Well, she hadn't. She'd felt him, and felt him leave, she was sure. But she'd seen Marion, for her sins. She didn't think Lil would want to hear that, though, knew that she wouldn't be doing a sick old lady any favours by telling her. Marion had done enough haunting since her death. Her sister didn't need to be haunted now that she was definitely gone.

Lil sighed. "Oh well . . . I suppose I'll never know for sure then."

Martha remained silent.

Lil pushed her hands against the table in an effort to propel herself upward, but failed. "So now you know," she said then. breathing painfully. "Now you know. Take them letters away with you. You may as well have them, I suppose. It's important that someone else knows what went on and you're as good a person as any as you're living up there now. They're no use to me. It's all in my head and I don't think I'll ever get it out, brain damage or no brain damage."

"Let me get you some water," Martha said, getting up.

Lil made a face. "No, I can't even drink water with the awful taste in my mouth. Jesus, Mary and Joseph, but it never leaves me. And do you know, the doctor gave me stuff for it and I used it once or twice before I'd go into town but sure isn't there alcohol in it? If I swallowed so much as a drop then I'd have my pledge broken and I intend to die with that intact, the one sure thing I have."

Mouthwash, thought Martha. It could sometimes leave a boozy smell on the breath – Dan used to use it before heading into work, she remembered, and she'd often give him a mint heading out the door as a joke – to freshen his fresh breath. Must have made things more pleasant for Paula, she thought, how kind of me. It explained though, she reckoned, why there had been a faint smell of alcohol from Lil Flynn on their second meeting in the pub. It confirmed the woman had been telling the truth: she was simply the victim of her own very slight disability and a smear campaign by a family who didn't want her talking to a town she didn't feel she could leave. What a life, thought Martha. What a waste of a whole life!

Lily made to stand again and Martha helped her to her feet.

"I won't see you to the door, there's a good girl," said Lil, leaning heavily on the table. "I'm not able. I'm going to go have a lie down for myself though. I'll feel better after that."

"No problem," said Martha picking up the pile of letters, careful to keep them in the order of the pile on the table. "You're absolutely sure you want me to take these?"

Lil nodded. "You're the only person who's listened to me since Robert and sure he went off to Australia with himself. Married a girl out there, had a family. Charlie inherited everything. Made damn sure that I stayed out here on the marsh, quiet and out of the way."

Lil stared wistfully into space and Martha again felt so sorry for her. She didn't know yet exactly what had happened, but she knew for certain that Lil wished it were her that Robert had married and shared a life with.

She realised then that she had got closure here but not what she had expected. That look on Lil Flynn's face told her just how lucky she actually was, to have been married and to have it end for a clearly defined reason, to have a beautiful daughter to love. Lil never had that, obviously had never had the chance to marry the man she loved for whatever reason, had lost the only child she would ever love. Martha felt like crying and kept her head down as she walked to the door. Once there, she turned to see the old woman walking painfully toward a door that Martha had failed to notice before, alongside the dresser.

"Are you sure you're alright, Lil?"

The old woman didn't turn, just waved her arm in dismissal. "I'll be fine after I have a lie-down," she said.

Martha watched her disappear and then let herself gently out the brown door. Then she paused, wondering if it was Lily's habit to leave the front door unlocked in this isolated place. It seemed she must do. Martha let herself out the porch door which she closed carefully behind her.

Once outside, she paused, turned her face to the sky and took a deep breath. If she was expecting to be rewarded with fresh air, she was disappointed, because there had been no let-up in the sultry conditions since she had entered the dark and dirty little house. There was still no sunshine either, although Martha was glad of that. She didn't think the temperatures would be bearable if the sun came out. She felt exhausted. First Mary and now Lil. And the story was even more complicated than she had first thought – new names, a bigger cast of people than she had originally expected. And so much sadness, both Mary and Lil deprived of their men because of the effects of that house. And this Marion person. Exhausted or not, Martha had to read those letters and find out who this Marion character was. To get to the bottom of the story at last.

Martha's mind raced as she drove back along the country road to Shipton Abbey. Her glance fell on the pile of letters from time to time – she was itching to start reading them. Lily must have been taking the medication the doctor gave her when she met her in the pub that time, the poor woman. She had seen no signs today of someone who wanted to scare her, just a woman who wanted the truth to be known about the events that had changed her life all those years ago.

Obviously with no witnesses – no living ones anyway – it would be impossible to prove, but Martha figured that Marion had smothered her son in a rage with a pillow before turning her attention to her sister. What had driven her into that rage though? And had she then blocked the opening of the fireplace itself with Henry's body in it or did she have an accomplice? And who were Albie and Robert? The Mountfords were mixed up in this too somehow, she was sure.

Martha's thoughts turned to poor Henry. Had he simply been unconscious when his mother bricked his little body up? According to Gabriel, that's what his spirit had told him. That he had woken in the dark, cramped and woozy. Hungry and desperately thirsty – that's what Gabriel had said – frightened at first but trusting that someone would come and get him – calling out and knocking.

He was probably afraid that his mother was in a rage and was timid at first, but then no one came for him and he started to feel panic. Martha imagined him searching weakly for any sign of light, any way of escape. Would any light have reached him from the top of the chimney? No – Lil had said the chimney had become blocked up. Did he try to climb upwards – no – the space was too tight. The mortar between the bricks was probably fresh enough for him to make fingerprints in it but it seems as though there was no way the small, weak four-year-old was capable of anything.

To die, screaming for the woman you called your mother, when the woman who *was* your mother had murdered you, or so she thought, and then tried to hide your body by bricking it into a wall . . . no wonder that Henry had still been at that house.

Martha felt tears prick her eyes again and had to pull over as it became too difficult to see. She didn't want to, but couldn't stop herself imagining someone doing that to Ruby – imagined *herself* doing that to Ruby. She couldn't – it was absolutely inconceivable that she could hurt her in any way. For God's sake, she had accidentally given her a spoonful of food that was too hot once and had cried herself. What in the name of God had this Marion person been like? This woman who had also pushed her sister down a stairs and left her for dead? Who had lived all those years in London before being killed by a train of all things. '*Should have died roaring*,' Lil had said.

Martha realised she was ravenous. Looking at the clock on

her dashboard she saw that it was nearly noon. She had plenty of time for a sandwich and a coffee and maybe a glance at one or two of those letters before heading for London. Wiping the tears from her eyes, she started up the car again and drove the short distance to Shipton Abbey. Once she had a rest she could think about getting the car packed up, picking up Ruby and getting on the road.

She parked in the village car park and made her way to the café on the high street. She was absolutely starving and ordered herself a huge chicken roll with garlic mayonnaise and a takeaway coffee. She planned to sit outside at one of the tables and eat it but, when she emerged with her lunch in her hands, she realised that the little café was beginning to fill up with the lunchtime trade. She needed somewhere quieter, she thought, somewhere that she could fully absorb what Lil's letters were going to tell her. Martha looked up and down the street and eventually figured out where best to go. She took the small lane that led behind the café and down the hill toward the estuary and the abbey.

Shipton Abbey itself towered over her, forbidding and grey, as finally a strong sun broke through the clouds. Martha wiped her forehead – each step, even downhill, made her hotter and the sunshine made it brighter but more uncomfortable. She crossed over the road to the abbey entrance and made her way through the foreground where a guided tour was being conducted by a middle-aged woman hoisting an umbrella aloft so that a group of tired and sweating tourists could follow her. She crossed through the small burial ground at the front with the most recent headstones, dating up to the 1800s, and then around the side of the huge ruined building. Once around the back, she made her way through the stones to a corner shaded by trees. There she sat down, placed her lunch on the grass and took out the bundle of letters.

She took the first from the top of the pile – they had been jumbled in her bag so she would have to sort them by date. She took one out of its envelope and noted that it had been folded in such a way that the date was the first thing she saw on the page. Lil had folded them all this way, so it was easy for Martha to sort them between bites. She noted that the dates started frequently enough – monthly, she thought, but by the end there was only one letter a year.

The first was dated February 1st, 1953.

'*Dear Caroline,*' it read. '*Happy St Brigid's Day to you and Happy 17th birthday to me . . .*'

33

Eyrie Farm,
Shipton Abbey,
Norfolk,
England

March 15th, 1957

Dear Caroline,

I know it is only a little over a month since my last letter but I feel I must write to you today if only to keep my hands busy for they cannot stop shaking. I have news both good and bad. The bad first – Albie has found out about Henry and has broken off his engagement to Marion. It is a disaster. For all of the months of goodness that she has shown, she has doubled it with badness since this terrible thing took place on Sunday last.

For weeks she has been trying to put Albie off coming to Eyrie Cottage to meet me lest her secret be discovered. He put his foot down, however, and insisted that last Sunday was finally the day when he and I should be formally introduced. He was insisting that I be her bridesmaid at their wedding in June. Little did they know that I will be far away by then, but more of that later.

She had been like a caged animal since he decided this, pacing up and down the house, shouting at Henry to shut up all the time, screaming at him that if he so much as breathed while Albie was here then she would kill him stone dead by ripping off his head with her bare hands. He is nearly four now, and old enough to understand and she frightened him terribly.

The terrible day dawned sunny and bright and I laid on a spread in the parlour for Albie of ham sandwiches and butterfly cakes and a huge fruit cake that I iced and decorated especially for him. He was due to arrive at three o'clock and that he did, on the button, in his great motor car with a bunch of daffodils for us.

Marion was like a cat on a hot griddle. I had put Henry into the back bedroom and told him that he should be as quiet as a mouse as he always is when the workmen are here. I served the tea to Albie, gave him sandwiches and cake, and was chatting politely, when all of a sudden there was a terrible crash from upstairs and a scream from Henry. I couldn't stop myself belting up that stairs. I know when his cries mean that he has hurt himself and sure enough when I got to him he was crying his little heart out and a big cut on his hand where he'd picked up a piece of what had broken. It wasn't his fault, I keep the picture of the Sacred Heart in there that Mammy sent us – it doesn't feel right having Him in the kitchen, Caroline, as we have so little faith between us here. The nail was always loose though and it chose that moment to crash down from the wall, as if the Sacred Heart himself were looking down with disapproval on the poor child locked in a room while his mother entertained.

Henry's scream was so loud that Albie came up the stairs behind me, and Marion behind him telling him to come down, that there was nothing to see. You can't imagine Albie's shock when he saw this poor bleeding child, his mouth wide open with roars, and tears streaming from his face. I thought he'd drop dead on the spot. I started to tell him that Henry was my son. I thought I could get away with that and then I'd be the one with the shame and Marion's big wedding could go ahead but Albie turned to Marion with a funny look on his face and said to her that he couldn't believe it was true, that he'd heard the rumours but he'd defended her to the very end, that his fiancée would never have had a child out of wedlock. He demanded his ring back from her and told her that their wedding was off and that he wouldn't make a fuss but that he didn't ever want to see her again.

He looked a broken man, Caroline, as he walked down the stairs with Marion after him telling him over and over that she didn't know what he meant, that Henry was my son and that I was the one with the shameful past. He didn't listen to her though and I was holding Henry in my arms when I heard his car drive away with Marion screaming and running after it.

When she came back in, I tried to lock the door on her but I didn't make it in time. She beat us, Caroline. She picked up a stick from the driveway and came up that stairs like the devil himself and started to whip us with it, first me, then Henry, then me again. His screams and cries were terrible, telling her to leave him alone, to leave his mammy alone but she's never listened to him and she didn't that day. Again, I managed to get him under me so that I got the worst of the beating. My back is just starting to heal a week later and I have a black eye where she caught me unawares. Henry's injuries are under his clothes and he is used to her beatings so he recovered by Wednesday and was able to walk again but she managed to thrash the soles of his tiny feet where they came out from under me and he could barely take a step.

She beat us for an hour, I'd say, Caroline, screaming terrible things, wishing us both dead, swearing that she was going to beat us both to death. We were only saved when she got too tired to beat us any more and she threw down the stick and stopped kicking me and stormed off outside.

I think my mother was watching over us that day, because not ten minutes later I heard another car pull up outside and who should come straight in but Robert. He didn't care if she was there. He just knew that there was something wrong because he had nearly crashed headfirst into Albie Forbes' car which was *tearing along the road and he guessed that he had been here. He bathed our wounds, kissed Henry better and then rocked him to sleep – the poor little man was exhausted from crying and the pain. Robert wanted to take us away with him there and then but I persuaded him not to, that I knew what to do with Marion and once Henry was safely locked away then she couldn't harm me.*

Robert was home for the weekend and had come only to tell me the joyous news that he had arranged our wedding – what a bittersweet afternoon that was! He stayed as long as he could but the fear was too great in me that Marion would go berserk if she returned and found him there and tell his father again and all would be ruined. "We must carry on as normal," I urged him and he reluctantly agreed. He was terrified of leaving us alone there but I made him go. After all, it is only now a matter of days before we are to be Mr and Mrs Mountford and no amount of cuts and bruises and kicks from my sister can take that away from me.

It is the one thought that has sustained me throughout this difficult week. I have scarcely seen Marion till today. She appeared in her finest dress this morning and said that she was taking the bike and going to Bickford to plead with Albie to take her back. I said nothing, just kept Henry behind me and watched her go. She has been too calm, and I fear that if Albie does not take her back then I don't know what she will want to do to us.

I am dressed and ready to go, however, Caroline. I am wearing the green dress that I wore to that first party when Robert kissed me, for he has said that is how he remembers me at my most beautiful. Our plan is set, only another hour to go and he will come and collect me and Henry and our bags and then we are away from here. Away from Shipton Abbey, away from Marion, away from Mr Mountford, away from the secrets that we keep in this little house.

We are to go to London, where a friend of Robert's from university keeps a place. I am to stay there alone, with Henry, and Robert is to stay with Iris but without saying a word. Then on Monday morning – only three nights to sleep before we are husband and wife – we will be married at a place Robert calls a registration office – he has made all the arrangements for us, and straight after that we are going to France, of all places! He has enough saved for us to stay in a hotel until we find somewhere to live and then we will settle there, reinvented as Robert, Lily and Henry Mountford, a proper family at last!

My bags are packed in the hallway, Caroline, such as we have. Ted, the bear that Henry has treasured – Robert's own bear from when he was a child in fact! – is sitting on top of Henry's little knapsack and he is dressed in his 'big man' shirt and a pair of short pants because the weather is very fine indeed and Robert has promised to get him new clothes in London, and indeed when we are in France it is so warm there he shall wear short pants every day and go to school with other boys and girls, and learn French and who knows – maybe Robert and I will have a little companion for him, or more maybe. The future is wide open to us, Caroline. My stomach is alive with butterflies and I can scarcely keep still.

Wish us luck and Godspeed as we leave today for our new life!

Your friend,

Lily

34

It was two o'clock when Martha reached the final letter, written the day that it had all happened, March 15th, 1957. She picked up her coffee cup and swigged back the last, cold mouthful inside.

So that was who Marion was. And poor little Henry, like a dirty secret up at the cottage, unable to play with other children, deprived of everything that a child should have except for the unconditional love of his aunt and the unfettered embarrassment and shame of his mother. Marion didn't care about Henry – Lil was right – had never done so from the day he was born and even less so when Albert appeared on the scene. And poor Lil – now she knew why she liked to be called Mountford – herself and Robert had been so close to being husband and wife. Martha sighed, feeling sadness on her shoulders like a burden. Everyone who had ever been to that place had ended up broken-hearted.

She leaned back against the tree she was sitting against and shut her eyes. They burned from reading through the letters, if she just rested them for a moment then she'd be able to drive up to the cottage – she had nothing to fear there any more – and pack up and finally get on the road.

She was roused by a distinct wet plop on her nose, followed

by another, and another – she was dreaming that she was trying to drive her car from the back seat, unable to reach the pedals and in too high a gear to go around the many corners on the road. In her dream, suddenly the sunroof was open and rain was falling in on her face, making it more difficult to drive . . .

She opened her eyes – there was, indeed, rain on her face, huge thick drops falling faster and faster. She sat up, unsure for a moment where she was or what she was doing. Then it hit her – the letters! She looked around her to where she had neatly piled them up beside her hip and gathered them quickly into her handbag to keep them dry. They couldn't be ruined! Lil had entrusted them to her care.

The rain started to get heavier – a drop stung her as it hit her directly between the eyes. "Ow!" she said out loud and gathered up her empty coffee cup and the wrapping her sandwich had come in. She scrabbled to her feet and looked up at the sky which was slate grey between the raindrops. It was still hot, however, and Martha felt a niggling fear in her stomach that a thunderstorm was on the way. She checked the ground where she had been sitting and seeing that she had gathered up all of her belongings, started a slow run back around the abbey and through the burial ground toward the car park.

The rain was coming in torrents as she reached her car, pelting the ground and bouncing back up again, causing small white splashes on the road. Martha eased herself into the driver's seat and slammed the door shut. She turfed her handbag over onto the passenger seat and started the engine before tugging her seatbelt around her. As she did so, the time on the dashboard clock caught her eye: 16.15 it said. She had been asleep for two hours! She couldn't believe it – she knew she was exhausted but she had never been able to sleep anywhere other than her bed – a couch or a train seat at a push – but under a tree? Dammit, she was going to be later on the road than she expected, later getting to London and it was going to cause havoc with Ruby's timetable. Oh well, she thought, can't be helped. Berating herself for having fallen asleep, she drove out of the car park and across the village the short distance to Lullabies. Time to get this show on the road.

Martha was disappointed in one way that Mary was absent from the crèche when she arrived there. Gone home early, Aneta said. Martha wasn't surprised, considering the morning they'd had. Aneta was on her own with Ruby and Ella and Ruby screeched with delight on seeing her mother. In another way, however, it meant that there was no long goodbye with Mary, no chance of reprising the conversation from this morning, of having to explain what she had been doing all day, why she was soaking wet with her short hair sitting stringy on her head.

Martha was in and out of the crèche in five minutes, Ruby in her arms and her belongings in her changing bag. The heavy shower had completely stopped by the time she left Lullabies and she noted that the road out near Eyrie Farm was completely dry as if there had been no rain there at all. She felt vaguely nervous as she reached the turn-off for the cottage but realised that was purely habit – she was just used to being afraid of the house. There was no need to feel scared any more, however. Gabriel had seen to that – and she herself had felt the spirits dissipate and cross over.

Martha gathered Ruby from the car and headed for the door. Will's car was gone, no sign of wiring or equipment of any sort left, as if the investigation had never taken place. She knew she should probably say goodbye to Will and Gabriel but she was sure they'd understand that she was keen to get away as quickly as possible. For all she knew at this stage of the day they'd headed for Edinburgh themselves. It was probable that Gabriel's bus was fixed and ready to go, she thought, and grinned to herself as she popped her key in the lock and let herself in, leaving the door open behind her. She knew this would be a quick stop – she needed to pack up the basics to survive with Sue in London for a few days until the packers came to the cottage and did what they had to do. She knew they needed clothes, the essential baby equipment and nothing more.

Martha meant to put Ruby on her playmat but then thought

better of it when she glanced into the study and saw the nest of cushions from earlier still on the floor. She sat her down with a kiss and an assurance that she would be back in a moment and carried on into the kitchen where she set to packing Ruby's food, bottles, steriliser and playmat into a shopping bag that she took from under the sink. Only the essentials, she thought. What she would do was telephone Rob Mountford in the morning from London and make the necessary arrangements about returning his keys and having her remaining belongings picked up by a removal company. There wasn't much – Ruby's cot, nick-nacks like lamps and ornaments, some pictures. Martha could do a mental tour of the house in her head and list out exactly what was hers and what belonged to the cottage itself. A full clearout of her stuff could be done in an afternoon.

She glanced into the conservatory, picking up a toy and her sheep mug that she had left there that morning – God, that felt like a different person! Funnily, though, she had expected the house to feel different somehow, lighter, but it felt exactly the same as it always did. Not spooky, necessarily, but somehow heavy, occupied. Martha brushed the feeling off. It was just her imagination that the house should have any sort of a feeling at all. And this oppressive weather certainly wasn't helping. She carried on upstairs, shouting another reassurance at Ruby that she wouldn't be long. The baby ignored her. She had found a tassel on a cushion that she was using to tickle her own face and was very preoccupied.

It seemed to take forever for Martha to get her 'essentials' into the car. She was a hoarder, a nester who loved all of her stuff around her and much as she tried to be practical there was stuff that she just didn't want to leave behind. The picture of herself and Ruby that had fallen off the wall the night of the storm when Alison Stockwell had baby-sat, a huge bundle of nappies even though Sue lived just around the corner from a Tesco Express. Wow, Tesco Express, thought Martha with a grin. She knew she shouldn't feel excited but she couldn't help it. She longed for city things – being caught in a cloud of exhaust from a bus – she adored that smell, even though she knew that it was filthy and harmful. She longed for the sound of sirens in the distance instead of birds and foxes, for an orange glow of street lights on her ceiling at bedtime, for the distant rattle of the Tube. She would get to Sue's about eight, she reckoned. Not too late for Ruby's bedtime, and her own nap at the abbey had probably done her the world of good and would keep her alert to drive on the motorway. She'd stop for a coffee and some petrol at the service station out at the motorway and then she was on her way home.

She made her way up the stairs to do a final gathering of items from her and Ruby's rooms. She gave her habitual glance upwards when she stood on the first step and then shook her head. No need to do that, she thought. There's not going to be anything to see up there. What did catch her eye was a glint of silver hanging from the post of the banister on the landing. Gabriel's rosary beads. He must have left them for her to find them. It touched her to think that he had hung them there to make sure that she wouldn't forget them, that she should keep them as some sort of protective talisman for the little girl on her hip. She stepped into Ruby's room to pack some items there and left the beads down on the dressing table.

It crossed her mind as she packed the last of her clothes that Sue might not be there when she arrived, could be off covering a story. It didn't matter – when Dan left, Sue had insisted that Martha take a key to her apartment so she could let herself in any time, day or night. She had even bought a travel cot for Ruby, bless her. In a way, thought Martha, that might be even nicer – to have that lovely modern apartment to herself for a night at least. No spooky corners or fireplaces. Nothing older than an unpaid phone bill or some stale bread in the whole place. She could have a bath, and order a pizza which would be delivered to the door. She could eat it in her dressing gown and then have a hot chocolate and get into a bed with clean sheets – she'd probably have to make it herself but what matter. The thought of being in Sue's apartment cheered her immensely, made her feel that once she got there then everything would be fine, carefree and safe.

Martha zipped up the final suitcase. She glanced around the room and remembered her next task – to empty the nappy-bin in Ruby's bedroom. She had noticed a faint unpleasant pong in there and reckoned that she'd be none too popular with Rob Mountford should she leave them there, in this weather especially. It would serve him right though – hadn't Lil said that he'd told her not to speak to Martha? Didn't want anything to damage his chances of making as much money as he could out of Eyrie Farm. Calling it Hawthorn Cottage, as if that could banish the past . . .

Martha crossed to Ruby's room and began to deal with the nappy-bin. Suddenly she started and swung around. She thought – was sure – she'd heard the door to Ruby's room squeak. She stood still, the end of the chain of nappies emerging from the bin in her hand, enfolded in plastic like a long string of sausages. There was nothing there. Get a grip, Martha, she thought and pulled the rest of the nappies from the bin. She rested them on the ground while she replaced the lid of the bin and secured the sides. She could give it a good scrub out when it came back to London.

Martha glanced around the room, at the picture of the hare leaning against the wall. That was something she might leave off her inventory. Donate a horrible picture to a horrible place, she thought. She didn't think she could ever look at it again without feeling a shiver down her spine. The moon and stars lamp too she would leave behind. She had come to regard the gentle, silent rotation of the shapes as something sinister rather than comforting.

For the first time something struck her – was Henry's body *still* in the fireplace? It had never even occurred to her that it might be. It must be. All this time she had been putting Ruby to bed in here . . . she shivered. Maybe that was why his spirit couldn't leave the place? Then again, Marion's body wasn't here – she hadn't even died here, but it was to Eyrie Farm that her horrible, restless soul had returned. To find her son. To shut him up so that no one would ever know he was there . . .

Martha shook herself. Stop, she thought. It's over and you are one trip to the car away from getting out of here. She glanced at the chimney-breast for a moment longer.

"Rest in peace now, little boy," she said aloud, a wobble in her voice. "Sleep tight."

Martha turned and left the room, bouncing the nappy-chain along behind her with one hand as she hoisted up the suitcase she had left on the landing with the other. The small table had been righted, she noticed, and the shards of the broken lamp cleared up and disposed of. She saw they were in the wheelie bin outside, along with chunks of tape used to secure the cameras and attach wires to the floor, when she opened it to put in the nappies. She bunched up the chain of nappies and threw them in on top and then turned her attention to trying to get the suitcase into her car. No easy task. She had certainly crammed too many 'essentials' in this time.

Eventually she managed to fit the case in along with the bags of toys and feeding items. She banged the boot shut, straightened her back and took one long look at the house. "Let's go!" she said and trudged back inside to the now bare study. "Right then, Ruby Doo!" she said to her daughter and held her arms out to pick her up. The baby was growing tired, she could see, her skin a little paler than normal, little red bags under her eyes. "Do we need a snooze, darling?" she asked and bent to catch her daughter under the arms which were outstretched towards her.

It was then that she remembered something. "Oops, one more thing that Mummy forgot!" she said and straightened her back. The rosary beads that she'd left in Ruby's room. They'd completely slipped her mind. For a second she contemplated leaving them but rejected the idea. She couldn't leave them for the removal men. They'd never see them for starters and then probably stamp them into the ground and leave them behind. She couldn't let that happen. Gabriel had been so good to give Ruby that extra protection, and they were clearly something precious to him that he carried around with him. She would retrieve them and then she could courier them to Will at the university to give back to Gabriel. She doubted he'd appreciate them arriving in a package at the bus depot.

Ruby gave a wail as she saw her mother retreat when she had come so close to being picked up into the safety of her arms. She was exhausted and hot and Martha felt guilty at depriving her of the cuddle she so clearly wanted. She bent and ran her hand around Ruby's chubby cheek. "Sorry, darling. Give me two seconds and I'll be back."

Martha turned and walked quickly down the hallway, Ruby's wails getting louder by the second. "Mummy's here, petal!" she shouted, hoping to provide her with reassurance. A thirty-second trip upstairs and then she could settle Ruby into her car seat and she'd fall asleep as soon as the engine started. "Coming, sweetheart!" she called again. Ruby's wails turned to sobs.

She had reached the bottom step of the stairs when the study door slammed. The bang echoed through the hallway and made her jump, giving an involuntary cry of shock as she did so. Martha froze. The door only ever did that when the window was open in there and the front door opened at the same time. The front door was ajar alright, but Martha was sure all the windows were closed . . . but she hadn't checked too thoroughly, just assumed. She jogged back down the hallway.

The bang had silenced Ruby but Martha knew it wouldn't be long before she reacted to her fright. She reached out and pressed down the heavy handle to the study door and pushed with her shoulder against it. It didn't move. She tried again, not a budge. The slam must have somehow tripped the locking mechanism. She bent down and peered between the wood of the door and the frame. Sure enough the bolt of the lock was visible in the thin gap. Martha felt panic. The key, she thought, the key is inside. Then she remembered. No, it wasn't – she had taken it from the lock the morning after she had slept in the study and put it in the pocket of her pyjama bottoms. But where were those pyjamas now? She didn't remember packing them. They must still be upstairs, on the bedroom floor perhaps.

She turned and, as she did so, was greeted by a sight that made her blood turn cold. There by the stairs she saw something she never thought she'd ever again see.

Marion.

The same chubby, pasty-grey skin, the dark short curly hair, the black clothes. The sight was exactly the same as before. Through her she could see the stairs, yet the apparition still managed to look as solid as a live human.

Martha screamed in fright and shock and flung herself back against the doorway, partly to get away and partly out of instinct, to somehow protect her daughter. Her mind flashed back to what Gabriel had told her – the study didn't exist for Marion, it hadn't been there . . . wait . . . Martha felt a pit of fear form in her stomach. He was wrong. The study *had* been there when Marion had lived at Eyrie Farm. Lil had said she had watched it being built – Duncan Stockwell had used it. For heaven's sake, Martha had *seen* Marion go into the bathroom upstairs – it hardly existed directly above without the study being there underneath it. How could she have been so trusting – how could she have left her daughter in there, unprotected, without thinking?

Marion's pupils were black. Martha could see no trace of anything human about them. They were only a few feet from her face now – the spirit seemed to be growing closer to her, not visibly moving but somehow gliding towards her – close enough to touch her – close enough . . . Martha gasped as the spirit glided *through* her. She felt icy cold, as though her skin and blood had been dipped into freezing water. As soon as it had entered her body it left, the coldness passing through her, the apparition gliding through the door behind her into the study. No, thought Martha, *no no no!*

Marion's spirit was now in the room with Ruby. The locked room, where Martha couldn't help her. Martha turned and jiggled the door handle frantically, banging on the door and shouting as loudly as she could. "*Marion!*" she screamed. "Marion, get out of there! Get the hell away from my baby – she's mine! Leave her alone, Marion!" She pummelled the door with her fists, the palms of her hands, rattled the handle, kicked the door with her feet. There was no give. She was never going to get in this way. What was Marion *doing* in there? What scared Martha the most was Ruby's silence. Just like Henry's . . . She had to get in.

She forced herself to step back from the door. It felt like the most unnatural thing in the world to do but she was on her own and she had to think logically. She took a step away, a step back, then turned with a moan and ran for the stairs. She had to get the key.

Martha sprinted for the stairway, taking the steps two at a time, running as hard as she could. She reached her bedroom, bare since she had cleared it out. The pyjamas, where were the pyjamas? "Where are the *fucking* pyjamas!" The laundry hamper – she had rolled them up and dropped them in the hamper the first time she had been here with Will. Dear God, let the key be there! Let it not have fallen out somewhere!

There they were. She grabbed them and there was the key, hard in the pocket. "Oh, thank you, Jesus," she moaned. Bizarrely, she thought of Gabriel telling her she had to have faith. She didn't know then if he had meant faith in herself or in a higher power. Still didn't.

The key in her hand, she dived for the door. "Mummy's coming!" she yelled and ran for the hallway.

It took a split second, but Martha saw the table suddenly slide at high speed out from the corner of the landing under her feet. She couldn't stop herself – she crashed straight into it and fell sideways, away from the stairs, knocking the table over with her as she went. She landed heavily on her right arm, the key making a *clunk* as it fell from her hand and landed on the floor.

"*No!*" she shouted and made to sit up, scrabbling for the key with her hand. She felt a sharp pain jolt through her shoulder as she did so. No sooner did she raise her chest to sit up, however, than she was slammed back onto the floor, her head bouncing back and hitting the wooden landing. She looked up. Marion stood – no – *hovered* above her. She seemed ten feet tall to Martha. She didn't know if the spectre had grown taller or if it was elevated off the ground.

Marion looked down at Martha, her chin spreading around her lower face, her eyes black and fixed. Fear gripped Martha and she tried to sit up but couldn't. She tried her legs and found that she could push herself along the ground in the direction of Ruby's room.

Again, as if it had happened in an instant, Marion's face was suddenly directly over Martha's. She got the smell of rotting vegetables and realised that it hadn't been the nappy bin creating the foul odour earlier, it had been Marion. Why hadn't she realised this and just got herself and Ruby out of there? Because she was certain Marion was gone, that's why – sure that she had felt her leave.

Rage suddenly filled Martha. "You're supposed to be *gone*!" she shouted into the spectral face. The foul mouth that Martha had looked into earlier suddenly opened wide, the eyes closed tight and with an overwhelming stench the thing started to growl, lowly at first, then louder and louder until the sound filled the air. Martha tried to cover her ears but something was pinning her hands to the ground. She could only turn her face away from the cavernous mouth, the rotting teeth, the black tongue . . .

The growl lingered in the air long after it had finished. Martha heard a cry from downstairs. Ruby. She was alive. If she was crying, she was breathing. She was fine. At the same time, Martha was sure she could hear a whimper from behind her. She tried to turn her head around. Henry? Surely not. Surely he'd crossed over that morning? She'd felt him leave . . .

The apparition was upright again, staring down at her, the hands folded demurely at the waist. Martha tried again to move her arms. It worked this time. She extended the fingers of her right hand and felt the metal of the study key beneath them. She scrabbled it toward her and closed her fingers around it. Whatever happened, she must not lose the key again. At the same time, if Marion were with her, then she wasn't with Ruby, was she? Did she have enough power? Enough energy to be in two places at once? Still Martha could hear Ruby cry. She tried to make her muscles move to get up but couldn't. The cry was loud and strong though, and it was an upset cry, not a cry of pain. That was all she had to console herself with.

Martha strained again to get up. The scratching had started from Ruby's room. She could hear little thumps, whimpers and a small voice. It was just like she'd imagined it. "*Mammy?*" said the little voice. "*You they, Mammy?*"

Martha tried to focus on anything but the voice. It was unbearable. Little Henry was going through it all again. Unimaginable suffering and fear.

"*Mam!*" shouted the boy, annoyed at being ignored like any other child. "*I come out now! I hung-ny. I thus-ty!*"

Martha heard the little speech impediment – the inability to say his 'r's', substituting 'n's'. "It's alright, Henry!" she called. "I'm coming now!" Anything to give him hope as he experienced the horror again and again.

Suddenly Martha was flipped over onto her stomach, as though she was lying on a rug and someone flicked it. She grunted as she hit the floor, banging her chin against the ground, winded. As quickly as she landed on her stomach, her body was spun around so that her feet were now lying in the doorway of Ruby's room and her head was near to the table that had slid out into her path. The movement was so quick that the room whirled around her and then suddenly she felt hands around her ankles, just as she had the other night. Hands gripping her like a cold vice and dragging her into Ruby's bedroom. She tried to sit up, tried to kick, but it felt as though she were bound, wrapped in cling film all the way down her body. The hideous apparition of Marion was nowhere to be seen but she could still strongly detect her awful smell.

Martha was dragged over the saddle-board into Ruby's room. She squirmed to avoid a screw that she knew protruded slightly from the saddle-board. It didn't work. She felt the metal edge rub against her jeans and then scrape her stomach as her clothes were pulled up with the dragging movement. She screamed in pain and frustration, her stomach exposed now, her T-shirt bunching up under her arms. She was over the threshold now, inside the door. She struggled again to turn or get up and was amazed to find that this time her movement was unrestricted, the vicelike grip on her ankles suddenly gone. She stood up quickly, stuffing the key into the front pocket of her jeans where it would be more difficult to fall out, straightening her clothes. She swung her head around. There was no sign of Marion.

The scrabbling in the chimney had stopped after Martha had spoken to Henry but as suddenly as it stopped, it started again. "*Mam, whey ah you?*" he said, his voice growing panicky. At the same time, a low rumble came from above their heads. The promised thunderstorm arriving at last. Martha heard a thump on the roof, then a second, as another thundery shower began.

"It's alright, Henry, love. I'm going to get a man to help you," said Martha in the most soothing voice she could manage. She had to get to Ruby but this little boy needed her as well. If she could just get Ruby and get out she could go and find Gabriel, get him to help Henry cross over this time. The thoughts came in an instant but they spurred her into action. She took a step toward the door, was momentarily halted as the first flash of lightning lit up the entire room, and then the door slammed in her face, as the study door had done downstairs. She stepped back, then turned in an instant as the blackout blind snapped down and the room was plunged into darkness, the rain beating an insistent tattoo on the roof.

"*Please, Mammy!*" came the voice from the wall.

"It's alright, Henry, I'm right here," said Martha, terrified. She stepped backwards, circling in the one spot in the middle of the room. "Stop it, Marion," she said. "Now open the door like a good girl and let me go."

There was another rumble from outside, closer now, a sonic echo lingering. Martha's heart boomed as the moons and stars of Ruby's lamp began to slowly circle the walls, casting their dim warmth. Dear God, no, thought Martha. Please, no.

"Marion," she said, as sternly as she could manage. "Now stop it. This sort of behaviour isn't going to bring Albie back." She yelped as the bars of Ruby's cot began to rattle fiercely. She didn't know what she could achieve but if she could get a reaction from Marion then maybe she could keep her going, wear her out, sap her energy . . .

The scratching from behind her grew more insistent. Martha gasped aloud, a picture flashing across her brain of what was being repeated in there, time and time again.

"I know what you did to Henry, Marion," said Martha.

The cot continued to judder, the rattling growing more violent. The legs began to move and it slid around an inch or so from its original position, making a scraping noise as it did. Martha stepped away from it.

"Did you smother him, Marion? Poor little Henry! He did nothing wrong, you know."

Suddenly, a cushion from a chair flew upward into the air and was hurtled at Martha at huge speed. She turned to avoid it but it caught her square in the eye. "*Ow!*" she shouted and covered it with her hand. She could feel it sting and tears begin to form. She blinked frantically, needing to keep both eyes open but unable to with the pain.

"You stupid bitch!"' shouted Martha, unable to stop herself.

"*Shuuut uuuup* . . ." came the reply, a growling, rasping voice coming from mid-air, from everywhere in the room at the one time.

Martha whimpered.

"*Go* 'way, *Mannion!*" came the little angry voice from the fireplace, through the persistent sobbing and scratching. "*Leeme alone!*"

Martha felt as though her heart would break, with sorrow for Henry; with fear for herself and with terror for Ruby. She couldn't hear if her daughter was still crying or not – the rain on the roof was too loud, the echo of the ghostly voice still rattling in her ears, the cot now jumping for want of a better description, the bars shaking and trembling fiercely.

Martha suddenly felt exhausted. She began to cry, overwhelmed by what was happening to her. "Leave us alone, Marion, please!" she begged.

The response was a disembodied snarl, like an animal about

to attack. Martha didn't know what to do any more, was overcome with fear for her child.

Martha looked around her helplessly, saw the rosary beads that she had come back for on the chest of drawers and reached out a hand instinctively to grab them. She grasped them in her hand, willing them to give her the protection that Gabriel had intended for Ruby. Almost without thinking she wound them twice around her hand and pushed them down to her wrist where they hung like a loose bracelet. Henry's sobs were growing in intensity, interspersed with gasps for breath. Dear God, no, thought Martha – he's running out of air or strength.

"Just stop it, Marion!" she screamed. "Everyone in the village knows what you did to Henry and Lil – I made sure of that!" She would try anything now to make her stop.

In an instant everything went quiet. The cot ceased to rattle, the scratching stopped from the wall. It worked, thought Martha. It's stopped, like being in the eye of a storm. She glanced around her and then took her chance, taking a step toward the door. She reached for the door handle and in the instant she did so, the entire room came alive around her as the storm began again. Henry screamed from the chimney-breast, an unnatural guttural scream of sheer terror and panic, as if he realised suddenly what was going to happen to him. The bars of the cot began to rattle more violently than before, the legs sliding from side to side, as though it was performing some ridiculous, unnatural dance. The lid flew from the nappy bin and skidded across the floor, the small side table where Martha placed the soothers flipped over and landed on its side with a violent thud. Martha raised her hands to her ears, unable to take in what she was experiencing. As she did so, another scream joined Henry's, faint at first but growing in intensity, like two voices at once, three voices, ten voices.

Slowly, a black mist formed in front of Martha, becoming clearer and more distinct. It grew clearer from the legs up – the old-fashioned shoes, the legs, the tight skirt, the round-neck jumper and then the face that was barely a face at all, a huge open mouth emitting this scream from the depths of another time and place, a scream not for the horror that her son was experiencing, nor for the lives she had ruined, but a scream for herself. The eyes were tightly closed, the head itself thrown back.

Martha could barely look. Her heart boomed in her chest and she burst into tears again, whimpers coming from her mouth. She didn't know what to do, had never thought it possible to feel such fear. She truly thought she might die of fright.

"Please, Jesus, this is too much," she said in a whisper of disbelief, her hand clutching the tiny crucifix on the beads on her wrist, her brain trying frantically to process what was going on. "*This is too much!*"

Suddenly, through the screaming and the rattling and the noise from the rain, came a voice . . .

"Let me in, Martha. What's going on in there?"

Gabriel.

A hammering came from the door. "Mrs Mannion!" he shouted. "I demand that in the name of Jesus and the Lord our God you leave this room now!" It was futile. The scream continued, the room continued to move.

"Gabriel!" shouted Martha. "Her name is *Marion*. I know all about her, what she did to Henry. She's locked Ruby in the study – please keep her out of the study!"

"Ruby's fine, Martha – now can you get this door open?" The door handle rattled as he tried to get in.

She tried to go to the door but could not. "I can't move, Gabriel – it's too much here," she sobbed and sank to her knees, aware that help was literally inches away but yet so far.

"Marion!" shouted Gabriel in a commanding voice. "I demand in the Name of God that you step back. Step away, Marion. Leave this woman be!"

Amazingly, it worked. In an instant, the room fell silent again.

Martha stayed on the ground, sobbing with terror. This was what had happened before that scream. She hadn't thought it could get any worse, but it had . . .

She was roused by the feeling of arms around her. Her instinct was to push them away. Her arms flailed wildly around her as fear grabbed her gut again and everything went blank with terror.

"Don't touch me!" she screamed, punching out as hard as she could. Strong arms restrained her. The fact that there was heat coming from them made her look up. Gabriel was looking down at her, holding her arms at her side to prevent himself being punched.

"It's okay, Martha, I'm here," he said. She continued to struggle against him, her brain too traumatised to fully take it in. "*I'm here*," he said sternly and she felt her arms grow still. Someone else was here. Gabriel. She was safe.

"She did this before, Gabriel," she babbled, looking frantically around her. "Everything went still and then it got worse. Poor Henry . . ." she pointed at the chimney-breast.

"I know," he said. "She blocked him from us this morning, made us think she'd gone but she hadn't. And neither had he. I felt there was something wrong. She's very strong, Martha, but we've got to be strong as well."

"I know her story now," she said, staggering slightly as Gabriel helped her to her feet. "She's Henry's mother but she never loved him. He loved Lil more. Ruby! Where's Ruby, Gabriel? If Marion's not here then she must be with Ruby!" She flung herself through the door and bounded down the stairs.

She ran along the hallway, Gabriel close behind her. She dug the key out of her pocket, fumbling, her trembling fingers caught up in the lining.

"Hurry," said Gabriel.

That made her panic even more. Gabriel was likely to know something of what was happening behind the closed door.

Ruby gave a sharp scream from inside the room and began to cry.

"She's hurt her!" gasped Martha, and struggled to get the key into the keyhole. It refused to go. She had never felt her hands shake like this – it was like someone else had them and was moving them around, preventing her from what she needed to do.

"Let me!" urged Gabriel and grabbed the key from her hand, slotting it neatly into the lock and turning it. It gave a click and the door swung open.

"Ruby!" cried Martha and pushed her way past Gabriel into the room.

Marion was in there. The air was thick with the foul smell from her and Martha stopped dead in her tracks at seeing her. She was kneeling at Ruby's head. The baby had been flipped onto her stomach, a position she hated. Marion's hands were poised on either side of Ruby's head, fingers spread, just about to grab her by the temples. Ruby was screaming with fright, her legs kicking and pushing against the ground, straining her little chest upward, pushing as hard as her arms would let her to lift her head and see what this horrible thing was.

Martha knew what Marion was about to do: what she used to do to Henry. She made a dive for her daughter and pulled her by the feet back toward her. Ruby screamed violently and Martha's heart almost stopped. Then Ruby was in her arms and safe. She stepped backward out of the room and drew her child closer to her chest.

"It's okay, Mummy's here, it's fine, darling," she crooned, turning Ruby to face her and scanning her for any signs of harm.

"Marion, you have done your damage in this world – it's time for you to go, and to let Henry go as well!" Gabriel boomed from inside the room.

Martha, backed against the stairs, glanced away from Ruby and over his shoulder. The spectre was there one second and gone the next, as she was so fond of doing. "Gabriel, be careful!"

"I know," he growled in frustration. "Let's try to get to Henry while we can." He stormed off down the hall.

Martha wanted nothing more than to go out through the open front door – she could see her car outside, and another vehicle beside it – Will's Volvo, she realised. She knew that Henry must be helped though, and it was safer to have Ruby with her. Where *was* Will? Was he outside, somehow watching this through one of his cameras? How could he do that? Realising that she was alone, she scurried after Gabriel, clutching Ruby to her for dear life.

There were no further signs of Marion on the stairway. Martha climbed as quickly as she could, terrified that somehow Marion would trip her or make her fall in some way. Ruby wasn't even safe in her arms, she thought, but at least she was with her. The little girl was feeling the fear from her mother and looked up at her with frightened eyes, giving a little moan of apprehension.

Gabriel's face was pressed against the blocked-up chimney when she entered the room behind him. Martha didn't want to be here, didn't want to see or hear anything more that was supernatural. She had been so close to getting away. Why had she gone upstairs to get the rosary beads? To think that she had put Ruby in mortal danger . . .

"Henry, love, are you there?" said Gabriel, ear pressed up against the wall. "My name is Gabriel and I'm here to help you but you have to listen to me, and we have to do this very quickly before the bad lady comes back, do you understand me?"

There was a silence at first, then a faint knock and a voice. "*I want my mammy.*"

Martha felt an indescribable sadness sweep over her.

"I know, wee man," said Gabriel. "Now I want you to look around you. There should be a light somewhere, can you see it?"

Silence again. Then the small voice. "*No. Where's my mammy?*" It was followed by a little weak sob.

Martha gasped. Gabriel didn't know who it was that Henry wanted. "The woman he calls 'Mammy', Gabriel," she said urgently, "she's still alive –"

She was interrupted by a voice from the doorway.

"Come here to me, Henry. I'll mind you," it said.

Martha froze again. Marion, come back, trying to draw him toward her again, to block his little soul from ever getting peace. Martha's back was to the door, Gabriel facing it. She saw the look of puzzlement on his face and turned fearfully to see what was happening.

"Come here, love," said the voice. "Mammy's here."

Martha stared, Ruby clutched to her chest, silent now. There was no terrible smell, she noticed. And the woman in the doorway wasn't Marion, but vaguely familiar to Martha. She was young, no older than her early twenties, she thought, slim, with dark hair and blue eyes. Like Marion, Martha could see her firmly but could still make out the hallway behind her. She was dressed in a green dress, her shoulder-length hair held back with a matching ribbon.

"Lily!" said Martha breathlessly.

But how could this be? She had spoken to Lil Flynn only earlier in the day.

The figure ignored her. "Come on now, Henry, before Marion comes back, love."

The apparition's gaze was fixed at a point behind Martha and it held its hand out in that direction. Martha noticed there was almost a glow from the hand that was extended and she followed it, turning her head slightly, taking in Gabriel looking to the same point. As Martha turned, she once again felt a warmth beside her, halfway up her thigh, a slight tug on the hem of her top. She could scarcely believe her eyes when she saw him standing there, shyly folding himself toward her legs, as if he were unsure of the person speaking to him. With brown hair, cut in a pudding-bowl style, a blue shirt and a pair of black shorts, barefoot, it was him. Henry.

Martha felt her knees sag underneath her. He was beautiful. A beautiful little boy, skinny and small, pale and sickly-looking. She had an urge to bend toward him and catch an arm around him, a longing to reassure him that he was safe now. She couldn't, of course, but he looked so real – *could she?*

She felt no fear of him, nor of Lil at the doorway. In fact the room felt warm again after the freezing cold she'd experienced while Marion had been there. The feeling was the exact opposite to how she felt around the other spirit. It was peaceful and almost comforting.

Henry eyed Lil cautiously in the doorway.

"Come here, darling," said Lil and crouched down, like any mother on seeing her child. She spread her arms out wide to receive him and Martha looked back to see a broad smile spread across the boy's face, a smile that she saw on Ruby's face first thing in the morning, the pure delight of a child as it sees its mother.

"*Mammy!*" the little boy said, joy in his voice.

Martha burst into tears and watched as the little spirit pelted across the room and was enveloped into Lil's arms. Tears streamed down Martha's face as she watched them embrace. Gabriel placed an arm against the small of her back. Martha sniffed loudly – it was almost like watching a film, she thought. Even Ruby was silently watching the scene unfold before her. She can see them too, thought Martha in amazement.

The room fell silent as they watched Lil press her face against Henry's, wrapping him in a firm grasp. She closed her eyes and nuzzled against him, as a mother animal would her young. In turn, his skinny arms were wrapped around her neck and clasped together as if he would never let go. Gabriel gasped as though he could see something that Martha could not and they continued to stare as the vision before them grew fainter and fainter. After a moment, Lil and Henry were there no longer.

Martha and Gabriel stared in silence for a long time at the place where they had been, unable to find words.

It was Martha who broke the silence. "They're really gone this time, aren't they, Gabriel?" she said, eyes still fixed on the spot where the ghostly reunion had taken place.

Gabriel nodded. "They are."

"What about Marion?" whispered Martha, keeping her eyes on the doorway, mesmerised by what she had just seen, but terrified in case the older woman would come back.

Gabriel fell silent, as if listening for something around him. "I don't know," he whispered back. Martha turned to look at him, clasping Ruby tighter to her. "I think she's still here, but I can't sense where or what she's doing."

A look of alarm crossed Martha's face. "Then let's go, Gabriel

– she hurt me earlier and I don't want her to hurt Ruby – we don't know what she's capable of." She could feel her stomach stinging where Marion had dragged her over the metal screw earlier and her mind flashed back to those ghostly grey hands, poised to close over Ruby's temples. Panic formed in the pit of her stomach.

"I don't think she can hurt us, Martha," said Gabriel. "She's still here, true – I can't find her, but I know she's terribly weak. She's used up everything that she has. And more importantly, her reason for being here is gone . . . Henry's gone."

Martha charged over to the window and pulled up the blackout blind, allowing blessed light into the room. The storm had passed as suddenly as it had begun and blazing sunlight shone in through the little window, dimming the moons and stars on the walls, taking some of the fear away. Martha looked again at the room, as if checking to make sure that there was nothing there.

"If she's here, Gabriel, then I want to go. I don't want to be where she is, even if it's only a hint of her."

Gabriel nodded and stepped out of the room, closing his eyes and muttering to himself as he walked, as Martha had seen him do earlier that morning.

They walked toward the stairs, Martha scanning the landing, the doors leading off it for fear that the apparition was watching her from a shady doorway. There was nothing. They began their descent of the stairs.

"Why didn't Will come in?" asked Martha, remembering that his car was parked outside.

"He's not here," said Gabriel, his voice subdued.

Martha turned, looked at Gabriel and then looked back at the stairs. Imagine tripping and falling now after everything they'd gone through. She peered down into the hallway. Nothing.

"How did you even know to come here?"

Now that there was calm, the questions flooded into Martha's mind. It suddenly made no sense that Gabriel had turned up out of the blue. They had reached the hallway and Martha stepped out into the glorious sunshine. Birds chirped in the trees above her and a gentle breeze had started to blow, the air cleared by the thunder and lightning. She turned her face to the breeze and breathed in. Ruby's hair blew gently and she jiggled her legs in delight. It was as if what she had seen had never happened.

Gabriel stepped out behind her and, with a final glance down the hallway, closed the door firmly behind him. "Last time we'll be in there, hopefully, eh?" he asked, giving the handle a final tug.

Martha didn't answer. She had thought that too many times to think it even once more, but she hoped Gabriel was right.

The tall man turned to face her. "I got a message to come," he said.

"But from whom? No one knew I'd come out here – I just wanted to get packed up and on the road."

"The message was from someone who looks after you," said Gabriel. "That thin lady that I saw that time?"

Martha was shocked. "My mum," she said.

Gabriel nodded. "I thought so. She was really worried about you – knew you were in danger and wouldn't leave me alone until I got up and went to you both. She was especially worried about the bairn."

Martha was momentarily distracted by a car pulling into the driveway behind her. "What now?" she thought, but focused her attention back on Gabriel. "She knows about Ruby?" She suddenly wanted to know everything that Gabriel knew. Her own mum was looking after her at last, properly. "What –" she began, but was interrupted by a car door slamming and the crunch of footsteps across the gravel.

"What are you doing with my bloody car, you great big ginger bastard!" shouted Will, charging up to Gabriel.

Martha looked at Gabriel who was trying to look innocent, to pretend that Will wasn't striding toward him with rage in his eyes.

"What the bloody hell is going on here?"

"You *drove* out here, Gabriel?" grinned Martha. It was

suddenly the funniest thing in the world. She started to giggle and couldn't stop, aware that it was hysteria after what had happened inside the house.

Gabriel shrugged an 'I don't know', and continued to ignore Will.

"You blew your cover for me and Ruby?" laughed Martha.

Gabriel gave her a barely discernable grin back and she threw her head back and laughed more.

"What the hell happened?" demanded Will. "I got your text to get up here to the farm but funny how when I got outside my bloody car was gone! So you *can* drive, can you? Or did the spirits get you out here? One of them turning the wheel and one on – bloody – *gear* – duty!"

Gabriel himself snorted, Martha doubled over with hysterical laughter.

"Jeez, Will, no need to insult *them*!" said Gabriel, pointing upwards and rolling his eyes around. "Christ, I shouldn't have done that," he said quickly, putting a hand to his mouth.

This made Martha laugh even harder and she bent over, Ruby starting to grizzle at the uncomfortable position she had been placed in.

"Martha, are you okay?" came a familiar voice and she felt Ruby being lifted from her arms.

"Sue!" she said. It didn't surprise her that her best friend was there, wouldn't surprise her if the Queen suddenly turned up in a Routemaster bus. She threw her arms around her friend who looked as bewildered as Will. It was her green Citroën that had brought them there.

"Christ on a bike, Martha, I had a few days off and thought I'd surprise you. Then I call to the village to get some stuff and then I'm driving out here and spot this fellow trying to wave me down with his face looking like something out of *Rocky*!"

Martha looked at Will. Sure enough his nose was bloodied and he had the beginnings of a swollen lip. "Will?"

He stopped glaring at Gabriel and hugged her. She felt her tense body relax in his arms and breathed in the smell of him, felt safe. She was suddenly aware of the pain in her shoulder, the stinging from her stomach – she wondered if it were bleeding.

"Are you both okay?" said Will, releasing her and looking directly into her face.

Martha's skin was pale, her eyes red from crying. She nodded. "We're fine. Gabriel got there on time. Look, can we go back to the B&B or something? I don't think I can drive to London tonight."

"London?" said Sue. "What are you driving to London for?"

"To see you, you bloody fool. Thank God you're here!" Martha released herself from Will's grasp and threw her arms around her friend again.

"Was it Mannion?" asked Will, breathlessly.

Gabriel nodded and looked back at the house. "She's still there."

"Is she?" interrupted Will, a tone of excitement in his voice.

"Leave it, Will," said Gabriel. "You need to hear what's happened before you go charging back in with the cameras. Henry's safe though – definitely gone this time. I had my suspicions that it hadn't worked the first time. Anyway, what happened to you?"

"Your bloody landlord, Martha," Will replied, dabbing underneath his nose and checking his finger for blood.

"Rob Mountford?" said Martha. Now she was really puzzled.

"The very man," said Will, sniffing. "He was staggering out of the pub and getting into his Land Rover when I came out of the B&B to come up here. He was in no condition to drive and I offered him a lift before realising my car was missing. But next thing I know he starts ranting on at me, about who did I think I was, and he was perfectly fine to drive his own car and he belonged in this village and I was no one blah blah blah! *Then* he bloody recognised me – someone must have told him about me, and he started shouting at me that I had no right being up at his farm and it was his farm and that I was to stay away from his woman and all sorts. Next thing he took a swing at me – I wasn't expecting it and this is the result. The man's bloody huge! Thought he was going to knock my head off!"

"Bloody bully," hissed Martha. "Bullying you, bullying me, bullying poor old ladies – that family is nothing but a bunch of bloody bullies!"

"Oh, he didn't bully me," grinned Will.

"Wait till you hear this," added Sue.

Martha looked at Will, who glanced down at his hand. She noted for the first time a trace of purple on his knuckles. "I bloody punched him, I did!" he said, in a mock Scottish accent.

Gabriel tutted at the stereotype.

"You what!" shrieked Martha.

"He might be big," said Will, "but I'm fast. He won't be bullying anyone for a while without a great big bandage on his nose. Of course I'm sure there'll be a court case, and I'll be charged with assault, but he started it!"

"Holy *shit*!" screeched Martha and impulsively she threw her arms around Will again, who staggered backward with surprise.

"Break it up, kids," said Gabriel. "Let's get our asses out of here. Things might be calm now but I really don't want to hang around here any longer, do you?"

Martha released Will but smiled directly into his face. He smiled back, beaming from ear to ear.

Sue climbed back into her Citroën, Gabriel into the Volvo on a nod from Will. "You can bloody drive us back to Edinburgh as well," he growled, as Gabriel slid into the driver's seat.

Will sat in next to Martha who had secured Ruby into her seat and was sitting behind the wheel, staring up at Eyrie Farm.

"You want me to drive?" he asked.

She shook her head. Her hand rested on the gear-stick and Will covered it with his own, turning to look directly at her.

They sat in silence for a few moments, watching the farmhouse while the others executed three-point turns and crawled down the drive. A part of Will longed to see something – a face perhaps, or a shadow move behind a curtain. Martha was just glad to see the house at rest, if only for a while.

It was Will who broke the silence. "Oh, I heard in the pub that Lil Flynn woman was found dead this afternoon, poor old soul. A man who drops off coal to her, it seems, looking for his money."

Martha closed her eyes. "I reckoned that," she said. "And her soul was very rich in the end . . ." She shook her head, letting the melancholy go, and put the car into reverse.

Without a backward glance, Martha, Will and Ruby turned and drove down the gravel driveway of Eyrie Farm for the last time.

35

Belvedere,
Brockley's Marshes,
Shipton Abbey,
Norfolk
England

July 15th, 2008

Dear Henry,

*My little darling boy, my own sweetheart, precious little angel.
Where are you, my darling? All those names that I once called you
when I held you in my arms from the day you were born until the
day I never saw you again? What became of you, my boy? I fear that
I know too well but all these years I have held a hope in a corner of
my heart that I should see you again and hold you once more to me.*

*If the worst happened to you, sweetest Henry, then I feel I
shall see you very soon. The doctors tell me I have cancer in my
stomach and that it has spread to other places as well but I don't
listen any more. Their tablets make me half crazy and with the
funny way I speak nowadays – you have never heard me speak*

this way – the villagers think that I am some sort of drunken fool and you know that your Auntie Lily never touched a drop in her life.

I am old now, Henry, discarded, out here on the marshes like a witch that the village cast out. Those Mountfords have had me over a barrel my whole life. They set me up in this house – this prison. Belvedere, they call it – it means 'a beautiful view' I think. Is it a joke, I ask myself? They didn't interfere with my scraping a living but they made sure that everyone thought nothing of me – they even managed to somehow destroy what friendship and loyalty I thought I had with Mrs Collins who delivered you, my only friend. She never came to see me once I moved and when I saw her on the street from then on she turned the other way, pretended not to see me. That can only have been their doing. I thought their hold over me was gone when old Charles died but only a month ago young Robbie, his grandson, a great hulking idiot of a man was out here telling me not to be telling my tales. I pray that soon they'll have no choice but to leave me alone.

Most of the villagers don't know me. Some do, but as the old drunk who spends her days in the pub. I do that, Henry, because I feel that if you, or Robert, were ever to return to me it is where you would go to ask if I am still here and I am afraid that the landlord would tell you a false tale about me and you would leave. Also, any news of the Farm would come to me through there. And it is company as I am lonely out here. My customers don't come here any longer. There's no need for my skills.

I am very tired today. That woman who has been living at Eyrie Farm has been to see me and I have told her what I think happened to you and what I know happened to the woman who gave birth to you. I gave her my letters, Henry, and if you should ever come back to me then you must go to Eyrie Farm and get them from her. I trust her because she has a child herself and knows what it is to love like a mother. The difference between us is that she gave birth to her own child where that is the one thing that I didn't do for you Henry, but I feel as though I did.

I have missed you every day for the past fifty years, my lovely dark-haired boy. You were the one constant in my life. Robert wasn't a constant after all but I hear that he found happiness and bless him for that. I've learned that you're best not building yourself up to love many folk, Henry. The more you love the more you lose. Good luck to the woman who became his wife, to the children that he bore all that distance away in Australia. Oh, that I were her, Henry, that you were his child like we planned. We were only hours away from that happening when Marion came home. Albie wouldn't have her back and threatened to set the dogs on her when she arrived at his house. I can imagine that she begged and pleaded and probably made a show of herself somehow. She had nothing left to lose, Henry.

When she came back early and saw our bags in the hall she lifted you by the arm away from me, dragged you upstairs, smashing and breaking things all around her like a madwoman. I remember your screams as she pulled you away from me and I heard the noise your arm made when it came out of its socket. I thought my heart would break there and then, little boy. And then it went silent, and then she came out to me and pushed me and the next I knew I was in the hospital and I couldn't speak at all and I didn't know where you were gone. I think I know now, my darling, I pray that it was swift and painless for you. For me it is slow and filled with pain but that is my penance for not protecting you, for letting her get you and hurt you. If I could go back and take your place then I would, a thousand times. Why didn't I leave with Robert when he wanted to take me away the day Albie discovered you, cut and bleeding with the glass from the Sacred Heart?

Robert told me that he came for us, darling. He didn't let us down that day, but Marion met him at the door and told him we were gone away ahead of him and that I would get in touch with him. She pretended that's all of my so-called message she understood and sent him away while she finished what she was doing.

It took Robert a day to come back, knowing then that something was wrong. He says I was awake and wandering through the house, bloodstained and confused, but I have no memory of that, just of being brought here to the house on the marsh and him handing over the paperwork for my mortgage and all of my things here from Eyrie Farm. I have never been back up there, Henry, can you believe it? In a village this size, and with all the tales the villagers tell of it, and I have never once in fifty years made the trip back to the Farm. I am afraid of what I would see there. In case I saw the fireplace that I think she bricked up using the tools that the workmen left and the skills she learned from my father back in Dublin.

I never again heard from my father, Henry. I tried writing to him to tell him my new address but I never received a letter back. For all I know he could have been dead by the time everything happened at Eyrie Farm and Marion left Shipton for good. Surely any father who cared would have worried at my news, that I was now living on the marshes, with no mention of Marion or indeed of you. I think my mother's death finished him, Henry. And he was so ashamed of Marion, of you, God forgive him, that he felt it easier to bear if we didn't exist.

I can't write any more, my darling boy. I am going to go to sleep now and perhaps I'll dream of you, your dark hair and your big smile for me, your mammy. I pray that you are alive and well somewhere. That your mother by birth took you with her when she fled after knocking me down the stairs and that somewhere along the way some kind people took care of you, like I wanted for you when you were born. I fear the worst though, my lovely boy, in which case I will see you very soon.

With all the love I have left,
Your loving mother,

Lily

36

December 10th

Martha crunched through the frost in the thick grass, glad she had worn a pair of low-heeled boots. She hadn't realised she was going to have to trek quite so far over uneven terrain.

The sun had begun to melt the frost, but it was still early and very, very cold. She pulled Ruby's hat down over her ears and tugged the zip of her snowsuit up as high as it could go. "Ba!" said Ruby, looking upward and Martha glanced up to see where the bird was.

Gabriel was already there, she could see, talking to a man she imagined must be the gravedigger. No sign of Will just yet but then again he had the most important job today. Martha waved at Gabriel who was stomping his feet to keep warm. He waved back, and Ruby joined in, clasping her little fingers in and out in her mittens. Martha was surprised the mittens had stayed on this long – normally she felt they needed to be glued onto her hands to keep them on.

Martha stumbled over some more rough ground, edged along the corner of a grave – she couldn't bring herself to walk directly on it – and stepped down onto the grass. As the gravedigger moved away to wait discreetly in the background, Gabriel came forward and kissed Martha on the cheek.

The two of them stared at the headstone.

It was small, made from local stone, a simple rectangular shape.

'Lily Alice Flynn – February 1936 – July 2008
He who does not love does not know God, for God is Love'

There was a small space open at the top of the grave, the rest of it covered in green material, the small mound of earth in a pile alongside the headstone.

"Look at her, tucked away in the corner again, like she was out on that bloody marsh," said Martha.

"Och Martha, she's not there," said Gabriel, taking Ruby from her arms. "Hello, precious!"

Martha grinned, remembering how disgusted he'd been at Ruby's existence the first time they had met.

"You know she's with Henry and they're happy," Gabriel went on. "Neither of them will be in this hole in the ground."

Martha squinted against the morning sunlight and saw Will's car pull up. The Lexus certainly was more impressive than the Volvo under the circumstances, although the Volvo was still used when he went on investigations. She smiled to herself as she saw him step out. He looked very tall in a dark blue overcoat and his suit. Bless him for going to all the effort, she thought.

He opened the back door and leaned over the seat, sliding something toward him. She saw that a man who must be Father Timoney had stepped from the passenger seat and had come round to hold the door for Will. The priest closed the car door behind Will as he straightened and looked across the graveyard, and set off toward them, the small white coffin in his hands.

It was Rob Mountford who had eventually found what remained of poor Henry Flynn, taking a sledgehammer to the fireplace with a policeman present. At first it was hard to distinguish the bones from the twigs that had been dropped down by nest-building rooks over the years but a shred of blue material was sticking out from between the twigs and a forensic team had spent three days at the cottage conducting their investigation. The letter that Lil had left cleared much up, and

Martha had given the rest of the correspondence to the police. There could be no verdict of murder, of course, no actual evidence of what had happened but everyone knew what fate had ultimately befallen the child.

The case was thankfully kept out of the papers – the one undertaking for which the Mountfords had volunteered. Heaven forbid that their name should be associated in any way with the murder of a child.

It had angered Martha at first that no one would ever know what they had done to Lil and Henry but after a while she began to think that Lil and her poor forgotten parents would also have preferred it to stay a secret. All the trouble that secrets caused, she thought.

Two wooden planks lay over the hole, with two long strips of cloth laid across them. Will laid the coffin on the strips. He stepped over the rough, frozen ground and crossed to Martha, touching Gabriel's arm as he passed and kissing Martha on the cheek before taking Ruby from Gabriel and settling her on his hip. She started to wriggle so he took out his BlackBerry and gave it to her to play with. A shadow of annoyance crossed Martha's face – she was trying to teach her not to play with phones and remote controls and here was Will undoing all of her good work. She'd have words with him over that, but for now it kept Ruby quiet as Father Timoney began the short funeral service.

When he had said the prayers, Will handed Ruby back to Martha. Then he and Gabriel caught hold of the strips of cloth under the tiny coffin and lifted it as the gravedigger swiftly removed the planks underneath. Will and Gabriel steadied themselves to lower it into the grave.

Martha became aware of some people approaching and looked up. She smiled as she recognised Mary Stockwell and her children Alison and Ryan. She guessed who the other three were and her heart gave a thud.

Mary gave a small wave and the group stood solemnly, watching Gabriel and Will finally lower Henry to his resting place. With Lil. With his mother.

Will had arranged for the stonemason to do his job as soon as possible. It would just say 'Henry Joseph Flynn, 1953-1957' under Lil's inscription. Will, who had paid for the grave to be marked, was insistent that Henry's name be kept a secret no longer in Shipton Abbey.

Father Timoney finished the prayers and the short service ended. He turned to Will and shook his hand and they engaged in a short chat. Martha watched Gabriel take something from his pocket and kneel momentarily, slipping something into the grave – the small silver rosary beads that she had gone to retrieve that day in July. If she hadn't, none of them would be here. That made her wistful and sad at the same time. Maybe Lil would never have come for Henry if things hadn't got so stirred up. Certainly she and Will would never have –

"Hallo, Martha," came a voice in her ear, and she turned to see Mary Stockwell beside her, the warm smell of her perfume coming from the fur collar of her coat.

"Mary!" Martha extended her free arm to hug her old friend.

"Hello, pigeon, remember me?" said Mary, bending slightly to address Ruby, who didn't, but who wriggled in delight at the attention nonetheless.

Ruby had slipped down Martha's hip and she hauled her back again into a more comfy position.

"You've got so big," said Mary and rubbed her cheek. "Martha, I don't think you've met everyone, have you?" Mary stepped back so that Martha could see the little group behind her. "You know Alison, of course, and Ryan . . ." They smiled and nodded at Martha and then continued to look bored. "And this is Claire and Oliver . . ." Mary pointed to another two who did the same and then stepped back to form a huddle with their brother and sister.

A small, balding man with a pockmarked face stepped out from behind Mary's shoulder.

"And this is Duncan," said Mary nervously. "My husband."

The man smiled and extended his hand.

Martha took the proffered hand and gripped it firmly. "I'm very glad to meet you, Duncan," she said and smiled. The man smiled warmly in return and Martha watched as he and Mary exchanged a look which told a thousand stories. She couldn't wait to hear what had happened after she had left, when the reunion had taken place and how, but she knew there was plenty of time for that later.

"You'll come back to the Abbott's, won't you?" said Mary. "John has laid on a bit of a spread, felt it was the least he could do – for poor old Lil as well as the little boy. I can't believe it was all true . . ."

"We're going to head back there now, Mary," said Martha. She couldn't talk about what had happened just now. Not in the cold, with the little boy only now where he should be after over fifty years. Not that he should be there at all. He'd only be in his mid-fifties, she thought. Maybe quite high up in his job, with grown-up children, grandchildren. "We're staying tonight actually," she continued, blocking the thought of Henry from her mind. "So we've plenty of time to catch up. It's been lovely to meet all of the children at last – and you, Duncan."

"We'll see you there then – Ryan has to get back to work and Alison should really be in school. We couldn't miss this though – it seems fitting that we're *all* here." Mary wiped a tear from her eye and, smiling at Martha, turned to usher her brood back across the graveyard to their car.

Gabriel followed behind them, deep in conversation with Father Timoney.

Will came over to join Martha. "That can only mean trouble," he said, nodding at Gabriel who was stressing some point to the small, bald priest.

"Poor Father Timid," said Martha, who had met him before, when Lil had been lain to rest. She looked back at the grave. "Sleep tight, Henry," she said aloud, and turned to walk back toward where she was parked. Will took a last look also and fell into step beside her, lifting Ruby from her arms and settling the little girl on his hip. Martha caught a whiff of his aftershave on the breeze and inhaled deeply, feeling butterflies in her stomach at his proximity. Will always made her feel like that, even after the time that had passed.

"So," he said. "You haven't answered my question."

Martha grinned, continuing to look down at her feet so as not to stumble on the rough ground. "And what question's that?" she said playfully.

Will sighed in mock aggravation. "You *know* which question! About Edinburgh."

"I'm not moving to Edinburgh!" said Martha with a laugh.

"You can't stay in Sue's forever, you know!"

"Can too," said Martha, in a petulant voice, laughing as she did.

They stopped and faced each other. Martha reached up her hand and idly brushed the sleeve of his coat, looking directly into his brown eyes.

"You move to London then, if you're so fed up with long distance," she smiled.

"No. I hate London," he replied.

"Well, then, we continue to commute."

"Martha."

"Hmm?"

"This time I'm actually serious."

Martha tilted her head to one side. "You really want us to live together?"

Will started to walk again. "Not *together* together," he said. "It's too soon for that. But I wish I didn't have a mammoth drive or train trip every time I want to see you. And that's all the time. I mean we're getting on great, aren't we? All three of us?"

Martha eyed him holding her daughter as they strolled. He was amazing with Ruby. When they were together she couldn't get used to how he did so much for her – lifting, carrying, feeding, getting up in the night.

"We get on better than great," she smiled shyly. "I just don't want to live in Edinburgh."

"But if we found the right place then you'd consider it?" Will couldn't keep the excited tone out of his voice.

Martha smiled. Why not? "'Spose so," she said coyly.

Will stopped in his tracks, a beaming smile spreading from ear to ear. "So we compromise then? Find a middle ground? Somewhere in between?"

Martha, a few steps ahead, looked back at Will and Ruby and smiled. "I guess," she said, and kept walking, unable to keep the smile from her own face.

"Glasgow then. Let's move to Glasgow," said Will.

Martha simply closed her eyes, smiled and breathed in the fresh air of the December morning.

THE END.